SOUPER MUM

KRISTEN BAILEY

Published by Accent Press Ltd 2016

ISBN 9781786150684

SOUPER MUM

SOUPER MUM

It's very easy not to write. So thank you to Shirley Golden, Sara Hafeez, and Claire Anderson-Wheeler who cheered me on from the side-lines and told me to keep at it.

Thank you to Accent Press, especially Cat Camacho, for their belief and all their hard work.

Grazie bella Helen per il vostro aiuto con la traduzione. Sei una stella!

And an even bigger thank you to Nick Bailey for believing in me when I'd given up on myself; for digging me out of that low point when I developed an addiction to online Scrabble and thought everything I wrote was crap. You told me I wasn't crap. I'm glad I married you.

For the mini Baileys.

J, T, O, & M

PROLOGUE

'We could sex it out?'

There are no words. I look at Matt as he eyes me up cautiously, wondering whether making love to his nine months pregnant wife would have her explode like John Hurt in *Alien*. The 'sexing it out' will not be happening, mainly because I'm teetering on the edge of the sofa trying to find the best position to accommodate my piles, but also because I know the sweaty and brutish effort that sex would entail is just not worth the indignity. The baby body-pops inside me and I imagine a very tiny me in sweatbands dancing to the Sugarhill Gang. She stops.

'The fact is, I'm never having sex with you again. You and your sperm are not allowed within a five-mile radius of my nether regions once this one gets out.'

'Single beds and onesies then?'

I nod. Matt pretends to laugh. I am deadly serious. This baby makes four. Four little humans. From now on, reading, wine, crochet, and addictive iPhone games will become my nocturnal activities of choice. He hands me my tea and starts to pat down the sofa looking for the remote. I smile secretly to myself because a) Matt makes great tea and b) my back fats have tight control of the remote. I am carrying this man's progeny past the forty-week stage, this TV is mine. He starts sifting through the toy box. I sip my tea loudly.

'Have you …?'

'Check the kitchen maybe?'

I return to my show, half-watching, half-comforted by a noise that isn't the high-pitched shriek of three children under the age of ten. Matt swears through the wall and returns scratching his head.

'It's bloody Jake, isn't it? He uses those remotes as car ramps.'

'Probably.' Winning. I am winning.

'What you watching?'

'Some cooking thing.'

Cookery programmes get me through pregnancies. When I am swollen, overtired, and literally stuck to the sofa because I can't lever myself off it, there is always comfort to be had from watching someone baste a ham or ice a gateau. Matt thinks otherwise.

'Can we switch to BBC2?'

'No.' Simply because I cannot endure another tedious programme about a man walking up the Welsh coast for no other reason it would seem than to be rained on. Not even a handsome man at that.

'Please, anything is better than this. Really, Jools. This bloke is such a tosser.'

I look up. Tommy McCoy: foodie hero, Michelin-starred, TV chef du jour. The sort you see splashed across jars of pasta sauce, shiny books, and your television, asking you to buy local, go organic, and sieve your own fruit. Sorry, in our house your fruit will always have bits. So maybe he's a bit of a cock, but that didn't mean his brand of cooking wankery was going to make me give up the television.

'*So, my love, it's me, Tommy. You know me, off the telly. Hahahaha, look how shocked you are! Class!*'

'I mean, the mockney geezer act is wearing a bit thin, eh?'

'*So ... balsamic vinegar – laaarrrvely on your strawberries. Who'd have thought it, eh?*'

Matt cuddles up next to me. 'Or, alternatively, you could leave the strawberries as they are, you dipshit. Why is that woman crying?'

'It's part of the show. He accosts someone in a supermarket, goes through their trolley, tells them how crap their food is, and then spends a week teaching them how to buy and cook proper food.'

Matt scrunches his eyebrows, trying to understand how the show's concept is worthy of a woman's tears. I surprise myself at how much I know about this show given I've only ever read about it in *Heat*.

'This is the part where he brings out the pictures of what her body will look like if she continues to eat the way she does.'

True enough, Tommy starts with graphic pictures of an enlarged heart and gastric ulcers. Matt grimaces slightly.

'Preachy. So really, he's getting paid millions to tell people they need to eat proper food. What a revelation. Some jumped-up Essex wannabe, probably makes more in a day than I do in a year.'

I nod, awaiting the rant – the money rant where for a moment, Matt slips back into his socialist student self and preaches about distribution of wealth, the rich getting richer and the poor getting poorer. Poor little church mouse Matt and his holey socks and sad life with his Jabba the Hutt wife. This is my least favourite rant given it always has a way of questioning mine and the kids' value in his life. Still, at least it's better than his 'teabags-in-the-sink' rant.

'Why is everyone hugging? What's in that bowl?'

I look up.

'Quinoa.'

There is no response as to how anyone can cuddle over grain. Matt starts to put his hand down the sides of the sofa in his continued quest for the remote. He pulls out a toy cow, a Tesco Clubcard, three Lego men, and something greying and round.

'For the love of … crap, Jools – is this a piece of meat?'

I look at the furry, leathery disc curiously.

'Nope, an old breast pad.'

He stares intently at it, secretly working out how long it must have been down there. Five years, to be exact. Then a look like he gives me when he finds solidified milk in the fridge or a huge, sticky mass of travel sweets on the passenger seat of the car – his health and safety look. I give him a look back.

'It's all right, love! I've got a great chicken dish for you. Stuffed with lemons, thyme, and a bit of bacon. What do you say?'

'I say I can't believe I am fricking watching this shite.' Matt's voice deepens, his accent slowly evolving into Angry Scotsman.

'Please … it's just TV … a stupid TV chef and you're getting your melons in a twist about it.'

I sit forward. The remote literally falls out of my back. That's not Matt's happy face.

'Seriously?' He reaches over. I let the remote fall to the floor and try to kick it under the sofa. The lunge action makes me topple like a Weeble. Matt laughs. This induces rage.

'Oooh, Tommy McCoy earns more than me for doing nothing … suck it up, Campbell.'

'Well, maybe we should get him round here. Teach you a thing or two about cooking.'

I pause. I half want to smother Matt with my pregnant boobs, but there's a definite need to stop proceedings for a short while. I look down. A wet patch grows in my maternity shorts like an angry, enveloping raincloud. I think two things: first, my tea? No. Second, damn my pelvic floor! Have I pissed myself? No. Then my abdomen tightens. I look up at Matt and grab on to the sofa cushions until my knuckles lose colour. Mother of bollocking bollocks. Tommy McCoy's face beams at me from the TV.

'Don't worry, laaarve, I'm Tommy. I'm 'ere for you!'

With whitened teeth and badly dyed blond hair, he prances around some stranger's kitchen in really terrible trainers. Please don't let this man be the first person my baby sees. Please. Pain sears through my back like someone ironing my spine.

'Matt … Jeeeeeeeeesus Christ, she's coming.'

And even though he's done this twice before, Matt stops in his tracks, the emotion hits his eyes, and he catches me.

'Wow. So we don't need to sex it out then …'

I laugh. I fall into him. Now. She's coming now. And all I hear is Tommy sodding McCoy's voice echoing around the room as I spread my legs, my undercarriage throbbing as if it might fall out.

'Now with your chicken, first check for the gizzards. Just pop your hand up the hole and pull them out.'

CHAPTER ONE

It's a dream I have almost once a week. I am in a room with the kids. The room has no windows or doors but has a strange padded quality to it. There is no Matt and Millie is almost always without a nappy. Jake notices first and declares she will pee everywhere and we will all drown. Ted is bored and picks his nose. Hannah sits quietly and asks where her father is and why I didn't bring my phone. I am wearing jersey catalogue pyjamas that have flattering flowy bottoms and a vest which magically supports my flaccid boobs. My hair looks frigging fantastic. In my pyjama pocket is a key. But there is no door? Everyone starts shouting for help and Ted gets anxious and starts eating the fruits of his nose-picking. I beat the walls with my fists. I feel along the sides of the walls with my fingers. They are ridged and leave a fine white dust in my palms. I know this. I hold the dust to my lips. It's sweet. The walls are spongy. Wait! Doughnuts! The room is made out of doughnuts! 'Eat!' I tell the children. 'Eat your way out!' They do as they're told. The walls are filled with jam; raspberry, apple, some with custard, which we all agree is an abomination. All the kids tuck in, grabbing handfuls of sponge. They have sugar around their lips, jam in their hair but they all look so content, so joyful. I smile. Then from a little hole that we've eaten through in the wall, I see daylight. We hear Matt's voice. I never recall what he says but he doesn't sound too impressed. The voice always gets louder. Millie always pees on the floor. Then I wake up.

'Jools … Jools! Get your arse out of bed.'

And I always check. No doughnuts. No jam. No fancy pyjamas. No key.

'Seriously? Jools, c'mon!'

Is there a key? It's happened again, hasn't it? I pull the duvet over my head to see my regular bedroom attire: an old

1

misshapen T-shirt and tracksuit bottoms, my hair looking like small mammals have nested in there to seek refuge from a harsh winter. A muslin, dry and crispy, is stuck to my forehead. Outside, a pigeon sits on the sill, has a crap, then flies off into the drizzle. I look down at a wet patch where fatigue or doughnut lust has seen me drool into the pillow. The bed undulates as a five-year-old boy bounces in next to me. Get up. Get up. Get up. You great big state of a woman, you.

'Jake … get your zombie mama out of bed for me …'

Jake does as he's told and tries to prise my eyes open with his five-year-old fingers. He's lucky zombie mama don't bite. A bare-chested Matt appears at the bedroom door wearing just his work trousers. If I squint in the lowlight of the room, he looks a little like Richard Gere in the beginning of *American Gigolo* except the only dancing he seems to be doing is with the Febreze bottle. He finds a shirt on the back of the bathroom door and sprays it frenetically, smoothing it down with his hands. Jake flashes the bedside light on and off in my face.

'Are you dead?'

'No.'

'Then can I go?'

'Yes.' He kisses me on the cheek and scoots off. I reach for my phone on the bedside table. 7.27 a.m. Matt eyeballs me with a foamy mouth. Now is not the time for Facebook, wifey. I eyeball back as he stands there with his chest on show and his flies undone. He looks over at Millie, her little pink tongue hanging out in fatigue.

'How many times was she up last night?'

The urge here is to exaggerate to garner some sympathy so that maybe, just maybe, Matt will volunteer to take the kids to school.

'Three.'

'You better grab a coffee then.'

He, who slept through each episode of waking, spread-eagled across three-quarters of the bed with only his erratic night flatulence keeping me company. To be honest, I forget now if Millie wakes in the night at all, the only sign I get being if in the morning one of my boobs is hanging out. I roll up my

2

T-shirt. True enough, the right is out – my nipple bowing its sorry head down to the floor. Matt glances over, a little disheartened as he watches me stuff myself back in my bra. Then he utters the words that no one really needs to hear.

'We're out of milk.'

We look at each other for five seconds to let the news wash over us. Crap. The big question though is whether it was anyone's fault. Will we survive? How will we address the matter? Breakfast is allocated Matt time in our house. He'll sit with the kids at the table and he has his quality time with them over Weetos and Rice Krispies while I either get fifteen minutes more sleep or tend to Millie. This sounds like some idyll of wholesome family time but no one really talks. They just stare at each other in a sleepy haze, milk often dribbles down chins, the twins will complain that someone's got more cereal than them, and they hate the world.

'The kids had a quarter cup each for breakfast but we are running low on everything.'

He gives me a look. This is your department: catering and beverages. Your department has underperformed.

'I'll go for a shop today. Is your pay in?'

'Well, this is food. The kids have to eat. You can put something like that on credit, you know?'

'But you told me …'

I trail off, not wanting to bring up the searing topics of finance and his casual condescension so early in the day, else my eyeballs seep out their sockets. Given I'm married to an accountant, it's always made sense for Matt to have the last word when it comes to our finances, something I don't necessarily fight, knowing it's for the best. Still, being twenty-nine and having my credit card usage monitored always makes me feel like I'm an errant teenager, like I might spend Matt's wages on Strongbow and Superdry. I salute him when his back is turned. Millie pops her little auburn head off her mattress and looks around to see where she is. There's a rosy blush in her cheeks from naughty, hurty teeth. I pat her head and put my legs over the side of the bed.

'Millie smells.'

'So do you.'

I stick my tongue out at Matt, who doesn't get the joke. But hell, he's right. I wrestle Millie on to the change table, pinning her down with one elbow as I fiddle with the wipes, praying there has been no spillage. No wipes. Bollocks. I take her into the bathroom and try to her wipe her down using some cosmetic pads and lukewarm water. Her face in the mirror says it all. This is undignified, Mother. I then pop her down on the floor as I put the seat down to have a wee. The door swings open. There are no boundaries in this house. I haven't peed on my own since 2006.

'Mum, can I have that white stuff in the fridge?' Ted stands by the entrance to the bathroom in that half-jog stance he always seems to favour; places to go, has our little Ted. He doesn't seem too perturbed by the fact I am mid-stream. I bend over to stop Millie going through the contents of the under-sink cupboard.

'It's in the measuring jug with the cling film.'

'No, hon – that's coconut milk.' I'm half glad he asked my permission, as I think that might have been in there since at least last Friday.

'What, coconut like in Bounty bars? I like them. Please?'

'This isn't a negotiation, Ted. If you drink that, you'll be sick.'

'But …'

'She's right, buddy.'

Matt nods and gives me another look. Look at our children scavenging in the fridge! Ted, like all the others, takes Matt's validation over my authority – slightly disheartening but at least it means I can wipe in peace. Or not. As I'm half hovered over the loo, half pulling up my pants, the door swings open again.

'Can you see my nipples through this shirt?'

Matt turns on the main bedroom light and I flinch from the light like a 1930s vampire. Matt stands by the door – no longer Richard Gere, but looking like a pastel blue Shar Pei.

'Kind of.'

'Shit.'

He looks over at the mountain of clothes in the corner of the

4

room then looks to me. He knows better than to mess with it; one false move and it'd be like a house of cards. I wash my hands then give him Millie while I sift through it. Go on, dance or something. I'll be Smokey Robinson. This has to be funny. Nothing. I find him a vest and retreat to the bathroom to brush my teeth, staring at the woman in the mirror. She looks familiar. I look down at the old T-shirt I'm wearing and the lovely wet patch over my left breast. I forgot to swap sides again. I take off my T-shirt and bra and grab a vest, shirt, and jeans from the top of the laundry hamper. I slowly pull up my jeans, breathing in to do up the button, and let my ricotta cheese mummy tummy relax over the waistband. Today's look is pale, uninteresting, and braless. It will have to do. I hear Matt's scowling from next door.

'Shit, I've missed the 7.47. Remember the Sky man is coming today. You need to pay the Vodafone bill and there was something else …'

'Milk?'

'No. But yeah. I'll text you.'

I watch Matt as he swears at his socks then stands at the mirror and smoothes down his ruffled blond hair, exhaling loudly into a resigned sigh as he studies his badly fitting white collar uniform. He then turns to me and there's a moment between us – we don't have to say it any more – no goodbyes, no kisses. We just look: a look which kind of says good luck. Let's go do this.

By the time I get downstairs, Matt is gone and it's 7.55 a.m. Time to move this up a gear. It's a school dinner kind of day, so I frantically count change, wrangle book bags, and scan the calendar for important events/deadlines I've probably missed. There is no time for coffee so I down some warm lemon squash, bundle Millie into her jacket, then rally the troops. Hannah sits on the last but one step doing her shoes while her topless brothers use the sofa as some sort of high jump mattress.

'But the question is, will Ted clear three metres?'

I then watch as he jumps from coffee table to sofa, twisting his body around until his head gets wedged in between the sofa cushions. Hannah rolls her eyes while I balance Millie on my hip and grab his ankles, trying to dislodge him. Jake sits to the side, laughing hysterically.

'A bit of help, Jake?'

'That was … awesome!'

Ted re-emerges, hair covered in old sofa lint but looking no worse than most mornings.

'Boys! Shirts! Shoes!'

They shuffle to the front door as I slip on my Converse. No time for socks.

'My shoes aren't here, Mum.'

'Well, where are they?'

Jake does what he does best, which is to shrug nonchalantly as he slips a sweatshirt over his head. I go into search mode, jogging between different areas of our small downstairs space, reaching under sofas and into black hole cupboards only to be assaulted by the vacuum cleaner and to find the remote for the DVD player which has been missing for three months. Then I go in the garage. Shoes! Yes! But … shit.

Seriously?

Bloody bastard shitty bollocks fuck.

'WHY IS THERE PAINT ALL OVER THE GARAGE FLOOR?'

Breathe, Jools. Just breathe. I squint my eyes and read 'gloss' on the side of the paint tin. My shoulders slump down so hard I swear my boobs bounce off my stomach. Jake grabs his shoes and is ushered out of the house by his sister. Silence. Why, little people? Why why why? I look at myself in the mirror. Don't scream and go hysterical and make your eyes bulge. Don't scream. It adds wrinkles and sounds horrible. They are but very little people. Your little people. I lock up the house, strap Millie in, and go and take my place in the car. Don't scream. Hannah turns her head around from the front seat, gesturing to her brothers in the back.

'I'm sorry, Mum.'

I don't respond. Ted's eyes glaze over.

'I'm sorry too.'

'They're both learning about road safety at school so we

thought we needed a zebra crossing,' adds their big sister.

'IN THE GARAGE?'

I turn around to give the last authoritative word on the matter. No going in the garage! Stop devaluing our house! The only paints you're allowed to use in the house are the crappy Crayola ones that wash out! But as I lurch my head around, I notice Jake's hand clawed around something contraband, something pink. Ted chewing. Silence must be broken.

'What the … where did you get those?'

'We found them in the back of the seat.'

I grimace. Now I must also clean the car, must throw up a little in my mouth, must get to school. I grab at half-eaten sweets and start the engine. I sigh heavily. I run over the recycling crate, hearing shards of plastic crunch under the wheels. Don't scream. I rub sticky sweet hands down my jeans and notice a tyre of flesh poking out where two buttons are supposed to be on my shirt. Pray Millie hasn't eaten them. I turn on the radio. Hannah sings along to a One Direction song which makes my heart break a little. School. Just bloody get to school.

'Sweets are not breakfast, guys.'

'Well, we were hungry,' Ted informs me. 'There was no bread this morning. Or cereal, so we had Nesquik.'

Bet Matt was thrilled by that.

'Daddy was going to make Choconana shakes but the blender was being a bastard,' pipes up Jake.

I swivel my head around.

'So in the end he just gave us the bananas and told us to dunk them in the milk.'

The b-word still out in the open, and me just being too tired and speechless to deal with it, I miss a gap in the traffic and a car behind flashes me. Someone else is being a bastard this morning. I swivel round and shout something I shouldn't. Millie laughs.

We pull up outside school with four minutes to spare and I stand by the car until all three are safely deposited, nipples on end in the drizzly cold as I forgot to wear a coat. And a bra.

'Jools? Hi! Good weekend?'

Paula Jordan leaps in front of me wearing head to toe hot pink Nike with toned abs and a thong on show. All our kids are in the same classes so it means a friendship has been forced upon us. She peers into the car. Millie has a moist Percy Pig covered in fuzz stuck to her forehead.

'Not bad. You?'

'Are those sweets for breakfast? That can't be good – all those refined sugars.'

I try to put my body in between her and the window.

'Oh no, it's one of those Play-Doh thingymajigs. You look well for a Monday morning.'

Her ponytail swishes with the compliment.

'Yogalates. Amazing class in the park. You get to breathe in that morning air, reset your chakras, really sets you up for the day.'

It's like she's speaking a different language. I scan down to her abs to inspect if they might be real or those spray on ones I've seen in magazines. The real test surely would be to punch her in the stomach. But I don't.

'The kids do it too. Actually, it has really focussed Harriet and Toby's energies – maybe it's something your twins could benefit from.'

Hidden insult #1. I nod, thinking how they usually focus their energy by running around in circles until they pass out and the energy ceases to exist. 'Maybe.'

'So I'll get to yours for 6.30?'

I nod again. It's my night for entertaining the Jordan children at my house, post-swimming club. Not that I mind, but I await the inevitable.

'Just to remind you again, the kids are allergic to gluten and dairy. But you knew that, right?'

I go into auto-pilot smile and nod mode. I know because you tell me every week, it's engraved into keyrings on their school bags, and you've even written me a laminated list for my fridge detailing everything they're not allowed to consume.

'It's just when they come to your house – no offence or anything but they always come back a bit … giddy. It's just

8

things like food colourings, flavourings – even cocoa. They just don't agree with those things.'

Hidden Insult #2. She has the habit of making it sound like I pour bottles of tartrazine down their necks when they come over. The fact is, she goes around school telling everyone how delicate her kids are, how the gluten we're giving them is poison, but little Harriet once came round telling me their dad lets them secretly feast on Peperami and Wagon Wheels in the shed when their mum's having her weekly colon cleanse.

'I mean, if you have nothing in, I have a bag of millet in my car. The kids love it steamed with red chard.'

I nod again. A bag of grain in your car. I look down at Millie who's found a lightsaber on my back seat. Different languages, different planets.

'We'll be fine. I'm just popping to the supermarket now.'

'Waitrose?'

'Sainsbury's.'

Then silence. I should have said Lidl.

CHAPTER TWO

Time to take a deep breath. In and out. And close your mouth, fool. Too late, coffee dribbles down my chin and onto my checked shirt. Millie looks at me, ponderous as to which of us is the infant at the table. We're sitting in Caffè Nero beside Sainsbury's having breakfast: double shot cappuccino with two sachets of sugar for Mummy, bad croissant for Millie; the sort of shrivelled-up pastry that would make the French weep and brick up the Channel Tunnel. Crumbs stick around her face like crusty cold sores and I spend half my time dusting them off. She giggles and dusts my mouth off too. I feel a level of guilt given this is probably the only time Millie and I will get to bond today. Too often these times I'm supposed to be feeding her and looking her deeply in the eyes to build the maternal attachment, I'm usually multitasking: reading a story, applying Savlon to battle wounds, stirring a dinner. Yet she's one of those babies who doesn't seem to mind. Sitting there just taking it all in, ginger curls, doughy cheeks like Marlon Brando.

The ginger doesn't come from me. With a blonde eight-year-old and twin boys with chocolate hair, I wasn't sure what to expect with this one. Not ginger, that's for sure. I just remember the look the midwife gave me when she was in our front room, my legs akimbo as Matt filled up the birthing pool. I froze, thinking something was wrong. The baby was stuck, she saw feet, my bikini line was so overgrown she'd have to tackle that first with a hedge trimmer. But all she did was comment about how many carrots I'd eaten in this pregnancy. I didn't put two and two together until a tiny, copper-headed missy was placed on my stomach. Gorgeous. But her head aglow like a pumpkin.

I write a shopping list on the back of a napkin with an old pen from the Manchester Team Building Exercise 2004 I found in my handbag. Matt always brings me the best souvenirs. First, the Holy Trinity: milk, bread, and eggs. As long as I have those in the house then we can survive anything. We definitely need cereal, wipes, and a plan for tonight's dinner. After Paula Jordan left me at the school gate choking on the back draft of fumes from her Nordic silver Honda CRV, I started to wish I'd asked for that bag of millet. What to cook, what to cook, what to cook? It's like the mantra around which my day revolves; a subtle equation whereby you have to balance the contents of your freezer with what the supermarket shelves have to offer and what your patience and time constraints will allow. And today, I have to balance in the added variable of the Jordan kids. Do I go raw? Paleo? Lacto-vegan? I think about Paula on her sanctimonious foodie bandwagon looking me up and down. I think about my garage floor. It's Monday. Time to go pescatarian; time for fish finger pie. An age old recipe of my dad's, it involves a box of fish fingers, a tin of tomato soup, lashings of grated cheese, served with cheap white buttered bread. It's comfort food at it's very best; starchy and dayglow and I have a fondness for it given my dad used to cook it for me once a month when I was on my period – his way of trying to offer a teenage girl solace.

I served it once to the Jordan kids on a day when Paula asked me when I was thinking about losing my baby weight. I remember Toby hoovering it up without actual cutlery. Yes, today is definitely a fish finger pie day.

As I scribble down the rest of my list and stop Millie eating lumps of butter like cheese, I hear the two baristas chatting. One checks her hair in the milk steamer, the other is restocking wooden stirrers.

'So it's today! Shit, you think we can get in on it? Pop up in the background?'

'Man, he is so fit. We have to at least get an autograph.'

I crane my neck to help with the eavesdropping while remembering we also need sugar and I need tampons.

'Didn't you see all them vans outside? They've got lights and cameras, it's well flash.'

I simultaneously correct their grammar while looking out of

12

the window. Vans, lots of them. I had assumed it was the mobile library doing the rounds. There's a lot of action. People in baseball caps mill around, trying to keep the drizzle off with their clipboards. A commercial, maybe? Photo shoot? My gawping is cut short as my phone rings and I attempt to find it in the cavern that is the change bag.

'Hello?'

'Mrs Campbell? Juliet Campbell?'

I always sit up straight when I hear my name in full. Definitely not Dad. It can only be a teacher, a policeman, or my mother-in-law.

'Yes?'

'Clifton Primary School here. I'm Mrs Terry, the school secretary. I'm afraid Ted isn't very well. He threw up during assembly. Could arrangements be made for him to be picked up this morning?'

Half-arsed banana smoothies and mouldy Percy Pigs would do that to young stomachs. Poor little mite. Bad Mummy. I look at my list. If I rush and pick him up now, then we'll have no food for the others when they get home. I'll have to give the Jordan kids tuna served out of the tin like cat food. I'll need white spirit to try and cover the twins' tracks from their father. We'll definitely need milk. I start crossing things out and look at the clock on the wall.

'Ummm, yes of course. I'm just in the doctors' at the moment. Could you give me half an hour?'

'Sure.'

There's a condescension in her voice that suggests she knows I'm lying. It's a 'he's sick and you don't even care' voice.

'I'll be as quick as I can.'

Few people shop on a Monday morning bar elderly couples stocking up on pork pies, rice pudding, and newspapers, which makes trolley dashing far easier given the circumstances. Pensioners are left for dust as we race around, Millie enjoying the lively pace, my boobs not too happy about the lack of support. When we get to the freezer section, fish fingers are on special at £1 a box (get in) so I dump three boxes in the trolley and get some plain crackers for Ted's poorly tummy. I emerge from an aisle to see mini muffins fresh out of the in-store bakery. Will I have the time to bake my own later? Will I bugger. I cave. This is going well. Maybe I'll only be twenty minutes. Next bread, eggs, tinned soup, locating the white spirit next to the lightbulbs, and then the milk aisle, scanning the lids for blue and green, the right amount, something that isn't leaking (this has happened before, the smell has still not left the car). I see a new product – toned milk. From cows with slim calves and flat stomachs? I laugh at my own joke and Millie looks like she's worried for me. Given it's Monday and the theme for today is comfort food, I also treat myself to a pack of mini scotch eggs. Damn the consequences. I head for the counters slightly smug, also worryingly out of breath. Behind me I hear crates rattling to get past so I stop hogging the aisle and move to one side, cupping my hands under each armpit as the icy fridge air hits me. But no one passes me. I turn around only to find a great, giant light in my eyes. For some reason I assume it's fallen from the ceiling and bend at the knee. But then, a face. Shitting mother of …

'Hello, darling. Right, don't be too surprised. I'm Tommy, it's lovely to meet you. And what's your name?'

I'm not wearing a bra. I've actually got a boob in each hand. I'm blinded by a light behind Tommy's head and a camera is pointed square in my face. Tommy McCoy. He puts an arm around me as I wave into the camera for some unexplained reason.

'Shit. Sorry, I mean … yeah, you are …'

Tommy and his cohorts all cup their mouths and laugh at my speechlessness. Millie glares at me wondering why we deserve such attention, her chin shiny with drool. I notice they're leaving a gap wide open for me to talk.

'I'm Jools.'

'Like Jools Holland?'

'Yeah. But I can't play the piano.'

That was funnier in my head. The blank expressions in front of me assure me that's the case. A couple of elderly ladies stop to ogle. Staff in uniform pinnies and fleeces emerge to stare at me. I'm still not wearing a bra.

'And who is this little carrot top here?'

Millie, who has heard this term of endearment a lot since her birth, looks immediately quite insulted. I urge her to throw up on him.

'This is Millie.'

'She your only one?'

'Nope. I have three others.'

'Cripes, love. You've been popping 'em out haven't ya?'

How the hell do you respond to that? Yes? Indeed, I have! Like cannonballs! I smile back. He's very glossy in real life. His hair looks like it's been dipped upside down in wax, and with his face close up you see the shimmer of face powder. The light blue eyes might be a redeeming feature if you could look past the distressed jeans, the slogan T-shirt, and the orange suede trainers. He hops about on his feet, addressing the camera every so often by winking at it, presuming his fame and looks give him licence to squeeze my shoulders.

'So tell me about yourself, love?'

Love? I'm not sure what he wants to hear. I'm also not sure how to stand. He's considerably taller than me so every time he grabs my shoulder for a one-armed hug, I end up in his armpit. I'm also wholly aware that in my current ensemble of comfy student chic, I'm going to appear ever so dumpy. I hover on my tiptoes.

'I'm a mum of four. I live here. Not in the supermarket … but in Kingston. I … errrm, I'm married to Matt as well.'

I hope Matt doesn't see this and wonder why I added him as an afterthought. Lots of beady expectant eyes watch me, taking in the short and meagre speech that is my life story.

'And do you work?'

'I'm a home … mother … housewife?'

I pause as I say it. I hate that term and the pitiful looks that come with it. Is that all? You're just a housewife? I'm tempted to tell him I'm an astronaut on Sundays. But I don't. Tommy continues.

'So, not sure if you've seen the show, we're here today looking for people we can help. Tell me what's for your dinner tonight. Can I have a look in your trolley?'

He hasn't quite asked my permission so much as told me what he's about to do. Maybe I can run. Or feign confusion. This isn't my trolley, never seen this baby before in my life. He starts with the fish fingers.

'Fish fingers? Really?'

I want to answer back. But I can't. Tommy nods, frowning and pulling a face like I've just told him I'm feeding my kids fried turds.

'And your family eats this a lot?'

'It's just an occasional treat. It's fish fingers ... I'm making a pie ...'

He pulls his lips back across his teeth.

'I mean, it's like comfort food. Being Monday and all. Just ...'

He looks at me and sighs a little. I want to question the sort of man who has never sought infinite amounts of joy from a fish finger sandwich. But I don't. His attention returns to the contents of my trolley. Tommy rifles past white spirit and milk and gets to the bread.

'Is this the sort of bread you normally buy?' he says, squeezing my loaves. 'The average household could save up to £250 a year by investing in a bread maker. You could do yourself all sorts of flavours: wholemeal for a start, multigrain, lovely Mediterranean loaves with olive oil and sundried tomatoes ...'

The bugger has pummelled my loaves and left huge depressions in them that I know will mean the bread will never return to its original shape and will leave the slices shaped like squashed clovers. His attention turns to the scotch eggs and mini muffins and he has his way with them too, poking at them and listing all the artificial ingredients to the camera.

'Such a shame, love, you know these things are so easy to make yourself. Bit of minced pork, herbs, and breadcrumbs. I have an amaaazing recipe.'

I nod. It's just for today. I needed a scotch egg pick me up.

16

The posse of spectators who have gathered are all shaking their heads like I've just peed in the middle of the aisle. I stand speechless, shocked but also narked. I don't have time for your judgement, I'm not dressed for this. I need to get to my precious Ted and his technicolour vomit. I can also feel my skin starting to glisten – these lights are bloody hot.

'Look love, I want to help you and I can see you're uncomfortable so I'm gonna ask you straight up. You're a busy mum of four and to be honest, I don't want to see you feeding your brood this rubbish. Can I help you?'

I look at my wrist and a watch that I'm not wearing.

'Ummm, the thing is, I really don't have the time. I need to get somewhere.'

The gathered crowd inhales. One woman in her sensible shoes, perm, and twinset seems to not understand what I am saying. You mean you are turning him down? Are you blind? Other Monday mums jostle to the front of the crowd, arranging their bosoms so the producers may pounce on them next. I smile at Tommy, who looks like the sort who's never been turned down without a fight.

'C'mon, love. You get me for a whole day, in your house, on the television, helping to turn your life around. Whaddya say? For your kids?'

By this point, I'm quite proud of myself because none of his bribes are luring me in. He could indeed turn my life around, if he had a cheque for a sizeable amount of money with my name on it in his back pocket. Alas, I suspect my pride would prevent me asking for cold, hard cash. He grabs my shoulders in a vain attempt to squeeze some emotion out of me.

'Sorry, I can't.'

I turn to leave, glad to have my back to the camera for once, but not before I hear him mumbling under his breath to someone with a clipboard.

'Let's find someone else. If she doesn't care, then why should I?'

This is where I should really walk away. I should canter to the tills, pay, pack, and run off to Ted who's going to be sitting on those orange polyester chairs by the school office wondering where I am. To be honest, it takes very little to rile me today. I'm not touchy, over-sensitive, or confrontational in the slightest. Take my parking space, spill my drink, show up on my door trying to sell me windows. It's all small things in the greater scheme of things. But today is Monday. I'm not wearing a bra. I'm coming off a truly bad school run. He thinks I don't care. I turn and see him still glaring at me while he adjusts his collar.

'Excuse me?'

'Changed your mind then?'

'Actually, no.'

The producer seems happy I've returned but the crowd seem a little bored of me now.

'I just heard what you said. I thought it was a little out of order.'

Tommy shrugs his shoulders, quite unapologetic.

'Well, like I said, love. It seems to me like you don't care. You've got a whole load of crap in your trolley, pardon my French, and you're gonna give that to your kids? Mums like you break my heart.'

My mind races like a high-powered computer, filtering everything that was wrong with what he just said. Firstly, crap is crap, it ain't French. Secondly, I'm not giving it to just my kids, there are two adults involved too. And lastly, mums like me?

'Well, please enlighten me about the sort of mother I am, seeing as you know me so well.'

The semi-dispersing crowd re-huddle for the potential drama about to unfold.

'What's your idea of cooking? Putting something on a tray to go in the oven? You've no fruit, no veg. You probably have your kids chugging away on snacks all day long.'

'I've got fruit and veg at home, my kids eat OK. I think it's a little rude to judge me on a shopping trolley and the fact you've just met me.'

'Really? You have the veg at home, is it?'

Why the hell would I lie about a bit of broccoli? A person from the production team hands him a Japanese radish that I half hope he'll slip on so it lands directly in his rear end.

'What's this called, then?'

'It's a radish. A daikon, I think.'

He seems shocked. I raise my eyebrows. C'mon, throw all your rare vegetables at me, you bloody condescending prick. Now you're just assuming I'm uneducated, stupid even? Seriously? Ted is sick. Granted, that's because he ate old Percy Pigs for breakfast but I'm not doing this now. Tommy's rifling through a basket fingering some physalis.

'Hold up there, missy.'

I freeze. Missy? I have the overwhelming urge to throw something at him, saddened that I haven't got a pineapple available. I am flustered, cold, and have a suspicion that Millie may have filled her nappy again.

'Really, please. I think you've insulted me enough today. I'm not sure I can handle any more lectures. Thanks.'

His eyes mist over. He puts a hand to my shoulder and cocks his head to one side.

'Sorry, look – all I want to do is help you, love. Not judge. Eating healthily can be cheap and convenient. At least take a copy of my book for some recipe ideas.'

He holds it up to the crowd. It's shiny, has his face on it, and is called 'The Real McCoy.' I open the first page to see that it's signed. My first thought is of eBay. A young upstart with equally fluorescent trainers hands out a few copies to the crowd. One woman holds her copy with Tommy's gleaming face at her bosom, smells it, and looks like she might be having a special moment. I put mine in my trolley.

'Don't you want to look through it now?'

'Errrm, no. Thank you. It can wait.'

He throws his hands up in the air like he's done with me. I'm a lost cause, obviously there must be something wired up wrong in my brain. Why aren't I in the throes of oestrogenic adulation, hanging on to his every word? I catch an image of myself in the reflection of the camera lens. My hair looks like I've been rolling around in static.

'You should think about your kids.'

'I do.' I furrow my brow to see where this is going.

19

'Because you need to …'

'I need to …'

'Do better by them.'

The hush descended over the crowd hangs like fog. Tommy stands back, knowing a line has been crossed. Walk away, Jools. Walk away.

'Excuse me? What right do you have to tell me that? God, yeah – if I was shitting money like you – of course, I'd buy bloody organic everything and make my own bloody bread. Thing is, I don't have your millions. I have four kids and a mortgage. So I don't need some hyped-up twat who's completely removed from reality giving me grief and judgment over a fucking fish finger.'

I said fucking. Millie looks up at me like a little distressed lobster. Mummy has her rage on. The fish fingers have made their way into my hand as if helping me fight the closing argument of a trial. The once frozen box is soggy in my fingers. Maybe I can bring up the fact they're 100% cod, the fact Captain Birdseye looks like the reliable sort. Tommy, for once, is speechless, while my transformation into raving lunatic continues. The entire supermarket seems to look on.

'We're all parents, love. We know how hard it can be.'

He announces this to the crowd. Some of the faithful nod. The irony is not lost on the others.

'Really, Tommy? How? Please explain your hardships to me.'

Tommy is silent and staring daggers at me. I'm on a roll.

'I thought so. Are you off on the school run later? Will you be changing nappies today? Making cups of tea you'll never drink? Wrestling your children into a bath? Grating cheese till your fingers are raw? No.'

People chuckle. A group of shelf-stacking teenagers have joined the gaggle of silent spectators. Somehow it goads me on in a playground mob way.

'You're not like me. It's completely patronising of you to compare our lives in any way. So please drop it with the mockney "best mate" act and realise you know nothing of my life, and even if I do mess up being a parent every so often, I

20

don't need you shoving it down my throat.'

Wow. That was quite ballsy, but also surprisingly eloquent, which is very unlike me. A man at the back applauds me. Everyone else is paralytic with shock, so I leave. I run. Literally sprint. Gripping on to my trolley and heading for the self-service tills to avoid any further human contact. I'm silent, maybe a light shade of raspberry, and a bit balmy around the armpit region, still breathless. I brought my own bags. Does that count for anything? I can feel the stares of staff and customers boring into the back of my head. Car. Just get to the car. Leaving the store, it's drizzling again and I run to the car using a spare fruit and veg bag to cover Millie's head. Everything loads randomly into the car and, all damp, I finally get into the driver's seat, checking myself in the rear view mirror. A rather fetching sweat moustache, hair like a straw mane, my eyes creased with an emotion I can no longer contain. Tears fall on to the steering wheel as I realise how bloody angry I am. Bloody, bloody idiot. That, and I forgot the sodding cereal.

CHAPTER THREE

Ted's in my bed with some water, crackers, and CBeebies. I picked him up from school, my clothes drenched in sweat, my cheeks still on high blush so much so that the school secretary asked if I'd come from the gym. I may have laughed. But Ted did what he does best; he feigned being sicker than he was, asked me for sweets in the car, then came home and threw up on the WELCOME mat where I found out from the smell that he'd definitely drunk that white stuff in the fridge.

So now while that mat soaks in a bucket in the garden, I do my usual zip around the house. Dad's been in. You have to love my dad, every morning after I leave he always lets himself in through the back with the key we've given him and potters about, does the washing up, hangs out the clothes. It's like having a house pixie with a penchant for corduroy and muted autumnals. Today, he's made beds, put pyjamas under pillows, replaced the empty loo roll holder, and left me a note:

Did a shark eat your recycling crate? Have rung Council to get you a new one. You also need milk and some white spirit for your garage. Dad x

Must remember that floor. Right, things I had to do, things I had to do? Put the phone back in the charger, change Millie, put crap in different places and pass it off as tidying. Vodafone bill. I open up the laptop and log on, skimming over the bill – the same every month – with me using up all our free texts to tell Matt to get milk, and Matt using all our free minutes to ask if we need anything else. I pay the bill then get on Facebook, viewing my Home page – something to quell the insanity of this morning. There's nothing much today: Lewis Young (met in first week of halls; used to eat toasties together; snogged once at a Hallowe'en club night) has holiday pics up of his trek up Machu Picchu. Lots of ponchos and llamas. Helen MacDougall (summer job friend; WHSmith alumni; we stole pens together) informs me in her status that '*Foo Fighters were ace last night! Thanks for taking me babe x x x.*' Joe Farley (went to primary school together; thick NHS glasses; now runs a used car dealership) is playing Mafia Wars and Farmville, encouraging me to help him buy a cow. Ben (younger brother; bound to our friendship by blood and genetics) is online. I message him, knowing he's the sort who lives by his phone so may reply.

J: Whatcha doing?
He replies immediately.
B: *I'm trying to catch a bus out of Acton. BIG NIGHT!*

I scowl as I'm reminded how his social life buzzes even on a Sunday night when I was in ironing miniature polo shirts and watching the *X Factor* results.

J: Acton is near IKEA. Meatballs for breakfast!
B: *One step ahead of you, sis. His name was Marcel.*
J: Too. Much. Information. Stay safe. Pick me up a new colander.

And with that, he's offline. I didn't even get to share my McCoy news. I examine my wall and then scan local parents' pages. Millie stares at me from the corridor, banging blocks together – go on, tell people; it's vaguely interesting compared to your usual posts e.g. *They've changed Jaffa Cakes! I swear they are less orangey now* ☹
Here goes …
Jools Campbell *met Tommy McCoy in Saino's this morning – what a dickhead.* A chat box flickers open. Annie. University lawyer friend and saviour.

A: *You met Tommy McCoy? You going to be on TV?*J: Jesus, hope not. I looked a state. Think I might have been a little rude to him as well.
A: *Hahahahaha :D What did you say?*J: I can't even remember. PMT induced ranting.

A: *Good for you. Can't stand him. You fancy a drink Friday night?*

Annie always asks me this but knows me getting a babysitter or indeed having the time and energy to doll myself up, get a train into town, and sit in a crowded bar elbowing skinny office minnies out of the way is not ever going to happen. Still, she asks and keeps me in her loop which is why I love her.

J: Maybe. Or maybe come here and we can do a curry?

A: *Sounds fab. I have to go – important stuff ... we're counting eggs today.*

J: They usually come in boxes of six or twelve.

A: *Nope, my eggs – hopefully there are still some of the buggers in there because the other option is that maybe I've reached menopause. Yikes!*

J: I did notice a bit of a 'tache on you last time.

A: *I was trying to channel your monobrow.*

J: Har-de-hah!

I feel my fingers reach up subconsciously.

J: Text me after your appt, tell me how it goes. Campbells love Aunty Annie x

A: *Speak later Missus x*

Millie crawls under the kitchen table, cruising in between our assortment of chairs, stools, and high-chairs, resting her head by my knees. Lovely Millie. I reach down and stroke her hair. Facebook sits there quietly, waiting for me to get sucked in, quietly judging me for having nothing else interesting to say. Tommy McCoy's name looks up at me and I look at my box of mini scotch eggs on the kitchen table. Instant pangs of guilt dart through me. So I resort to carbs, E-numbers, and unidentifiable meat products in times of crises and personal lows? I pick up a pear from the fruit basket in the middle of the kitchen table. It's also about balance. I flick open my mobile to call Matt. He answers after three rings like clockwork.

'Matt Campbell?'

'It's me.'

Matt's voice always relaxes when he hears my voice. His throat opens up and his voice goes a Scottish semitone deeper – the same voice that lured me into bed the second we met. Scotland has a lot to bloody answer for.

'How goes it?'

'Rough, rough morning. Ted's at home – threw up at school.'

I can hear Matt's chair roll away from his desk.

'Tummy bug?'

'More a dodgy breakfast combination. He's in bed with Mr Bloom. The other two are fine. Anyway, had an even more surreal moment this morning in Sainsbury's. You'll never guess who I ran into?'

'Who?'

'Guess.'

Eight years of marriage tell me he'll never play this game with me.

'Tommy fricking McCoy.'

'Hope you told him he was a talentless prick.'

'Pretty much.'

'What …?'

'He was trying to recruit me into that programme of his and I went off at him. It was actually a bit embarrassing.'

'And the accounts manager will be in the office on Sunday. You could talk to him then?'

'Boss?'

'Yes. I could call you later to confirm the details.'

'Yes, that would be most satisfactory. Love you.'

He'll never say it back, not at work at least. 'Yes, thank you for calling.'

I smile. Then I receive a text from him two minutes later:

<In meetings til 5. Want details. Big hug 4 Ted. Pay that bill, buy milk. Sky man coming before 2. Don't shag him.>

I reply.

<Sky man coming? I'll put on my best knickers.>

Best knickers? Do I still own a pair of those? Black, lace, French. The last time I wore them was probably when I met Matt. Matteo Campbell. My rebound sex man. The man I ended up marrying.

It had been 2001 at Leeds University. I never wanted to go up North and had hoped to stay closer to family but I followed then-boyfriend Richie Colman who was studying civil engineering and who I thought I'd marry and have babies with. Richie thought differently and unceremoniously dumped me after our first year to shag a blonde biochemist called Dawn. To ease the distress, I went to the cheesiest night Leeds had to offer and got very, very drunk. Matt would be in that club. Of course, I can't tell you how and when we met but my then-housemate Annie told me our meeting pretty much went as such; it was the end of the night and having drunk my own weight in B52s and Slippery Nipples, I had my arms linked with a group of people I didn't know, Matt being one of them. Annie remembers when the lights came on our faces were attached to one another, our lips locked and intertwined like cod fish. When she tried to detach me from him to drag me into a cab, I held on to Matt's hand and brought him home with us. I don't remember the sex but Annie does because she heard it, with the bonus of listening to me throwing up shortly after. She always tells this story with a smug air, but she also took someone home with her that night – a rugby player with arms like hocks of ham who came into the kitchen the next morning in just his pants scratching his undercarriage right before rifling through our drawers for a teaspoon.

Yet my one-night stand turned into something more. Matt left that morning but I'd bump into him the following night at the same club. I was in mourning for Richie, I wanted to mask his loss with fruity alcohol and messy snogs. Matt spied me from across the bar, came over, and boom, the sweet Scottish voice and he was back in my bed again. From there in, he became, and I cringe to call him this, a booty call. He started buying me tubes of Munchies and sharing spliffs with me. He was studying Social Policy and Philosophy, I was a psychologist. He had so many ideas about the world, global development, and changing things one person at a time. He wore beanie hats and in the mornings I'd find him hidden under the duvet, his sandy hair all fuzzy like a lost hamster, his slate grey eyes a little bleary from the weed and snakebites. He was completely likeable. Completely. But I'd spent the last four years with Richie Colman, I needed distractions, space, time. He was just the rebound guy – so I knew in the back of my mind that even though Matt was pleasant enough, our dalliance would have an expiry date. We were both twenty years old, our biggest concerns being cheap alcohol and scraping through modules. Then everything changed; the condom split.

CHAPTER FOUR

Clifton Primary Swimming Pool. Possibly the most humid place on the planet north of the Equator, where the windows are constantly misty from all the excess heat, which in turn transforms non-swimming children into manic whirling dervishes, and the parents, sweating elegantly in their fleeces, sit dotted around the viewing terraces chatting on their iPhones trying to handle the rubbish acoustics. I'm feeding Jake and Toby the rest of the mini muffins washed down with apple juice and watching to make sure Ted doesn't leapfrog down the benches and end up in the pool himself. The power of distraction does wonders for a poorly tummy. I sit and stare at the azure of the pool wondering why I feel so tired and rough. Probably the scotch eggs I ate in the car. It's been a quiet afternoon. The Sky man did arrive at 2 p.m. and told me he was here to fiddle with my dish. I resisted the temptation to respond with innuendo, given 'Stuart – Here to Help!' was five foot tall and three foot wide. So I just made him some weak tea like a good hostess and Ted offered him a Rich Tea finger which he ate like a wood chipper, leaving crumbs all over the freshly washed doormat.

'Mummy, Toby's had three muffins and I only had two.'

Toby looks especially pleased with himself, chocolate crumbs lining his collar. Must remember to attack him with wipes before his mother sees. I hand Jake another one as he runs off and I am almost a little impressed that he has been able to count and determine the numerical difference. But that's always been Jake. Even when he was little, there was always a Stewie Griffin look about him like he knew more than he was letting on. Matt calls him the mastermind, like he might have even sent Ted out first to check on the situation before making his appearance in this world. Ted is different, a follower – but the ever-faithful henchman, the one who'd defend his brother to the core but who probably drew the zebra crossing because he was told to. Must remember to clean the garage floor when I get back.

'All right, Jools? Paula offloaded the kids on you again?'

I turn to see Donna, mother of Ciara (Hannah's class), Justin (two years younger), and Alesha (one year older than Millie; always dressed in Bisodol pink) and who lives five doors down from me. I like Donna immensely. She's amiable for the fact she is completely ballsy, no holds barred, always says what's on her mind, which makes for entertaining company in the bear pit of try-hard mothers and their competitive ways. She's dressed in skinny jeans, knee-high boots, a maxi cardigan, and a T-shirt emblazoned with a slogan I'm glad the kids can't read. I'm still wearing what I had on this morning but have added a grey hoodie and a bra. I'll never leave the house without a bra again. Donna being Donna puts her hand in my plastic bucket of muffins and helps herself. She flicks her poker straight black hair away from her face.

'That bitch is doing my 'ead in I tell you. Told me Harriet couldn't come to Ciara's pizza party 'cos she's allergic to wheat.'

I don't want to fuel the fire by telling her I'm going to stuff Harriet silly with gluten tonight.

'Aah, let her be. Sunday, right?'

'Yep, and tell Matt to come too, bring all your kids. You know what it's like at mine, friggin' free for all.'

I watch as Donna feeds Alesha muffin crumbs out of her perfectly manicured blue nails, each nail with a spray-on Celtic pattern. Donna, it could be said, is a little rough around the edges with her tattoos, key chains, and overdone mascara, but I think that's part of her appeal. In any case, I think I'm closer to being her than someone like Paula Jordan; she from the herd of parents who pretend their children are being educated at Clifton Primary because they're *Guardian* reading lefties when in fact they'd sooner go private if they had more money. At least with Donna, what you see is what you get. She's also full of gossip, which keeps me on my toes.

'Anyway, did you see Jen Tyrrell this morning? Might as well have mounted Mr Pringle at the gate.'

Jen Tyrrell – Paula Jordan's BFF but ten times worse. I'm surprised she doesn't leave a trail of wheatgrass and diet pills everywhere she walks. She's the sort of mother who also feels the ridiculous need to be queen bee. Recollections of those sorts of girls from school always urge me to give those kinds of folk a wide berth. Mr Pringle – the twenty-something, freshly qualified teacher of the girl's class – a dewy-eyed looking fella who most of the mothers take great joy in ogling from the school gate. He's pleasant enough to look at but his youth and energy often make me feel a little woeful about myself.

'You heard? She's started a "parents' discussion forum" so she can go rub her tits in his face every Tuesday night.'

'What are they discussing?'

'Crap. Fundraisers, school plays, fucking do-gooding bullshit.'

I laugh. It's always been the case at Clifton Primary: two very different crowds – one who twizzle the occasional turkey, their kids' looking they've been thrown up on by a Claire's Accessories; next to the Boden crowd, competing to be the most organic and involved mothers in the land. I'm on neither team, just watching from the middle of their stand offs at the school gate, watching the divide that will never be united. Not by Donna at least who scans the stalls. But there's no one here to pick a fight with unless she go for the au pair sat waiting for little Maisy: bag of organic dried fruits in one hand and rice cakes in the other.

'Did you see Hugh Tyrrell at that parents' meeting last week? I tell you, if I was porking that you'd need to take my eyes first.'

Hugh 'Huge' Tyrrell – for want of a kindly word, a 'portly' man with hair that sprouts out his collar like errant weeds. I laugh and nod but to be honest, I have become a bit lost for words given my emotional and physical fatigue. Donna picks up on it.

'You all right? Little quiet.'

'Crap day. Guess who I bumped into this morning?'

Donna shrugs her shoulders.

'Tommy McCoy.'

'What? The real McCoy? You're joking! He's fit as.'

'Maybe, but a real tosser. He was in Sainsbury's and I think I had a fight with him. It was surreal.'

Donna loves this idea of me being confrontational. Actually, anyone in a confrontation will do for her.

'Bloody hell, a fight? Was it fisticuffs over the frozen foods?'

'Fish fingers, actually.'

'Hope you told him where to go.'

'I think I did.'

Donna smiles and puts one arm around my shoulders and the other hand into my muffins.

'That's my girl! Shame, though. I always thought he was fit. Rumour is he's hung like a ruddy donkey.'

My muffin lodges in my throat, just as she spies her Justin with his trousers around his ankles about to pee in someone's handbag and hurdles down to stop him.

CHAPTER FIVE

Before long, the kids, having been illegally loaded into my car, are now filled to the brim with fish finger pie. Something I'm still unapologetic about – comfort food needs come first but given McCoy's damn voice still haunts me, I'm now cutting apples and plucking grapes onto a plate. Something still riles about this morning – there was the judgement, the presumption, but also the fact he pigeonholed me so quickly; how he was so quick to turn around and judge one day of junk as a fail. I think about what he said and turn to look at empty plates, thinking about processed food zipping its way around my kids' bodies, turning into bad fats and making them stupid. Maybe I should have gone with a spag bol tonight. Maybe I should have baked my own muffins. I pluck at a few more grapes.

Upstairs, I hear some sort of boyband-like anthem pulse through the ceiling. That would be the girls, while the boys are gawking in front of the television which is allowed, as the alternative would be them hurling themselves off the sofa and swinging from the lampshades. Millie sits in her high-chair and catches bits of grape in her mouth like a trained seal. Half an hour until Paula Jordan arrives. So I've hidden anything with artificial colouring and gluten and I have my two best mugs out. I even have the kids watching the Discovery Channel which is thankfully now less fuzzy since Stuart the Sky Man came to fiddle with our dish.

'Daddddddyyyyyy!'

It's a sound I hear every night. Like he's just returned from war or the children haven't seen him in months. I hear the front door open and shut and watch from the kitchen as the boys hurl themselves at him. Toby Jordan watches in adulation. I suppose Paula calls for more restraint in her house. Kids generally like Matt because of his *Balamory* style accent and the fact he launches them through the air and over his shoulders.

'All right? Ted? You OK, buddy.'

Ted immediately remembers he was sick and pulls a face. Matt bundles him in his arms and returns him to the television. There's two minutes of wrestling before he comes to find me and to give Millie a kiss.

'Correct me if I'm wrong but we have just the two sons, right? Or are they multiplying on their own now?'

'The Jordan kids. Eaten?'

'Nope.'

'There's some fish finger pie if you want it.'

'Yeah, why not? Put a brew on as well.'

Matt always returns from work with pink eyes and a doughy, bloated expression on his face, like part of his soul has been extracted through his flesh. He's always worked long, hard hours to support us but I know that being an accountant was not what his heart desired. To avoid being a corporate clone, he therefore hangs on to the last vestiges of his youth that he feels still keep him young and relevant: the vintage satchel, the big earphones, the Kruder & Dorfmeister playlists, the unstyled Blur/Parklife haircut. Hell, if he could, I'd bet he'd wear his tie around his head like a Cherokee as soon as he left the office. I'm not sure what Matt would have done had we not got pregnant at the age of twenty and instead used our degrees to lead other lives. He'd probably be on a Greenpeace boat giving whalers hell, maybe a renegade journalist in East Timor, or an anti-war campaigner helping mine victims find new limbs. Instead he signed his life away to Price Waterhouse Cooper. I can't even remember what I wanted to be.

Even before removing his bag and shoes, he does what he always does and that's to sift pointlessly through the cupboards. He sits down next to Millie, his blond hair all ruffled, stretches his arms behind his back, and takes a long sip of tea. Then he stops.

'So what do you know?'

It's his line. He knows I have a million and one things to tell him when he walks through the door and this line is permission that he is ready to take it all in. I lean on the counter sipping from a cup and dole out the rest of the Rich Tea fingers.

'Start with Tommy McCoy.'

I tell him all the details and he nods, laughs, and finishes my explanation with a hug. Hugs are what Matt and I do. For the longest time, I've realised this is our ritual way of maintaining some level of intimacy in our relationship given we lack the energy to kiss or think of anything complimentary to say to each other. So our groins slightly touch, his stubble grazes my freckly cheek, we literally prop each other up. Today, his hair smells of mangoes which makes me think he's run out of shampoo and had to use the kids' but the contact is surprisingly drawn out and I see Millie smile to see us embrace, like she knows this is how the world should be.

'Well, don't let the bastard get you down. You're an all right cook.'

I look over and give him half a smile, knowing that popping fish fingers in soup and slapping a thick layer of butter onto cheap white bread doesn't really qualify for much affection. But all right? I'll take that. He points to the fridge.

'Well, you do what all mums do, you get on with stuff. End of.'

I stare at the fridge and the numerous recipe cards and magazine cuttings stuck on with alphabet magnets. He may be right. Maybe that is something that also niggles. Not that I'll ever be a McCoy league chef but truth be told, I thought I quite liked cooking. I have a feeling that in my harried existence, it's one of those things I seek some sort of joy from, even some feeling of achievement. From creating something in the kitchen to seeing it being wolfed down and the kids asking for more, it's definitely one part of being mum where I feel almost useful. Even feeding the husband makes me feel that I can at least provide him with some joy after a fraught working Monday.

I watch him sit down to eat when there's a knock at the back door. Adam. Adam, the elder of my brothers, lives around the corner in a bachelor pad with a flatmate the kids have christened Smelly Seb. When Adam runs out of money for a takeaway, he comes round to ours.

'Matteo! Juliet! How goes it?'

'Eaten?'

'Nope.'

I get him a plate. 'So are we still on for tonight? You got the TV fixed?'

My raised eyebrows reveal to the boys that an explanation is wanting. Matt nods and winks to Adam. 'It's the Champions League semi-final. Liverpool vs Inter. Adam and I are making a bit of a night of it.'

I flare my nostrils. 'Anyone else I can expect?'

'No. Could you rustle some of those nice chicken wings you make?'

'No, I can't make bloody chicken wings.'

Adam holds his imaginary handbag up. Matt smiles at me hoping it will summon up some goodwill. Not likely, Matteo Campbell.

'Well, I won't mind if you both get the kids bathed and ready for bed before you sit down to your game.'

I pat Millie on the head and Adam and Matt mumble their acceptance of the terms and conditions then wolf down what's left of the fish finger pie.

'You know Dad used to sprinkle the fish fingers with Tabasco, crisped them up under the grill. Proper legend.'

I stand open-mouthed wondering how he has the gall when he's shovelling it all in double speed. Jake walks in and does what he always does in the kitchen – sniffs his nose around on the hunt for sugar. His face lights up to see my reprobate brother.

'Uncle Adam! Are you here for the football?'

I realise there has been a plan in place all along, so stand closer to Millie to garner some form of female solidarity.

'Sure thing, Jakers. How's it going, little man?'

'All right, but Alfie Lingham called me a pube today.'

A bit of crust flies out of Matt's mouth which Millie finds highly entertaining. Adam looks to me for some back-up – this goes beyond the call of duty for an uncle.

'Do you know what a pube is?'

'No.'

He's five. For some reason this fills me with a sense of

36

relief.

'Well, it's hair that grows around your underwear area.'

Matt laughs and piles more food into his mouth so he doesn't have to explain.

'What, like Daddy's? He's got hair all over his beanbags.'

'Yes, that would be correct.'

Adam is going purple trying hard not to laugh and erupt in a messy fish finger fit of hysterics.

'Well, that's stupid. How can you be a pube? Anyway, Toby's mummy is here.'

We all freeze as a cloaked figure hovering in the hall awaits her entrance to be announced.

'Paula? Paula! Hey, come in. God, kids, eh?'

Seemingly unperturbed at learning about the state of my husband's balls, she sashays into the kitchen. The boys even rise to greet her. Luckily, her eyes seem more focussed on the bright orange concoction laid out in front of her and the fact Adam seems to be creating a sandwich involving crisps, sweet chilli sauce, and iceberg lettuce.

'Thanks again for looking after the kids. Are they ready?'

'Yeah, sure. HANNAH!'

Paula still can't seem to take her eyes off the food.

'Can I get you something to eat, perhaps?'

She forces a smile, staring at the loaf of bread on the counter. Her bread is probably brown with bits and a chewy crust, not neon white and doughy. She shakes her head.

'Did I tell you about the new wholefoods section of Waitrose? We've tried the tempeh bacon and it is delicious. You really wouldn't know the difference.'

It's a comment so out there that even Millie looks perplexed. I think it's a lead in so I will confess if I've tarnished her kids' insides with fish fingers. It's also a sanctimonious way of telling me how clean living she is, why she's so skinny and her skin glows like a ripe peach (which Donna says is nothing to do with her vegan lifestyle but all to do with the dermatologist she sees and the tummy tuck she had to get rid of her baby pouch). Matt and Adam look quizzical.

'I'm sure. Next time I'm in there, you know …'

I notice Adam mutter, 'Tempeh?' trying to resist laughing.

'Ummm, Paula, this is my brother Adam.'

She turns to greet him as he takes her hand and shakes it rigorously. I'm scared her arm will detach from her socket. In Adam's unsubtle way he gives her the once over: boobs and face. I think Paula enjoys the attention.

'Our kids are all in the same swimming classes.'

'Wow, you're a mum too. Would never have guessed.'

Please, Adam. Not Paula Jordan. To interrupt a potentially rather ick-inducing situation from proceeding, my voice gets shrill as I urge Hannah and Harriet to come down from upstairs and the boys to make an appearance from the living room. Paula doesn't sit but does what she always does: scans the cracked paint on the walls, the year-old school newsletters on the fridge, my hair twisted on the back of my head like a cockatoo's backside.

'What about a drink?'

I point to my best mugs but again she shakes her head, knowing that I probably don't have the organic ginger and elderflower cordial she's used to. She flicks her hair. It smells warm and chemically which makes me think while I've been looking after Harriet and Toby, she's been with Toni and Guy.

'So are you joining the parents' discussion forum on Tuesdays? We're thinking we could hold the meetings in parents' homes. Thoughts?'

I smile to myself, thinking of what Donna told me earlier at the swimming pool. Now they're going to lure poor Mr Pringle into their homes and seduce him in their downstairs cloakrooms.

'I'm not sure I have the time, Paula.'

I look over at Matt and read on his face, what the hell is a parents' discussion forum? Paula reads it too.

'The parents want to welcome Mr Pringle into the fold and are going to hold a fortnightly forum where we can discuss ideas with him over the children's extra-curricular activities.'

'Poor bloke.'

I laugh, maybe snort a little. Paula suddenly looks offended. Matt continues in the way I've come to appreciate him, i.e. in his inimitable Scottish accent mixed with some inventive swearing.

'No offence, Paula, but he's a young lad. Probably wants to spend his Tuesday evenings down the pub – not in a room full of overzealous mothers talking about the children he's spent all ruddy day with.'

I close my eyes. Very slowly. Offence might have been taken – just a smidge. I shout up the stairs for Harriet to get a move on. Paula stands there looking at the crumb trails on the floor. Harriet appears looking sullen at having to go home. Toby appears and smiles at me as he puts his shoes on like he might want me to adopt him. As they tackle their coats, Paula throws in a last ditch attempt to win me round to wasting my Tuesday nights at the bigger, better, and more colour co-ordinated houses of the Organix crowd.

'Well, I think it's a way for us to use our time better.'

I can think of another. *EastEnders*.

'Put me down as a maybe. I'll see.'

She creases her eyes at me – a look which perceives me to be either a wastrel mother who just sits there using prime-time TV to fill her sad life, or one that tells me my disinterest means I don't care. In any case, it feels overly familiar from this morning, so much so that I don't wave to her as she trots out to her Honda CRV. Bye then. Thank you for taking care of my children? I settle the kids back into the living room, trading sensible nature programme with nonsensical alien cartoon and return to the kitchen to find Matt washing up and Adam making space in my fridge for beers.

'Forgetting the whole Victoria Beckham thing, she's a bit of a MILF.'

'Adam, you're such a scrubber. She's married, and ten years older than me.'

'The word is experienced, sister.'

Matt laughs in his Marigolds.

'And what's this, Matt was just telling me you had some run-in with that foodie berk McCoy? Good for you. He's such a knob.'

I smile and nibble at the last soggy fish finger in the baking dish. Matt turns to me.

'What did you give Millie for her dinner? Looks like vomit.'

I inspect the bowl.

'It is vomit.'

Adam takes this as a cue to leave and terrorise the three children in the living room. Millie looks decidedly pale.

Ted threw up again, having the good sense to deposit it in a toy truck in the living room, then Jake followed suit. Hannah holed herself up in her room telling me she wasn't coming out because everyone had the Plague and she was going to die. I got a phone call from Paula at about seven o'clock to tell me Toby was not too well and asked if my kids' vomit was bright orange too. I made Matt Google 'orange vomit' to try and come up with an explanation I could fob her off with that avoided the truth about fish fingers. Ted and Jake were given plenty of water and cuddles, wiped down, and put into our bed with buckets nearby. Millie stayed downstairs with the football fans, lying on the sofa having only mildly vomited just the once. Having brothers like hers has aided her ability to sleep through anything. By some miracle, there is no bit of carpet, bed linen, mattress, or clothing that needs scrubbing so I'm in Hannah's room as we make our way through the *Harry Potter* novels. Hannah has a thick section of my hair and twists it around in her hands as she nods off.

'Mum, can I go to the cinema at the weekend?'

'What do you want to see?'

'The 1D movie.'

Hooray.

'OK, maybe. We could go in the morning.'

'Oh, not with you. I want to go with Tash.'

'Oh. With her mum?'

'No, just us. Lucy's mum lets her go the cinema on her own and she's got her ears pierced.'

Lucy's mum also dresses like she's fifteen in unflattering arrays of midriff tops and harem pants. I stop for a moment. I look at Hannah's soft ear lobes, thinking about them being poked with hot needles and my baby girl looking like a shiny pageant queen. I'd forgotten about peer pressure at school or had thought I wouldn't have to deal with that for another five years at least.

'We'll see.'

'That's what you always say.'

'That's because I love you.'

What the hell did that mean? Hannah doesn't buy it either. She never has. I reckon she knows she was born to a mother who was never really old or ready enough to know where she stood on certain matters, so always gives me a look like I'm just pulling my parenting skills out of my arse. She sits there unimpressed, still twiddling my hair.

'Look, it's late. How's your tummy feeling? You OK?'

She doesn't respond so I kiss her on the forehead and turn off the lights. It's late for her so she won't get out of bed in the morning without a shove and a kick. On my way out, Matt is checking the boys as they sleep in symmetrical star shapes next to each other.

'Ted's got a fever. Just gave Jake some more water. How's Han?'

'OK, just having a strop because I won't let her go to the cinema on her own.'

'But she's eight.'

'Exactly. Millie?'

'Asleep with your brother.'

For some reason that makes me want to dash down the stairs, but Matt stops me for a quick embrace and I relent. Another hug, this might be a weekly record. We've had it easy tonight. The worst so far was the flu of 2009 when the boys were babies, Hannah was three, and we were all sick. So sick, Jake had to be hospitalised, Matt pulled a muscle in his ribs from coughing so hard, and Hannah threw up over the new carpet in the landing that we've since covered with a rug.

'So what else do you know?'

'Too much. I'll tell you later.'

'I'm sorry I didn't tell you about the football.'

To be honest, I'm not sure how angry I was about that. It pales in comparison to what other wives apparently worry

41

about. From Hannah's class alone there are sordid whispers of infidels, gamblers, and Tinder fiends. Empty beer bottles on the coffee table and crisp crumbs all over my sofa isn't a big deal.

'Well, I'll trade an evening of football for a morning shopping, on my own, with the phone turned off.'

'Phone on.'

'Phone off and I'll only go to Primark.'

'Deal.'

He smiles and we stand in the darkened room almost mid-moment, both of us too tired to take the emotion to the next level, whatever that may be. Hugging with stray hands, I reckon. But the moment is gone as shouting from downstairs starts up again.

'You're missing the match.'

Matt looks at the clock in the room.

'No, it's half time.'

'JOOLS! JOOLS! Shitting hell, come quickly!'

We skip down the stairs, both fretting something's up with Millie, hoping she hasn't thrown up on the sofa. But as we enter the living room, Adam is crouched in front of the screen listening carefully. Millie is still asleep. The three of us gawp as we listen to the news report. Blood drains instantly from my face.

'... the woman, only known as Jools, has found herself a YouTube sensation. Twelve thousand hits in a matter of hours, the clip filmed by a worker on their mobile phone of her quarrelling with renowned TV chef Tommy McCoy as he tries to recruit her for his hit television show, Off Your Trolley ...'

The clip is unbelievably clear. It is me standing by the yoghurts: hair, boobs, the jeans, the horror. Matt is transfixed. Adam is rubbing his chin hanging on every word.

'... in the clip, the mother of four berates Mr McCoy's ideals and rejects his offer of help by questioning his intentions and indeed his own TV persona by referring to his 'mockney' accent. Mr McCoy has been unavailable for comment ...'

The clip replays. Adam is the first to say something.

'Shit. Look at Millie's hair. It looks like a ginger afro.'

It does. If you squint it looks like her head is in flames. But really, all I can see is me. Am I really that big? I've heard the adage about the camera adding ten pounds, yet why are five of those pounds on my face? I look bloated, pale like a middle-aged, lard-eating man. We won't even talk about the hair. And the lack of a bra is wholly evident; my nipples, which should protrude nicely on a level with my armpits, are halfway down my torso. The buttons missing from my coffee-stained shirt reveal a strip of podge above my waistband. I'm also shiny with sweat like I've been jogging.

Then there's the rant. Did I really say that? Who is this beastly woman? Why am I standing on my toes? Why is Millie not wearing socks? Matt puts his arm around me when Tommy McCoy starts laying into me about bread. Adam claps when I correctly identify the radish. Matt squeezes me when I tell Tommy I can't bear to be insulted by him any more. They both laugh when I talk about him shitting money. Then the clip ends on a grandiose note, when I tell Tommy he'll never be like me and storm off. I thought I'd strode away quite confidently but in the clip my bulbous behind is all I can see, the backs of my jeans all torn and frayed, three inches darker where the hem soaked up the rain.

'And in other news ...'

We stand silently as the news moves on to the next item, a dog who can bark along to Adele.

'Oh my god, I'm so sorry ... that was...'

Horrendous. Completely horrendous. From my coat hook nipples to my pre-menstrual rant to looking like a mess of cheap blouse, badly fitting jeans, and scuffed trainers. I am mortified beyond belief.

'... that was the possibly the best thing I've ever fucking seen, Jools ... come 'ere ...'

Adam envelops me in his gangly arms and lifts me up. Matt shakes his head in bemusement, alternating between the screen and me. This is good? Humiliating myself on TV is good? I'd rather get naked with Gok Wan in front of the entire world than people see me like that. YouTube? Matt and I are speechless as Adam, who's forgotten about the football, heads for the computer to search for more.

43

'Any more beers, Matt?'

Matt saunters off to the garage while Adam starts to investigate this unlikely news item, my head spinning from the shock value of having seen my mug in HD, huge bags under my eyes, frizzy mane, and my appalling dress sense. Until a voice booms from the kitchen.

'JOOLS! WHY THE HELL IS THERE PAINT ALL OVER THE BLOODY GARAGE FLOOR?!'

CHAPTER SIX

The next morning, I find Adam lying across our sofa wrapped like a battered fish in early copies of all the major tabloids and broadsheets. It's a strangely calm morning. Last night, if I wasn't perched on the bathroom floor, stroking a twin's head balanced over the toilet, I was staring into the computer wondering why 352 people suddenly wanted to be my friend on Facebook. Matt went through the phone messages and web stuff. Adam went through the beers, running to the petrol station at six a.m. to pick up early editions of all the papers. So now the house sits like after a party on a school night – stinking of booze, vomit, and everyone sleeping way past when they should. Except me. Millie has bounced back and sits on my lap while I pick up a paper and finish my coffee. It's *The Sun* and I've made page eight. They do what they always do: headline in bold, thoughts in italics, and scratchy black and white pics that make me look more pickpocket on CCTV rather than confrontational, have-a-go, ranty mother-type. *The Sun* is very happy for me and ends its story asking if Tommy has bitten off more than he can chew. Hahahhh!

Doesn't look like I've made the *FT*, *Telegraph*, nor *The Times* but *The Guardian* has a column about me standing up for the everyday woman and how I'm a better exemplar of our times than McCoy. The column is a little despondent though, writing as if to say this is all there is – a scruffy woman and a box of fish fingers.

When I turn on the TV, I seem to have fallen off the headlines, for which I'm thankful, bar a lively debate on morning television where a lady in a primary coloured shift dress waves her fist in the air in support for me. The computer is hibernating so I switch it on and notice the YouTube clip that started everything is still up. What the hell? 867,423 views? I figure we must account for two hundred of them. Last night, we reviewed the clip from every perspective before we got bored and explored the newspaper and Tommy McCoy fan sites instead. Matt appears in his sea-green towelling dressing gown, his sandy hair all tousled like a nineties boy-bander.

'I'm having a sick day. I'll take Hannah in later.'

He comes and sits down beside me and puts a wet head of hair on my shoulder. Millie does what she always does and rakes the hairs on his legs with her tiny fingers.

'So, what's new?'

We scroll down the YouTube page to read some of the comments. There's a mixture of social commentary, vitriol, and support. The bad stuff is pretty damning. MrsMccoy4eva thinks I'm rank and ugly and need to get a life. TommysBabe thinks I'm ungrateful and wonders if all my babies are ginger mingers. I tell Matt not to wade in but he and Adam set up their own YouTube account last night under the creative pseudonym of McCoyIsACock, defending our honour by replying to anyone who'd posted a bad word about me or poor little Millie. As grateful as I am for their support, I was less bothered about nameless people insulting me on the web than I was still reeling from how ridiculous I looked on the television. Matt types away another cyber rebuke as I place Millie next to Adam, hoping she'll claw his eyelids open.

'What are you writing?'

'I'm replying to Eve, Weymouth, Dorset on the *Daily Mail* website who says that you are a state and obviously had bad PMT.'

Eve, Weymouth, Dorset may indeed have a point but I let Matt post his comments. Millie, meanwhile, has taken to thumping Adam on the head with the remote control.

'Yeah, yeah. OK, Millie. Thank you.'

'Working today?'

He grunts in response. Adam works in sales, has done for five years though I'm no wiser what it is he actually sells. It involves a Bluetooth headset and an embarrassing-looking Nissan. He makes a bid for my coffee and picks up the closest paper to him – *The Express* – flicking between football bulletins and scouring articles for information about last night. Matt starts laughing to himself as he types.

'Listen to this one: *"We're here for you Tommy. This bitch is nothing. She just wishes she was you. Love you! From your biggest fans."* With two rows of kisses. I mean, they even address the comments to him, like he reads them. Deranged.'

'What are you looking at now?'

'The Tommy McCoy website. Did you know he has a wife called Kitty?'

Some stupid beanpole beauty with a closet full of Hermès handbags, Louboutins, and hair extensions comes to mind. She has lent her name to a line of baby foods and organic soaps. Matt chokes a bit on his own tongue as he reads out verbatim from Tommy's own bio:

'*Kitty and I met on a yoga course in Cornwall. We bonded over our desire for a more holistic and ethical approach to living and my amazing recipe for butter bean casserole!*'

A bit of coffee spurts out of Adam's nose, which amuses Millie no end.

'Looks like they also have a ginger.'

'A ginger baby?'

'No, the kid's name is actually Ginger. He has four like us: Basil "Baz", Mace, Clementine, and Ginger.'

There's a moment of silence as we take in the names and think about those poor children. Adam interrupts.

'He should've called one of the boys Chip, or Crispin. Crispin McCoy. The endorsement deals that kid would've got would be legendary.'

We snort with laughter, me a little unladylike as I double over grabbing my sides. The sleepless delirium doesn't help. Even now, every so often, I am ambushed by awful flashbacks of standing in that supermarket aisle, seeing my face on the television. Hannah emerges at the door of the living room, powdered sugar all over her jumper like dandruff.

'What are you laughing at?'

I smile at how her bunches are at funny angles coming out of her head. I haven't said a word to her yet about what happened.

'Just something in the news.'

She has something soft and spongy in the palm of her hand, something that doesn't look like it came from my kitchen.

'Where's the doughnut from, missy?'

'Grandpa's in the kitchen. He's been to the shops.'

I get up while Matt continues to type and Google and Adam stirs from his semi-comatose state. I tell Hannah to go and wave the doughnut in his face, hoping that might rouse him. True enough, when I get to the kitchen, Dad's boiling the kettle and wiping down countertops. My memories of Dad all seem to be him in the kitchen: sat there watching us open exam results, swearing at the washing machine, fighting with the oven gloves, watching us eat our tea. By trade, he was a design technology teacher and would come home with recipes scribbled out of old Home Economics books and experiment on us. The day he discovered pasta was a revelation. The tripe, deep fried with mixed peppercorns, less so. Needless to say, he soon realised food was the one way he could connect to us – as proven today where he knows one of the few things that might be able to help is an old-fashioned jam doughnut: raspberry jam – vermilion and sticky – wrapped in foamy dough and served in a white paper bag with greasy patches soaking through the paper. He's got a bag of ten and a pile of today's newspapers. I give him a kiss as he lines up the mugs on the counter.

'So tell me, Jools, what's all this about you beating up some TV chef?'

My eyes widen like saucers.

'Beat up?'

'The *Daily Star*. Page five.'

I turn to find the article accompanied by a still picture from the clip where the angle looks like I'm about to head-butt him.

'So I was at my ballroom dancing class last night and then I get home and go to bed and ten thirty, nearly eleven, your bloody aunt Sylvia rings and tells me someone who looks like you is on the telly. And there's me thinking, it's Aunt Sylvia, she's probably put her bifocals on upside down or something but lo and behold, I switched over and there you are. My Jools laying into that bugger off the telly.'

Dad dunks the teabags in and out of the mugs of hot water.

His salt and pepper hair is brushed over his bald patch like usual. He's wearing the spotty socks the twins gave him for Christmas.

'So what did Aunt Sylvia think?'

'Crikey, don't know. She was just excited to see you on the telly.'

'And you?'

He's finished dunking and moved on to stacking the doughnuts on a plate.

'Where are the boys?'

'Still in bed. They're having the day off. Dodgy tummies.'

'Your cooking?' He laughs under his breath.

'A bug, actually.'

He pulls up a chair and sits down, flicking through the papers with one hand and chewing on a doughnut in the other. I'm waiting with bated morning breath for his response, knowing deep down his opinion is probably the one that matters the most to me.

Like that day nine years ago when Matt and I drove down from Leeds in his battered Punto to tell him I was pregnant and I was going to be keeping the baby. I couldn't give a rat's arse what anyone else thought, but Dad ... I worried about Dad. You see, I was his golden girl, the alpha female in the house who was all shiny and set for greater things now she was going to university. And in my second year, I was going to be having a baby. Christ, in all of that I never worried about me, the baby, Matt – only Dad. He was quiet for a very long time when we told him. His questions were all very practical, sounding out all the obstacles we'd have to face. He never judged nor chastised us at any time. Yet I'm not sure if I can bear to see that same look of disappointment etched in his face again, the one that told me that this was not what he had hoped. He grips on to his mug and takes a large swig of tea, his finger rested on an article in *The Mirror*.

'This bird has some gall. She's called you a "poster girl for desperate, unkempt mothers everywhere." Like she's some bloody oil painting herself? Face like a cat's arse.'

He pushes a cup of tea in my direction.

'You all right?'

I shrug my shoulders.

'Never nice reading about how "desperate and unkempt" you are. Must say my self-esteem has taken a bit of a knocking.'

He edges a bit of doughnut my way too.

'Jools love, it's a funny old situation you got yourself caught up in here but you did good. That bloke's a prize tosspot if ever I've seen one.'

'So you don't think I embarrassed myself?'

He smiles. 'Oh yeah. You look a state, girl, you're not even wearing socks. But you stood up for yourself. That's all I've ever told you kids to do.'

And with that he picks up the plate of doughnuts and heads into the living room.

'Your brother here?'

'Which one?'

'Adam. The git was supposed to help me plumb in my new dishwasher.'

I nod and he wanders off. The mumbles of morning greetings and excited grandchildren echo through the walls as I sit in our cold kitchen and watch the windows steam up, tears in my eyes, from what I'm not exactly sure. There's a strange, nervous excitement that bubbles through me, almost overwhelms as I read the headlines mentioning Millie and our adventures in Sainsbury's. Until I get to *The Sport* and read:

JEALOUS EX-LOVER ATTACKS TV CHEF MCCOY

I laugh. And cry. Each emotion doing its best to outdo the other.

By 8.30, the tears still make my eyes glow so Matt leaves to send Hannah to school and drop Adam home, while Dad stays to help to look after the boys and spend time with me because I'm 'looking all fragile.' This involves stuffing me with more doughnuts, offering to make his famous chilli con carne for dinner, and skimming the news channels for mention of me and my McCoy-based antics. I make *BBC Breakfast* and Dad rings in to give them an earful only to be put on hold for fifteen minutes and give up. We watch though as Kate Silverton calls me the 'leader for the revolution against middle class food snobbery' to which Dad cheers a little. On *Lorraine* the TV chef of the day, who is actually quite pleasant and who I'd gladly watch as he's very into puddings, is apparently not a fan, which upsets me a little. He tells the viewing public that I'm one of those mums who thinks cooking and buying organic is a chore but can actually be quite cost-effective. To back up his claims, he bakes a simple fish pie that he costs at a fiver whereas my fish finger supper cost me much more than that. But he doesn't know that fish fingers were on offer for a pound. Dad tells me his fish pie looks like a dog's dinner and that he doesn't know me, he doesn't know that I cook other things. My lamb chops are apparently very tasty. I smile back at Dad for trying to cheer me up and stare at the empty plate once piled high with doughnut.

At about nine-ish, the boys get up and I'm fixing them some toast because I've eaten all the doughnuts when Ted comes zooming into the kitchen.

'Hon, you want to throw up again?'

'Nope. Grandpa says you've got to come now. Now, Mummy.'

He grabs my hand and drags me into the living room and there on the television is Clifton Primary in the background: familiar cars, faces, and landscapes behind a female reporter's head. The boys gawp at the screen.

'*The woman's name is Jools Campbell and it's been reported that three of her children attend this school, Clifton Primary. We've asked some of the other mothers today what their opinions on the matter are and whether they are reflective of the parents here.*'

'Mummy, why are they at our school?'

I have no words. The soundbites come thick and fast, between parents and teachers and someone who I think is the school caretaker. First up, bloody hell, is Jen Tyrrell.

'I try and give my children organic all the time. I mean, you only want what's best for your kids, isn't that right?'

Then it's another mother.

'Organic's very good and all but I can't afford it most of the time.'

A random stranger.

'She was a bit hysterical but I know what she means.'

A familiar face! Pooja's mum, Sivani, in that dusky pink fleece she always seems to be wearing.

'She's a lovely woman. I think Tommy McCoy was wrong to criticise her. I know her kids and they're lovely. She's lovely. Her family are lovely.'

Overdoing it with the lovely maybe, but I shout thank yous at the screen, making a note to get little Pooja round for tea one day. Then, Christ ... Paula Jordan appears with a flick of her hair and pashmina.

'All my family eat organic. We're vegans. It's a lifestyle that suits our family very much.'

Dad sneers to see her face.

'I know her. She's been round here before, right?'

I nod, not wanting to tell him she was here only last night.

'She seems a little proud of herself.'

The boys get a little overexcited to see her on the screen and start putting their peanut buttery fingers all over it to point out friends in the background. I see Donna at the gate staring over and waving, before strutting over to have her say.

'Jools Campbell is a friend of mine. And I'm glad she said what she did. The bloke's a ...'

She scans the children around her in order to self-censor.

'The bloke has no idea. He really doesn't. He should try living off my budget for a week. He really should.'

Thank you, Donna. My eyes crease around the edges to take it all in.

'Mummy, are you famous?'

I have no answers. Especially when I see our little red Fiat Punto pulling up outside the school. Too late, they've been tipped off.

'Mr Campbell? Matteo Campbell? Can we have a word?'

Matt looks infinitely better on screen than I do. Maybe it's the combed hair or his doey eyes but he's also very good at standing his ground and controlling the furore around him. I see parents freeze in the background to take it all in. Tuesday mornings at Clifton Primary just got a whole lot more interesting.

'I really have nothing to tell you all. We're shocked at the absurd amount of attention the situation has received.'

I see Hannah wrapped around Matt's lower half, her big blue eyes scared, one hand shielded across her face because of the lights.

'Hannah? Hannah, is it? What do you think, darling?'

Matt says nothing, like a true professional, and ushers her towards the school gate where Mrs Whittaker stands, resplendent in florals, and uses her rather large bosom to form a fortress into the school entrance.

'Now please, if you will, there are children here and I will not have their school day disrupted. Please leave before I have to call the authorities.'

She grabs on to Hannah who has tears in her eyes and takes her inside. I'm crying. Tears are rolling down my face, which upsets Ted who comes over to cling on to me like a limpet. The feeling now is to run to the school in my pyjamas and scoop Hannah up. I see it in Matt's eyes as well as he stands by the gate not knowing whether to follow her in or leave. He turns to the reporter who's still trying to get a comment out of him. Shit, that's not a happy face.

'Mr Campbell? Mr Campbell? Where is your wife today? Can I get a comment about yesterday and what she meant?'

He's properly riled. His hair is starting to frizz at the edges. He waits by his car door and then turns around.

'Yeah, I've got a comment for you. Anyone who insults my wife and my family insults me. Tommy McCoy can get f ...'

The report gets faded out to someone on the news desk who apologises for the disruption to the interview and the words that may have upset some viewers. The boys are suddenly jumping about on the sofa excited to see their father on the television. I'm still crying. Dad has Millie in his arms and looks over at me.

'Well, it could have been worse, love.'

I give Dad a look as he retreats into the kitchen to put on the kettle.

Ten minutes later and Matt's car has pulled up outside the house. The boys meet him at the door, throwing limbs around him as he enters. Dad stands by the living room doorway with a cup of tea.

'Matt, you all right, son?'

Matt is speechless and stares at me as I stand by the kitchen door looking sheepish, guilty, and pretty much a wreck. Dad takes the boys into the living room to entertain them while Matt marches towards me. He rubs at his temples which he does when the kids are running around the house and his brain can't quite take it any more. It makes me burst into tears and crumple into a chair. Matt comes and puts an arm around me.

'Don't cry, you. This has just become bigger than needs be. But we have to think about the kids. I'm going to ring Mrs Whittaker to apologise formally. She did really well with all of that.'

I nod.

'Oh, and my mum rang.'

Great. Really fucking great. Gia Campbell. Matt's Italian Catholic mother who dislikes me enough already given how I corrupted her only son and made him settle for a life more ordinary. Given her English is about as good as my Italian, I'm unsure how to make the customary explanatory phone call.

'Don't worry. She was just worried. I covered for you. I think she was concerned seeing all our faces on the television.'

'All our faces?'

Matt turns the screen to *The Sun* website where they have drawn up an interesting article comparing my life to Tommy McCoy's using columns and, disturbingly enough, family photos.

'Where the fuck did they get the photos?'

'Facebook?'

The Sun is being incredibly kind, though. Apparently, I beat Tommy as two of my kids are twins, they have better names, and I speak on behalf of many mothers out there. However, Tommy beats me in the looks stakes, the fact he has oodles of

54

money, and is a far superior cook. It pains me to see our kids up there being used for this exercise.

'Aren't there laws against this sort of thing? Invasion of privacy?'

Matt shrugs his shoulders as he returns to my Gmail inbox.

'You know, I was thinking on the way back. Some of these emails were from magazines requesting interviews. Maybe we should say something, draw a line in the sand. I mean, some of them even offered to pay.'

With the house mortgaged to the hilt and credit card bills to pay, this gets my attention and I sit down in front of the screen. I scan the page and there are the names of familiar women's magazines, papers, and one e-mail from the producers of a daytime filler show. Matt is scanning and deliberating the contents of each one.

'Here. These people are saying you could do a phone interview. This might be good. Get us some closure.'

Matt has a point. I indicate to a name on the screen.

'Who's she? Luella Bendicks? Sounds like a porn star name.'

Matt scans through the email, cupping his fifth cup of tea of the day.

'A publicist, apparently. Can offer comprehensive media training and representation.'

'I like her name.'

Matt gives me a look. Now is not the time to make decisions so lightly. He points back at the phone interviewer and starts making notes on the back of *The Sport* while hastily reading the article about me being Tommy's ex-lover. He laughs. For the first time today – though I'm not sure if it's because he thinks the story ludicrous or because of the fact that I'd never be able to obtain a lover of such calibre. I cast a look over his scrappy notes:

- state for the record the surprise that this situation has blown out of proportion
- jest about physical appearance, stand by your comments in a more dignified way without shriek ranting
- defend the fact that your children eat very well without

Tommy McCoy's help.

He picks up the phone and starts dialling. We're doing this now? I haven't even brushed my teeth. Not that it matters, but I re-tie my hair and straighten my pyjamas so I can talk to John Elswood, freelance journalist at large. It's a very dependable name. This will work. In fifteen minutes' time, my eloquence and his articulate journalistic stylings will stop this matter being drawn out any more.

'Johnno Elswood?'

Johnno's Estuary accent throws me, making me slightly nervous.

'Yes. Hi. Yeah, I'm Juliet Campbell, you … errmm … you emailed me earlier this morning about an interview, maybe, perhaps …'

'Yeah, shit. Crikey, thanks for getting back to me. How's it going love?'

'Ummm, yeah. It's certainly been a crazy twelve hours. I've really been shocked that it's been blown up into such a big thing.'

Matt puts his thumbs up as he watches me speak.

'Well, let's start with the first thing. How would you like to be paid for this?'

Matt and I forgot to talk money. I sound hesitant, not really knowing what the going rate is. He speaks before I have the chance to suggest anything.

'500 quid sounds fair, eh?'

'God, yeah. Whatever, I guess.'

I hear the click of something in the background as he launches into the questions. My hand seems to be gripped firmly to the side of the table.

'So, in your own words, love … just tell me what happened.'

'Well, I guess it's like you saw it in the video. Tommy tried to get me to be part of his TV show and I think he did so in quite an offensive way.'

'Offensive how?'

'Oh, like just the way he assumed that because I had fish fingers in my trolley it meant that's what I gave my kids to eat all the time. It was the assumption that irked me a little.'

56

Matt mouths the word 'irked' back at me questioningly. I shrug my shoulders back at him.

'So he just assumed you to be some chav mother who doesn't give a toss about her kids and feeds them crap. That sort?'

'Ummm, I guess. I'm not sure I'd put it …'

'So you've got four kids, right? Hannah, Jake, Ted, and Lily.'

'Actually, it's Millie.'

'And so what sorts of things do you usually cook for them?'

'Oh … bit of everything. Pasta's big here … rice, potatoes, soups …'

It's the open-ended question to beat all open-ended questions. We run the gamut of every kind of dish here from beans on toast to full-on roast dinners to everything else that's improvised in between.

'And tonight, what they having?'

'My dad's cooking his chilli.'

'So … you're not cooking?'

'Errrm, yeah?'

'And little Lily's having chilli too? Ain't she a bit young for that?'

'Her name's Millie. Errrm, no. She'll get whatever's in the freezer, maybe. Then some milk, I suppose.'

He pauses for a while amidst all his scribbling and rustling of papers.

'So you breastfeed?'

Huh? What has that got to do with anything? He's asking me about my breasts. I blush and pat down on pieces of paper on the table searching for answers.

'Well, Millie, yes.'

'You breastfed all of them?'

'Well, the twins it was harder because I had a problem with clogged nipples so I …'

The colour from Matt's face drains at this point. I look up at the ceiling. Matt points at things on our piece of paper that I should be bringing up. The fact is, I don't have control of this interview at all. My arse is firmly in the back seat.

'That's great, and is there anything else you want to tell Tommy McCoy?'

Christ, there's a lot but I'm not sure if it's suitable for print. I just want this to stop. I see Hannah's eyes from this morning and if that's what a bit of media attention gives you, then I don't have any need for it whatsoever. I don't need my checked shirt image to be plastered across any more papers, I don't need my kids harassed or my husband having to sort my mess out. I've realised I've left a sizeable pause as I think these things through.

'I guess I don't want to draw this situation out any more. Tommy McCoy is free to do his show and I'm sure many people can benefit from his expertise but we're OK in this house. We are really shocked to be receiving so much attention on this so we'd ask our privacy just be respected especially as we have young kids.'

Matt does a thumbs up again, a bit more slowly this time since the nipples comment. There is no sound at the other end of the line. Has he fallen asleep? There's a few mumbled 'hmmms' as I hear him writing.

'So do you have any idea which publication you will submit this interview to?'

Again, no response.

'Do you think this will put an end to all the news stories? It's been pretty crazy.'

He hasn't heard me. Not one bit. He also may be eating as I hear gums smacking against each other in the background. And something that sounds like a pelican crossing? Wait, is it a pelican crossing? He's driving?

'We'll send the money on to you, Mrs Campbell, in the next couple of days. Thanks again.'

'But I didn't give you my …'

And then he hangs up. Matt waits for me to respond. I hold the phone knowing that has not gone as planned. Not one little bit.

CHAPTER SEVEN

I'm sitting in the kitchen looking at the clock on our wall that hasn't quite sat right ever since Jake flew a toy helicopter into it. It could be nine, it could be ten. It might be the middle of the night for all I know. In my hands, the remnants of Dad's chilli, which I eat with a teaspoon and a bag of ready salted crisps. There is something wonderfully gutsy about my dad's chilli, the way the heat hits the back of your mouth then spreads to the rest of your torso. Covering the table are articles that he has expertly cut out of today's rags that strangely look like some primary school collage project. Yet all I see are pictures of me: in the shirt I've now thrown out, lips pursed, and hair on end, fifteen times over. Matt comes in holding empty cups of milk and Millie's blankie slung over his shoulder. He opens the cupboard above the fridge and gets out a dusty bottle of gin and pours it into two mugs, then comes to sit next to me.

'How are the kids?' I ask.

'They're OK. Hannah asked me some more questions. I think she got the brunt of it at school.'

Matt puts his hand in mine as he arranges the articles on the table. I down a bit of what I thought was gin. It may be a liquor Adam brought back from his last stag do that might have Hungarian roots. It scorches the insides of my throat and I wonder if it might help me get the gloss paint off the garage floor. Matt has no problem necking his as he approaches the sink to wash up. He holds up a frying pan with some unnamed yellow mass on it. I do my best to reassure him.

'Not vomit. It was the beginnings of an omelette.'

The twins' lunch that in my current state had turned into cheesy scrambled eggs that had turned into primrose-coloured inedible goop when I had to separate them after a fight about the scraps of grated cheese on the chopping board. Cheese: the

59

epicentre of many arguments in this house. You have more than me! Who didn't cover it properly? Ask Mummy to cut a chunk for you, don't just bite into it! Matt prods at the goop curiously and slides his Marigolds on. Dare I say it, I am a little turned on.

'How do I make this all right for her?'

Matt shrugs his shoulders and moves on to the dinner plates. The twins have taken the news of my supermarket showdown quite well, water off little boys' backs. But I was always more worried about Hannah: our sensitive soul. I think spending the first two years of your life in a student bedsit might do that to you. I spoke to her when she came back from school but my explanations fell short of what she had actually heard. According to Lisa and Zara, I was going crazy and she would have to live in a home while I was driven off in a white van. When I explained my supermarket antics, I then rather surprisingly got told off. Apparently, I had always told my kids to never answer back. I should just walk away.

'Well, Mummy was naughty and should have walked away. But I didn't. And now, see? I'm all over the papers. So this should teach you all that it is always better to walk away.'

Again, she didn't look convinced. Neither was I. Will lacking, I just pulled her head to my chest as she lay on her bed and told her things would be all right. It'd all go away soon. I hoped.

'Well, did you hear what your dad told the twins to say if anyone started badmouthing them?'

I give Matt a suspicious look, rather like the one I'm giving the big purple lump on the chair next to me. Poo or Play-Doh? No, uneaten kidney beans – that would be Ted.

'Well, he said that if anyone says anything bad about them then that means they're just jealous because their own mothers gave them up for adoption since they were too ugly, and they were only adopted because the orphanage ran out of babies.'

Several hairs on my head feel tight, like they might be turning grey. Matt's shoulders shudder as he swears at our spaceless and uneven draining board.

'Maybe you should have come back at McCoy with that one,

eh?'

I laugh, noticing some lettuce smeared under the table like wallpaper. That would be Jake.

'Was work OK? Did anyone call you up about it?'

'Please. Half of them don't even know I'm married nor have the time to watch the news. I wouldn't worry.'

I pause for a moment thinking whether that inferred he hid me from society like some Elephant Man secret. Matt and I don't even wear rings. We did. Cheap ones we bought from a goth shop in Leeds town centre for the purpose of our wedding. But there wasn't even an engagement ring. The proposal had happened in my Headingley flat, in my bed. I was distraught with morning sickness and worry and Matt had become this permanent fixture in the flat nursing me back to normality. I couldn't stomach anything except Sprite and Haribo up to this point so Matt used to come by with fruit and vitamins, worried our baby would come out looking like a gummy bear. Hannah was going to happen, this much we knew, but the how and why was uncertain. The why was an amalgamation of Matt's lapsed Catholic guilt and me determined to not be some lost teen mother. But there was also a weird concoction of emotion that despite not being ready, this was a good thing. Despite an innate hesitancy to refer to the religious, a blessing, if you will. It never felt like the wrong thing to do. This was never going to be a mistake. So when Matt approached the underside of my duvet that morning, me a little green around the gills, I saw a plate with an assortment of crackers and fruit slices and a pick-'n'-mix jelly ring on top. I assumed it to be there for decorative purposes until I saw Matt's blue-grey eyes, bright like wet pebbles. Let's get married. I want you to be my wife. There was, as there often is with us, little messing around. I was a big bag of hormones. I was also excited, like any twenty-year-old would be to be on the receiving end of a proposal, filled to the brim with fear of the unknown so my gut, apart from wanting to retch, told me yes. I nodded and accepted and the next week we went one rung up on the ring stakes and bought a couple of stainless steel bands. Three months later, Matt's became too tight, I lost mine down the sink, or in the sink, or next to it?

That bit I couldn't remember. Since then we've never replaced them, mortgage and bills taking priority. It does make me wonder if women at work think he's available. Does he talk about his kids? Does he talk about me? I know that Matt is not the type to have our faces paraded around on a mouse mat or screensaver.

'Thank you for today. I did lose it in the middle there.'

'Hey, you know. You're only my wife.'

I pause again. Does that make me a chore, an obligation as opposed to helping me because his love for me has overpowered him so?

'I think it'll die down and we can get back to normal. I told Hannah what to do if she gets any more stick at school.'

I furrow my brow at him.

'So did I. What did you say?'

'That if anyone said anything bad at school, then she should walk away.'

'Ditto.'

Then a look. That look that makes me wonder if we do and say the same thing now because living together for so long has finely tuned our algorithms in the same way women who live communally always menstruate at the same time. It's what we do. Nine years later and you fall into rhythms where you know how things best work. We prop each other up (usually in this kitchen). We get through it. Of course, the other explanation is that our spirits are intertwined in some way. I watch as he stares at my reflection in the kitchen window and smiles. One or the other.

In our small moment, a knock on the back door gets our attention and we both turn tentatively to see who it might be. A well-groomed head and skinny jeans peers through and I smile.

'Ben! Crikey, mate, you scared the crap out of me.'

He punches Matt on the shoulder then heads towards me with one of his hugs. Good Ben hugs are what got me through my A-Levels. Ben is the antithesis to man lad Adam. He drapes his shoulder bag over one of the chairs and rolls up the sleeves of his yellow V-neck jumper with leather elbow patches.

'You silly bint. A checked shirt for one.'

I glare at him as he steals my crisps.

'How goes it?'

I shrug and collapse into my chair.

'Just been round Dad's, he filled me in.'

I turn my nostrils up and stuff my face full of mince.

'And what do you think?'

'I think it is hilarious. But you were also surprisingly eloquent for one so hormonal. I am almost proud.'

He comes to sit down next to me, resting his head on my shoulder as he examines the patchwork of black and white which is now my kitchen table.

'You know Dad said there was a bloke with a big camera outside before?'

Matt hears this and scampers with soapy hands into the living room.

'He asked Dad what was in his bag and Dad told him jars of Tommy McCoy sauces.'

Ben laughs. I don't.

'But I wouldn't worry. Dad gave him an earful, told him to sling his hook. And we checked, you didn't make the news again. Your space was filled by twin pandas in a Beijing zoo … so maybe this is it.'

I bob my head through the door to see Matt twitch the curtains, inspecting cars and lamp posts and double locking the front door. A little nervy but relaxed by Ben's last sentence. Just as I thought; the proliferation of extinct species, war, and Beyoncé have made for far more interesting news. I am beyond relieved. Ben chokes slightly as he takes a sip from my mug.

'Anti-freeze? Times can't be that hard, sis.'

I point to the cupboard that he then filters through and finds an even older bottle of Kahlua.

'But you're OK? I was chatting to Dad before and he said you'd taken a bit of a beating. It's all been a bit savage.'

I shrug and he hugs me again. The Kahlua is so old it won't even leave the bottle.

'You did good though. I mean, you're semi-famous, halfway up the Z-List. Almost as famous as the woman who threw that cat in the wheelie bin.'

I smile. Ben's ambition is to be on some sort of list as his career progresses – though hopefully, his fame could be attributed to something far more worthy than a supermarket rant. He turns his attention to some old wine in the fridge.

'You could be the new face of Bird's Eye. I think you've done them some fine promotional work. You could be Captain Bird's Eye's wife – put all those gay rumours to rest.'

And for once this evening, I laugh heartily and from the bosom. I can picture it now. Me in nautical stripes and a hat, maybe a little bolero style jacket with gold tassles, serving my kids fish fingers on our makeshift ship. Bless you, Ben, with your trendy trainers and 80s Morrissey haircut. I put my arms out for another hug and he comes over to let me rest my head against his stupidly flat and non-existent stomach.

'I think we should have a toast. To celebrity mediocrity and the fact that next week no one will know who you are.'

He smiles and raises a glass to me, before realising he might have poured himself a glass of old red wine vinegar and spraying it across the kitchen floor.

That night, sleep is wanting. I have crazy dreams that involve Tommy McCoy juggling jam doughnuts. My kids love him and tell me they want to go and live with him but I say no – they should live with me for ever in my house made of fish fingers. It means that every half hour I wake up in some feverish delirium asking Matt if he's up but roll over to find him with his tongue hanging out, his shoulders framed around the duvet. The kids sleep through tonight and seem to have recovered from whatever virus they were suffering from, and Ben is downstairs on the sofa watching television, hopefully not some late night call-in porn show. I desperately want to close my eyes and sleep but something's wrong. Not sure what it is.

Then at 6.36 a.m. (I know because that's the time glowing on the clock next to the bed) I sense a figure standing by the bed. My first thoughts are vomit, pee, or nightmare so I roll over and put an arm out to pat a head but instead get a handful of denim. I look up and pull the duvet up in fright to see Ben standing there. At first I ponder whether he's having one of his infamous sleepwalking episodes (we once found him in the shed) but he kneels next to the bed.

'Jools, you better come.'

'What the hell, Ben? Is it the kids?'

He shakes his head and I tiptoe out of bed, pull on my bathrobe and slippers, and follow him down the stairs. Outside is that navy-blue twilight hour where you know everyone, everywhere is asleep except for you and you secretly hate them for it. He leads me into the living room where there's a selection of chocolate bar wrappers, Adam, and the morning papers.

'Hon, what you doing here? Aren't you working tomorrow? You really should get some sleep.'

'I'll call in sick if I have to. You ... you should sit down.'

The TV screen is still buzzing. I notice someone has also been rolling cigarettes on a children's encyclopaedia.

'I went down to the petrol station to get the first editions of the morning papers and ...'

'And what?'

'You should have a look at *The Express*.'

I dig through the papers to find my face on the front page, a picture of me from Facebook – a night out, I think. No, a hen night in London for Annie. I look ridiculous in one of the baby pink shirt her sisters made us all wear that was far too small for me and my milk-bearing bosoms. Not only that, but I am far too drunk on cheap cocktails and someone is waving a plastic penis in my face. The headline – THE TRUTH BEHIND THE SAINSBURY'S MUM. I quickly see I have taken up pages four and five with an exclusive interview by Johnno Elswood. And I read, every word making my eyes crease up with horror.

'*When asked about payment for the interview, Mrs Campbell was flippant about the suggested fee with a reply of "whatever". She then went on to say she wasn't "some chav mother who doesn't give a toss about her kids and feeds them crap" but did say that she was going to feed her baby "whatever was in the freezer" – presumably more fish fingers? Maybe that's why little Lily Campbell's hair is so orange?*

Although reticent to talk about McCoy, one only has to go to her Facebook page to see she has proclaimed him to be a "dickhead". Colourful language from someone with young children.'

Adam has his head cradled in his hands.

'But ... I never ...'

The paper creases in my hands as I read on.

'... *when probed, Mrs Campbell also had quite lax views about breastfeeding, which the WHO recommend in children at least until six months of age. But this is hardly surprising behaviour from someone whose idea of nutrition involves a stodgy loaf of white bread. As a mother who had her first child when she was barely out of her teens, one baulks that she is the epitome of what young mothers are in this country: someone who has no problem bringing children into this world but has little to no idea on how to raise them in a healthy environment.'*

The newspaper starts to blot with my tears. Big, dark patches on the off-white paper as I look at a selection of pictures I had left up on Facebook because to remove them meant I possessed some sort of vain streak. Pictures of me looking drained and frazzled with the kids, nights out where I'm swinging from lamp posts, a particularly terrible one where I've raised my middle finger at Matt for pointing a camera in my face at 3.30 in the morning. And such horrible words, twisted out of sense and meaning into something incredibly mean. Ben comes and sits next to me as I turn into his shoulder.

'C'mon, sis. Just, you know, it'll be tomorrow's chip paper.'

'What will be?'

It's Matt at the door, with Millie and her bed head. My damp cheeks give me away and I hand him the paper. The colour rises in his cheeks to read it as Adam takes Millie away to distract her with the kettle being boiled for teas.

'Complete and utter fucker. If I ever get hold of this ...'

I'm a wreck. Sobbing into Matt's dressing gown, I'm a complete and utter sleep-deprived wreck. Matt keeps patting me on the back between sentences as he reads on. I hear the kettle steaming into action and watch as the sky changes colour behind his back. Light streaming into the kitchen. But all I see is grey, a little like mouldy meat.

CHAPTER EIGHT

'Please tell me that's not poo.'

Annie looks down at the chair where something brown and foamy is smeared across the seat. I study it hard and give it a sniff. Annie, in a wonderfully luxurious cashmere suit, cranes her head around, studying her backside.

I raise my hands to the air. 'Nutella! All clear.'

I dust her bum off as Millie looks on from her high-chair, curiously trying to work out our relationship. You're that woman who sometimes comes round and hugs me relentlessly because you really want a baby. But you always look smarter than Mummy and you have an actual hair style. You also don't seem too fazed that you nearly sat on some chocolate/poo and ruined your three-hundred-pound suit. Nor does Mummy when you ring her up post-copulation to ask her how many pillows you should put under your bum for the sperm to swim down at the most advantageous angle. Some would call that a friend.

'So tell me again what Matt did?'

Annie is here this morning in some sort of professional legal friend capacity to lend counsel and listen to how I, Jools Campbell, lowly mother of four, has seemingly got herself involved in the most bizarre celebrity situation ever. She sits there cradling her Bob the Builder mug while entertaining Millie with her burnt orange Kate Spade bag. I look over at my New Look carryall – suffering from a bad case of handbag dermatitis as bits of faux leather peel off to expose the lining.

'He phoned the paper to get them to print a retraction but they refused so he threatened to sue ...'

'... which resulted in ...'

'Well, nothing. I think the lady may have even laughed.'

Annie shrugs her shoulders as if to say rightly so. That sort of thing would take power, money, time, and more money:

something the Campbell collective weren't really known for.

'So then he called this woman.'

Luella Bendicks: publicist/media strategist/celebrity agent. Which is the reason Annie is here today: to hold my hand and appear official when Luella comes round this morning to give me the onceover. Not knowing where to go to after being so sorely misrepresented in the Elswood article, we emailed Luella asking for some advice. She got back to us within minutes to tell me to free up Friday morning, she was coming round. It was very direct, very to the point. Matt said maybe that's who we needed.

So as we await her arrival, I scrape Nutella off chairs and Annie and Millie make their way through the articles plastered to our stained kitchen walls in the same way a serial killer might plot out potential victims. My current *bête noire* is the magazine that has me in their 'Circle of Shame' section, where a big flake of croissant sits nestled on my neck like a huge wart.

'"*Maybe Jools Campbell could fill in for Kerry Katona and her infamous Iceland ads ...*" That's a bit harsh, I still go there occasionally to get potato waffles.'

I laugh. She cradles Millie's little head in her hands.

'Look at the scraps your mama gets in, eh? Lucky she's got me on her side.'

Annie was my saving grace at university. When other friends found out about the pregnancy, there was mostly pity and platitude and people who claimed to be friends but skulked away into the shadows of the pubs and £1 a pint clubs thinking it was far less damaging to hide away and not be around this big rotund reminder of alternative realities and how skewed one's life can become. Annie was not one of those people. She helped Matt and I find somewhere to live, she chose us a cot, she was there in the waiting room at the hospital. And she has been there ever since, a sobering reminder of what my life could have been (young professional; going on city breaks; proper skincare regime) but championing my family every moment she can. She goes on to start reading the printouts Matt has made of the Mumsnet boards; some of the people on there have really got their jute knickers in a twist over me, using it as a chance to have a bragathon over who is the most organic person in the land.

'How's Matt been in all of this?'

The one thing about Annie is that she knows all too well the circumstances under which Matt and I got together and the precarious state of our foundations. I secretly think she's not entirely sure how that came about or how we've lasted this long.

'You know. He's Matt – he's just been there. He's been sorting my shit out.'

She nods. That sentence defines Matt and I down to a tee. It's never been fireworks or raging passion – just a sweet man who's stuck around and got me through the everyday. She knows I could have it a lot worse. I could have a liar or a cheat or a wife beater. But once when we were drunk, she asked me if I'd settled for him. I was indignant at the time, exclaiming my love and how I was lucky to have such a wonderful man in my life. But she said what I guess everyone had been thinking: did I marry him because that was the right thing to do as opposed to what I really wanted? I'd lie to say I don't think about that now, but when you have a family everything becomes counter-weighted against the children, and their opinions on relationships, life, and beyond being forged by this paragon of marriage belonging to their parents. All I knew was that abandonment had the capacity to tear big holes into some part of your brain, making it one of the worst things you could do to anyone. It had always left me where I am.

The doorbell rings and I go to answer it, seeing a fuzzy image of someone with hair like lacquer in the glass. A shiny, short-fringed bob, the sort you see on Lego men or medieval serfs. I open the door and it's almost as if she's attached to the letterbox with how quickly she seems to get through into my house.

'Luella Bendicks. You must be Jools. A real pleasure.'

The handshake reverbs through my arm and into my spine as she gives me the once over. I'm braving some black jeans and a vest top, along with trainers and a cardigan. I'm feeling very Fearne Cotton with a baby pouch, minus the eyeliner and rainbow manicure. Luella is bedecked in a printed wrap dress along with black tights, ankle boots, and a black military trench. The accessories are very vintage, the bag is most definitely very expensive. I pray she doesn't put it in a Nutella patch. I invite her through to my kitchen and introduce her to Annie. There's a bit of territorial eyeing up as Annie stands, looking superior and important in cashmere.

'Annie's a good friend of mine. After the whole Johnno Elswood debacle, I thought I needed someone here I could trust.'

I hope that doesn't make me sound cynical and cagey. Luella doesn't seem to mind as she starts to rant.

'Hmmm, don't get me started on that wanker, Johnno. The bloke is an arsehole. Don't worry, we'll get him back. Is this the Millie from the clip?'

Millie's been staring at her since she entered the room. I think it's the shiny hair and the accessories. She doesn't see those too often.

'Yes.'

'And the others?'

'They're in school.'

'Of course.'

Annie shrugs her shoulders at me as Luella dives in her bag, making herself comfortable. She pulls out a couple of folders decorated with Post-it notes and scrapbook cuttings.

'Can I get you a …'

'Tea. Green if you have it, if not then just black, no sugar.'

I nod as Annie opens her eyes widely at me.

'So I'll get down to business. Bar the Johnno Elswood thing, have you spoken to anyone else?'

I shake my head. I'm wondering if she's meaning literally because I have spoken to other people in terms of not being completely mute.

'Well, then let me lay it all down for you. The Elswood thing was a big fucking mess. The bloke wanted to drag your name through the mud to sell a few copies of the paper. I suspect though – actually I know – that Tommy McCoy and him have a history. I wouldn't be surprised if he paid him to dish the dirt.'

Annie and I nod to keep up. Millie's still staring at her hair.

'But put that to one side, this thing has drawn out quite the debate. Everyone's got something to say about it. Look at this.'

She pulls out something that looks like a pie chart with my name on.

'You were the eighth most talked about person in the newspapers last week. That's not bad.'

I turn to study the chart. I beat a *TOWIE* pregnancy and the fact that Primark have started selling high heels for toddlers. I'm not sure what to say – surely the idea would be for no one to be talking about me at all, to have this disappear into thin air. I feel my reaction is not as animated as she'd like. She pulls out several articles that I haven't seen before.

'The thing is, you are quite a big fly in the McCoy camp and he's come back fighting, even got the wife on his side.'

She puts a picture of the perfect waif that is Kitty McCoy out in front of me, cradling a watermelon like she might have given birth to it. Her hair is beauty queen, her teeth sparkle like nuggets of chewing gum. I wonder how she housed those four children inside that body. I skim the article and, when asked about me, she says that it's a shame I *'flew off the handle like that; my husband was only trying to help.'*

'Condescending little vixen, eh? Don't worry, if we want, I have early modelling shots of Kitty back from when she used to pose in cheap cotton nighties for the covers of romantic fiction. Some of it looks like porn.'

My mouth flies open at the thought.

'They don't want anyone telling them their brand of healthy living bullshit is just that. So Tommy has upped his game as well. The whole incident increased his media presence threefold so he's taking advantage. We've got chat show appearances, recipe corners, and next week ...'

She dives in to get flyers.

'The signing of his new book in Covent Garden while he tries to break the world record for pancake tossing. You are a big problem to them and their type of brand management.'

I cock my head to one side to get to grips with being this big a problem to their food empire.

'McCoy is everywhere. Newspapers, TV, books, and radio; he has his hand in everything and it's all fricking press manipulation. It's like subliminal advertising, the more you see his face in the press, the more you're reminded you want to eat his sauce and buy his book.'

But not for me. The sight of his face now provokes a response not unlike nausea.

'So when someone like you comes along and says different, that his brand is bogus, it snaps people out of their McCoy love fest and makes them question their brand loyalty. Which is why I fricking … love you.'

Luella is a hurricane of information. I am at a loss for words but must admit to feeling quite impressed by her wealth of knowledge on the matter. Yet I'm not sure what her intention is. Something in her tone and behind her eyes speaks that she wants to ruin the McCoys in painful and intrusive ways. I just want to let people know that my kids eat all right, my daughter's name is Millie, and that Johnno Elswood is a prick who deserves to get a bad case of genital warts.

'Errrm, so what do we do from now?'

'Well, first up, I've got you an interview with Jill Robertson over at *The Guardian*. She's the Family editor. And that trumps Johnno and his shit journalism and tabloid crappery. We can get your story across and print the truth.'

This makes my whole body lighten a little as the stress, worry, and fatigue of the last few days seems to evaporate off me. This is what I want. Yet *The Guardian* is a little highbrow. I'll have to get my thesaurus out, work out how far left I really am. Luella is flicking through papers while Annie keeps her distance, studying her every move.

'So, first things first. I need to know about you. Can you cook?'

'Well, I can throw meals together but I'm no Raymond Blanc.'

Luella laughs. Not really laughing, kind of like a big horsey chuckle. I'm slightly offended.

'Oh, I didn't think you were that for a second but on a scale

74

of one to ten.'

I think for a moment. Being asked to rate your skills as a chef is almost like asking someone to assess their skills in bed. Surely you need to ask the other person involved? I mean, even when the food/sex is average at best, it's still there and it's still edible/pleasurable. I have flourishes of good cooking – I can whip up macaroni cheese with my eyes closed. I have flourishes of days when the meatballs could break holes in the windows. Again, like sex, it ends up being very experimental, it sometimes doesn't work, and sometimes I'm too lazy to do it properly.

'I'd say a safe six.'

She furrows her brow.

'And a half? I did Home Economics at school. I got an A for my fruit scones.'

Annie interrupts. 'She's selling herself short. The girl's got some skills. You do that nice cake with the stuff.'

Annie grips my hand while I sit there trying to work out which stuff cake she's referring to. Luella scribbles something down.

'I mean, could you win *MasterChef*?'

'Ummm, no.'

Luella twists her face around, looking a little disappointed.

'But that's not how I cook. I don't do fancy molecular gastronomy restaurant food. To be honest, being in the middle of a crowded kitchen while a balding, middle-aged man shouts at me is not my idea of fun.'

She laughs a little under her breath, seeming a bit more interested by me.

'But you like food?'

'Well, yeah. Not sure if it always likes me though.'

I pat my thighs at this point. Luella smiles.

'And do you have a food ethos?'

I scrunch my forehead. Ethos? 'Not sure if there's a niche for "5 a day with a little of what you fancy and not too much crap."'

She laughs again. I may be winning her over.

'I mean, it's trying to be healthy. But we indulge in stuff we shouldn't and I cheat and it's not macrobiotic and organic but somewhere in the middle.'

She scribbles this down. My upside down reading skills scan 'needs definition.' I hope that's not a reference to my thighs. The fact is, I'm somewhere between Nigella and Delia, I reckon. I don't dangle baby courgettes pornographically in my mouth nor have a larder full of imported ingredients but it's sensible, reliable cooking replacing the twinsets with something a bit funkier. Again, not sure if there is a niche for that.

'And I don't know enough about your husband. Matt, isn't it?'

I nod tentatively.

'And what does he do?'

'He's training to be an accountant.'

Luella's shoulders drop an inch. I think she was expecting something more glamorous, more edgy. I think Matt was too.

'Well, one thing is that he's all right-looking. We can use him, the kids too. I like this one here. The hair is brilliant. Personally, I think McCoy's kids look a little inbred but that's what will happen if you just give your kids pulses and nuts.'

A bit of Annie's coffee seeps through her nose. Millie smiles, knowing that her hair is pretty special and she's glad it's been noticed.

'But for now, my advice to you is to get your story out there properly. Say what you want and don't let the McCoys attack your lifestyle and your family to try and prove their point.'

I nod. This is rational, sane. This is how to make my life normal again.

'And then after that, the ball's in your court. I quite like you. I think you're personable, young ... we could work on the cooking bit but this has the potential to be quite big. Nearly one million hits on YouTube, it's got over to the US, we could get you some chat show appearances, guest spot on *Saturday Kitchen*. Think you could do television?'

I look at Annie, who suddenly seems very interested.

'You mean there's further mileage with this?'

'Hon, I'm the best in the business. I can get you a makeover in *Closer* by next week, a cookbook deal by Christmas. Hell, if you wanted I could get you on *Strictly* this time next year. Tommy McCoy is coming to the end of his fifteen minutes, love. The backlash is starting and there's enough people out there who'd love to see someone like you steal his thunder.'

'But I have nothing against him per se. I mean I do ... but ...'

'C'mon. Who doesn't want to see someone like that, with all his preachiness, all his money, all his highfalutin' thoughts on the world, brought down a peg or two? And you? I think you might be the girl who can do it. The public wants someone like them, they're sick of these two a penny skinny minnies and jumped-up TV chefs. They want proper housewives, women in the trenches. I've been in this business for a long time. I don't back horses that don't win.'

Annie has bought into Luella's spiel and is clapping her hands like a seal, far from the po-faced lawyer I wanted her to be, sitting there defending me and looking over paperwork for missed dots and uncrossed t's. I think the *Strictly* comment did it – she's been trying to get tickets since forever. That's not to say that Luella being here doesn't fill me with some hope, some comfort too. But she's evolving this into something else. Drawing lines in the sand I can do. But battles where I am supposed to be this epic housewife/mother-style David character taking on the behemoth that is McCoy and his Goliath empire sounds tiring, time-consuming. Plus, I have no slingshot. Not even any rocks to put in it. Man, I even look stupid in gladiator sandals. They make my legs look like trussed-up sausages. Annie and Luella sit down to plan my course of attack while I nod and grab the plate of biscuits in front of me, breaking them off and sharing them with Millie, beige coloured crumbs becoming dust in her fingers.

CHAPTER NINE

It's Saturday. This means two things in our house: no work, no school. It also means that, whereas breakfast every other day of the week is hurried cereal and buttering holes into toast, we get up and make extravagant breakfasts that usually revolve around pancakes and bacon and setting off the smoke alarms. Our rituals do not seem to have been interrupted by this week's events bar a new inclusion to the proceedings: a newspaper at the breakfast table being scanned through by Matt and myself. It means I don't notice Ted squeezing half the honey bear on to his plate. Jake peers over when he sees my picture on the front.

'You in the papers again, Mum? You look nice there.'

I give him a hasty kiss on the forehead. Jake, ever the charmer. Hannah's face is all scrunched up and she entertains Millie with a strawberry.

'Yeah. But this time, this woman has written some really nice things about me and not told lies.'

The children are not that bothered. Matt reads between mouthfuls as Ted realises retrieving his pancake is going to be like tackling fly paper. Matt left the house this morning at seven to buy ten copies of *The Guardian*. I'm not sure what he intends to do with ten copies but this is the seventh time he's reading the article.

'You know, I think it's good. I think you come across likeable and more importantly, as though that Elswood fella was talking out of his arse.'

Jake and Ted always like it when Matt says this. It gives them an excuse to grab their butt cheeks and make them talk. Over pancakes is not the place, though. I grab another copy of the paper, re-reading things Jill Robertson wrote:

'... *what is most evident is that Mrs Campbell is a far better spokeswoman for the modern family. Her life, although frenetic, is a much better indicator of what mothers endure on a daily basis and her honesty, to say that at times she finds the domestic ennui difficult and overwhelming, more realistic and less condescending than when it does come from our celebrity peers ...'*

I read the word ennui again. Meaning boring? I keep looking over at Matt, hoping he's not taking too much offence.

'... in trying to manipulate what McCoy assumes to be her domestic failings to bolster his preachy attitude towards food and gain a few more viewers, he has shown himself to be part bully, part food snob ... she'll be the first to admit her culinary skills no way match McCoy's but she can identify a daikon and her children "usually" get their five a day ... "Maybe three and half most days," she says, laughing ...'

I stuff some blueberries into Millie's mouth when I read that bit. I scan again, looking at the picture they took of me in the restaurant where they interviewed me. I'm wearing a green jersey dress that Luella chose for me from Zara over tights and some brown heels. Big knickers and an even bigger bra held everything in. I see Matt's eyes scan over the picture. I say nothing.

'I don't look too mumsy? I wanted to wear jeans but Luella wanted me to look a bit more elegant. I don't look like I'm trying too hard, do I?'

Matt shakes his head.

'And what about the bit about Dad? Not too much? You think he'll be OK with that?'

The journalist asked me where I learnt to cook. My mother? I froze a little to hint at my shock and went to tell her no, I learnt from my dad. With two young brothers in the house, learning to fix cheese on toast for them after school, heat up tins of beans, and boil pasta a necessity. By fifteen, I learnt all the other bits and bobs from watching *Ready Steady Cook*. Ainsley Harriot once taught me very interesting things you could do with a red pepper. The piece is sympathetic about that yet not to the point where I sound like an orphan in an apron. Neither does it draw out the drama too much.

'No. I think he'd approve. It's a great piece. I think we've done well.'

He envelops a whole pancake in his mouth to the wonder of his boys, who try the same but end up with honey all over their chins, noses, and hair. The phone rings and Matt goes to answer it.

'Buongiorno, mamma ...'

I swing my head around. When it's in Italian, it's Matt's mother. Ringing to dissect the article and my skills as a mother and give her five pence share to the proceedings. I study Matt's face, trying to listen out for the words I know.

'Si, mi fa piacere che hai letto l'articolo. Hai comprato quante copie? Si, si ... sono sicuro che questa sai la fine. Si, certo, i ragazzi mangiano bene.'

Something about chairs, children, and eating? I pretend to clean the boys' faces.

'Beh ... è molto gentile da parte di Zio Dino, ma cosa me ne faccio con dieci chili di mozzarella?'

Cheese and dinosaurs? Must get that Italian for beginners book out again. I wonder what Gia Campbell makes of all this attention. Maybe she's happy someone's pointed out what she's been harping on about for the past eight years. I don't bake enough, I seem to have a food philosophy based around potatoes and mince. Matt dips in and out of English.

'Mum, you're always welcome here but really, I'm sure the article has wrapped everything up. Really? OK ...'

The hairs on the back of my neck stand to attention.

'Is Nonna coming?' asks Jake. Matt puts his hand over the phone receiver.

'She wants to talk to you.' I grimace, taking the phone reluctantly, knowing I have to at least play courteous and dutiful in front of the kids. This has little to do with monster-in-law clichés. It's just that because of her thick Italian/posh Edinburgh accent, I can't make out half of what she says. I try to recall my basic Italian. Como va? Come stai?

'Gia! Comma sty?'

There is a short pause as she tries to work out I'm not talking about punctuation or a pig's place of dwelling.

'Juliet?'

'Yes.'

'Good morning. I am reading the paper. I like your hair.'

'Thank you, Gia.'

Awkward silence #1.

'I am so sorry this whole thing got blown out of proportion. I didn't mean to embarrass the family.'

'I am not being embarrassed for you. I am good.' There are words in between that I didn't catch.

Awkward silence #2.

'I am sending you trees.'

'Oh, like something for the garden?'

Awkward silence #3.

'No, for eating. *Formaggio!* Chess!' I am lost.

'OK. Thank you. I will look out for that.'

'Give me to Matteo. Ciao, Juliet!'

I hand back the phone and shrug my shoulders. Matt smiles and mumbles something before hanging up.

'She's sending us some mozzarella.'

'How? In a jiffy bag?'

Matt shrugs his shoulders. 'She'll find a way.' He turns to tackle the boys with the box of wet wipes. I look over at Hannah, who's pushing bits of pancake around her plate, staring into the honey bear more meaningfully than anyone should have to.

'You OK, Han?' She shrugs her shoulders as I look to Matt, hoping for some back up.

Hannah finally pipes up.

'Is this going to make people at school gossip again?'

Matt listens in to the conversation while retrieving a blueberry from Jake's nose.

'Like what?'

'Well, people have been saying stuff. Imogen says her mum said ... she said you're a ...'

'A what?'

'First, she said I was an accident ... then she said you were an embarrassment.'

Matt squeezes that little bit too hard so the blueberry and a large piece of dried-up snot flies out of Jake's nose and onto

Millie's tray. Millie proceeds to eat it while Matt and I stare at each other.

'Well, Imogen's mum can hardly talk. She's got a mullet.'

'Matt!'

I turn to Hannah in my best motherly pose, considering I'm in a badly fitting vest top and cow print PJ bottoms.

'Hon, there were no accidents. You were a surprise. A good surprise.'

Matt nods. Surprise is a slight understatement. My period was six days late. I put it down to exam stress, drinking, and a shoddy diet. Three days later I took a pregnancy test with Annie. Two weeks later I told Matt. He cried. Big fat man tears rolled down his cheeks. It was the same sort of shock I expect people feel when they hear they've been adopted or this whole time they've been raising you the wrong sex. That a seismic shift in your identity had occurred, skewing a once flat and calm horizon. I felt nothing for days. The surprise of that little blue line numbed me into paralysis. Matt intervenes.

'Imogen's mum is just jealous because she got lumbered with her instead of you. I reckon her mum …'

I kick Matt under the table, knowing the sort of explanation that will come out of his mouth.

'Were we accidents too, Mum?'

I look over at the twins. If Hannah was our accident, the twins were our bolt-from-the-blue, knock-you-for-six type of surprise. We were going to try for one more, a boy to complete the family. Then the scanner thought our son had an exceptionally large appendage or that was another leg. Twins. Twin boys, no less. Matt stared so hard at the screen a little bit of drool came out of the corner of his mouth. I look over at Millie. She was the one born out of laziness. You go down the shops and buy some condoms. I can't be bothered. Oh, let's just do it, if it happens, it happens. Probably won't.

'No, no one here was an accident. And to call someone an embarrassment is not very nice.'

Hannah nods in agreement.

'She says that about Ciara's mum too. And Liam Baxter because he has two mums.'

Matt and I look at each other, slightly horrified a mother could be so indiscrete.

'Which is silly. Because Liam Baxter still has a dad, it's just that his mums are gay and she doesn't get it.'

Matt and I hold our breath as little boys' ears prick up.

'What's gay?'

Hannah interjects, 'It's like when a man and a man love each other. Or a woman and a woman. And they can get married and stuff and have babies.'

The boys don't look too perturbed by the idea.

'Like Uncle Ben. He goes out with men.'

'Hannah, how do you …?'

'They showed us a video at school about liking all different types of people. Gay people, Muslims because everyone thinks they're terrorists, and if you've only got like one mum and your dad's run off like Carly Matthews at school. I know about Uncle Ben because last Christmas he brought that bloke with him that you told me was his friend but I saw them kissing in the garden.'

Matt and I stare at each other, trying to take it all in. The boys have heeded Hannah's reasoning without as much as a hint of a need for further explanation. They simply shrug their shoulders and ask to be excused so they can turn the living room upside down. I usher them away as I clear up. I guess to them such ridiculous stereotypes that a man should be with, and only be with, a woman have not yet been set in stone, a fact pretty much exemplified by the fact that up until last year, Jake was pretty certain he wanted to marry The Little Mermaid. She wouldn't be able to walk down the aisle, Hannah had told him. Jake didn't care. He said he'd have an operation to become half fish and live under the sea. I guess people had done far worse to suffer true love.

'So when Imogen's mum talks crap …' adds Matt.

'You shouldn't really listen?' finishes Hannah. I'm still reeling from Matt having said 'crap' and it being out in the atmosphere like that for Jake and Ted to hear, memorise, and repeat in school.

'Pretty much. Try not to listen to them. Just remember we're all nice people and should try and be nice to everyone.'

I've overdone it with the nice. I can tell as Hannah has her eyebrows all arched and her mouth scrunched up like she knows I'm trying to be a parent and it isn't working. Matt laughs under his breath.

'And what about that stuff with that TV chef man?'

'Well, it's done with, Han.' Matt draws a line in the sand by holding up the newspaper article, showing me at my normal, non-crazy mum best. I look to Matt. It's done with. The end. Hannah looks semi-satisfied and runs off to be with her brothers. That leaves Millie around the table wondering if she's still hungry, tired, or in need of a nappy change. She looks up to both of us.

'Is that what you told your Ma then?' I ask, cradling a lukewarm cup of coffee. Matt starts to pile sticky plates on top of each other in his efficient Saturday husband way.

'Pretty much so. I mean, no point dragging this out, eh? Look what happened to Han at school – the girl doesn't need that sort of grief.'

I nod, a little sheepishly though, given I know what I'm going to say next.

'But what if this wasn't the end?' Matt looks at me curiously. 'I mean, that publicist said this could go somewhere. There's the possibility of an extended career as a media chef-type mother.' Matt bursts into laughter. I try not to act offended.

'What? Jamie Oliver in a skirt?'

'I don't know. She just said there is mileage in this. What do you think?'

He looks at me like I've just said I'm going to fly to the moon in a spaceship made of sliced ham. He shakes his head and starts to transfer plates to the sink – his silence pretty much confirming what I thought he'd think.

'I mean, maybe we should capitalise on the moment. If there's a quick buck to be made out of this, it could be good in the long run.'

Matt turns from the sink, annoyed.

'Or not? The last week has been manic – look how emotional it made you to have our lives under scrutiny from people we don't even know. I'm not sure it's worth it.'

'It doesn't have to be like that.'

'Well, it has been so far. I say think it through properly – the market is flooded with these chef types and most of them are TV saps. Why be one of them?'

'Why not? I could shake the market up? Be that down-to-earth mum who's more in touch with the public.'

'With one difference ... you can't cook.'

I inhale sharply. The best/worst thing about Matt is that he tells it like it is, straight from his Scottish hip. There are advantages of being told the truth, of not having someone blow smoke up your arse, but sometimes you crave the little white lie to feel like he might care enough to temporarily bolster your self-esteem.

'Excuse me? I cope. The children have survived this far ... you too. Last week, we were in this very kitchen and you said I was all right ...'

He shakes his head. 'All right for a mum but you're not chef standard ...'

'Exactly ... millions of mothers out there and who really knows what they're doing? I'd be speaking for them.'

'Did you tell Luella about the lasagne you dropped on the oven door?'

Matt often brings this up. He uses this story in the same way I bring up the time he dried the bed sheets without noticing Ted had been storing a carton of Ribena in the dryer.

'It was an accident.' It was me having slaved a whole afternoon trying to cook a lasagne to impress Matt's mother. A young Jake hovered behind me as I bent down to retrieve it from the oven. An oven glove slipped. A tray of lasagne fell to the oven door, cracking it and taking it off its hinges. I sat there crying, trying to scoop it off with a fish slice. Often, if the oven is hot enough, you can still catch the smell of two-year-old béchamel.

'I am sure there are millions of mothers out there who have done similar.'

He shrugs his shoulders. 'Well, you're asking me and I think this isn't a good idea. It's not us at all.'

He talks about us collectively like he probably should but it doesn't mean that it doesn't make me feel resentful that the decision has pretty much been made for us. I'm about to tell him as much when the phone rings. Please don't be Gia again.

'Hello?'

'Jools. Luella here. Great, great article. Loved it. Think it struck a very genuine chord and you look radiant in the photo. This is all very good.'

I'm well, thank you for asking, Luella. Matt moves over, pretending to wipe down Millie's high-chair when really, he wants to eavesdrop.

'So, I've been doing some research and this is what I know ...'

She then launches into further analysis of the article from the exact number of column inches it's scored to a scarily in-depth analysis of the message board reaction. HelenOfTroy thinks I'm brave to be deprecating the McCoy empire; Lewes4256 has a crush; MotherofFive thinks I'm trying to be a martyr for housewives everywhere but we all don't need to be pitied. I nod and take it all on the chin.

'And so we now have to await the Sunday tabloids. My sources tell me there might be a comeback. I need you to be prepared for this, so I'll be around at about four o'clock.'

'Well, four is fine. I'll bake a cake.'

'Lovely. I'm allergic to walnuts but everything else is good.'

I was being sarcastic but now, along with the school laundry, the dishes, the upstairs bathroom where Ted missed the toilet bowl, the homework, and trying to cut Millie's nails so she doesn't claw her eyes out with her little talons, it's another thing to add to my list. The phone still to my ear, she bids me farewell as I flick through recipe books. Matt looks at me and mouths Luella's name. He looks confused as to why I haven't ended this conversation yet. Cake, cake, cake.

'So when you say prepared? I mean is there another interview involved? Do I have to read anything?'

Comeback? That sounds like the actions of some fallen pop group. I inhale deeply, knowing Matt has heard what I just said. This is the end of this. But it isn't. Part of me feels there are downsides that could manifest as newspaper articles for gossip-mongers to chatter about at school. But there is something about this that feels different – something I can't quite put my finger on but it takes me out of this house. It moves everything in a new direction.

'Errrm, no. Don't read anything but just prepare yourself emotionally.'

She's strangely silent.

'Ummm, yeah. I don't quite get what you mean??'

Matt starts washing the dishes next to me, plunging plates deep into steaming foamy water.

'Well, tomorrow, *The Sunday Mirror* has an exclusive about you. Johnno Elswood has an article with an ex of yours, a Richie Colman?'

The breath hangs loose in my mouth on hearing his name. My hands tighten around the Delia Smith in my hands. Matt watches on, curious.

'And … I'm sorry … he's also … I mean …'

Luella is surprisingly hesitant. I turn to the baking section. Chocolate brownies, maybe? Or do I go safe with a Victoria sponge?

'They've managed to track down your mother.'

And with that my fingers loosen. Delia goes for a swim in the sink, Matt swears profusely as he gets covered in bubbles, and the phone tumbles to the floor.

CHAPTER TEN

All I know is that it happened in October. The leaves were just starting to change colour and at school, I had started to wear tights. That's all I remember. There were no fights, no dramatic exits, no letters, no taxis leaving like in a soap opera where people cried and looked out of rear windows. It was one day she was there and the next day she wasn't. Looking back now, it was as much of a shock to Dad as it was to us, so much so that he didn't actually tell us what had happened and spent a week fobbing us off with excuses about hair appointments, bingo, and sick aunts in Suffolk. Being kids, we just took it all in. As long as the television worked and the spaghetti hoops were on the table, it didn't faze us.

Then one day Ben noticed something. A duck on the mantelpiece, gone. He panicked. Mum loved that duck. Something had obviously happened. He turned and told Adam he was going to tell on him. He must have broken it. Adam shrugged his shoulders. He ran in to the kitchen to tell Dad. Dad was heating up something. Soup. Leek and potato soup. I followed Ben into the kitchen. Where's the duck, Dad? He didn't answer. Mum loves that duck, she's going to go mental. Then he broke. Soup fell to the floor, looking a little too much like vomit. A ladle clattered against the tiles. He backed onto the cooker and tears fell down his chin. I don't know, mate. I just don't know. I felt Adam's presence behind me. I remember running up the stairs and looking in her wardrobe, hearing empty hangers swing back and forth. That's all I remember. An argument about a duck and soup on a kitchen floor. That's all. She had just gone.

After that, to bring up the issue again with Dad felt a little raw and untactful and could have brought about more tears and his leaving, which was something we never wanted. So we never dug for any information nor talked to him about her again. We all had our suspicions: new loves, mental breakdowns, Ben's dramatic take that she was wanted for being a drugs mule. But her abandonment and reluctance to try and find us or stay in touch, while it lingered, never consumed us; we avoided the issue, swept it under the subconscious, thinking one day it might re-emerge. One day. We just didn't know when.

So it turns out to be today, in the early hours of Sunday morning while I'm sitting at the kitchen table sobbing my heart out in my sheep print pyjamas. I sip at lukewarm tea and study her face: still the same. Whereas Dad has lost most of his hair (he blames us) and lines are etched onto his face like old leather, she hasn't aged one bit – her hair is still a mousey, shoulder-length bob, the lipstick still dark and plum. The clothes have been overhauled into a white shirt and jeans, not the eighties leggings I remembered with baggy tunic dresses, no Alice bands. But the headline. I'M NOT ALLOWED NEAR MY OWN GRANDKIDS. I read on, literally foaming at the mouth with tears.

'When did you leave Jools, her brothers and your husband?'

"It was back in 1995. Juliet would have been ten. Adam was seven, and Benny was five."

'And was the split amicable? What happened?'

"I left because I fell in love with someone else. He was someone my husband worked with. When he found out, he went ballistic. He told me I had to leave. I wanted to anyway, but he said he was going to keep the kids and if I tried to take them, then he'd kill me."

'Really? Why didn't you report this to the police? Go through the right channels to try and claim your kids?'

"Because I loved the kids and didn't want to put them through that. After that, he told me the kids didn't want anything to do with me and to keep away. So I did. I tried to get in touch when I heard Juliet was pregnant for the first time as I thought that's when a daughter should have their mother around. I sent cards and gifts but I guess they never got to her. Until this day I still haven't met my grandchildren, it breaks my *heart."*

The article is complimented with pictures of my mum looking painfully into the air, trees in the background as she strokes pictures of us. Johnno doesn't seem to want to let her words speak for themselves though, and has a final dig about someone who'd renounce their own mother and let a poor old woman not have ties with her family. I wipe the tears from my cheeks as the kitchen lights turn on and Matt put his arms around me from behind.

'How bad is it?'

'Shit, Matt. I don't even know if it's true or not. Why is she doing this?'

His arms squeeze tighter as I hear footsteps behind him. I wipe my face to think it might be the kids.

'I found these two at the front door.'

It's Adam and Ben. Ben with briny tracks down his cheeks, Adam all pale and withdrawn. Matt puts the kettle on and gets the leftovers of my brownies out of the fridge as we all sit there in the early hours of the morning, this routine becoming a little too familiar.

'This is my fault.'

Dad shakes his head as Adam and Ben sit around the table, grey and staring into space. I have my suspicions that Adam may be drunk. Dad is quiet, wistful; Ben is teary, silent; whereas I am hyper-emoting, more on an asthmatic, foaming snot level. The littlest brother comes over to embrace me.

'If I hadn't done that *Guardian* interview and just let things lie, this would never have come to light.'

Nobody answers, everyone probably exhausted from this having materialised so quickly in the space of twenty-four hours. One minute, we're motherless and quite content to be so, the next there's hours of phone calls, tears, and conjecture. She's back. Adam picks up the newspaper and stares at it with a good dose of venom.

'Must be the money. Not that I expected differently.'

Ben shakes his head.

'Maybe they twisted her words. Like they did with Jools.'

A possibility. But Adam's not buying it. Neither am I. Dad doesn't respond. I just stand there staring at her picture, willing it to talk or move so I can slap it. I'm wondering how she thought this scenario would pan out? Oh, I haven't spoken to my kids in twenty years, here's an idea, I'll do it through the national press. And while I'm at it, I'll spout a whole load of bullshit too. Why? Whywhywhywhwhy? The question fills my guts with such incandescent rage I want to run through the street, release some sort of primal scream from deep within my being, and wave my fists at the sky. I keep looking at Dad, who just stares into space, like he knew this day would come but still has little to no answers about how to approach it. Adam looks enraged, verging on demonic with disdain, Ben is paler, like he might just want to go lie down in a darkened room.

'It sounds like she wants ... you know ...' says Ben, tentatively.

Adam and I look at him curiously.

'... to get back in touch.'

I see Adam's palms roll into fists. I shake my head at Ben. Never. She burned those bridges many years ago – burnt them to the ground, down to the river below taking the cinders far, far away. I feel the emotion swell inside my torso and stand up. Must do something else. I bend down in the kitchen to keep an eye on my chicken. Matt has taken the kids to Donna's party and given us some space to talk. Thinking it might help, I've decided to roast a chicken, like in some way being domestic and doing Sunday things might lift me out of this weird emotional plateau.

'Are you doing roasties?' asks Adam.

I was. But I over-boiled the potatoes so they're becoming mash. I take out my chicken and he sits there, a little burnished, a little fragrant, a little like he's wearing wet tights. Everyone is still strangely quiet, the room just fizzes with a million and one things that need to be said. I don't know what to say any more so I just take my chicken out of the roasting pan and sit him on the chopping board. Then I hack away at the poor bugger like it's done me some great injustice, flesh flaking onto the counter, gravy seeping into my drawers.

'Shouldn't you leave that to …'

Dad stands up to quiet Adam. I really go for it, stabbing at it until all that's left is a carcass with its legs askew like it's mid-yoga pose. Until Dad realises the knife needs to come out of my hands. He comes over and pats me on the back.

'That's a big bird. Leftovers will be good for sarnies.'

I stare at him as his eyes remain fixed on the chicken. You need to talk. You're not allowed to be practical Dad right now. Someone has opened up these massive floodgates into an event which will always hold epic importance to us. It's not time to talk about sandwiches.

'Tell us what happened.'

Adam and Ben shake their heads with worry. Dad just looks at me and knows. He sits down and scratches at his corduroy-clad thighs.

'What do you want to know?'

'Who was Brian?' I ask.

'Bloke from the school. Taught geography. I didn't know him that well but your mother did. All I remember is that he had a beard like David Bellamy.'

He rubs his chin at this point, wondering if his lack of facial hair meant their relationship was doomed from the beginning.

'And they fell in love. She told me one day, she told me she wanted to be with him but he didn't want to be father to another bloke's kids. So that was that.'

We all sit there quietly as he says it. Like that's the end of the story. But he tells us she did get in touch with Dad every so often (every year if she remembered our birthdays) and Dad would not have a lot to say to her bar the fact we were all right. She'd blether on about her new life with Brian as a lead in to find out if Dad had ever replaced her like she may have hoped, but Dad always replied no, even when he dated that woman he'd met on the internet who was nice enough but somewhat obsessed with all things crochet. Dad said that the one thing that was true was that she did send a card when Hannah was born. It had a pink teddy on the front and Mum wrote inside how happy she was to be a grandmother. Dad didn't know if that was meant sarcastically so he kept it from me. I had a lot to deal with in any case. I wasn't sure if I minded. We all believed Dad, of course, there's no reason not to, and the portrait she and Johnno Elswood had painted of Dad being a "push a woman up against a wall by her throat and fighting tooth and nail over his kids" kind of man was as far off a comparison as we could think for the old fella. As he tells us everything, all I can think is that Mum maybe did this as some deluded attempt at getting our attention and coming back into our lives. Yep, way to go, Mum. Talk down the man who's single-handedly raised us for the last twenty-odd years. That'll work.

'I should have told you this sooner. I'm sorry. I really am sorry.'

Ben cries a lot at this point. Adam shakes his head like he's going to uproot things and tear at bits of paper with his teeth. I'm pissed off at his need to apologise.

'Dad, you have nothing to be sorry about. We only wanted to hear things when you were ready to tell us.'

The boys nod their heads and look over at him as he looks at her picture on the table.

'She still looks the same though, eh?'

I watch his expression, wondering when and if he ever shed any tears for her. He never did in front of us, I'm not sure if we ever gave him the time, but I think about lonely nights in bed when he would have thought about why and how things had come to be as they were. It makes me twist my lips around each other and go over to the carving board again to hack at the chicken while apologising at it profusely. That poor bloody chicken.

My chicken hacking is soon interrupted by the phone and Dad again, who is a little scared for my chopping board and the fact I've managed to spray gravy all over the ceiling. I grab at the phone.

'Jools? Luella here.'

The need to rant still simmering in me, I don't think she'll mind being a soundboard for all my woes.

'Hon, how's it going?'

Her tone is matter of fact. She's been a little furtive since yesterday, reticent because she couldn't block the publication or

94

intervene with the paper as much as she'd have liked. She also met everyone for the first time yesterday; she liked Matt and his stripy jumper, my motley crew of children even more so. But meeting my fifty-five-year-old dad and realising he was going to be attacked most in the tabloids tomorrow really got to her, at least halving her normal rate of words per minute.

'How are Frank and the family holding up? That was a shitty piece of journalism if ever I saw one.'

I retire to the hallway and back up against the wall.

'We're all right. But Luella, I'm so pissed off. This isn't about me, that article made my dad out to be some sort of tyrant. It really isn't fair to him.'

'So it's all lies, yeah? We could force them to print a retraction, come back with a counter story. It's what I would advise.'

Yet again this idea of putting my story out there and going at it tit for tat feels useless, like I could be doing that for the rest of my life without anyone knowing the real truth.

'I just think I want to stop. It's really not worth it in the long run.'

I feel relieved as I say it. I look at the clock. 4.56 p.m. This would normally be the time when *Antiques Roadshow* would be on and you knew your weekend was coming to an end. The sky is changing colour and that Sunday gloom just sits in the air waiting for the working week. And I think about what Matt said. This isn't us. This is where it needs to end.

'Really?'

'I just seriously don't have the energy to do this. I want to kill Johnno Elswood, I really do. But I can't sit back and let them tear into my family like this. I just can't.'

She pauses for a moment as I inhale deeply. I've made my decision. No more spotlight.

'It's just, love, I didn't want to be the one to tell you this but I've been doing some digging. Turns out they found your mother through a private investigator that was paid for by …'

My ears prickle for a second.

'By who?'

'McCoy. He's on a mission, love. He's using you in the

worst possible way, really trying to ruin your credibility.'

I pause for a moment, clutching on to the phone, knowing not to drop it this time. If I didn't feel anger before, I felt it now. Searing through my veins, bubbling through my nostrils like a bullock on heat, making my eyeballs fizz in their sockets. How fucking dare he.

'Jools? You there?'

'Yeah. If he wants war, I'll give him a war. Let's take this bastard down. Call me tomorrow.'

And with that I hang up, a little abruptly. But there is something I need to do. I burst into the kitchen, stride over to a cupboard retrieving the Tommy McCoy cookbook I have in my possession, and throw it in the sink, before grabbing a box of matches and setting them alight. Ben has his hands over his mouth, Adam runs around the kitchen realising he can't get to the sink to get water. The book goes up pretty quickly. Of course, as I stand there in my temporary fit of insanity, staring at his pretty face go up in flames, it's Dad who knows what to do. He backs away casually from my semi-carved chicken, before grabbing the kettle and throwing it over the mini bonfire, using the other hand to switch off the smoke alarm. He looks down at the embers.

'You scalded the sink, love. That will need replacing.'

I just stand there as Ben reaches over to embrace me and Adam starts to laugh. If Tommy McCoy wanted war, he was messing with the wrong, if slightly demented, woman.

And now it's evening. I'm not sure what I've started. I haven't spoken to Matt about it at all, and the sink is black and looks like a cauldron, Hannah says. The pizza party at Donna's was a success. Matt, however, said the parents who were present mainly used it as an opportunity to fire questions at him. Was it true I'm estranged from my own mother? Am I getting paid for my interviews? Is it true I slept with Tommy McCoy? In the end, he said he probably ate more pizza than he needed just to have something in his mouth which meant he didn't have to talk.

So now I'm sitting in the kitchen doing what I do best:

staring at the wall, sipping tea, and avoiding chores. I wonder if this is what my mother did days prior to her leaving. Did she just sit around, dreaming about a better life with her bearded lover while a half-eaten chicken sat on the kitchen tabletops? When she was on the edge of the loo watching us in the bath, was she just plotting the best ways to abandon us? My mother was this grey area I never really thought about too often. When I did now it was in comparison to my own adventures in motherhood, so for every time I licked a tissue to wipe my kids' mouths down or gave them oven chips for dinner, it came with the reasoning that I could do a whole lot worse. Nothing was resolved today with Adam, Ben, and Dad. While we talked more readily about the circumstances surrounding her departure, we came to little conclusion over why she had done what she did or what we intended to do with the information. Except procrastinate and stare at the wall. Or begin a personal vendetta to take on an almighty TV chef. My last words to Luella still ring in my ears. Let's take the bastard down. With what exactly? A half melted spatula? Fish fingers? What exactly have I started? I think about the kids again. Maybe I'm doing this for them. I stare at a half-sodden copy of Delia on the counter top. Doesn't she have enough money that she can buy football teams? Money. We need money. This could give us money we don't have. I hear the creak of Matt's footsteps upstairs, hovering in the bathroom, and feel myself tearing up again. Shit. I go to the fridge to distract myself and grab instinctively at a Muller Corner and a bottle of Matt's beer. I then open the laptop on the kitchen table, looking for distraction. Facebook. Chatrooms. Maybe they can provide sanctuary and diffuse the stress so instead of being riled by mothers and chefs, I can read what people I don't give two hoots about think of me. Mumsnet. Wow, there's even threads dedicated to me. I say me, but it's mostly mothers talking about themselves and how much better they are than me. So you make your own fish fingers, good for you. I log on to Facebook. I scroll down my homepage. Nothing. Friend requests at twenty-nine. I click on the link. Don't know you, may have gone to school with you, definitely know you. Then a chat box flickers up.

R: *Jools? Hon, how are you? We def need to talk.*

I have no instincts at this point. I'd even forgotten I added him as a friend all that time ago. I just stare at the computer screen, at the stamp-sized picture of one Mr Richie 'Love rat' Colman.

R: *Jools? You there?*

I haven't even read the story he sold to the papers. With all the emotional fuss and confusion over my mum, it seemed irrelevant to even bother. We def need to talk? Intrigued, I scramble through the papers on the table and flick through to the article. In the meanwhile, I reply in the most nonchalant way I know how.

J: Hi

I finally find him, relegated to page ten and eleven. A double spread where a picture of us from college is used as the centrepiece. I gag a little to see it – mainly because my jeans seem to be halfway up to my chest but also because of how young and happy I look. He looks like he always did – kind of like Ryan Giggs with brown, curly hair that I thought at the time was luxurious and cute but in truth, made him look like a spaniel.

'... *when we finished she just found the next bloke, the first bloke who came along, and the next thing I hear, she's pregnant. I tried to meet up with her, tried to make sure she was all right but her bloke, Matt, warned me off. He was really angry, like we had a proper fight about it; he even hit me. To be honest, from that point I was just worried about the sort of bloke she was now with ...*'

My eyes fizz with tears as I read on:

'I mean, I knew when we were going out that was what she wanted, to have the family and be the mother she never had. But she did it all really young and then she got married well quickly. I knew her heart wasn't in it. I knew she still had feelings for me ...'

I freeze for a moment to process everything.

R: *You must be so angry with me. Really I can explain.*

My fingers hover over the keys. How dare you insult my husband like that? How dare you assume so many things about my life, about my family? But the thoughts don't process themselves as such.

J: What do you mean Matt warned you off? You came back? You tried to meet up with me?

I press enter and see my haste there on the screen. Part of me is simply curious, thinking that Matt and Richie were always separate threads in my life never destined to meet. Had they done, the universe might have imploded. I wait for his reply and scan through the rest of the article, the photo of him now. He looks different: receding hairline, in double channels down the front, and yes, yes, yes – quite a sizeable paunch – an affliction many of our male comrades from university seemed to have fallen victim to given they seem to have survived for the past ten years on combinations of takeaways which slower metabolisms won't forgive them for. I click on his profile. He's working for some top-notch engineering company that his photo albums seem to suggest send him around the world. Other albums suggest nights out in exclusive London bars, a flat in Putney, and a flashy hairdresser's sports car. He still likes the same dance music, his favourite film is still *Back to the Future*, and his favourite quote is from Terry Venables circa Euro '96.

R: *Do you remember that girl I was with?*
J: Dawn the Biochemist.

Pause. I maybe shouldn't have remembered her name with such speed.

R: *Yep. It didn't work out with her.*

Not surprised.

R: *When it didn't I tried to get in contact to patch things up but Matt and you were already together and you were pregnant.*

I'm not sure how to reply.

J: Yes, I was.
R: *I mean it happened so quickly, of course, I was worried about you. When I called round yours to check on you, Matt went off on one. It got pretty nasty.*
J: I don't believe you. Matt's not like that.
R: *So he never told you.*
J: Why are you lying like this? The article is a joke, Richie. Why would you talk about Matt like that? Why would you trash me like that?
R: *I'll admit, a lot of it was twisted about. That Elswood journo bloke wrote a load of crap but that stuff about us fighting was pretty true.*

I don't reply. If it is the truth, I half hope that Matt left a great big imprint in his face. On the other hand, I'm now asking myself why I didn't know about this – why the secrets? Was I too emotional and pregnant to have not sensed the furore going on around me?

R: *BTW, no one's called me Richie for a long time. It's Rich now* ☺

I still don't reply. I stare at the screen and the picture of him in the paper on the table.

R: *How are you anyway? This stuff with McCoy and your mum must be getting to you. I know you.*

I re-read those last three words.

J: You knew me.

I remember a time when I was a lost teenager without a mother and Richie Colman persuaded me to go to Leeds with him. He'd look after me, he said. He knew all the angst and turmoil her absence had caused and knew it was deeply embedded in my psyche. We used to sit in his bedroom on his Argos bed sheet set and talk tearfully about loss and aching and wishing one day she'd come back into my life. To know he knows as much is both heartbreaking and a tad disconcerting.

J: You knew a very different person then. I've changed a lot. For a start, even if you and Matt had a fallout all those years ago, I think it's highly inappropriate you go and tell a national paper about it.

That's good. That's conveying my annoyance with him and a loyalty to the man I'm now with. And I am a very different person to the high-waisted denim girl I was back then.

R: *Why did you think we fought?*
J: If you did ever have this 'fight' …
R: *Maybe we fought over you.*
J: Really? *sarcasm* Pistols at dawn to win the lady was it?
R: *I just didn't get how quickly you jumped into that. You and this guy. I guess I just assumed it to be a passing phase, that maybe I could win you back.*
J: But I was pregnant. … with his kid?
R: *How was I to know the baby wasn't mine?*
I've never moved my fingers so fast over a keyboard in my life.

J: Because she isn't. Hannah is most definitely Matt's daughter. You got an A in Biology – I thought you knew how that all works.

I'm slightly unnerved to think I've never given that another moment's thought. They were sexual partners at least five months apart when we found out I was pregnant.

R: *Crumbs, A Level Biology. Blast from the past there. Didn't we have sex in one of those labs in the science department?* ☺

I simultaneously want to blush and throw the computer out of the window. How do you respond to that? Yes, we did. Thank you for having fond memories of the occasion but if I remember correctly I ended up with ladders down my new tights and I'm not sure it was entirely pleasurable from where I was perched. I don't reply. I should log off because this is bordering on weird. This was supposed to be a distraction from mothers, from emotions, from the shittiest day I've had since this all started. I should be angry with you. I should be laying into you; about the way you unceremoniously dumped me, the way you forgot about four years of a relationship we'd cultivated over sixth form discos and exam halls. The way you're talking so lightly about something as important as my daughter's parentage. The way you've talked to a newspaper when we were done a very long time ago. But instead I'm shocked into silence, unable to take any more information into my little brain.

R: *Do you ever think about the what ifs?*
Don't look at it. Don't respond.
R: *I'm sorry I treated you the way that I did. I loved you very much – I was just young and stupid. I wish things could have turned out differently.*

And that's when I do slam the laptop shut, my heart pounding like it could fall out of my mouth. But an ache. Like a very tiny heartstring being plucked. The what ifs? As much as I hate him right now, how he wishes me all the frigging best, I hate how the sentiment pokes at that little bit of my heart that thought life would end up differently. With him, maybe. With a mother. It's what this whole day has been about – greener grass, a life different to the one I have now. The emotion yo-yos inside me, playing tag with my insides.

Matt. Think about Matt. Good, dependable Matt who could have easily buggered off eight years ago but didn't. I think about when he'd stay up with Hannah in our crappy Leeds studio apartment and play her Zero 7 CDs to try and get her to sleep. I think about someone who would carry me to bed even though I was six months pregnant and probably weighed the same as a small walrus. Think about your kids. Think about how life wrote you another ending and in the greater scheme of things, you ended up with the better lot in life. Think about your own mother, how she went with her different ending and it ended up hurting so many. Think, think, think. But all I can see is my life having veered off the beaten track, a life over which I've never had much control. Fricking Richie Colman. On the other side of the fence waving at me. It makes me wonder, it makes my heart beat a little faster. Think, think, think. But not too much or Matt will tell you off for ruining the laptop with your tears.

CHAPTER ELEVEN

So you learn a new thing every day. Green rooms are not actually green. This one is white with hints of broccoli green. And they have cappuccino makers with little dispensers of cinnamon and chocolate next to them, posh German chocolate biscuits and all you can eat croissants. I know about the cappuccinos as I'm on my fifth one. When you've lived with Nescafé Gold Blend for the past five years, you grab any opportunity you can to have a bit of real, from proper beans-style coffee. Of course, now I look properly wired, like I'm in a state of drug withdrawal. My hands shimmer, I can feel every inch of my fingernails, and my eyes are very big. Or maybe that's all the eyeshadow the make-up people put on me. Lilac? It makes your eyes look bigger, I've been told. I think it might make me look a little intergalactic. I feel the make-up as well. I feel like my face has been set in sand for all the foundation they put on me to cover up the rings under my eyes, twenty-something acne, and, well, the list could go on. Luella storms about with a clipboard and keeps asking questions to people dressed head to toe in skinny black. I sit with my coffees wondering how one should sit in a dress. I think about the last time I wore a dress. Do nightdresses count? Maybe it was in the summer. Matt made a joke about legs coming out from hibernation. Matt. Matt would be good right now. I think about what I did the other night – my very mild online flirtation – and my mind starts to race again with guilt and questions. Did they really have a fight? Like a *Fight Club*-style free for all? Who threw the first punch? I think about what would have happened had Richie fought harder for me, had I not got pregnant. But then there wouldn't be a Hannah, or twins, or Millie. I ponder such things as I attempt to cross my legs and nearly fall off the sofa.

After the McCoy bonfire as it's come to be known in my house, Luella got in touch with *This Morning* and, lo and behold, here I am on a Monday morning at an unfeasibly early hour. In the corner of the room is Phillip Schofield in colour and literally fifty feet away from me. I want to tell him I once got through to a phone-in on *Going Live*. But I won't. The idea is to tell Phil and Holly what happened in Sainsbury's, talk about my life, and correct all the mistakes that have come to print in the past twenty-four hours. That said, I always have my secret weapon. She's small, ginger, and dressed in purple. Millie. Luella said that if I get nervous or can't think what to say, then talk about the baby. She says she hasn't given them any subjects to avoid as that speaks volumes about celebs even before they walk through the door, so the field is wide open. Mothers, babies, McCoy, they could pick my brains about the state of the NHS for all she knew, so the idea was just to go out there and speak my mind and speak it well. When she said that I gave her a look, realising this woman obviously didn't know me too well.

So now I'm sitting here while Millie is fast asleep. It breaks my heart that soon I'll have to wake her so I can use her as a shield. I spy the pastries and biscuits but I am wise to that game. No crumby chests or pastry-style wart things again. I just go up to the machine and make myself another coffee, attacking the foam with both cocoa and cinnamon sprinklers but dispensing a bit too much given my hands can't seem to stop shaking. A wrist appears at me from the side grabbing mine. Luella.

'God, you're not nervous, are you?'

I laugh, 'Of course not. Just me in front of two million people while my life is being analysed. What's there to be nervous about?'

Luella laughs back. I'm not getting the humour.

'Just relax. I could have put you in front of Jonathan Ross, Graham Norton if I wanted. They'd have ripped you to shreds. These two are pussy cats.'

When do I tell her I'm allergic to cats?

'Anyways, you're on in five. They're talking about spring wedding fashion then going to a break and then you're on the sofa. We're OK, yeah? I'll be right by the cameraman if you need me.'

She's nice. Unfeasibly nice. I want to ask her whether she'll do the interview instead but I just take a deep breath and lift Millie from her pram and follow her out of the room, feeling a little like someone else should be here. Matt. I definitely miss his hand right now.

When we take a right out of the room, all eyes are on me and the baby who's still asleep and drooling a large patch of wetness onto my left shoulder. For some reason this doesn't feel like it's of any great concern. I'm in black today. A black shirt dress over some skinny jeans and ballet pumps. The skinny jeans are a new thing to me. Aren't they just leggings made out of denim? They're not entirely that comfortable either but Luella has told me they've shifted pounds. They've shifted them over the waistband into a tyre of flesh. But the shirt dress does wonders to hide that. Just don't breathe out. Or in. Maybe don't breathe at all then you can collapse and the interview will have to be postponed. Or not.

As I sit down on set, the first thing that strikes me is how I can't see Luella at all. The studio lights blind me so much that all I can see are faceless black figures roaming around the background like ghoulish pixies. The second is that this microphone pack sticks out of my back but under my dress like I've got some horrific hunchback growth. Millie finally wakes up and perches her chin on my shoulder wondering where I've brought her now. She always has this look about her like I'm not showing her the world but simply dragging her along behind me. Phil and Holly come over to introduce themselves and pat Millie on the head, they're nice enough. Holly is incredibly pretty but I'm reminded in the back of my head of all those mornings Matt would spend watching Saturday morning television with Hannah, pretending he was bonding with her but secretly was just ogling Holly's bosoms. People are waving limbs about in the shadows and then a light starts to flash. I'm squinting a lot until I realise Phil and Holly have started talking.

'So one week ago, our latest guest became an unlikely household name after a clip of her on You Tube received over one million hits. Jools Campbell, a mother of four, was filmed ranting to TV chef Tommy McCoy after he accosted her in the supermarket and tried to attack her lifestyle. And we have her here today...hello, welcome and you've brought a friend I see …'

I'm still squinting reading everything he just said off an autocue. Shit, that's me he's talking to then.

'Yeah, this is Millie. Thank you for having us here.'

Holly makes cooing baby noises and there are comments about the hair. Poor little Mills has received such a commentary that I'm half tempted to dye it or shave her head. Millie looks over at them, not too impressed as always.

'So one week and you're in every paper, your name is on everyone's lips. How have you coped with this deluge of commentary on your life?'

I find myself adjusting Millie's position on my lap as I can see a large roll of fat in a small screen to the right.

'Ummm, it's been a bit crazy. I … I guess when it happened I just assumed it'd be this one crazy event in my life and nothing would come of it, but everything has blown up to crazy proportions. My family have been put under the microscope, my life, my kids … crazy.'

Crazy? I can see the look in Holly's eyes. This woman is crazy. I smile a lot but I feel my head is sweaty under the lights and hope all this makeup can soak it up. Time to stop saying crazy.

'I just … I think mums today have a hard enough time. We don't need reminding when we're not doing the best job in the world. I think I was just trying to defend myself that day. I just can't believe everything's got to this stage.'

They nod.

'Like the article with your mother?'

I pause. Luella was right – nothing is out of bounds. My mother situation still sits a little raw. The media have picked at that scab and I kind of need to let it heal over a little before I can deal with it. For now, it just stings. I really need to talk.

'Erm, you know … I guess … sure.'

As eloquent and concise as ever, Jools Campbell. My eyes

glaze over for a moment – could be the eyeshadow, could be the emotion coming up into a slow simmer. This isn't about her, it can never be.

'Also the fact that *Heat* have me in their worst dressed pages this week because I didn't wear a bra to the supermarket.'

The diversion tactic to beat all diversion tactics, talk about my tits. Phil's eyes scan down. Holly laughs. Job done.

'So if you wanted to rewrite a lot of the media coverage about you, what would you say?'

I smile. Time to get my word out there. Here goes.

'At the end of the day, I'm a mum in a semi looking after four kids on a budget. I'm a cook, not a chef, and sometimes that role, while enjoyable, is also a chore. I'm like any other mum out there trying to do the best by their kids but sometimes falling short.'

I sigh as I say this, realising the depth attached to that last sentence. Christ, woman. Don't get emotional again. They nod again. I can't tell if it's sympathy or boredom.

'I just think McCoy doesn't realise that we don't need his condescension. His smirking and finger pointing because we don't know what an artichoke is or because I occasionally dole out fish fingers. We don't need that sort of help.'

I nod to myself hoping I've not come across as too offensive.

'... so tell us what do you think would help you in the kitchen?'

I pause for a moment. Am I supposed to refer to ingredients, kitchen appliances, or what I would really want which is a houseboy called Juan to chop my onions for me.

'I guess sometimes you just want reliable recipes, new twists on old favourites ... that and an extra pair of hands?' That hasn't drummed up nearly as many smiles as I thought it would.

'Well, funny you should say that because we might have those spare hands for you today. Let's bring her on.'

The first thing that runs through my mind – not my mother, please not my mother. But the person who appears from behind the curtain is probably a thousand times worse.

'Kitty McCoy! And she has brought with her today her little

one, Ginger.'

I freeze, holding up Millie as a shield. What the holy crap of mother? I look over but can't see Luella's face, only a figure marching up and down and waving her hands about. Kitty approaches me and shakes my hand while Phil makes a lame joke about Millie's hair colour and the youngest McCoy's name. The first thing I notice is how perfect her fingers are, soft like baby's skin, yet her handshake is a bit feeble, the eye contact slightly menacing.

'So lovely to meet you, Jools!'

I still can't speak. I have been ambushed. Worse, I have been ambushed by someone who guided me through my younger years on children's TV and looks particularly happy with himself. How could you do this to me, Phil? Kitty looks me up and down. Next to her I look like the before shot of a makeover shoot. Her skinny jeans are far better fitting, her top has nautical stripes: the sort of horizontal patterns that magazines always tell me to avoid because they'll make me look as wide as a freighter ship. Baby Ginger sits wonderfully still on her hip, wearing a beautiful checked dress and tights. Poor Millie in her casual get-up. But Millie has more hair and she's got nicer eyes. Look at me comparing the poor babies, I have got really desperate.

'So we thought today was the day to get you two to meet, you both have babies the same age and I know Kitty has some things she wanted to share with you.'

I can see Luella in the corner of my eye waving her hands about. Like telling me to stop? Or not talk? Kitty turns to me and puts a hand on my knee, I flinch as she touches me. I don't want to hear it.

'Yes, Jools. I know how hard it is for young mums nowadays so I have my own brand of baby food and I thought I could show you some recipes from my new book that I think all new mums should try. So …'

Everything is a flash of exclamation marks and Kitty's new book, *Kitty's Kidz!* 'Organic! Everyday! Family!' – as people run on set to usher me to the kitchen set-up less than twenty feet away. A bosomy woman comes to take baby Ginger away, a person with a clipboard offers to take Millie. I decline. Phil and Holly follow us. I still can't speak. I stand there next to the kitchen counter while Kitty gets down to business tossing her ice blonde hair about her shoulders. Jesus, she is tiny. How the monkeys do you get so skinny after four kids? From her profile side she looks about ten centimetres across, like she could fit through prison bars. I've read all the articles; I just bounced back! I ate sensibly! I breastfed all the fat away! Part of me wants to believe there was lipo, faddy diets, and girdles involved. Part of me knows she probably didn't get through three packs of Maryland cookies a day nor use the excuse that pushing a double stroller up a hill is a proper cardio workout.

'So Jools, I have this gorgeous recipe which is great for babies coming up to their first birthday. My kids love it and in our house we call it Baby Ganoush.'

Everyone laughs except me. I smile like I'm passing wind. Kitty proceeds to grab some pre-prepared roasted aubergines from an oven and blends them with yoghurt, lemon, garlic, parsley, and adds other assorted clear bowls of spices and such. The blender comes on and Millie starts to cry. Ginger in the meanwhile is quiet from over in the wings.

'Aaaah, is she scared of the blender? That can happen with unfamiliar noises. My kids don't mind it, it's just on all the time in our house.'

I'm not taking anything in. One, I'm still stunned by the ambush, and two, I'm all too aware that Millie has just peed in her nappy.

'It's just so incredibly easy and my kids love it with veggie sticks or with pitta strips for a quick and tasty lunch.'

Phil and Holly tuck in as someone from the side creeps a large plate of crudités on to the counter. There's lots of oohing and aaahing. I'm offered a cucumber stick and dip it in to the light green gunk in front of me. Phil turns to me.

'So Jools, what do you think?'

This is my chance to say something. Anything.

'It's lovely. Thanks.'

'So with recipes like this, I really don't think there's any reason to cut corners.'

I smile through gritted, bearing-into-my-gums teeth. I just can't believe they've gone and done it again: brought me and my abilities as mother down a peg or two, but this time on live television.

'And Kitty had some pudding ideas she wanted to share with us too.'

'Yeah, I mean my kids are really loving exotic fruits at the moment. Papayas especially. So easy to mash up for babies. We're also really into drying our own mangoes.'

Phil, Holly, and Kitty all turn to look at me. I have trouble drying the kids' clothes in time for Monday mornings, she wants me to dry fruit as well? I want to cry. Maybe stuff my face full of crudités to make me feel better. Yes, I am rubbish. Thanks for telling me. I eat Baba Ganoush out of a tub, sometimes with a spoon. I don't use my blender too much as it's a bastard to clean. Then from in front of me, a little hand reaches out and grabs a stick of cucumber and starts to gnaw on it. I want to lift her into the air. Look! She eats vegetables! But everyone has their gaze fixed on Queen Kitty. Millie turns her face to smile at me. That one little dimple on the left cheek, the gappy, translucent baby teeth. That smile that says she's happy because the cucumber is cold and helping ease her teething woes. But also a smile I see a lot, the one that I believe to be her acknowledging me. I'm that someone who's been there from day one and hey, it hasn't all been a bag of fun (you fashion my infantile hair so I look like a little ginger Susan Boyle; Jake pushing me off the sofa was a particular low point) but you're my mum. Here, perched on your rather large hips, I am usually safe and warm and cosy. You're not perfect. I get it. I look down and smile back. You have to say something, Jools Campbell. You must.

'Papayas are quite expensive though.'

Phil and Holly nod so as to say they agree with me. They've earned back some brownie points they may have previously lost.

'It's just two, three quid for one papaya, and I could get two bags of apples for that.'

'Yes, but the point is to introduce your children to new

tastes. Papayas are stuffed full of vitamins and fibre. In the Far East, they're everywhere.'

'Yeah, but I live in Kingston.'

No one seems to know how to respond. I'm also trying to recall the last time I ate a papaya. Possibly as small, unrecognisable lumps in an exotic Ski yoghurt.

'It's just there is also a cost in importing exotic fruits – I thought being organic was also about eating local produce.'

Phil and Holly are still being wonderfully impartial and nod their head, following the conversation with sudden interest. I see Luella has stopped jumping around in the background, and a quiet hush descends over the set.

'But it's also about educating your children about variety.'

'Don't get me wrong. I appreciate your advice but what if you have a budget to think of?'

Kitty gives me a look, the same look her husband gave me when I told him he could take his TV show and his misguided attempts at helping me and leave me alone. This all makes for a fabulously awkward moment which I predict might make some list of annual awful moments in a magazine somewhere. Kitty, slightly speechless, just puts some of her Baby Ganoush on the end of a celery stick and pops it in her mouth, mumbling something through roasted aubergine.

'I was just trying to help. You said …'

We all strain our ears to hear her.

'You said before that you feed this poor girl out of a freezer. I'm just thinking about her, that's all.'

Phil and Holly inhale sharply. Millie grabs on to my shoulder knowing all too well that my chest has tensed up and I'm ready to lash out. But I keep my cool, I think.

'I'm sorry. That interview was taken out of context. I do freeze a lot of Millie's purees in ice cube trays. That's what I was referring to.'

'Well, even so, this recipe freezes very well also and is mentioned in the book.'

A copy is pushed over to me and I push it back in her direction.

'I'm good, thanks.'

'Please take it. All mums need a hand every so often.'

'Well, if you want to help, you could come around and do my ironing?'

Holly chokes a little on a pepper stick, laughing. Kitty just smiles and proceeds to munch her way through some carrot. I want to get said carrot and ram it into her forehead.

'I also have a new snacks section in there. You will find that childhood obesity is linked to an overconsumption of processed snack foods.'

I look at Holly and Phil, who realise this little segment has become about her, her book, and her agenda. She couldn't give two hoots about my ironing. Phil starts flicking through the book.

'Crisps? You make your own crisps?'

This has suddenly got everyone's interest as we imagine her drying her own fruits in the heat of the North London sun and deep frying batches of crisps for her children with her cashmere jumpers and non-existent backside.

'I do. I use a mandolin and use anything from sweet potato to parsnips to kale. The kids love them.'

'But how do you get the smoky bacon flavour?'

Phil laughs and all is forgiven. Kitty gives me the evil skinny eye.

'The crisps you speak about are incredibly unhealthy. I would never give them to my children.'

She sounds so resolute. I don't hasten to add that Millie is probably thirty per cent salt and vinegar given that was all I could keep down in my first trimester.

'I mean, even processed, overly sweet cereal bars: they are the enemy. I always make my own. I always have an array of healthy snacks with me. Like here: dried fruit and honey bars.'

The book comes out again. There's a picture of Ginger munching down on one, radiant in a mink sequinned dress, her face shiny with health and Photoshop.

'This is the perfect snack for young babies.'

I glance over the pages.

'How young?'

'Of any age. There's no limit to how young you can start

healthy eating.'

I arch my eyebrows.

'Well, there is if you're giving babies honey. Here, you say these are a suitable finger food from nine months. You're not supposed to give babies honey until they're one year old.'

Kitty's face goes grey as she looks down at the book. Phil looks over at me.

'Really?'

I attempt to sound like an authority on the matter.

'It can cause infant botulism.'

He'd better not ask me what that is because I don't know myself. Phil and Holly look back to Kitty, who's looking over at a man in a suit. Behind him, Luella appears to be doing a little jig on the spot. Kitty scans the recipe with her well-manicured finger and realises this rather big typo is not going to go away on the five gazillion other books in circulation.

'Well, it's just a bit of honey. And ...'

The set is silent. Phil, ever the professional, expertly leads into a break. Camera lights flick off. Luella storms over, along with a man in a suit, obviously part of the McCoy entourage. Phil and Holly are ushered away with make-up brushes and people with wires in their ears.

'What the hell was that? We were not informed that Kitty was going to be here. You ambushed Mrs Campbell here and used her for your own purposes, and that was to publicise your little book.'

The man in the suit turns to Luella and they embark on their own little argument as regards to my fame (fame?) being contingent on theirs and how it was all the producers' fault. I look around to see Kitty striding off set to Ginger and the bosomy nanny. So much for being here for my benefit, she doesn't seem interested to impart her culinary wisdoms now the cameras are off and I've pointed out the rather large mistake in her book. There are hair flicks aplenty as she strops off. I look down at Millie, who is fascinated by the lights on the ceiling, her little mouth wide open. Luella grabs my arm.

'We're out of here. This is the last time I come on here. I have this year's *X Factor* winner and their family ready to sit on your sofa but it's not happening, you hear me.'

And in a storm of swear words and fumbling about trying to get all my belongings together, we leave.

By the time we get home, it's nearly time to pick up the kids and I find Ben and Dad preparing dinner in the kitchen. When it comes to my kids, I always send a tag team in to help with any babysitting – one to wipe, one to catch. It looks like another Dad classic: toad in the hole. When I enter, the kitchen is silent, making me think they've watched the interview and the way Kitty McCoy basically mauled me on air. Luella follows behind me, slightly sheepish. She's apologised ever since we left the studio and was still mid-explanation when we hit the A3. It was wrong of the producers to think they could create some sort of celebrity duel on their show, worse for Kitty to capitalise on what was supposed to be my air-time for her own selfish purposes. She's mightily peeved, to the point where I know she wanted something different for me, not that. In the car, I spoke to Annie and Matt. Annie was kind as always, saying my comebacks were good and collected, my dress looked very chic. Matt said what I needed to hear, which was he wouldn't do her for a month of Sundays. It'd be like shagging a rake. That, and that it was quite obvious that Millie had had her wee face on halfway through the interview. Ben and Dad are more reticent to show their opinions. I hand Ben the baby while Luella goes over to air kiss my father, something which has caught him unawares both now and the several other times she's done it.

'Frank, put the kettle on. This girl has been through the ringer. Did you watch it?'

Dad nods, silent, and does as he's told.

'I mean, talk about being waylaid. It's so the McCoys though, they have press manipulation under their belts, that's for sure. But you did good, Jools. I was worried for a second, your face when she came out was a picture, but you held it together and that's what's important. I don't take sugar, Frank, and green if you've got it.'

I shake my head to Dad. He smiles and looks at me for that moment too long, like he might want to tell me something.

'Dad? Everything OK? The kids got off OK this morning?'

'Oh yeah. It's just … something happened when you were out.'

I go through the list of possibilities: kids are at school, Matt is at work. This means it's something to do with the house. I think about our dodgy guttering or the fact someone may have blocked a toilet.

'Your mother called.'

Luella stops her babbling to stare at Frank for a bit, then back at me before realising her mouth needs to stay very much shut for the meanwhile.

'You better speak to Ben, he spoke to her and now he's gone all quiet. I don't know what she said …'

I rush into the lounge to see Ben disrobing Millie from her coat as she's perched on the sofa. He always seems to do it much better than I can and that's saying something since I've had four to supposedly practice on. Millie has a soft spot for Ben, I think it's the constant singing and comedy hair.

'Dad told you then.'

'I'm sorry, hon. Are you OK? What did she say?'

'She didn't even register who I was. She thought I was your husband and I said no, it's her brother and then she called me Benny and launched into lots of hasty admissions of love, how sorry she was. It was quite touching.'

I grab him, sandwiching Millie in between us, hoping the hug will do enough to squeeze any hurt out of him. Ben has always been this dynamic, happy sort, but talk of the darker side of life has always led his face to drop a couple of shades as he fights off the anguish with sarcasm, lots of it. We settle into the sofa, leaving Millie free to explore the television and find the remotes to snog.

'I told her it was best not to call here again. I wasn't sure what to say. And then she started with the sorries and I hung up on her. It was … I don't know. It's like, you left me when I was five so I'm gonna hang up on you to get back at you. I don't know. Maybe I'm crazy. Yes, what a crazy situation. So crazy.'

Ben always has a way of harnessing bitchy humour to change the tone of a situation. I hit him with Millie's blankie which makes him giggle.

'Was it awful?'

'Well, you started a blethering fool but you reined it back in the end. I forget how feisty you can be.'

'Feisty?'

'I mean you've got chutzpah. You were always standing up for me and Adam when we were little. Remember Wendy Bird in Juniors when she called me a nancy? You cornered her in the toilets and cut off her hair.'

I cringe to think that was once me. I was in my teens and had launched into a vaguely gothy-type persona which meant nothing more than some stripy tights and scowling a lot. Wendy Bird was a blonde princess who said too many things about my family so I accosted her in the school loos and cut off a chunk of her hair. However, I'm ponderous that Ben thinks I would exact my revenge on Kitty McCoy in a similar fashion. He rests his head on my shoulder like he did when we used to watch *Rainbow* together.

'Do you think she'll come and find us?'

'I don't know.'

'Because if she does, I might need to prepare myself. Get a monologue prepared.'

I laugh because he knows I have the same plan.

'You OK?'

'I'll be all right. I just … sometimes I think she just royally fucked up some little part of my brain, you know? I don't know how I feel about her.'

I hold him close and feel his little head sigh with the weight of something a child shouldn't really feel for a parent. The problem is, I know exactly how he feels.

CHAPTER TWELVE

It's Sunday today, six days since the *This Morning* incident and nearly two weeks since Sainsbury's. This is the sort of action that usually fills a year. It's quiet in the house for once. Quiet because I've plonked the kids in front of the television, still in their pyjamas mid-morning, and Matt is persuading Millie a nap would be a really good idea. Quiet also because someone showed up on our doorstep earlier. She was small, in a velour tracksuit top that matched her Autumn Magic curls, and was here to pinch Matt's fats and make sure I was still feeding her grandchildren. Gia Campbell is in the building; hence the hush descended over the house, and I suspect most of Surrey. Gia and I have a wonderfully strained relationship – the main feeling that sits between us is 'You're never going to be good/Italian/Catholic enough for me' versus 'Whatever, you married a tall Scottish Protestant.' It means we share smiles and half-hearted hugs and M&S two for a tenner Christmas presents, and when she feels like it or when Doug, the other Daddy Campbell, goes fishing, she shows up on our front door unannounced and usually with a waxy cat shopper foaming with basil and other assorted goodies. This time, however, her reasons for visiting are slightly more covert. She keeps giving me looks like she's read all those articles and is trying to burn scarlet letters into my forehead with her eyes.

'She can sleep in Hannah's room. It'll only be for a bit.'

Matt whispers in the hallway as we hear Gia rustling around in my cupboards, probably rearranging spices and wondering why half of them are past their use by date.

'Do you think she hates me even more now?'

'Probably. We might have to have another kid to get her back on an even keel?'

Matt laughs but it gets stuck in the back of his throat when I punch him near the groin area. At least that was one thing I was good for, producing mini Campbells for her to fawn over so she could pay tribute to her son's strong Italian sperm.

'Juliet! Juliet!'

I am being summoned. I must admit I do like the way she says my name, like it's supposed to be said, as Shakespeare would have wanted. Matt ushers me in and goes to sit with the children. I take a big, deep breath.

'Gia? Is everything all right in here?'

'You are not having sage?'

Right now? No. I prefer one sugar in my tea. I shake my head.

'Then good I bring. Come. I bring nice pancetta.'

I look over at my kitchen counters and the usual array of school letters, bills, empty crisp wrappers, and hamster food is replaced with a sleek and shiny work surface. An onion and three cloves of garlic sit on the chopping board awaiting their fate.

'I think you help me cook. Come, come. This I teach. We chop.'

I take five seconds to process the sentence. I get the word chop, so stand there to attention and approach the board. Before I pick up the knife, she grabs a shoulder. I smile back hesitantly.

'What are we cooking, Gia?'

'Something great. Simple risotto. Nice pancetta, onion, and we roast the butternut squash. The children like this one.'

Only too well. When she cooks this, well, when she cooks anything, from bolognaise to zabaglione to the simplest tomato sauces, the children always lick their bowls clean like feral cats. I stop for a moment to take it in. You want us to partake in an activity together? OK. I see her take some of my stock cubes and hold them to her nose, sniffing them strangely. I start to peel at the onion and chop it in the manner I've become accustomed, like the way a chimp might use a rock to break something open. Gia looks at me curiously.

'I no like this McCoy.'

I stand there and nod. That's probably the first and only thing we have in common.

'I no like how he go on the television and he cook Italian when he no Italian. He think he go there on holiday and then he teach people how to cook my food. He is wanker.'

I freeze to hear her curse. My onion is a jumble of small squares, bits, and slithers. Gia eyes it up, grabs the knife from my hand, and dices it further.

'Rock the knife from side to side, you try.'

I take over as she stands next to me examining my work.

'You are well, Juliet?'

I nod curiously at this sudden enquiry into my wellbeing as I watch her stare at my bottles of olive oil, shake her head, and go into her bag for her own.

'I thought I should be coming down. I read so much in papers and I know it must be very hard.'

A large lump forges itself in my throat, waiting for the knife in my hands to end up in my jugular, especially if she read about one Richie Colman.

'I … I don't know what to say, Gia. I am sorry such lies were printed. It really means nothing.'

Gia purses her lips. I feel duped. What was once a bonding exercise was just a cover for discussing other matters. Not so clever when there are sharp objects in the area.

'I know. I just always worry. I … I also read about your mama. I am sorry.'

I fish around in my drawers looking for a garlic press. I find it full of Plasticine and pick all the crusty bits out, trying not to look her in the eye.

'I was not knowing before why you have no mother. Matteo no speak of this. But now I read the papers …'

'The papers were not very accurate, Gia.'

'Oh, nononono. Matteo explain. But I feel like now I know.'

I can feel tears in my eyes. Onion tears, not mother tears, but Gia looks up and perceives them to be the latter. I wipe my eyes on my shoulder and look at Gia. There's a look on her face. One I'm not sure I've seen before. She pats me on the shoulder and nods. I feel like she might think we are bonding, that this is a key breakthrough moment, perhaps. I will share a recipe with you because it is obvious that my shortcomings as a temptress

121

harlot and non-Italian mother may not be my fault at all. There is silence for about five seconds. Hell, for her to believe that is good enough for me if it means she teaches me some closely guarded recipe and I go up in her estimations a bit. She puts a velour arm around me and squeezes lightly, in the same way I've seen her pinch ciabattas to check they're still fresh.

'Jesus Christ, Millie.' It's something I hear every night. Matt's voice through the ceiling as he changes a nappy and acts like it's the first time he's seen how much a small infant can actually poo. 'It's all over your frigging back.' I hear swearing at the wipes, the new pack of nappies, and all the while, Millie chuckling her little heart out. At the front of the house, I hear the kids with Gia and the faint mutters of pirates, curtains, and walking the plank. To her credit, the kids love Gia, her Italian glamour and pockets full of fudge help, but despite any disdain we have for each other, we're both mature enough to realise the relationship she has with the little Campbells is important, mainly as she's the only granny they've got.

I am in the kitchen, (the only room I ever seem to frequent any more) and am busily writing down recipes into my file (provided by Luella). This is all part of Luella's master plan for me: get all my cooking knowledge down on paper and try and get my skills out there. So she's planned for me to cook on *Saturday Kitchen*, like in front of proper adults instead of the four wailing banshees that are usually hanging by my ankles, telling me they're starving and they may die if dinner doesn't make an appearance soon. Butternut squash and pancetta risotto, I print in my best writing. I stare at the empty bowls piled by the kitchen sink smeared in clementine-coloured goo – the risotto was a success, something to add to my cooking repertoire, even though all I feasibly did was chop an onion, some garlic, and stir the pan, learning things about steam and stirring. I scribble down Gia's wise words: a risotto should be *all'onda* and ripple in the plate like a delicate stream. It shouldn't land like old porridge. I continue to doodle in my folder, getting my head around writing and forming actual sentences, then finish the recipe with a flourish and try to

122

annotate it with pictures.

'What are you doing? Why are you drawing a giant penis next to my mother's recipe?'

Matt peers over my shoulder curiously.

'It's a butternut squash.'

'Seriously, I have never seen poo that colour. It's like we solely feed her mushy peas.'

I nod, grimacing, always pleasant to hear Matt's descriptions of stools as food. At least it wasn't korma.

'Now the others want pudding. I'll whip something up.'

He heads over to the fridge, rooting through the drawers to find some fruit, yoghurt, and assorted goodies, then starts assembling mini trifle/parfait desserts for them with a snap of his hairy wrist. I look over and scowl a little. Although I hate to admit it, Matt's always been the better cook; he thinks on his feet, he doesn't need scales, he knows the magic formula when it comes to seasoning. I'm at a loss why Luella hasn't thought he'd be a far more worthy adversary for McCoy. I remember when Hannah was starting to wean he was the one who'd be whizzing up purees, and even now the one who on a Sunday when energy is lacking is still chopping and making soups from the remnants of the roast. That's not to say my skills are lacking but when the honour of cooking three meals a day, five days a week is forced upon you, it is easy to fall out of love with the process.

'So what else has Mum planned?'

Yes, it seems she's not only here to teach me about risotto. She has decided to lend me her services as cooking guru so that maybe, just maybe some of her genius may impart itself into my blood, pretty much like it has with her son. I look over now as he's hulling strawberries and cutting them into star shapes. I might hate him, just a little bit.

'Well, she wants to teach me her chicken cacciatore, her gnocchi, and how to make tortellini. Hearty Italian fare. She says McCoy may be able to cook restaurant food but he lacks spontaneity. He's not a cook like she is.'

Matt nods as I lose his face in the fridge again.

'She half has a point. Mums are different breeds of cooks,

you're more instinctive, spontaneous – you have to think on your feet more. Is this granola?'

He holds up an old Tupperware.

'Hamster food.'

He puts it back in the fridge and I watch his denim backside as he bends down, a slice of fraying underwear peeking up over the top. I scribble down a bit of what he just said about being spontaneous. Hell, I like that. Many a night has been spent with three potatoes, a tub of Philadelphia, and a carrot, wondering how this could feasibly be turned into an evening meal.

'Hey, is my shepherd's pie worth writing home about?'

Matt shimmies his head about. Yeah, thanks for that.

'But you do a decent chicken pie.'

I scribble things down.

'Is this for that *Saturday Kitchen* thing?'

I nod frantically.

'Do the pie.'

'But I always buy the pastry in.'

'And? I don't know anyone who makes their own puff pastry. That could be your cooking niche. Jools Campbell Does Pies.'

'It sounds like really bad porn.'

I see his body shaking with laughter. 'Free DVD with every cookbook.' I look up from my folder and stare at my husband as he continues to root through the fridge, finding half a furry cucumber. I pretend I'm too busy to notice. He returns from the bottom shelf with some marshmallows and a jam jar then heads over to the counter and rolls his sleeves up, lining everything up on the counter.

'How about … Jools Campbell: the Mother Forker …'

I fake smile.

'Chez Jools? The *Sort of* Yummy Mummy?'

He laughs at his own joke. I don't. I doodle a little pie in my file with stars all around it but squint and notice they all look like flies. I then look over at kitchen rat Matt, doing what he does best, which is to line up all his utensils and pick out bits of something from a 'clean' mixing bowl that wasn't washed up properly. He then stalks around the kitchen, sticks a tea towel in his waistband, and this is when I know I've lost him. He's playing chef. Like when he puts on his B&Q tool belt to screw in a lightbulb, I am doing serious things that deserve my attention and I shall not be disturbed in these endeavours. I, of course, sometimes feel the need to poke fun at his surly alpha male ways, which often results in a scrap of sorts but deep down, I think that's what I've always liked about him. He gets on with things in his own pensive, sensible ways. He never says much unless needed and then when he does it's sometimes still incomprehensible, but always earnest. Even the Matt I met at university was so annoyingly honest and straight down the line. After our second one-night stand, I remember he woke me up fully clothed and with a cup of tea, his fluffy hair was poking out of his beanie, his duffle coat had shades of the Paddington about it. I assumed he was leaving so didn't think much of it. It had been a lovely night, he was sweet and considerate. But this was drunken, incognito sex that was, in a way, fuelled by a need to get back at Richie bloody Colman. I remembered him looking at me with fuzzy eyes.

'Ummm, I have to go. I volunteered to do some stuff at the Union.'

I was intrigued by his excuses and smiled.

'Anything interesting?'

'I'm collecting signatures for a petition for the release of some Thai prisoners in Cambodia.'

I remember not saying too much as I thought this was either the most elaborate excuse I'd ever heard in my life or the actual truth. When I realised such, I remember being quiet, knowing I knew sod all about the geography nor the politics of the situation. He launched into explanations, yet not in that preachy way I'd come to expect from bohemian sorts who'd accost you outside the supermarket with pictures of drowned cats. He was sad and wistful, his eyes looking as if he knew what he was doing could probably lend very little to any outcome but he was at least going to try. I pulled the duvet back to try and locate my knickers.

'But I mean if it's all right, I was thinking of coming back? I'll be about two hours and then maybe I could bring back some food? We could have some tea together. Ummm, that's if you want to.'

I just smiled and nodded, pretending to cover my mouth to mask the smell of stale cider, and went back to lying against my pillow as he got himself ready. I noticed little things about him, the sort of things that stick in the mind because they're novel and exciting, and the things I refer back to now when he's left skid marks in the loo or wet towels on the bed. A slice of midriff when he stretched his arms above his head, tatty little holes in his T-shirt, a dimple on his left cheek, eyes that went the size of large almonds when he smiled.

'So this is a little embarrassing but it's Jools, right? Not Julie, or Julia?'

That may have taken away the romance of the situation a bit but the fact was up to that point I thought his name was Toby.

'Well, it's usually Jools. Or Juliet if you're my grandma.'

He said my name out loud to himself a couple of times as he smiled.

'Then I'm Matt. Or Matteo if you're my mother.'

I smiled. There was something slightly exotic about his name that made me swoon a bit more. I mumbled the name to myself.

'So Matt, what time can I expect to see you back?'

'Say three o'clock?'

And with that we had a cheeky snog and I went back to sleep, thinking he might not return because my morning breath had been particularly bad. But he did. Three minutes past three. And with him a bag of iced buns.

I'm still daydreaming about that incident when I'm disturbed by Matt swearing at the kitchen.

'Jesus ... Jools, this kitchen is a fucking tip.'

My immediate daydreams evaporate into nothing as I watch the scowl, the look about him which says this is my responsibility. Yet with his mother upstairs and within earshot, I feel reticent to draw this out into an argument. Maybe I can blame her? But I can't. At the end of the day, this is how I cook. It involves soiled tea towels, every teaspoon in the kitchen being used, and kitchen tiles splattered in sauce. I look around. Matt tuts and starts piling things up by the sink.

'I'll do it later. Anyways, I've decided that's my cooking style. Neat and tidy does not a great cook make. You have to throw some love and wild abandon in there.'

'Not sure you can have wild abandon with two countertops the size of ironing boards. You need to clear up as you go along. You don't see Nigella cooking in this sort of pigsty.'

'No, you see her cooking in a kitchen that's not even hers.'

'Still, she'd put things in the bloody bin.'

He pushes ends bits of squash and onion peelings into a plastic bag. I'd love to see Nigella cooking in here – not sure she'd survive without her freestanding cake mixer and mezzaluna, having to make do with my IKEA scissor selection and scratched non-stick pans.

'You don't need a whole countertop to spoon out some yoghurt.'

He gives me another scowl, piling dishes by the sink and balancing crusty pans next to them using talents he's probably accrued from many a night playing endless rounds of Jenga with the kids.

'And don't leave this to "soak", I don't want to have to deal with soggy bits of rice in the morning.'

Preachy Matt! I give him the eye from my folder. If we're starting on pet hates, then please could he not throw the dirty tea towels in with the baby clothes nor leave an inch of juice in the carton. This little exchange is quite indicative of how we fight: serious Matt vs sarky Jools. It's petty – I'm usually defending the way I do things, he'd preach how he'd do things differently. Then we compare stress levels when it comes to our work. Juggling four children and a house vs commuting/audits. He tells me he'd gladly trade places with me, I tell him he ruined my earning potential when he impregnated me. And then my humour is completely lost on him. That's the one thing about his earnest sensibility – it does not sit well with scatty tomfoolery.

'I think I've got a name for your brand then: the scummy mummy. Or the crumby mummy. Forking hell, she's loose in the kitchen again!'

I cast him a look to let him know he's hitting a nerve. He stops what he's doing. I can just about handle preachy Matt but there are times when it borders on the cruel and I have no humour left to combat it with.

'Too much?'

'Just the bit about me being rubbish at my job. Always a winner, Matt. Proper confidence booster.'

He comes to the table with a bowl of perfectly cut strawberries for us to share. 'I was attempting to be funny. You know I think you do a perfectly good job. It's just this celebrity thing, it's going to be a full-time gig and you're going to have to get your shit together before you run off and do this …'

As soon as the words leave his mouth, he knows he's worded it completely wrong. I already know as much but that doesn't mean you couldn't cut the silence with a big fat knife. It was that bit on the end about running off. Away, out of here like someone we know. He pauses, not knowing what to say next or whether to broach the subject at all. The problem with the situation with my mother is that it's never brought up between the two of us. I leave it to swim in the darkest recesses of my mind, he never probes the issue – it just sits there like the Coco Pop-sized mole on his lower back, the credit card bills, the strange sound the car makes – because if we were to talk about it, it might lead to a whole ball of madness. Emotion makes my chest swell slightly. Matt returns to the counter, even the double cream that he's been whipping seems to droop slightly.

'I mean, I know you're not going to run off but …'

I can't seem to answer him.

'Jools, I just …'

'I know. You've never been totally keen about me doing this …'

Matt waves his hands about, backtracking with impressive speed.

'Shite, Jools. I was just saying you needed to keep the kitchen in order. Don't start.'

Again, indicative of how we do things – when mundane and petty gets picked at to mean more that it is. He stares at me for longer than he needs to. *Don't do this when my mother's in the next room.*

'But you haven't even told me if you think this is the right thing to do. You said before you thought that *Guardian* article should have been the end point. But then it snowballed ... I don't know. We didn't even make this decision together. Should I be home more?'

'Jools, when have I ever tied you to the kitchen sink? You're free to do what you want.'

'But don't run off like my mother?'

'No. Just ... this has nothing to do with that. If you think this is the right thing to do, then go ahead, you're just going to have to multitask, that's all.'

I raise my eyebrows at him, insulted by the further condescension; even more so that he thinks I don't multitask every hour of every day, it's all I do.

'So you don't think I'm capable of handling both? You think I shouldn't do this?'

He throws his hands up at me, his voice slightly raised.

'Christ, Jools. I am never going to tell you what to do with your life but if this works out, you're going to be a working mum now. You'll have a lot to fit in.'

I sit there, confused at how this conversation has evolved but also at what he's trying to tell me. I can't do this? If I do this, that's fine but it's not changing my life – off you go?

'I mean, I am doing this for you guys too. Luella says if we get momentum behind this, it could get somewhere. That could mean a lot for us.'

Matt looks confused and pulls up a chair next to me.

'Well, that's a load of shit.'

I sit there, indignant. There are a lot of reasons to do this: to get back at McCoy, to stand up for the everyday mother, but he can't deny the financial rewards that the situation might bring have a lot to do with this as well.

'Matt, this could be us paying off a bit of the mortgage, putting money aside for the kids. This is important.'

He looks a little angry. Matt gets angry in scales (1 – someone, usually me, leaving the garage door open; 10 – paint

129

on garage floors) – this is about a six and a half. He looks a little hurt at the suggestion that his financial contribution to our household needs topping up.

'Sod the money. This is more than that. You need to do this for yourself, I get it.'

And this is where I pause because to say it out loud – I want to do this for myself – sounds so completely selfish, almost neglectful of my family's needs, their emotions. There needs to be another reason why. Because it's what my mother did – listened to some instinct greater than being a mother and a wife, decreeing that this just wasn't good enough for her and she needed more. I refuse to say that out loud. Matt looks over at me.

'But I just can't understand why you want to do this?'

'What do you mean?'

'All of this, with the telly and the papers, it just feels hard, it feels like a lot of work and a lot of tears. You've let that TV idiot come into our lives, our kids' lives and tell us we're not good enough – that our lives are not good enough.'

'I've let him …'

'Well, this could be over. But it's not. I was all for one with you standing up to him and having that moment to speak up for yourself but you're drawing this out. Into what? Into being some half-arse celeb … the sort we used to take the piss out of all the time. You have a degree … you're smart. You could do so much more.'

'Like what?' Matt shrugs his shoulders. 'Seriously, Matt … tell me what I should be doing with my life?'

'I don't bloody know … just maybe not this …'

His voice is slightly raised, almost trembling, but he stops. He steadies his hands on the countertops and finds three little teaspoons to put into three plastic IKEA bowls and walks out of the room.

R: *Hey, Jools. Did we get cut off the other night?*
J: Ummm, yeah. I didn't like the direction of the conversation.
R: *Sincere and apologetic?*

J: Hmmm, I gauged it more as deceitful and trite.

R: *Well, take from it what you will. I am sincerely sorry. I've complained to the papers. They are printing a retraction on page 4 of tomorrow's paper.*

J: Taken out a full-page apology? Really? How sweet.

R: *You were never this sarcastic.*

J: I've changed, Mr Colman.

R: *I can see that. You were always funny, not sarky – never cruel.*

J: No, you were the cruel one.

R: *Harsh.*

J: True.

R: *So I'm supposed to apologise for dumping you when we were 19? I'm sorry. Can I blame being young and foolish?*

J: You can blame the fumes from all that hair wax you used to use.

R: *She's back in the room.*

J: That funny girl you used to know?

R: *What happened to you?*

J: I had babies. Lots of babies.

R: *Was that always the plan? I knew you wanted a family but going into uni, I always thought you wanted to do something else.*

J: Well, yes. I write my doctorate at the weekends. Evenings, I run a small business empire from my kitchen table.

R: *Selling what?*

J: Car bumper stickers and iPhone covers.

R: *:D But you're happy?*

J: Of course.

R: *You sound so resolute.*

J: Why wouldn't I be? I have a heavily mortgaged house, my health, my kids AND all my own teeth.

R: *Humour aside, are you happy? Really?*

CHAPTER THIRTEEN

'Mrs Campbell. Half an hour until you're needed on set. Do you need anything?'

A stiff drink, a hug, and a second pair of knickers, maybe. The boy stares at me, hair styled into a quiff like Tintin with a clipboard and moon boot trainers. When did men start wearing old hi-tops and getting away with it? I just shake my head and smile.

'I'm fine, thanks.'

'OK. Oh, and someone left these for you at the front desk.'

He enters the room with a big bunch of flowers and a padded envelope. Given I never get flowers, I squeal a little, which confuses Tintin a bit as he closes the door slowly behind him. Then a thought goes through my head – anthrax? I stare at the envelope before opening it gingerly with my forefinger. Inside is a drawing of me whereI seem to have no neck and I have giant cupcakes in each hand. Or are those my boobs? I delve my hand in again and feel a rectangular object and pull it out slowly. It's a black and white framed print of me in a birthing pool holding Millie for the first time. I look a mess of hair, placenta, and sweat but ecstatically happy. Behind me is Hannah, who missed the main event but made it downstairs to meet her sister within the first few minutes of her life. She's in her spotty pyjamas and has a hand up waving at her. The boys slept through the whole thing. They assumed she came down the chimney in the same way Santa does. Millie's all wrinkly and placid. We stayed in that pool for ages. Given there were now six people in that house, it was the most peaceful it's ever been. A card is stuck to the back:

'*Mummy! You baked us all for nine months. We came out OK! xxxx*'

I feel my eyes mist up. Firstly, to see myself topless for the first time in history. When did my boobs turn into flaccid water balloons? But secondly, to think what I really should be doing. I should be in my pyjamas, dodging my children who trampoline around my bed, wrestling them for cuddles and away from the television, wondering what to do for the rest of the weekend, an arm draped over a half sleeping, disapproving husband. Matt. That's what Saturdays used to be for. Now they're spent in Saturday Kitchens.

A knock on the door and Luella parades in holding a big pile of newspapers and coffee, with her phone tucked under her neck.

'The coast is clear. Unless they have hidden him under the kitchen counters, McCoy is definitely not in the building.'

To avoid a *This Morning* style ambush, Luella has been on a mission today, confirmed as she is a vision in khaki green with big black military boots.

'You just get to go on, cook, do your own thing. It'll be fab. Now tell me how many times have we practiced this risotto?'

'Enough.'

Nine to be precise. My freezer is now rammed full of the stuff, next to my fish fingers, baby food cubes, and some peas. Even though I can reel off the recipe in part Italian, part English and have been seen to be muttering about crispy pancetta in my sleep, I still think Luella's plan to have me cook this on national television is bordering on the absurd. I wanted to do something a tad easier perhaps; something involving mince, something I could do with my eyes closed. Sausages, they're easy enough to lay in a pan and serve with some mash. But Luella said I needed to cook something with a bit of flair, something that didn't involve meat and two veg and sounds harder than it is. So she told the producers risotto. Great. *Saturday Kitchen* is a big deal though. Apparently, appearing on hangover television will connect me with the hungover 18-25 demographic and bolster my campaign to be taken seriously as a housewife cooking domestic type as opposed to a tabloid headline. According to Luella this morning, we also need to boost our media presence given McCoy and company are going for the big guns. She opens the newspapers for me at a picture of Kitty McCoy in a leopard skin cut-out swimming costume. 'I'M A JUNGLE KITTY! GET ME OUT OF HERE!' No stretch marks and boobs as nature intended. Luella snarls in the same way she always does when she sees Kitty's picture.

'Thing is, this might work in our favour. Nobody likes the mums who go in and abandon their kids. Plus the ones who always pose in the waterfalls never win.'

'And it's been scientifically proven that watching anyone in leopard skin can induce the gagging reflex.'

Luella laughs. She likes having someone to bitch about Kitty with. I have a feeling her phone bill might be dedicated to voting Kitty through to all the Bushtucker trials in the next few weeks. She pulls out another paper.

'This is their pièce de résistance though. *Piers Morgan's Life Stories*. Take a gander at this, makes me want to rip my eyes out.'

'I WANT TO CHANGE THE WORLD!' screams the headline, below stills of him in an imposing empty studio, glassy-eyed and blowing his nose. 'MY FATHER WAS EVERYTHING TO ME ...'

It's primetime viewing tonight and Luella is not happy.

'Please. Number one, changing the world, my arse. The only thing he wants to do is change the size of his bank balance so he can be famous and live next door to the Gallaghers on Primrose Hill. Number two, he hated his father. They hadn't talked in years and even then Kitty used to send him jars of humbugs every Christmas just to rub it in. Poor codger was diabetic and everything.'

I look at his swollen, damp face in the pictures, feeling a little remiss to be talking about his father's passing so casually but wondering if like Luella suggests it's all staged to garner the public's affections. I'm also curious as to how she knows McCoy's dad is diabetic. Surely that goes above and beyond the duties of a publicist.

'Nice bloke as well. Not sure what he makes of all this tripe.'

I swivel a bit in my chair again. She knows his dad? She notices and smiles.

'I bet you're wondering …'

'Well, kind of. You know Tommy's father?'

She nods. 'Promise this won't throw you off kilter?'

I'm not sure much can. Given the tumultuous turns my life has taken of late, I'm pretty sure I could withstand any curve balls she threw at me.

'Tommy and I were once an item.'

A heavy sigh makes her chest sink into itself like a fallen soufflé. I, on the other hand, am floored, completely off guard.

'You what?'

'Yep, dated for three years if you can believe it.'

I sit there agape, a few dozen mutterations falling out of my mouth. Her and him? Together? I'm suddenly confused. Is this why she's been helping me all along? Because she had some sort of vendetta against the man?

'Oh, it was a lifetime ago. I won't bore you with the details but he was an up and coming chef and we'd been going out since college. Then everything started going well and his publicity machine got hold of him. They persuaded him an opinionated brunette wasn't going to sit particularly well with his brand and I was laid to rest as it were.'

She pirouettes a pen around her fingers as she talks. The way a woman talks of a past love, all misty-eyed and doleful yet with enough hatred to know if he walked into that room right now, she could probably skewer one of his testicles. I hold her hand and nod to take it all in.

'I'm sorry. No wonder you …'

'Tommy never even stood up for me or thought about our relationship. All the time I had sacrificed so he could follow his dream, all the support I gave him. Anyway, ten months later and he's engaged to blonde and skinny and three months later, Basil Brush was born.'

Her fingers have now started drumming the table, every inch of her seizing up to have to recount the details. I'm not sure what to do but hand her the bottle of wine that's been sitting on my dressing table. Hell, it's before midday but the information I've just been made party to deserves to be absorbed with alcohol. I open the bottle badly and pour her a plastic cupful.

'So you see, I know his story. I know everything with him is a crock of shit. It's brand management at its very best, it's selling a myth to people who suck it in and believe it. So when I see a person like you being shat on by him, I feel compelled to help.'

She glugs the wine like Ribena and puts the glass down, her hands picking bits off her tongue that I suspect are cork. Yet she doesn't seem to mind. I study her face, trying to read the sincerity.

'So, I have to ask, is that the only reason you're here? To get back at him in some way.'

She smiles.

'God, no. Of course, I'm all about exposing him for the fraud he is, but I liked your style. I thought you were someone worth supporting, someone quite endearing. And that is water under bridges that flowed past many years ago.'

'You're not still … I don't know … pining?'

Such an awful word. I've made it sound like she's a lovelorn wolf baying at pictures of him by the moonlight. Luckily, she laughs in response.

'Christ, no. I found myself a new man. Gorgeous Frenchman called Remy who's fabulous, but you know how it is with a past love.'

She pauses as she says it, looking at me for signs that I may want to divulge any information regarding one Richie Colman. Since the whole palaver with my mum, she's discovered I may be quite the sensitive soul when it comes to rehashing moments from my past so has let it lie. I like her all the more for it.

'Anyway, now is not the time to be talking of such things. Bad publicist. I'm sorry I sprung it on you. This is about you today. Time for focus.'

She bends back the newspaper in my hands.

'There's a bit about you in the interview. Third line from the bottom, page ten.'

I scan the words until I find it:

When asked about the growing popularity of Jools Campbell, the woman who stood up to him when McCoy tried to recruit her as part of his foodie army, McCoy shook his head, tears in his eyes again. 'She just didn't get me. My heart is and always has been in the right place and that's to help everyone. It's all about the next generation, about being as organic as you can and doing the best for our kids. It's all about the kids.'

A wave of bile surfs over my stomach. Luella's snarling a little again, possibly foaming behind her teeth. All this talk of someone who treated her so callously can't be good. I feel a need to calm her down.

'Look at his wrists. Must have left the watch on in the spray tan booth.'

She pulls the newspaper to her face and scans the photo and stops snarling, possibly smiles.

'You'd think someone who loved kids so much would also give his own proper names.'

Another smile. She studies his picture for a moment too long.

'Shitbag. He really is. Such a ploy for attention.'

She stares a little at the newspaper before putting it to one side.

'But I'm confident today will help our cause and I have some magazine things lined up. We'll get you out there, we'll get earthy, honest Jools Campbell out to the public to piss all over this.'

There's a knock on the door as Tintin makes his appearance again.

'Are you ready?'

Earthy, honest Jools Campbell. It sounds like some marketing campaign for organic peanut butter. I peek over at the picture glimpsing at me from behind my flowers: two little girls beaming up at me. Ready, steady, cook as a wise person once said.

'So Jools, tell me about this scuffle with McCoy then, sounded like a right old barney.'

The host today is northern, tall, and dare I say it quite good-looking. Casual in pastels and brown suede shoes, he leads me around this shiny kitchen set as I attempt to stand in some ladylike fashion. According to Luella, I am prone to slouching and always seem to have my hands in my back pockets. So I stick my chest out a little. But did that look like I was bouncing my boobs in his face? I hunch my shoulders in again and pretend to laugh.

'Scuffle? It was just an exchange of opinion. I'm no expert in cooking. But there are certain TV chefs out there who try and make us mums look bad and it all gets a bit preachy.'

He nods and smiles so his veneers shine at me like newly polished car lamps. I think I might want to hug him.

'I mean, when I cook, it's not perfect but it's about my family. And sometimes we eat great big hearty homemade dinners and sometimes it's a tin of something with toast. But we eat together and we keep the kids informed about making good food decisions.'

Tall Northern Chef smiles.

'I like that thinking. So fish fingers?'

'A once in a while treat. Who doesn't have happy memories of fish fingers from when they were little? I think that can be the best sort of food – the stuff that makes you glow when you think about it.'

I don't add that certain brands probably use breadcrumbs that make your complexion glow a faint tangerine afterwards, but he seems to like my reasoning, as does Luella who beams from off camera.

'I hear you on that one. So you've not really cooked before this then?'

I furrow my brow. 'Well, kinda. It's in my job description ... just not like this.'

'Well, don't worry, we had Ken Hom on here the other day nearly burn the place down so you'll be fine.'

I laugh, still tense, but approach the work bench and start manhandling my ingredients, all of which have been measured into little bowls.

'So first things first, don't bother with the little bowls. I mean who wants to create more washing up for themselves?'

Tall Northern Chef laughs. Look at me, cooking and making people laugh, I believe that's multi-tasking at its best.

'Yep, so it's a risotto. I can't take credit for the recipe, it's my mother-in-law, Gia's, but it's one of those great one-pan dishes that takes half an hour and my kids love it.'

I sincerely hope Gia is watching, given I gave her a little moment in the media spotlight. I pick up my squash and grip on to it tightly.

'So we start with your butternut squash. You just wrap it in foil and just pop it in a mid to high oven.'

'You don't cut it beforehand then?'

I give him a look. There'll also be questions while I do this? I didn't expect questions. I thought I would just have to cook. I shrug my shoulders.

'I guess you could but these things are pretty tough. If you've got a range of crappy knives like I have, you'd probably need a hacksaw.'

I laugh. Then stop. Crappy. Is that a BBC 10 a.m. kind of word? It would seem not given Tall Northern Chef looks mightily uncomfortable. I look over at the camera to see Luella shaking her head at me.

'But to wrap it up and just pop it in is the easiest and quickest way, I reckon.'

I walk to the oven to demonstrate, open the door, and realise it's way too hot without oven gloves and end up chucking in my little foil package like a rugby ball. Did anyone see that? Only half of Great Britain. I scamper over to the counter and then start fiddling with my hundreds of little bowls, all unlabelled.

'So then the risotto base, which is dead easy. So in a hot pan, you need some olive oil then a smallish onion, two or three cloves of garlic, and fry that off.'

I'm feeling a little calmer now. One, because everything is actually cut up for me so all I have to do is turn on the hob and chuck stuff in the pan. I can do this. I show off chunks of glistening pancetta and make the chefly suggestion of substituting streaky bacon. Then I add my rice and glugs of my pre-prepared stock. It almost looks edible. Tall Northern Chef smiles and grips on to my shoulder.

'So contrary to what McCoy's been saying, you can cook then? This looks great.'

'Yep. I try. I mean I cheat sometimes and sometimes the

food doesn't quite work out but I give it a good go and any mum will tell you there's nothing more gratifying than a clean plate and a happy tummy.'

I turn my head to the camera where Luella has two thumbs up. I am stirring with one hand, chatting away, clouds of steam puffing out my rice. This is fine. I can do this. Someone slides a crinkly, burnished squash on to the counter.

'Then when the rice is cooked, I just scoop the roasted squash in … like this … and add some salt, pepper, some dried sage, and Bob's your uncle.'

And to prove a point, a pan of already cooked risotto makes its appearance from the side, from Tintin with the earpiece and the skinny jeans. It's swapped with my half-made dish and Tall Northern Chef, who I could very easily hug right now, compliments me with how great it smells and how easy it was to make. Well, yeah, when half of it's done for you, when you don't have to wash up or scrape it off the walls because Millie thought it'd be fun to missile it at her brothers.

'And it's bright orange so in our house that means it gets eaten in half the time.'

He laughs. The guest panellists laugh. Luella jumps about by the camera from foot to foot like a little kitchen pixie. I hand him a fork and he tucks in as do I. It's actually OK. But shit, it's hotter than I expected. I roll my tongue up into my mouth to try and force it down my throat. Why isn't Northern Chef struggling with this? He must have a mouth made out of asbestos. And then I cough.

'So … weee. It a lic-kle … hoooock …'

I cough again. A little more abrasively. The risotto flies out of my mouth on to Northern Chef's beige trousers. Worse than that, down his crotch so that I and most of the televisual world can see a) how tight they are and b) the possible outline of his undercarriage. I turn a deep shade of beetroot. I grab a tea towel from the counter and go to wipe at him, before realising what I'm doing. Tall Northern Chef looks like he might die laughing. I just might die. Right here, right now.

CHAPTER FOURTEEN

That evening, I'm sitting in the kitchen staring at the walls, despondent and a little drunk. After manhandling a chef on live television (who actually wasn't so upset about everything, I think he might have enjoyed the moment), I came home to find Matt, Gia, and the kids in fits of hysterics. Television gold, my dad texted me. Ben also rang to say Northern Chef had become his new crush. Who knew he was that well-endowed? Luella is not as upset as I thought she would be. It made for great television and the real reason we went on there, the risotto, was a success. I, however, feel rubbish. My plan was to be graceful, likeable, and elegant. Instead, reviewing the tapes, made myself out to be a cooking pervert. So now I drink. And to partake in the evening's events, I've invited Luella, Donna, and Annie and a very big bottle of tequila.

'Your mother-in-law made this? Shit, I should be her publicist.'

Luella drinks less, more interested in eating Gia's braised veal leftovers. Annie is here to be an emotional prop, Donna to cheer me up. I hear the thunder of footsteps upstairs as Matt and Gia wrestle with the children in the bath. Luella continues to chow down and pours me another shot. I stare at it, before licking some salt off my thumb, downing it, and, because we have no real lemons, squeezing a squirt of Jif lemon into my mouth. Donna cheers. Annie shakes her head.

'It really wasn't that bad. If you'd spat it out then said it tasted shit, then that would be terrible, but it was an accident,' she says.

I shrug my shoulders.

Luella intervenes. 'She is right. People have been Tweeting about this all day and everyone thought it was very endearing.'

I pull a dazed and confused face as Luella hands me her iPad and shows me pages of people showing their support. Annie suddenly looks very excited.

'Hey, we should get you on Twitter.' Luella's eyes light up as well. I shake my head.

'I don't know. It's a bit much. I'd probably get like, two followers.'

Annie opens the Twitter page for me to have a look. I can do Facebook. For one, there's a unique satisfaction you can get from stalking old school friends who used to be bitches in school, seeing how karma has left them single or with crow's feet in their late twenties. But there's also the way you can keep in touch with so many scattered across the country and globe, inspect their new-borns, weddings, birthday celebrations, and still feel you are part of their lives. It's the lazy social option. Twitter asks for people to be interested in you, to be thrilled to hear you're doing the school run or have just changed the sheets. Maybe the point is, I'm not sure if my life is interesting enough for commentary. Annie's fingers dance around the keys.

'There, I've signed you up. I'm going with a Campbells theme: you're SouperMum. Here, see I'm your first follower. I'm AnnieTheLawyer.'

'I will be your second. LuellaInc.'

They type so quickly, throwing the iPad between them, that I don't have time to interject. 'We could post recipes and mummy-style anecdotes and recommendations. It's a good move, believe me,' adds Luella.

Annie adds her husband as my follower to bulk out the numbers. Donna looks over and starts typing. I'm still trying to think what is relevant that people might want to hear. I read as she presses enter.

'HAVIN IT LARGE WIV MY GIRLS! TEQUILA 4 EVRY1!'

My eyes widen as I see it there next to my name along with my avatar, which Annie has chosen as Marge Simpson. Luella and Annie laugh. I can see the headlines in the papers now. 'Not only does she feed her baby tequila, she has it large! She can't spell!' Something in me can't be urged to care. I leave it, knowing Annie and Chris are probably the only ones who'll read it, moving my fingers about the touchscreen to read Annie's Twitter updates.

'Jus had appt with doc and my womb is inhospitable! Next time C's up there, I'll tell it 2 smile more and bake cookies! ☺'

Annie has got to the stage where she'll talk about her fertility to anyone. Donna reads over my shoulder while Annie realises what we're doing.

'It's something about my pH levels.'

'Well, mate, here, squeeze a bit of Jif up there, that will change your pH.'

Luella spits out a bit of veal. Annie, who is the lightest of lightweights known to man, thinks this hysterical. Donna takes her cardigan off and I'm sure I can see a new tattoo across her left bicep of someone's name.

'Mate, what positions have you been trying? I swear every time I've got preggers has been when Dave has been going at it missionary and I've got my ankles round by my ears.'

Annie seems to be taking mental notes while I wonder why I didn't introduce these two sooner. Luella is particularly blasé about everything.

'You got kids, Lulu?'

'Two. A boy and a girl.'

I swizzle my head around, realising I've never really even thought to ask Luella about her private life. She gets out a picture from her handbag.

'There. Xavi and Clio.'

They sound like car names but I don't tell her that. I just examine the photo and smile. They have the expected designer haircuts but behind them stands a very bohemian-looking man I assume to be her fabulous Frenchman.

'That's Remy.'

Donna looks over.

'Oooh, a Frenchie. Bet he's a good lay.'

I cringe to hear Donna be so comfortable with those she's just met but Luella doesn't seem to mind the inquisition. She just laughs, knocking her head back.

'*Il est magnifique!*' Donna snorts with laughter. Annie looks over at me.

'You mean the positions are important? What about you, Jools?'

The tequila has left me warm, a little like I might take off because I can't feel my feet. I turn to Gia's veal, hoping the tomato sauce licked off my fingers might be able to soak up some of the booze.

'Ummm, well you know about Matt and me. Condom broke the first time. Can't remember the life of me what the position was?'

'Means his little swimmers were busting to get out. Broke through the sodding rubber.'

I smile but Annie knows talking of Hannah's unplanned birth always hit a nerve, like to mention how random it was means it was less important in any way.

'Those sperm knew that they were meant to be with that egg and create the most beautiful little baby girl I've ever seen,' she adds. She grabs my shoulder.

'You all right? C'mon. More tequila. This will erase today completely.'

I fake a smile and look down at my drink, thinking about what she said. That in the greater scheme of things, Matt and me were just meant to be. Our inner workings decided our fate for us and made us a baby. Like magnets, it was a force uncontrollable. I think about that. And I think about Richie Colman.

'I spoke to Richie the other day.'

I'm not exactly sure why the words leave my mouth but all I feel is relief when they do, to be able to share without too much judgement. Luella looks over inquisitively on hearing his name. Donna rubs her hands together in preparation for gossip. I guess she'll know as much as was in the papers but she can see there's more to tell. Annie goes a bit quiet to hear his name. She was always very supportive of me at university, always on my side, I thought. When we were together, even though she found the idea of childhood sweethearts a little trapping and thought we would never last through the slalom course that was university, she allowed us to be. She then turned ape-shit on him when he dumped me and poured all her efforts into liking Matt even

146

though she knew I was diving into everything head first, fully clothed.

'Just via Facebook. We had a little chat thing going on. I just, he said some things. I don't even know.'

Annie pushes a shot glass towards me.

'I read the article. Did Matt really hit him?'

Luella closes her eyes.

'You know, I haven't even brought it up with Matt. With all the stuff with my mum and the cooking stuff, I pushed it away. It just didn't seem important, but he's just … niggling away a bit …'

Everyone looks over inquisitively.

'Was he a total shit to you?' asks Annie.

'No, he was apologetic, just wanted to explain himself … take a walk down memory lane. To be honest, it was all a bit of a non-event.'

But it wasn't. It triggered something inside this brain of mine, that much I know, which is probably why I've brought it up. I see Annie looking slightly worried, anxious about what I'm about to say.

'I hope you told him he was a cock. Those kiss and tellers who are in it just for the money get on my tits,' adds Donna. Annie agrees. You get a sense that is how Luella might make some of her living so she's quiet. They still all turn to me, expectant that this story will have a more interesting ending.

'I didn't know what to say. It was at the end of a crazy day after that article about my mum came out and it got me thinking.'

Annie looks like she's on edge. Thinking and me don't really mix too well.

'He was a first love. Plus he was harping on about the past and the what ifs, it just stirs up questions.'

Annie grabs me by the hand when I say the first love thing. She knows my relationship with Matt wasn't founded on some strong, intense love but has since gained momentum and four kids later still exists. I hope she's not drunk enough to pass comment like last time. Luella interrupts.

'Hon, we all do that. We've all got a Richie. I always say it's healthy – past relationships are what shape you, what move you along. You'd be crazy not to think about them occasionally.'

I smile at her, knowing all too well who her Richie is. She gives me a look that suggests it needs to stay secret for now. I raise my glass to her as she smiles and downs the red wine in hers.

Donna pipes in. 'Freddie Lyle. Squaddie who went off to Afghanistan. Wrote him a letter every week when he was gone but turned out he'd been shagging my cousin Felicia the whole time.'

Luella nods along, glad someone's half reinforced her point. Annie nods her head slowly.

'Mark Cadbury.'

I grab Annie's hand. Tall lawyer who rowed boats and had blond, floppy hair like a golden retriever. Broke her heart to search out the more dynamic social/work scene in Hong Kong where he 'needed to be single' but got there and married a society girl called Pearl Amoy within four months. She grabs back.

'There's always that one who gets under your skin. But you and Matt are solid, right?'

Solid in a sort of dependable, unmovable way. Like an Ashford and Simpson song, solid like a dependable, if rather uneventful, rock. I bob my head about to Donna's unease.

'Hold on, I saw that bloke in the papers. Matt's much better looking than him.'

Luella grabs her iPad and starts typing. Suddenly my Facebook page opens and she scrolls down to find Richie's name on my friends list. Profile open, everyone ogles the page – Annie bursting into hysterics.

'Jesus Christ, he got old. Is that a paunch?'

I ache to see his picture again. A sort of ache like a blinding migraine – that maybe if I see his picture again it might hypnotize me into thinking things I shouldn't about a man I don't really give a monkeys about.

'He's balding, Jools. That's not good hair genes,' adds Luella. Donna continues to scroll through the pictures.

'Good lay?'

'My first.'

Everyone turns to face me. I think back to walls covered in posters of Lamborghinis and teen girl insecurities. Everything was done under the duvet so we spent the first half hour thinking we'd had it down when really he'd been dry-humping my inner thigh. The ladies realise what this means. Yep, along with Matt, I've only ever slept with two men. My frame of reference is sorely lacking compared to the double digits I suspect at least two people around this table are on. Donna continues.

'So pretty shit then?'

I laugh and raise my eyebrows. Not that it got better, being turned over like a side of meat when he wanted a change of position, looking over a bony shoulder as it jutted into your cheek. He was young, my pleasure was a mere afterthought, oral was misaimed and lasted as long as he could be bothered, orgasms were what I read about in magazines. Then Matt came and changed everything. I mean, it didn't go all *Fifty Shades* crazy but he'd look into my eyes and would spoon me and cup my face like it meant something. When did we last have sex? Maybe a month ago, before all of this happened; I was paranoid that Millie would hear everything so we did it in the bathtub which proved a good move given we could clear up much easier afterwards. And it was the sort of sex we had become used to. One could say it scratched an itch. He was satisfied, so was I. We held each other for thirty seconds after with the I love yous then smiled at each other through the mirror as we brushed our teeth. It was and always is with Matt, we get the job done.

'Pretty much.'

We all laugh, when suddenly a text box pops up in the corner of my computer.

R: *Hey hon. We must have got cut off the other day? How's it going?*

Donna's eyes open up into Frisbee-sized saucers and she grabs the screen. To say I freak out is a slight understatement. I grab the computer in time to read:

J: Husband and his big cock lured me to bed.

Luella is in fits of hysterics as Annie goes ashen to read it.

R: *Ummm, OK. RU drunk?*

I am. We all are. But I have enough sense to know that this sort of talk should not be encouraged. I try and grab at the screen but I must be drunker than I thought as I end up grabbing at air.

J: Pissed up on Cristal. That's wot I drink now I'm famous.
R: *Ummm, is this you, Jools? The Jools I knew would prefer to get pissed on tequila shots.*

I let go of the glass in my hand as Donna taps the screen to make sure it's not attached to some sort of webcam. I grab the screen from Donna.

J: Yeah, it's me. Sorry that was a friend messing about.
R: *Thought as much. You never guess who I bumped into yesterday. Pete from A Level Biology ;) ;)*

Three pairs of eyes glare at me to explain the winky emojis.
'It's just from something he mentioned the other day.'
This is not enough.
'We had sex in a lab at school. He just …'
Annie's face goes from ashen to cadaver white. Donna laughs while Luella seems to eye me curiously over how that might have come up in conversation.
'Were you sexting each other?' asks Donna.
'Christ, no!'
My fingers move over the keypad with impressive speed.

J: Yes, it was highly inappropriate. I'm married.
R: *To Mafia Matt.*

Annie sucks air through her pouted mouth while Donna grabs

the screen back from me.

J: 2 some1 without a jalfrezi gut nd who still has all his hair.

Luella laughs, slightly inebriated, slightly goading Donna on in a rabid mob way. Annie smiles. I grab the screen back.

J: To someone I love very much.
R: *Your mate again?*
J: Maybe.
R: *Tell her this is none of her business.*

Ooops. This is enough to set Donna off. She jumps out of the kitchen chair trying to grab at me. Luella and Annie are in hysterics.

'Come here! Fricking needle pricked, up his own arse wanker – none of my business? Give me that iPad.'

The kitchen door swings open as Donna half mounts my back and Matt appears with a pair of wet pyjamas and Millie cradled in his arms.

'Ladies, I see we're feeling a bit better about things?'

Donna straightens herself out and I stand to attention, half guilty, half with an ache in my back that makes me think my body is too broken to give a grown woman a piggy back ride. Luella smiles to see Matt, given he's all trendy in his old Ramones T-shirt and frayed jeans, like to question a relationship with someone so fashion forward is insane. Annie decides to escape the awkwardness of knowing we've just been talking about Richie by grabbing the baby. Do I feel a bit better about things? I feel drunk, that's for sure.

'So who's a needle prick?'

The room freezes. A lump forges itself in my throat like a golf ball.

'Who else? McCoy!' says Luella. I look over and see how easy it is for her to lie. I, on the other hand, am going a light, sun blushed tomato red.

Matt shrugs his shoulders.

'Well, maybe next time Jools can feel his crotch up and find

151

out.'

And everyone laughs except me as the iPad glows in the corner of my eye and Richie's picture looks up at me.

CHAPTER FIFTEEN

Hannah and I look down at the cupcakes on the counter and she pats me on the back like we might be looking at the carcass of roadkill. If there's any moment where one feels they've failed as a mother, it's when the cooking goes awry. Because it should be so simple. It's raw ingredients and, most of the time, you are just applying heat to them and changing their physical state. You chop, you stir, you mix and when in doubt, you add a stock cube. But no. Every so often, these simple laws of home economics fail you. Beautiful, raw ingredients that animals suffered for, that were destined for greater things, become sorry pitiful sights that even the neighbour's cats reject. And you will have failed. People will go hungry, time and money would have been wasted, you will have doubled your washing up quota for the evening. Worse still is the look your daughter will give you. You are my mother. I am thankful for that and every effort you make to care for me. But please, please don't make me take these to school.

'Maybe we can pick the tops off and smother the tops with Nutella and Smarties.'

Another look. Even Millie looks over from her high-chair, unimpressed by my baking efforts. It's the Year 3 cake sale today and expectations are high for the new 'celebrity chef' at Clifton Primary. I was excited to be given the chance to prove myself to the mummy masses. Because I can do cakes in every sense of the word; from the eating to the making and creating foamy dollops of buttery goodness, cake is generally something that is very right with the world. That is until a teething toddler means you don't get round to making them until 10.30 p.m. And then you set the oven to grill so said cupcakes, which should be lovely, tanned, and wearing little icing turbans, are charred, black, and looking like my sink ever since I tried to set my Tommy McCoy cookbooks alight.

'Or we could dust icing sugar Batman motifs on them?'

I may have got a smidgeon of a smile. That will do. She sits down and reaches for the Weetabix, breaking out two biscuits and painting happy faces on them with honey like she always does. Millie, meanwhile, smothers hers in her hair, down her pyjamas, along the bottom side of the table, and across the newspaper on the table folded back at an article droning on about McCoy's new quest to try and revolutionise the bread industry. Never mind rogue bankers, coalition governments, and no money in the NHS, it was crappy bread that was bringing this country to its knees. To prove his point, my picture is there and probably the worst thing that's ever been written about me. *Jools Campbell, 31.* Yes, I've aged two years in a matter of mere months. I sigh to see it again and Millie flings more Weetabix over it. That's my gal. Try working some of that magic on these sad looking cupcakes too.

'What are these?' Gia shuffles behind me in her slippers, her eyes drawn curiously to the cupcakes on the kitchen table. I won't lie, I like the way she wears velour in the morning, looking all toasty and regal. The looks of disdain I can do without. 'I tell you, let me help you. But no, Juliet.' She picks up a cupcake and sniffs it curiously then flicks her finger over the top. I half expect them to echo. Then she turns her nose up and looks at me. What gene are you missing that means you cannot bake? She shakes her head, shuffling over to the counter to retrieve a tin hidden behind the microwave.

'Hannah, *bella*. Here, you take these. Chocolate biscotti. I think you can sell at your cake sale.'

Hannah's eyes speak relief. Gia's speak that she may have made this under the cover of night just to cover my back. I am part grateful, part embarrassed, maybe a little peeved she knew I was destined to fail so had hidden baked goods waiting in the side-lines.

'Thank you, Gia.' She doesn't respond but nods quietly at me like her work is done, before looking at Millie and tutting that I maybe should have stepped in before allowing Weetabix Armageddon to have happened.

My cupcake failure and being usurped by the baking goddess continues to haunt me at the school gate as I see my little people jog into their classrooms, Hannah clutching her cake tin like a trophy. Gia's presence has, no doubt, been helpful in our current predicament, yet she still seems to have her beady eye over my shoulder, watching, maybe judging, definitely beating me hands down in the cooking stakes. She's also a reminder that as I try to become this media incarnation of the all-cooking wonder-mother, there was always someone who would trump me in that department. It makes my shoulders slump slightly. Maybe I need to buy a Paul Hollywood book. Maybe I need to buy something in velour.

'Mrs Campbell. Morning, can we have a chat? It's about Jake.'

I stand to attention and take a huge breath.

'Morning, Mrs Whittaker. Is this about Saturday? I had hoped it wouldn't cause too much disruption, at least not like last time.'

She ruffles her brows at me. I guess she didn't see it, guess she'd be more of a *Countryfile* sort.

'Oh no, it's just due to health and safety regulations we would like Jake to come into school wearing underwear.'

My mouth drops open a little. Look at this woman, revelling in her newfound celebrity so much she forgets to put pants on her son!

'Oh! Sure. I will talk to Jake.'

She nods her head, not in judgement but in expectance. This was the woman who appeared on the television and most of the national press without a bra, maybe it's a strange family aversion to undergarments.

'And one more thing, Mr Pringle was hoping to have a chat. He's through by the office.'

I smile and nod again. Hannah. The thought that I haven't had our 'little talk' yet comes into mind and I wonder what emotional distress may have carried itself into her schoolwork. I picture Key Stage tests completely failed, artwork drenched in grey, black, and blood red.

I like Mr Pringle. Not in the way most of the mothers do, the ones who look on fluttering their fingers and walk past him with their shoulders out to boost their flagging bosoms. It's just outside of school, he might be a little trendy and in class he'd be the sort to perch himself on the edge of a desk and roll his sleeves up. Case in point as I find him signing registers, a Crumpler bag slung over his shoulder, wearing a big, billowing shirt that makes the lower half of his back look inflatable. He tells me to have a seat at the main reception area on the giant orange sofas then brings Hannah out. She stares at me intently and I freeze. Is this about me?

'So how are you, Mrs Campbell?'

I don't know how to answer. I'm having a bizarre celebrity food feud with Tommy McCoy, the ghosts of my mother/ex-lover are back in my life, and most nights, I get about five hours sleep, proven by the dark circles under my eyes and my electric honey frizz. I go for the safe, 'I'm-in-front-of-my-child' option.

'I'm OK.' Hannah comes and sits on a child-sized chair, hooking her arms underneath my knees. Mr Pringle smiles.

'Is everything all right? I understand the past fortnight has been pretty hectic and I did speak to Mrs Whittaker about it.'

He smiles his orthodontically stunning smile and shakes his head.

'Oh, that. It's fine. I guess. It's just … I wanted to talk to you about Hannah.'

I sit up straight in the chair for reasons I'm not entirely sure of. That it might make me look like a more morally upstanding parental type, perhaps.

'It's just … this is awkward. I mean, has Hannah started menstruating yet?'

He blushes. I blush. I open my mouth in horror, like I can suck enough air in to rid the room of oxygen. Why are you saying this in front of my daughter? I want to put my hands over her ears. She looks at me, confused.

'God, no. I don't think so. I think she would have said something. Definitely.'

I think about that sentence again. Have Hannah and I drifted apart so much that in her hour of womanly need when she would have been scared and confused, she'd not been able to tell me? She was eight, for god's sake. Although I'd read enough parenting/trashy magazines to know this was not an impossibility, there was no way she'd have been able to cope seeing blood in the gusset of her knickers without freaking out. Definitely. Hannah still looks confused. Mr Pringle blushes from his cheeks to the backs of his ears.

'It's just … the other day she brought a box of tampons into school and was giving them out to her friends.'

'Like presents?' I stare at Hannah. You give out stickers, you give out sweets. Not my sanitary wear.

'I wasn't entirely sure. But I don't think she was doing anything malicious.'

Hannah, who has sat there looking like we might have been talking another language, pipes in. 'It was Billy Tate.'

Billy Tate's started his period? Mr Pringle and I look at each other. 'Billy said his mum didn't use tampons and he wanted to see some so I brought some in.'

I nod my head. OK, that's not terrible. That's not handing out something like cigarettes or a crack pipe. Worse, it could be condoms. Still, my aghast face speaks volumes. Mr Pringle looks just as embarrassed with having to look me in the face and talk about the fact he knows I use super flow Lil-Lets and Fiona Tate doesn't.

'Ummm, well … maybe next time, just the one – you don't have to take the whole box.'

Mr Pringle nods, as does Hannah. Awkward conversation over!

'Obviously, we are very sorry. I guess it was just curiosity and I will have a chat to Hannah about well, keeping such … products at home from now on.'

I'm not sure where else this discussion needs to go. 'I didn't give them all out. Harriet didn't take one. She told me dolphins can choke on tampons so her mum uses a mental cup.' Well, there, obviously. I try to stifle my giggles. Mr Pringle looks at me for back-up as his eyes glaze over.

'You mean a menstrual cup?'

Hannah nods and lays her head across my knees. Mr Pringle

looks at us, relieved, slightly thankful, and smiles. Hannah just picks at threads in my jeans. How long before she stops doing this? Sitting intently, letting life-changing information just pass her by. I wince a little to think of her being older, some moody, pre-menstrual teen that hates and blames me for her female circumstance. She pipes in again.

'You're talking about periods, right?'

'And you know what periods are?' Mr Pringle asks.

'Some girls in Year 6 told me. My mum tried to explain it to me once. It's kind of gross but I get it.'

Is it terrible to think I can't for the life of me remember what I told her? From the corner of my eye, I see Mr Pringle nod in agreement. Yes, I agree they are gross. But you also appear to have some level of knowledge on the matter. No harm done. Hannah just smiles, looking over to her classroom to see what she might be missing. I brim with what could be relief but what I think might be pride.

'Of course, later on in juniors they'll be PSHE lessons to cover all of this. But I just thought …'

'No, it's good to know. Thank you. Anything else, just … yeah …'

'Sure. We should be going, Hannah. And I'm looking forward to seeing what you've brought in for the cake sale.'

Hannah looks at me and smiles. 'Mum made some awesome chocolate biscuits.' I smile back.

R: *You're up late.*
J: Seriously?
R: *The other night was interesting. Friends of yours?*
J: Seriously?
R: *I'm sorry, J. I just want to say sorry, J.*
J: No one's called me J in years.
R: *That's because I was the only one who did.*
long pause
R: *I saw you on TV the other day, Saturday Kitchen.*
   Friggin' hilarious. You're quite the chef.
J: Glad I was there to entertain you. I can do many things now I'm a grown up.

R: *Bet you can :D*

J: Oi!!!

R: *Please tell me you accept my apology.*

J: Whatever.

R: *How adolescent of you.*

J: Seriously?

R: *I am a prize idiot.*

J: That's a better apology. More like that please.

R: *I am a fool.*

J: ☺

R: *I should have stayed in contact.*

J: Seriously?

R: *I mean this is nice.*

J: Is it?

R: *Well, if it wasn't, then why are you still here?*

CHAPTER SIXTEEN

I stared a lot at Matt last night once we'd got into bed and he'd passed out within seconds of his head hitting the pillow. He's not classically handsome, his nose is a little off-centre and his face a little too round. But he has a good chin and his hair has never lost its appeal, the sort of straw-coloured fuzz that looks a little Damon Albarn circa the late nineties. He's always had good dress sense at least; he's very into his jeans and band T-shirts and zip-up tracksuit tops and till this day keeps the duffle coat from when we were at university.

There's no six pack or well defined garden path down to his groin area. The chest is, I'm afraid, slightly pigeony and the legs a tad hirsute. But he hides it well. No Speedos, for example, when we go swimming and he doesn't do tapered old man shorts in the summer. There's also the way he loses himself in blankets, duvets, and jumpers. He'll put a hood on or disappear into the bed to find the warmest, safest place to fall asleep in the spirit of a hibernating hamster. He says that's the Scottish in him learning to forage and keep warm. The last week or so I've been doing this a lot, coming up with ways to remind me of why Matt and I are together. Damn Richie Colman, Facebook, and his nonsensical hypotheticals. Yes, Matt often has no sense of humour and swears at inanimate objects. He hates that I have entered into this weird celeb cooking world. I resent that he doesn't understand it. We live in a house that is far too small for six people. We have sex when it's convenient and haven't done it during the day since, well, university.

But for everything that is bland and wrong with us, there are many more rights. However, with such deliberations always comes the question about whether others have these doubts. Are there couples out there who don't have to question because the love that binds them is stronger than that? I hope not. Because I hope Matt thinks the same things too. That what keeps us together is far more important, that his practical streak will know kids, house, and love come with responsibilities that you don't chuck out the window when the love flame is a little dim.

Which is something I definitely hope he holds on to, as the next morning when Luella appears at my door at 8 a.m., there is something to suggest something's wrong; the love flame is flickering. It's a typical morning Chez Campbell. The kids flutter around the house, I am quite literally half dressed, in a dressing gown, a green vest, some knickers, and my cosy Ugg-style slipper boots. On my head, Jake has asked me to wear a tinfoil hat as Gia got the boys *Wall-E* on DVD and the in-thing are robots who clean things up. This may be good if it encourages the boys to keep order of their belongings, less so if they assume I'm a robot who doesn't mind such things.

'Is that what you're doing the school run in? It's very Gaga.'

I smile and usher Luella in, immaculate in a teal jersey dress and black leggings. She's grabbing the newspapers to her chest and double air kisses Gia, who's been up since the crack of dawn preparing French toast for the kids. Gia's holding on to Millie, who's very glad to be receiving the full attention of someone who is covered in icing sugar. She chases the kids up the stairs while I walk to the kitchen, encouraging Luella to follow my lead. She's being a little cloak and dagger which is never a good sign, and closes the door behind her.

'So, you need to be totally honest with me, OK? I need to know this. Are you having an affair with anyone?'

If my chin were made of rubber, it would bounce off the floor, swing back up, and knock me out. I always am amazed by the insinuation. When would I have the fricking time? Quite literally. Like I'd just leave the kids in front of the TV while I popped upstairs for a shag? Maybe I could get it on mid-school run? Under the cover of darkness when everyone was in bed? Luella looks me in the eye for a long time, nodding and studying the directions my pupils seem to move in, then puts her bag down.

'Thought not. But …'

Matt enters the kitchen, curious at my get up and why Luella seems to always frequent our house out of office hours. I am trying to find the Febreze to freshen up a school jumper that smells a little of hamster. Luella passes a newspaper to Matt, who cradles his cup of coffee.

'Jesus, they dream these things up, eh?'

He reads, scrunching his forehead up while I have my bottom sticking out of the cupboard below the sink, one of the many black holes of this house.

'Is this McCoy again?'

Luella nods. 'I suspect so. But it's not even front page, he's clutching at straws.'

'They say here that it was a secret, covert conversation …' reads Matt.

'I know. They make it seem like some sort of grand flirtation.'

And that's when I pause. Who am I supposed to be having this affair with? I make a mental sift through the men in my life. Shit. No. I suddenly realise who they might be talking about. I look up at Matt, who seems confused by my mortification.

'I'm so sorry. Truly we were just chatting and he started with the innuendo and talking about the past and … really, it was nothing.'

Luella also starts to look confused.

'You know I haven't spoken to him for years. It was just he wanted to apologise about the article and explain himself …'

Matt puts his coffee down while Luella looks from behind his shoulder, shaking her head and gritting her teeth. He passes me *The Mirror,* showing a grainy photo of me and Mr Pringle. I stare at it for ages, and the accompanying headline: *Mummy Campbell and the Toyboy Lover.*

'Who were *you* talking about?'

'No one.'

'Jools?'

Luella looks like she might want to be anywhere else but here. I can't lie. I shouldn't lie. It was nothing.

'It was Richie … Colman.'

Luella takes this as her cue to leave and barricades the door

163

from eavesdropping mother-in-laws and little children. I have to think on my feet here.

'We were Facebook chatting and it just snowballed. Seriously, it was nothing.'

Matt's body language turns defensive, almost hurt. His shoulders slump, his eyes mist over.

'It was him being inappropriate and making references to the past. It was wrong and I told him as much.'

'But it was enough for you to think that someone could take it the wrong way.'

My silence speaks volumes.

'And for you not to tell me about it.'

He turns and places both hands on the kitchen counter as I see his anger boil up to a rolling simmer. I have no answers. Yes, we had some brief conversation that dredged up hypothetical questions but this really meant nothing in the greater scheme of things. I put my hand on him to calm him down and he shrugs it off. I put my hand back on his shoulder.

'I told you this was all a really bad, bad idea.'

'Matt, seriously. Don't make this bigger than it is.'

'And why can't I? From the moment this all started, it's dredged up so much bloody crap. And now him? Of all people, *him*?'

'And?'

He looks up at me, shaking his head in disbelief.

'Well, you might like all this attention but I think it sucks. I think this sucks for our kids and when you start telling me shit like this, it makes me bloody … fricking furious. I can't …'

'Can't what?'

'Him! He was a shit to you and sold your story to the paper and you have the gall to humour him? What the hell is wrong with you?'

'With me? Why are you acting like this? We talked. We didn't do anything else. Calm the hell down!'

He then grabs a cup of coffee from the kitchen counter and throws it across the room. Rivulets of coffee drip down walls, across chairs, onto the tiles. I flinch and shield my face like it might hide my shame. The rustle of footsteps outside the kitchen door get shepherded into the living room by Luella. Gia swoops through the door.

'Matteo! *Che cosa succede*?'

'Niente, mamma. Lascia stare.'

She glares at him then her attentions shifts to me. Brownie points earned over the past week evaporate into the air like mist.

'Come ti permetti di arrabbiarti cosi, davanti ai tuoi ragazzi!'

I haven't the faintest what they're saying but given it's reverted into Italian makes me think it must be about me and driven by emotion that the English language cannot convey.

'Non dirmi cosa fare. Ti deve piacere! Mi hai sempre avvertito di questo!'

She bangs the kitchen counters with her hands, which is enough for both of us to stand to attention, her eyes fixed on Matt as she points a finger at him.

'Enough! We can discuss this later when children are not in house. Take the children to school. We are late.'

8.32 a.m. Shit. What the hell just happened? Matt? I stare at him but he can't even make eye contact with me. Please don't leave it like this. It was nothing. But he doesn't utter a word, just pushes past me and grabs his coat from the banister in the hallway, ushering silent children out the door, Hannah turning to look at me for reassurance I'm not sure I even have. I turn and Gia already has the kitchen towels out and is cleaning the floor. I feel the need to make peace with at least someone.

'Gia. I'm not sure what you heard but …'

'Not now, Juliet. Go and change.'

I shuffle to the front room to see the children sitting bolt upright in the car, the twins clutching on to book bags. I wave them off but only Hannah responds with a small wave back, leaving me with tears still on standby waiting to roll. What the hell was that? Matt and I never fight, or at least not like that. We argue over messy kitchens, never grander things, and the guilt starts to stake me through the heart to imagine how awful it must be to have that set up anyone's day. Millie hangs off Luella's hip, staring curiously at the fuss at such an hour

'Jools?' asks Luella.

But nothing. I just turn, pretending to take gazelle-like leaps up the stairs to get dressed when really it's because I don't want her to see the tears in my eyes.

When I get downstairs, Luella is like a one-woman machine with the phone calls and the web print outs. Gia seems to have tidied up all signs of previous coffee flinging and even scrubbed and hung out the chair cover. I mooch about downstairs but she doesn't seem to be anywhere in sight. Dare I say it, I think I might be a little scared about retribution.

'She's gone to the supermarket.'

I sigh a little with relief but am hardly surprised. Whereas most people eat, smoke, drink, or partake in exercise to de-stress, Gia seems to do this in the kitchen. A fiver says she'll bring back some cut of meat which needs heavy tenderising. Luella is in the kitchen with Millie, who sits in her high-chair eyeballing me. Where have you been? Dad went off in a huff, Nonna's disappeared so I've been left with this one and she won't let me near her iPad. I go over to appease her with a rusk, hoping neither of them will notice I've been sitting in my bathroom, crying in a ball on our apple red bath mat.

'Thanks, Luella. Sorry for the drama and the tantrums and the mug slinging.'

All my sarcasm can't hide the emotion weighing on my shoulders like great, fat boulders. Luella urges me to sit down and pours me a cup of coffee.

'Talk about putting your foot in it,' she says, sucking air through her teeth. 'I would have thought you and him would have talked about it. That Richie Colman thing was in the papers weeks ago.'

I shrug my shoulders. That's not really Matt and I at all. We've always had some unspoken pact where we never really talk too much about the foundations of our relationship given we know how shaky they are. Yet in the same way, I've never laid myself bare to Matt. We never talk about my mum's abandonment, we hardly talk about the future. I think about Richie for a second. It was a very different relationship in that aspect; as immature as it was, our conversations were always open, long, and used up all my free minutes. Everything with Matt has always had sweet, romantic undertones but momentum has carried us through. Nine years of momentum, just swinging back and forth and not really going anywhere.

'Was Gia fuming?'

Luella twists her brow.

'She didn't say much. I think she was just confused.'

'What do I do?'

Luella puts a hand in mine.

'You should just let it lie for a while. Let him cool down. You're not ... you know ... with Richie though?'

I open my eyes wide like they could fall out their sockets.

'No! Why ...'

'It's just you sounded guiltier than you were.'

I cradle my head in my hands. The guilt stemmed less from a couple of Facebook conversations but more from the fact I've let myself think about him, comparing him to Matt, thinking about those what ifs and parallel situations. I'm guilty of having mentally erased Matt during daydreaming moments and replaced him with Richie.

'Well, then seriously, let it lie. And we definitely know you're not banging the teacher.'

I shake my head.

'Can I ask what this picture is about? Why are you looking at his crotch?'

'Hannah was sitting next to me and we were having a talk because she had given out tampons to her friends at school.'

Luella's whole body stops for one moment except her fingers, which move with expert precision over her iPad. She then gives me a look, almost like she was expecting something that random to come out of my mouth.

'Well, I've covered for you on Twitter.'

I freeze as she says it.

'Annie linked it to your Facebook account. You did know that, right?'

I look down and lo and behold, so it is, and I have five thousand followers on my Twitter account. Bloody hell. Five thousand people waiting anxiously with handheld devices and computers to hear of my next move.

SouperMum: *Sam Pringle is my kid's teacher FFS. Nothing to see here people! #happilymarried.*

I feel too embarrassed to bring up the fact I have no idea what FFS means. Still, at least the humour lends itself to taking the accusations not that seriously so I don't take offence to the fact she's hacked into my accounts. My phone rings and I see Donna's face pop up on the screen. I go to answer it.

'Jools, babe. Where are they getting this shit from?'

'DidyouseeMatt? WasheOK? Whataboutthekids?'

Donna takes a moment to translate. 'Calm down, babe. Matt seemed all right, gave the kids big hugs when they went through the gate. Chill.'

I tear up a little to think of my family in a big, collective huddle outside school like penguins seeking warmth.

'I just had a huge barney with Paula and Jen though. Geez, those women have mouths on them. Gossiping hags.'

Now there's a surprise. I am slightly taken aback by Paula's indiscretion given our supposed friendship but Jen Tyrrell is no great shock. She's the one who's often accosting Pringle at the school gate, presuming they have a friendship of sorts. The kind of parent who knows all, sees all, and has no problem flaunting this knowledge on social media and at the school gate with her Tannoy voice.

'What happened? Were they the ones who took the pictures?'

'To be honest, love, I don't know. I wouldn't be surprised but it could be anyone, really.'

I simultaneously feel betrayed and disappointed, sifting through all the mums I know at that school. Some I know, some I've sat next to at charity concerts, one whose car I once reversed into, one who always wears shorts, even in winter. All of whom I know have phones with cameras, phones that can take grainy pictures inside school gates and sell them to the national press. I feel the need to curse, be angry, yet residual information from this morning leaves me static.

'But them and their gossip; having the gall to talk about you and Matt when we all know Paula's hubby's been shagging that au pair? But I put them in their place, never you mind. We had it out. Chav? She should watch her gob.'

I close my eyes to see how that would have panned out. Donna (Superdry hoodie/ Reebok Classics) taking on Jen Tyrrell (Per Una denim/sensible, not meant as a style statement, moccasins). I pray physical violence wasn't used to defend my good name.

'And Mr Pringle, did you see him?'

'Nah, but seriously? The guy just got married. I think he'll laugh it off. Shit, look, Alesha just poured a Frube down me. I have to run. Call me if you need me.' Donna hangs up quickly, leaving me listening me to a bleeping tone. I have nothing left in my mind to give. Luella continues to type while Millie gives herself a rusk facial.

'Are we good?' she asks.

'Drama at the school gate ... and I should really ring Mr Pringle to apologise.'

'Got the Pringle thing under control. I rang the school and got his contact details and sent him a hamper as an apology. I hope he likes cheese.'

I turn my head slowly to meet hers. Cheese, yes. I hope he does. If only my problems could be solved with a bit of Gouda. She looks me in the eye as I appear drunk in thought and emotion.

'Jools, we are OK. Richie Colman was nothing, Pringle was tabloid filler pap.'

'But Matt ...'

'Will calm down. Give him some space. We flung this info at him at god knows what hour? He flew off the handle. You'll be fine.'

Admittedly, Luella speaks sense and my inner crazed worrier calms for a second. It was nothing. Matt will see that. We will go back to normal. Still, I attack the fingernails on my left hand, tearing them between my teeth. Luella gives me a look.

'And to counter this tabloid pap, I've lined up something for us on Friday. Are you free?'

I'm always at a loss how to answer this question. Time wise, owing to the children I am always occupied. On some other social scale, I am always free. I nod.

'Well, I have a gem. BBC breakfast news. You and Tommy McCoy and some politician on a sofa discussing food. They want some sort of debate over families and food and you have been invited to represent the modern mother, be the voice of the people. What do you say?'

I say nothing. Matt made his feelings very clear about the matter and that argument still echoes about my head. But there is also the fact I will be within spitting distance of one Tommy McCoy. The last time I saw him, everything changed – for better, for worse I haven't yet decided – but part of me wonders if seeing him again might make me launch myself at him and rip his eyes out with my unmanicured nails. Not sure if the BBC is the best place for that. For one, it sounds a little grown-up and I feel intimidated. *This Morning* and *Saturday Kitchen* I can handle given they feature segments devoted to omelette challenges and how to lose two stone by only eating baby food. BBC breakfast news asks for you to be demure, intelligent, and relevant. I'd have to put my serious *Guardian* face back on, learn how to cross my legs to appear ladylike on that formidable sofa. On the other hand, I'm starting to wonder if I'm scared of the McCoy dynasty. While I have made it a point to try and bring them down for their intrusive elbowing into my life, it feels tiring to have to do such battles on live television where so much can go so wrong. I did have a plan last night where maybe I could just start Facebook groups dedicated to hating them and burning their books at bonfire events.

'Christ, are we ready? BBC news is a pretty big deal.'

'I'll make you ready. Tomorrow I'm sending a stylist around and then you and me can have a huge powwow session to prepare you. This is the one where we can do some serious damage. No ambushes, no hiding behind his entourage and tabloid nonsense, we can take him apart bit by bit.' '

It's incredibly savage. If Luella had claws, she'd be ripping out his viscera and gnawing on the bones. I'd like to think it is down to the fact she wants to see my good name brought to rights and is supporting all mothers out there. But part of me thinks how we view our ones that got away is very different. I haven't even got the energy to get up from my kitchen chair at the moment, let alone fight McCoy in vicious, no holds barred ways. I just stare at my kitchen bin and see bits of shattered mug on top of last night's rubbish. I think about Matt, everything we need to talk about, conversations that have been on hold for nine whole years.

CHAPTER SEVENTEEN

It's 5a.m. in the morning. I'm sure I never used to think this time of day existed when I was young and studenty and could sleep like a warm, hibernating bear. Now twilight and I are good friends and I sit in my bathroom watching Millie in the bath because she decided in the middle of night to have a giant poo that not even wipes and concrete nappies could contain. A poonami if you will. But to be honest, dealing with excrement at such an hour is a welcome distraction.

Last night, when kids, husband, and mother-in-law returned to the house, things got slightly painful. Gia was impressively quiet with me about the coffee flinging. At times, she stared me out like she was angry and mumbled Italian under her breath. Other times, she seemed guilty and I was strangely reminded of toddler Ted's 'I think I might have pooed myself' face. All in all though, we're back to square one on that weird emotional plateau where all that links us is the fact I married her son. Matt, on the other hand, was being wonderfully mercurial in avoiding me, which is no small feat given how small our house is. When he got home, he ran to the children to avoid confrontation and even sat with Millie at dinner to not have to look at me. One day we will sit like adults and have a conversation over what could make a mild-mannered accountant turn into some fury-driven Neanderthal coffee flinger, but for now he just keeps quiet, spending that moment too long in the loo so we won't even have to walk past each other in the hallway.

Now he sleeps, the ultimate way to not be near me while I try and entertain Millie, who doesn't look wholly impressed with the world. Poor Millie. It's been quite a month for her. I wonder if she sits there internalising everything, making lists over how this rates as a poor life moment. Does this rate worse than Tommy McCoy in Sainsbury's? Worse than when I forgot to put a nappy on her one school run and left her peeing through her sleepsuit, car seat, and blankets? The boys pushing her around in a cardboard box pretending she was for sale? I owe this girl a lot more hugs and cheap plastic presents for what we make her endure. I slide my hand over her head and watch the curls flatten out before springing back into place.

By the time I wrestle her into a nappy, new pyjamas, and dry her hair it's too late to get back to sleep, so we mooch into the kitchen where I give her a bowl full of her favourite raisins and Cheerios and check the kids' schoolbags for signs of decaying food (Jake), small animals (Ted; one day I found a dead bird in a sock), and letters to tell me of events that happened last week (Hannah). No dead birds or biscuits but some interesting finds. According to Hannah's pencil case: 1D for ever! Really? Already? I make a mental note to introduce her to an alternative music source. But there's also a letter informing me that the end of year school play is coming up, 'The Giraffe and the Dolphin', and parents are in charge of their own children's costumes. I scan down the page to see that in this 'wonderful song and dance tribute to the animal kingdom that celebrates diversity and acceptance' my twins have been cast as rhinos and my daughter is going to be a hula dancer. Costumes will be needed for three weeks' time. I remember the time Dad used to give us tea towels to wrap around our heads so we could be shepherds/Joseph/innkeepers. Rhinos? Inside the boy's bags, I find spellings for next week. Words beginning with the letter K. Kite, kettle, koala, and knife (there's always a tricky one), some old remnants of paper planes, and a picture Ted has drawn of a rather good bus; he's even remembered wing mirrors. Given there are six passengers, I assume them to be us. Ted is driving, of course. Jake seems to be some sort of navigator with a map. And a gun? Hannah sits to the back – she won't like that. And Millie seems to be hovering in mid-air. That leaves myself and Matt in the back seat, our faces touching like we're 'having smoochies' as the boys would say, but really it looks like we've been melded together in a horrible genetics experiment. I had a chat with them yesterday about the Pringle incident and they've been cavalier about everything. Jake told me there was no way I would kiss Mr Pringle because I was too old (a tad heartbreaking) and Hannah said it was nonsense because he'd just got married. So that ended that. I hoped.

The kitchen door creaks open as Millie and I sit in the semi-darkness and it's Gia with a fleece over her pyjamas and her slippers with the giant velour bows.

'Millie. *Piccola!* She is not well?'

I shake my head as I stroke her cheek. She looks slightly happier than half an hour ago. I think it's the raisins. Gia starts rustling through the kitchen like she does.

'She needed a nappy change so we got up early. Gia, it's only 6ish. No one will be up for a while.'

She puts her hands up in defence.

'No, no, no. I make light breakfast. Luella coming at 7 a.m. for training.'

Training. This makes me think I need to wear a tracksuit and put on *Rocky*. With the BBC thing looming tomorrow, Luella is ready to turn me into a one-woman foodie express prepared to strap McCoy to the tracks and run right over him. Well, at least we'll be well-fed. I watch Gia with a slight mixture of admiration and confusion. She still seems nervous around me, as I am with her, but bless her for rising so early to entertain my guests. Seriously, who the hell gets up before the sun has risen to make breakfast? I figure the only time I ever rise out of bed to cook is on Christmas and even then it's to put on the oven and get back into bed.

'You like my pancakes, no?'

I nod. Pancakes in any form are always good. I watch as she breaks eggs with the one hand. How does she do that? Does she just have bigger palms than me? She then shakes sugar into the same bowl and starts groping the mix. No scales, no measuring. How do you do *that*? She then pours out the right amount of milk and whisks lightly like that's what her hand was made to do. I'm waiting for her to toss the pancakes with her toes. But she doesn't.

Soon after, the kitchen door swings open and Matt stands there in his stripy pyjama bottoms and an old Che Guevara T-shirt he kept from Uni. Gia tuts to look at it with all its holes, but I've known never to throw it out given it's a piece of his political youth he so desperately wants to cling on to. In his hands, the morning papers, which he flings onto the kitchen table. Since McCoy we get them delivered to the house every day. If nothing else, having a wealth of Sudoku to complete every day keeps me on my toes. Gia comes and puts a cup of coffee next to me, seemingly whipped out of thin air. I sip and turn the first page of *The Sun*.

'YOU WANT SOME MCCOYS WITH THAT?' screams the opening headline. Apparently, Kitty's run in the jungle is not going so well. Next to the fact most of the attention has been focused on a love affair between a fading soap star and Premiership footballer, Kitty has spent most of her time being needy and teary, which has not endeared her to the public who made her eat a wallaby penis as penance. Luella will like this. I make a note to keep the article for her. Matt sits opposite me with the *Daily Mail* and the computer open, his knuckles rested against his cheeks. He scrolls down then pauses. His eyes look up at me for a moment then down at the screen. Then up again. No smiles. He closes them and grips on to the edge of the table. Something's wrong. Shit. Not frigging Richie. I can't do Round Two just yet.

'What is it?'

He shakes his head. Gia goes behind him, stirring her ricotta cheese. Her stirring gets slower, more laboured.

'That is …'

'Non adesso, mamma. Glielo diciamo dopo.'

I scrape back the chair to go over and see for myself what could be so covert it needs Italian to keep it from me. Matt tries to cover the screen. I pull his fingers back.

'JOOLS CAMPBELL: HER MOTHER'S BATTLE WITH CANCER AND THE DAUGHTER WHO DOESN'T CARE.'

There was a time back in 2005 when I thought my life was near the point of implosion. The twins had just been born and went through bags of nappies, sucking on my nipples until they were raw and clogged, never sleeping in tandem, and providing enough washing to fill the Thames. Hannah was three and while she liked having real life dollies to play with, was going through a phase of wanting to be naked all the time and feeding the DVD player breadsticks. I used to cry rivers of tears at how bloated, unkempt, and tired I was. I used to feel as though my brain would seep out of my ears because it couldn't take the noise, the emotion, the sheer pressure. It was a low point.

Today rates up there with that time. It is 8.23 a.m. and point in hand, this is what I have to do today:

- Learn everything about the food industry with Luella
- Wax my eyebrows
- Send three of the children to school
- Talk to my husband
- Come to terms with the fact my mother had cancer
- Ring my brothers
- Ring my dad
- Cry
- Cry more

I haven't really thought too much about my mother since she sold her story to the papers and talked absolute shit about the circumstances under which she left. Bar Ben telling me she'd rang, I'd relegated her back into the deepest, darkest recesses of my mind where she'd always been, playing Frisbee with my thoughts over maternal matters. She wasn't worth the time. But here she was again, in my face with stories of illness, toying with me yet again. I read the article over breakfast wondering how she had the gall to speak more lies. If she was ill, I didn't know; if she was alive, I didn't know. All I knew was that I cried over breakfast, thinking Gia had put far too much salt in her ricotta pancakes when really they were just flavoured with my briny tears.

Luella arrived at 7.01 a.m. with hugs, knowing how much the article would hit me for six, apologising that her radar hadn't been big enough to stop the story going to press. Although she'd promised an entourage to style and preen me, she's decided against it and instead has me brought five bags of clothes, shoes, and her own tweezers to attack the unsightly caterpillar-shaped things above my eyes.

Now I just stand in the hallway and the house has become that nest of activity where the children launch themselves at me, demanding to know the whereabouts of jumpers and asking me to fashion their hair into something presentable. I stand there as they waltz around me, not knowing what to do. I just bend down and grab the closest one, Ted, and hug him, stroking his hair and looking into his eyes.

'Have I done something wrong?'

I shake my head. In the doorway, I see Matt looking on at this manic display of emotion, car keys in hand.

'Kids, car, please. Daddy's taking you to school today.'

There's a chorus of whys and cheers as they clamour to the front door and Matt and I have a moment standing one metre apart where we stare at each other for five seconds.

'Call me if you need me.'

I nod.

By 10 a.m., I don't have to ring Dad or the brothers because they each show up at my house of their own accord, traipsing in with cakes (Dad), alcohol (Adam), and the greyest, saddest face I've ever seen (Ben). Adam, who has been drinking since he read the headline, is sprawled across my sofa, legs akimbo. Dad tries to force feed him some chocolate éclair.

'Did you know, Dad?'

He shakes his head. Gia appears at the living room door with a tray of tea, cakes, and freshly baked biscotti. The boys sit to attention.

'Gia, you shouldn't have,' says Dad.

She blushes and shakes her head. Gia has always liked Dad. I think single men of a certain age whether widowed, divorced, or abandoned always bring out the sympathetic edge in woman of Gia's age. He is all the more attractive for having raised three children singlehandedly and for the fact he doesn't sit like a lonely spinster at home eating pies for one. To be honest, I think she likes a crowd when she's being the Italian Nonna.

178

Ever since they arrived, all I've been able to smell is cheese and baked meat wafting through the house. Luella stays in the kitchen as chief taste tester, no doubt.

'I can't believe she's gone and done it again,' says Ben.

'I can.'

Adam, fuelled by alcohol, is quick to respond. It's very much Adam's style. When Mum left us, I was very analytical about the situation even at the age of ten. I became obsessed with the reasons why she would have left and by the age of twelve was researching theories of maternal attachment. Eight years later, the psychology behind the situation still lingered enough in my brain to want to study it at university. Yet Adam's reaction was the polar opposite. After she left, she no longer existed, she was merely a ghost. He used to badmouth her every occasion possible and would get riled to see her picture or come across an item that once belonged to her. Twelve years later when girlfriends and sex became a preoccupation, he always found it hard to nurture any relationship, instead depending on multiple liaisons with multiple woman. I cross my fingers one day he'll find that girl to change his mind, to change the idea hardwired into his brain that women leave.

'Seriously, we expected different? I for one am done with her. I really don't care if she was sick or not. I really don't.'

Ben's bottom lip quivers. Ben's reaction was always more skewed when it came to Mum's leaving. His attachments still in their very rudimentary stages, they were never allowed to grow, like roots stuck in the ground unable to surface so stunted to live underground for ever. Ben attached himself to Dad, Adam, and myself at the time but he always looked a little lost, cried that bit more than Adam and I ever did.

'But she … what if she had needed us? I think I would have at least liked to have known.'

I think about that word need, imagining some Picoult style situation where she may have needed a kidney or bone marrow. Would I have been willing to sacrifice that to a mother who abandoned me all those years ago? Would I have wanted to hold her hand on her death bed?

'She's a bitch, Ben. A complete bitch. I needed a mother and where was she? Now she's using this to make us feel bad about her leaving. That's really magnanimous of her.'

I hear tutting from the kitchen door as Luella says something to Gia. The door closes.

'Adam. You shouldn't talk about your mother like that,' Dad says. Adam shakes his head.

'I'm sorry. But my mother left me when I was seven. Whatever happens to her, that's called karma.'

I am torn. Torn between a brother and his anger and another little brother who's crying at the suggestion that we can be so heartless. I'm speechless for once, so just grab Ben by the shoulders and go to hug him. It's always been Ben to be vulnerable and taken in by such emotional circumstances. He retrieves a crumpled newspaper from his shoulder bag and starts reading aloud.

'Of course, I wanted my children with me. I wanted to make amends. The doctors told me I might have six months max so you think about putting things right and saying your goodbyes. You think about meeting your grandkids. Even if I hadn't been ill, I still think about my grandkids every day.'

'Fucking hell, Ben. I can't believe you'd fall for her bullshit, her emotional blackmail.'

Dad is speechless. The wonderful thing about Dad is that he's never said a bad word against the woman in all these years, well, not to our faces at least. Even when Adam was launching into one of his tirades when she'd forgotten a birthday or we weren't celebrating Mother's Day, Dad would be silent to look at him, his face contorted with rage. He stares at Ben a lot who's a big mess of tics, tears, and general all out confusion.

'But Adam, it's been so long. And life is just too short for us not to …'

Adam doesn't even let him finish.

'What? Meet up with her? Play happy families? This article changes nothing. If she wanted to meet us and the kids, then all she had to do was show up, not go to the press.'

I have to agree with Adam here, but Ben slumps into his seat. His loyalty straying over the line, he can't quite bring himself to say anything to Dad yet nor look him in the eye. I say nothing. Half my brain, the half that has coped so well thus far without a mother, thinks this is not my problem. We are as much family as I am related to Mrs Pattak next door. Yet there is that other half of my brain intrinsically linked to hers, still fit to burst with questions and conjecture over the sort of woman she is, dreaming of that one-to-one confrontation we were meant to have that would solve any wrongful effects from twenty-odd years of her not being there. Dad sits down and puts a hand on Ben's shoulder while I look at Adam. If it were possible, this is where comedy fumes would come from his head. But he is angry, indignant.

'What are you trying to say, Ben? You want to meet her?' I ask.

Ben shakes his head and looks down at his hands.

'I don't know. I think so, yes.'

I look up at Dad, still looking at his socks to try and mask what he really thinks. Adam is so against the idea that he says nothing but leaves the room, slamming doors as he goes. Ben grabs my hand.

'Jools, I'm sorry. I don't want to start anything but this article makes me realise I know nothing about her. I just feel if I don't talk to her, see her at least once, then I'll always wonder. I'll really properly regret it.'

Christ, he's serious. He really wants to meet her. Dad is doing very well with the banal patting of the knee.

'Dad, what do you think?' I ask.

He again doesn't look up but hopes his knees will provide the answer. I repeat Ben's question.

'Dad?'

He looks up.

'At the end of the day, kin is kin. You're a part of her. You're an adult so I'm not going to tell you what to do.'

I look over at Ben. Little Ben. He can't do this alone. She'd take advantage of him and his vulnerability, she'd turn him into a big ball of emotion. I take his hand, trying hard to make the words that are coming out of my mouth sound convincing on some level.

'Well, I'll talk to Luella. Maybe she knows who wrote the article and can get us in touch with her. Because if you're going to see her, I want to be there too.'

It's only then that Dad looks up and straight into my eyes. The same look he gave me when I first told him I was pregnant all those years ago. Not anger, not shock. Some type of resigned disappointment. I'm not going to fight you on this one. But I always thought you'd do things differently. It stakes through me to see those eyes again, my own glazing over to think he thinks I've betrayed him. I then watch as he gets up and excuses himself to go to the loo as I grab Ben and let him bury his head on my shoulder, all the while my tears dripping onto his chocolate brown hair.

By the time it gets to evening, conversations about my mother have formed a cloud over the house that refuses to clear, almost like that stale milk smell in the car. Adam left soon after for work, Dad after that. Ben stayed around to help Gia wash up but moved the sponge around slowly, the way he does when things prey heavy on his mind. Now it's 7 o'clock and the kids are upstairs with them and Matt listening to stories, while Luella quizzes me on types of mushrooms and the benefits of eating goat. Luella has known not to pry too much about what happened earlier but she every so often squeezes my knee and puts two thumbs up at me. Either that or she stares at the raw space in between my eyebrows, studying her attempts at preening me. Not that it's made much difference. Now I've spent the last two hours grappling with the twins and trying to get Millie to eat any dinner, I look like the Gruffalo. Had the Gruffalo liked to wear badly fitting denim and an old nursing bra.

'So Jools? Did you know that forty-five per cent of children under the age of eighteen do not eat breakfast? What say you about this scandal?'

I'm staring at a browned patch of wallpaper below the sofa. It's either a drink, a leaking radiator, or very possibly wee.

'Jools?'

Luella looks up at me, doing her best BBC News presenter

impersonation.

'Oh, ummm, yeah, that's terrible.'

She pulls her best fake smile and suddenly falls out of character.

'A bit more enthusiasm, Jools? You need to have some witty opinions on the world. Spice it up a bit. The difference between you and McCoy is that you're relevant and can be pretty funny when you want to be.'

I nod, cupping my head in my hands. Luella comes over and puts an arm around me.

'It'll be all right, you know? Ten-minute segment, nothing can really go wrong.'

She's right. Yet if the past few weeks have taught me anything, it's that a few seconds of a misplaced comment, an obscurely angled piece of body contact and it can turn into twenty inches of column space. Never mind ten minutes.

'What about the kids? Getting them to school and stuff? I think I'm missing an assembly tomorrow?'

'Gia and your dad have it covered. You shouldn't worry.'

It's like telling the sea not to be salty. It weighs heavy in my heart to think that I'm missing a recorder recital to take on a wanky TV chef. Will they remember such incidents and take them with them into adolescence to use against me? Luella looks just as fraught as me. When she hasn't been cornering me today just to inform me about battery hens, she's been holding clothes up to my slouched frame trying to cobble something together for me to wear. Even on the school run, she was trying to accessorise me as I drove the car.

'You know, I've been thinking. You said before that McCoy paid Johnno Elswood to do some digging. You think he planned this too? To waylay me before the BBC thing.'

It was a thought which came to me today when I was thinking of how well timed this all seemed. Given all he's done so far, I don't think it's beyond Tommy McCoy to stoop so low. Saying that, I'm now worried that he'd involve my mother in the conversation tomorrow so as to rile me and get a more virulent response. Luella shakes her head from side to side.

'Kind of. The papers wanted to draw out the story with your

mum a little anyway but I'm sure McCoy would have had a hand in the timing.'

'Then why don't we ever bring this up? I don't get why we can't just drag this bastard's name through the mud.'

Luella looks up, sympathetic.

'Because that's not how to play things. Trust me, I have enough crap we can throw at the McCoys if we want but people have been far more impressed that we've been restrained and not been in the public's face the whole time – nobody likes a try hard.'

I shrug my shoulders. My whole life feels like I'm always trying way too hard. Luella looks at her watch.

'Now I have to go. I am confident this will be fine tomorrow. Please trust me. Just remember about those cooling eye-pads for tomorrow. You think people won't be able to see but HD is a real sod.'

I don't want to tell her that they'll probably be useless given I will hardly sleep tonight. She also points to a carefully stacked mountain of literature on the coffee table.

'And if you have the time, please. As much as you can. Great articles there on the great organic hoax and something to keep you up to speed on Tommy's work with pigs. I just don't want him to bring all this stuff up and have you not knowing what to say.'

I stare at the pile and back at her in disbelief.

'I will send a car for five in the morning. Just dose yourself up on caffeine but not too much. Last time you were all jittery.'

She's packing Tupperware into her bags because Gia has taken it upon herself to cook for everyone involved in my life at the moment. Luella is more than glad to take it and slings her bag over her shoulder. Her hair still remains very fixed in style and doesn't seem to frizz into a huge mane during the day like mine.

'You've got the Spanx?'

I nod, accompanying her to the door.

'Then one less thing to worry about. Look, I have to get back to my *bambini* so tell everyone I said bye and … you can do this tomorrow, I know you can. I have every faith. Bye, bye,

bye.'

I close the door on her and take a deep breath. Like a huge hyperventilation of air, my will to live seeping out of me as I exhale, hearing small twins upstairs leaping off bunk beds. I back onto the door and curl up into a small ball. Like a small distressed hedgehog. Suddenly, I look up. Matt stands at the top of the stairs and sees me. He edges his way down and comes to sit next to me. We say nothing for two whole minutes. Then he points to the dress hanging on the living room door.

'Is that what you're wearing?'

I nod. A black tea dress with some canary yellow shoe boot things that will apparently draw the attention away from my misshapen hips.

'What do you think?'

Matt eyes them up curiously.

'You'll look like some large fashion-forward cooking elf.'

I punch him in the arm and for the first time, we laugh. Together.

'I like the casual look on you. Trainers and jeans and stuff.'

He looks down at his hands. It was very me at Uni. My Converse and jeans were like a second skin, the stomach was flatter, the hoodies a little trendier. My hair used to be bundled atop my head stylishly, unlike now where most of the time it looks like a small squirrel's drey. Not sure Luella would let me get away with such scruffery. There's a moment of silence between us before I speak.

'We need to talk, eh?' I'm not sure why I say this now. Sleep, a long bath, and a bottle of rosé would be nice. To pick at a scab that is still raw and bleeding is not going to be productive. Matt buries his head in his hands.

'I didn't want to if you were still fretting over your mum.'

His courtesy jars with me a little, to suggest our relationship was less of a priority.

'How are you over that? Ben mentioned something about youse all meeting up with her.'

I shrug my shoulders and stare at him. I want to tell you so much, I want to pour my soul out to you over my mother but I can't. I'm not sure why.

'I'm sorry I threw that mug.'

I shrug it off. If a broken IKEA mug is a measure gauging my husband's reactions, then it's a small price to pay. I'd drive over to Croydon and buy a whole case load of crappy porcelain if it meant he got to air his true feelings with me.

'I should have told you Richie got in touch. I'm not sure why I didn't.'

Knowing the conversation might drift upstairs, Matt gets up off the doormat and walks into the living room. I follow him reluctantly.

'What did you talk about?'

'Stuff. He was sorry about the article.'

'Did you … I don't know, Skype, swap photos … you know …'

My response is impressively quick. 'No! Jesus, it was just talk. He brought up all that stuff about you hitting him. I told him it was a load of crap.'

Matt turns to face me, his expression looking exactly like Jake's when he's about to own up to something monumental. Though I suspect this has little to do with joining up his sister's freckles like a dot-to-dot puzzle. He fiddles with the loose threads on the end of his Kings of Leon T-shirt then looks up at me, square in the eye.

'Well, not complete crap.'

My eyebrows, raw and pink like carpaccio, arch into my forehead.

'He did come around when he heard you were pregnant, he was worried and wanted to see you.'

I am speechless, a little tired, a little confused. So they did meet? Well, at least the universe didn't implode.

'He said youse two had unfinished business, all sorts of things about having history and I was just this bloke you'd met. He was so cocksure, so bolshy. It kind of blew up.'

'Blew up how?'

I picture fisticuffs over our paisley sofa and mismatched curtains, a lot of swearing.

'He was adamant that you and I were just some passing phase. He came in checking me out like he still had power over you, like he still had feelings for you, that you did for him. I panicked. I ...'

I wait for the punchline, quite literally.

'I had words with him. I told him to sod off for a start but he was pushing to see you. So I did what I thought was right at the time. I mean, you know I'm not a violent person, I don't hit people. And even then it was only his nose ...'

'You did what?'

At this point, my mind is fuzzy with disbelief. I'm trying to get my head around Matt hitting someone and the fact I stood up for him against Richie looking like some stupid, clueless wife.

'I just, I mean, he just left after that. He didn't report it to anyone so I left it and we never saw him again so ...'

This is where I should say some word of disbelief, but air just pours out of my mouth.

'Did you apologise?'

Matt gives me a similar look of disbelief and shakes his head.

'I told you what he said, I panicked. It was a moment of madness.'

I think about Richie and his broken nose, not that I'm actually too bothered about that, but there is something inside me that is also extremely hurt.

'But you thought ... what made you think I'd choose him? Or go off with him? What the ...? Matt, I was pregnant with your baby. I would never have ... you thought I would have left you ... for him?'

His eyes glazed over, he looks up at me.

'I was confused. I was young, I knew you'd dated for quite a while, right? It was just the thought of you going back to him was so ...'

'Never going to happen. I can't believe you had that little faith in me.'

Matt nods. I want to sleep, I want to throw up, I want to throw something heavy at my husband. I slump myself on the sofa while he stands by the window watching stationary cars.

'Well, I was fighting for your honour, I wanted to be with

187

you. Some women would be flattered by that.'

'Some women would wonder why you've hidden this information from them for nine years. Why did you never say anything? Why did you never tell me he came back?'

'Well, what was I supposed to think? This man knew you far more than I had did at that point. I didn't know you well enough back then.'

Then we both pause, looking at each other. No, he didn't. All I knew was that he was a cute Scotsman who had good taste in coats. I was a Southern girl in a hoodie without a mother. Nine years together, something happened. I just can't tell what it was – nothing and everything changed and looking at my husband now, and everything we're deciding to bring up, I wonder if we've just had nine years of telling each other the rubbish needs taking out.

'Everyone thought that, not just me.'

I pause realising who he's really talking about.

'By everyone, you mean your mother. Is that what we were jabbering on about with her the other morning?'

I semi-translate what she must have been saying. *I tried to see past the fact she was a harlot with cooking skills nowhere as good as mine but I was obviously right! I always have been!*

'Can we just leave it? I really don't want to talk about him.'

And this is where I stand up, indignant.

'Well, I want to. If it's something that pisses you off, then it's something we need to talk about. Did you even read the article? It was a load of crap.'

'I read your Facebook messages.'

'You what?' My face acts offended but to be honest, I'm almost a little glad that he can see they are not as salacious as he might have thought.

'You're not happy?'

'I never said that.'

'You never said you were.'

I pause to look at his face, so defeated, so serious.

'So this cooking thing, you think this might make you happy. It could give you something me and the kids aren't giving you?'

I shake my head. 'That wasn't what it was about at all. I resent that you think I don't know how lucky I am.'

'But your life could have been different. You could have been with him.'

'Or not? I might not have ended up with either of you and joined a cult and changed my name to Steve.'

'Stop it.'

'Stop what?'

'He was your first love. That means something.'

'It means nothing.'

I say that knowing that, despite any frisson of emotion I may feel for him, a past love means nothing when you've made the decisions I have. You don't turn your back on four children because you picked the wrong box. You don't doubt that life is far more important than a whim about someone you once loved.

'Then why be friends with him on Facebook?'

'It's Facebook. He's not my friend-friend. You know how it is.'

'I know it's you stalking him to see how differently your life could have been.'

Damn you, reading me like a book. Thing is, it's a lie. I stalk everyone on there, not just him.

'Jools, play it down all you like but that bloke's always going to have a hold over you and I'm entitled to feel a little jealous. I mean, supposing you and I hadn't got pregnant when we did. Supposing we'd just been shagging casually and going out. You think we'd still be here?'

I freeze. It's that question: the one that always niggles in the back of my brain like a little gnat. I hate him for bringing it up. I hate that I have to pause to answer it.

'And supposing two, three weeks into going out, he rocked up and said he wanted to be together again. I think we might not be here. That's what I think.'

His face is sullen and serious. I shake my head.

'You're talking crap. That's what I think. In an alternate universe, I could be with Simon Seabrook who I snogged at my Year Five disco.'

Matt gives me a look as if to tell me I should be taking this more seriously. I interject.

'You think I don't know about alternate universes? I've known people who've disappeared into theirs following the supposed loves of their lives.'

He pauses.

'Are you saying Richie was the love of your life?'

I think about what I just said, my head swirling slightly.

'No. I was talking about my m ...' But he cuts me off.

'Jools, I just know all too well the circumstances under which we got together. We were pissed, we were young. I was stoned half the time. It's just ...'

All these half-finished sentences make me want to hit him.

'Your life could've been very different. You could be with Richie, you could have worked and got a good job. I see all this celeb stuff and I think about whether you're happy just being here, whether you're always thinking about ...'

'The what ifs?'

I freeze again to hear those bloody words. The fact is, life sent me down this path, and even though the past weeks have seen me wondering about how I ended up here, nothing would ever see me leaving the family I have now. I'm not sure whether to feel hurt. I'm not sure what to feel.

Matt turns from his window to go and sit on the leg of the armchair. I don't think I'd be with Richie now. No. Of course, Matt will feel some discomfort from my relationship with him. I knew Matt for a matter of months, Richie I'd known since I was five years old. My love for Matt was different; it did not come swooping in and envelop me because I still had feelings for Richie that were not going to dissipate overnight. That love faded, another was certainly entered into unexpectedly but it matured and developed and children were made and born. And for so long it's been Matt and I and four little people who have come along for the ride, and it's fit together so perfectly.

Matt and I are like a well-oiled machine (well, maybe not so well-greased from my end) – we run a house, we are great friends, we have embarked on this business of a young family, and been attempting to keep our heads above water. I know he will always be there for me and vice versa. But sometimes you question it. You question whether this is a relationship built on any semblance of raging passion, whether love has fallen into some realm of practical necessity. We're not a perfect couple, we're far from it. But we work on a very practical and sane level, devoid of mad wild man on the moors-style passion that any Brontë or Shakespeare will tell you is just a lust-riddled recipe for disaster.

'I just wondered whether you and I …'

'You and I what?'

'Whether you and I were supposed to end up like this.'

And the answer here should be simple. I should stand up and say both matter-of-factly, yes, Matteo George Campbell, this is it, the best it's ever going to get. I fricking love you. Maybe even give my husband a kiss. But I say nothing and stare at the floor, at which Matt gets up to leave.

'I just want you to … just … shit, Jools. I don't want to fight. I just want …'

Because to fight would mean energy, would mean fire that we're too tired to exude right now. I wonder what he wants. He doesn't finish his sentence. He just stares at me for a moment too long then leaves.

CHAPTER EIGHTEEN

Day is night and night is day. I stare at my alarm clock, the neon making my eyes fizz, and watch as numbers change, the house lying static with only Matt's indigestion and a baby keeping me company. Millie flits in and out of sleep. When she's out, I sit her in the bed next to me and she seems to pass looks my way that have more meaning than ever before. As we sit in the twilight together, she studies my face and grabs for my nose. As if to say, hey, laugh you daft bint, why so serious? With brothers who have a penchant for treating her like a rugby ball, and having been born into the carnival that is our family, she always seems to have this knowing look about her, like she's not sure why she's here, what contribution she makes to this family, but it's all immensely entertaining. I will hate leaving her tomorrow. This is not what I should be doing. Tomorrow is not about even earning money, which I could balance against abandoning her. While the fee being paid is nominal, enough to keep the kids in shoes for six months, something inside, something that rings strong tells me to just stay here. This is where I should be. Matt wakes every so often reminding me to sleep.

He's quiet, pensive, and the way he buries his face and curls his body around a pillow is like he might be trying to get some comfort out of it. He went to bed before me last night so we didn't have to draw out any other painful conversations. I just stayed in the living room and cried on Ben's shoulder when he came downstairs, trying to palm them off as tears for our mother. He bought it. Gia didn't.

She stood at the doorway and watched, then looked upstairs to hear Matt slam the bathroom door. She then did what Gia does best and headed into the kitchen to bake a batch of bread for breakfast. My brain feels like the consistency of marshmallow. Questions stab at my temples like arrows. What will I get asked? Will I be expected to cook? Will those yellow shoes make me look like a traffic bollard? Does Gia hate me? Does Matt hate me? Am I the love of Matt's life? I bloody well should be and he mine. I ask Millie in the monochrome of the room, asking her for her thoughts. But she is quiet, her little hands reaching for mine as she nestles into my chest like she always does, ear against the hollow part where my heart beats the strongest.

By the time it gets to morning, Millie is asleep and I am in the bathroom at 4 a.m., staring at my pallid face in the mirror. I've scrubbed my face within an inch of its life trying to draw the colour out, but my skin is still asleep, doughy and pale; my eyes look like they'd like to retreat into my head. Maybe I could just do the sunnies indoors thing. I cross my fingers that the make-up department at the BBC have industrial strength concealer.

When I exit the bathroom, the room is empty and Matt and Millie are downstairs making me coffee and toast. Over the years, Matt seems to have let the sleep deprivation become a part of his constitution. Instead of ageing him, he seems to draw strength from it, even if his hair resembles a ball of mousey tumbleweed. Everything is strangely silent bar the hiss of the kettle, the morning still quiet. Maybe I should just stay here with my daughter and my husband. Next to all of this, supposed tabloid affairs and my views on organic squash seem irrelevant. Matt places a mug next to me dosed with sugar, knowing that I need both that and the caffeine to function. Nine years has taught him that much. When the taxi driver knocks at the door, he bobs Millie around on his knee.

'I love you.'

If there are three little words you start to resent in a marriage, it's those. Not even because you don't hear them enough, but because you hear them too much. They're bandied about because they fill the silence and heal over the cracks. You don't have to mean it any more because you reckon to be there in a kitchen at 4.30 a.m. with an insomniac baby on your knee must mean something. That must be love. I look over and decide at such an unearthly hour, it's the only way forward too.

'Love you too.'

By the time I'm sitting in my make-up chair I'm still debating about my life with Matt. I've made this assumption that he is here to stay, that we will be together for decades to come but for what reason? For the kids sounds like some trite cliché that won't stand the test of time, but I feel awful that when I file everything that needs to be sorted in my head, Matt always seems to be low on the list. I try to think it's because he's mature and understanding enough not to take umbrage with the fact I'm neglecting us, but really it's more to do with him just not coming up on the radar and that is worrying. Anyway, in amongst the Matt issues are the Mum issues, and they're all encircled by Gia's disapproval, and looking at the make-up artist's silver wet-look leggings wondering if she'd let me buy them off her so I could make the boys some rhino costumes. Luella comes in, sees my face, and clicks her fingers in front of my eyes.

'Focus, Jools! C'mon, you look grey with worry. More bronzer, I think. Can we do anything about the bags?'

The make-up girl looks like Luella has just asked her to reattach a limb using a Pritt stick. I just think and think and think. Not even noticing the person who's come in and sat next to me.

'Morning.'

The last time I saw this man was in the supermarket, striding away from him having laid into him about my fish fingers. He's dressed in a striped shirt tucked into his jeans and one of those leather watches with a strangely conceived clock face. His hair fashioned into a messy quiff and his blue eyes wide and hypnotic, he looks into the mirror while my makeup girl douses me in foundation.

'Just some powder for me, I think.'

I want to talk but the large brush and hand in my face prevent me from doing so. So I wave like a six-year-old girl. He doesn't respond. His make-up girl giggles and drapes her hands over him like shoulder pads, caking his face with her magic dust. Luella glares at him through the mirror. He catches her eye and they look at each other for that moment too long. They would have been an interesting couple, I think; she would have been his equal, telling him what's what, while he would have admired that tenacity about her. I can see it. She then stares into the empty space where you look to ponder about a moment in your past. She's angry. The hand clutched around my chair handle tells me that much. He doesn't say a word. I put my hand on hers and whisper out the corner of my mouth.

'Focus, Luella … you look grey with worry …'

It makes her smile as he gets up to walk off. I look down at his jeans and see pointy boots. He looks ridiculous, though I think my fledgling pirate sons would quite like them.

'God, I want to push that man out the window. Please take him down.'

Luella may as well have a spit bucket in her hand. My mental quandary has pushed today and the next half hour out of my mind. This may be a good thing to help calm my nerves but it means I do lack any form of focus. I'm half expecting McCoy to ambush me like last time. Maybe he'll come out with that basket of vegetables from the supermarket again, maybe the MP joining us today, Ed Hellmann, will speak of legalisation and food policies that will whoosh over my head like a small plane. The fact is, I have nothing to prove – this half hour will mean nothing in the long run. My relationship with Matt will still be peppered with long, unanswered questions, I will be on the cusp of being reunited with my mother, Tommy McCoy could now go on air and tell the world I'm a shit mother and even strip me naked and throw tomatoes at me and I'm not sure how much I'd care. The way I feel is not important right now. Not even that, I don't even know if I'm feeling anything at all.

Hair and makeup done, I then head down the corridors to the BBC news centre, a weird empty room where all the fake red, swirling logos will be superimposed later. For now, the room is just some large control room, very NASA.

Actually the whole BBC thing has been a slight disappointment. I'm not sure what I was expecting – Daleks and Gary Lineker swanning along the corridors? It's more a very large rabbit's warren, lots of doors and corridors and normal people milling around. I might as well be in IKEA.

I'm invited to sit down on a leather, low-backed sofa and someone grabs at my dress to attach microphones and a large battery pack to me. Tommy's sitting next to me, his arms caressing the back rest, and Ed Hellmann reaches over him to shake my hand. He's in a suit and has great teeth amidst a bulbous nose and a bobbly cauliflower chin. The presenters, Bill Turnbull being one of them, are being briefed, and flick through inches of A4 paper, ignoring us. Luella stands in a well-positioned place by the cameras so I can see her this time as opposed to her being some leaping shadow. I see a ginger cameraman and can only think of Millie. I wish she was here again as my human shield. I called her Milli Vanilli when she was a baby. During our early hour mornings, I used to tell her about the lip sync scandal of the late eighties just to fill in the quiet and amuse myself. She'd stare back at me like I was completely ridiculous. We hadn't really worked each other out yet.

'And Juliet Campbell, an unlikely hero for all mothers, who recently came to media attention after a scrap between her and Tommy was aired on YouTube. So, tell me have you both made up?'

What? We've started? Luella is whisking her hands and staring at me while I feel a hand creep onto my knee.

'Sure we have, Bill. We're all entitled to our own opinions.'

He's holding my kneecap like an apple. He is actually quite lecherous this close up. I feel the urge to shrug him off like a pesky fly. I'm pondering whether to question the fact that our reconciliation has been decided by him. I, for one, still want to slap him really hard, not so much for anything food based but for the fact he's spent the past two weeks trying to damage my good name, caused great big rifts in my family, and used his money to do so. What was that Luella said? When we fight back, we do it clean, we do it noble. Throwing shit back at someone does nothing but sully your good name too. I dig my molars into my tongue, rendering me speechless for two seconds before smiling and nodding. Bill, who's probably the most sprightly and alert amongst all of us, takes that as his cue to continue.

'So Tommy, you've launched a new campaign, backed up with a new programme concerning families cooking at home. Affordable, back-to-basics cooking, getting people back into their kitchens. Tell us more.'

Blah, blah, blah. Tommy talks a lot with his hands and whips out from under his seat a copy of his new book, featuring him dressed in a mortarboard holding a whisk as a blackboard pointer. The book is called *Cooking it Old Skool!* I smile to see it, given that Luella told me it's a simple rehash of all his old books and recipes, with some colour photos added in of his kids simply to cash in on this recent furore. Ed Hellmann intervenes.

'I think it's an admirable attempt at getting people back in their kitchens but there is little in the book to make me think you've thought about budget, for example. The weekly household only has limited means per week.'

Tommy nods as I sit there flicking through the book, taking in its glossy cover and photos of people with their mouths open in rapturous delight at being in the presence of McCoy and his cooking. I pause at a picture of Tommy in his kitchen, the kids tucking into homemade waffles and fresh fruit, the kitchen resplendent in light wood, and saucepans hanging from the ceiling. Ed has brought with him images of bar charts and graphs about average spends and budgets and lots of numbers that at such an early hour make my brain twitch. Tommy agrees, but counters the argument with organic food being the most important beginning you can give your child, apart from love and time. My nostrils flare. I hear women in the background orgasm a little.

'Wouldn't you agree, Juliet?'

I nod. Luella is still whisking her hands about. I'm on mute. I'm really not sure what I should be saying. Bill is getting tetchy with me too. We're paying you to talk, woman, not browse and respond silently. I think about my four kids sitting around a similar table in my house, the once well thought out colour scheme in the kitchen drowned out by artwork from school, dry cleaning tickets, and streaks of jam. The children less eating than mauling their food, getting it stuck in their hair, talking with their mouths open, or not eating, being grumpy, tearing up bits of food to give the hamster. Where is our hamster? Is he still alive? Talk, Jools. Talk.

'I'd agree that Tommy here is feeding people hype as opposed to recipes that a real family could use.'

Crumbs, where did that come from? Tommy stares at me. The same death stare that his wife used on me all those weeks ago. How dare you be the fly in my ointment and stop my empire from expanding and taking over the world! I flick through the book and that page with the picture.

'I mean, whose breakfast table really resembles this? Most mornings I'm gathering the kids ready for school, rushing out the door. It's chaos.'

Ed Hellmann smiles at me. I think and hope he finds me strangely endearing. Tommy less so.

'Well, maybe for you. Mornings in my house are actually quite zen.'

I must not mention the hired help. I must not mention the hired help.

'Well, that's very nice. Must be all those pastels you have in your kitchen.'

I smile, thinking about my patchwork kitchen, wondering who it is out there whose crockery and table wares aren't peppered with hand-me-downs, children's tumblers, and Christmas gift mugs. Luella is jumping but this time with a bit of merriment in her step. I'm impressing myself with my restraint and ability to not get his book and break his nose with it.

'All I'm saying, Tommy, is that this book, bar being a rehash of your previous books, is quite disconnected from real life.'

Bill is starting to take an interest.

'In what way?'

I flick through the book, fuelled by my need to make this point as clear and well-founded as possible.

'Here. Japanese marinated salmon?'

Tommy nods as I hold up the picture of his perfect pink fish on its white square plate, looking so perfect I suspect it's been airbrushed.

'With a ginger-infused drizzle, sesame rice, and snow peas?'

Tommy still nods. Ed is finding it hard to contain his giggles.

'It sounds delicious. But this is restaurant food, this is so removed from my every day. I mean, for a start, I have four kids. That's six pieces of salmon that would cost me more than a tenner. That's a big chunk of my weekly budget. You're asking me to pan fry six pieces of salmon. And mirin? You're asking me to have mirin in my fridge? A whole bottle of mirin at four quid each for a dish that I'll only cook once every couple of weeks and will otherwise sit in my fridge doing nothing.'

There's a moment of silence. Bewildered silence as my rant is processed and pondered. I think through what I've just said. Was I offensive to the Japanese in any way? Maybe more so to the salmon. Or not. I hear salmon are on the verge of becoming extinct, maybe I did the species a favour. Bill laughs to try and break the silence.

'I'm sorry, that was a bit full on. We love salmon in our house but I bake it so it's less time-consuming, or put it in a pasta dish or fishcakes to make it go further.'

Tommy looks a bit lost for words. I have nothing left to say about salmon except that I like it smoked on Christmas day or on top of a canapé. Do I stick with salmon or move on to something else? Bill is looking to Tommy, whose fingers are digging into the leather like an overzealous cat.

'You mean the boring way. I'll think you'll find that people want new and exciting twists on dishes and to try different ingredients. Mirin is great in salad dressings and for teriyaki marinades.'

I pause for a moment, knowing I don't have anything else to say about mirin bar the fact I think I may have seen it on a Wagamama menu once. He's going to trump me with his foodie London culinary college knowledge. Go back to what you know.

'And you have a section here about making your own pizzas?'

McCoy nods.

'And you list the tool that every family should have being a wood fire oven in their back gardens.'

He nods again.

'Seriously? I don't know what your garden is like but I have a broken swing, a rotting apple tree, and a sandpit/litter tray in mine.'

Bill laughs.

'I make pizza and I do it in an oven in my kitchen, not in a one-thousand-pound appliance that can only be used four months of the year.'

Tommy sits there, stony faced. I refuse to give him the time to speak.

'I agree with Ed; you make no allowances for what normal people can afford in terms of kitchen appliances and ingredients, so how this is a reflection of "family cooking" I really don't know.'

My fingers have become imaginary sardonic speech marks. Bill turns to me.

'So how would you define family cooking, Jools?' I smile to have been recognised and given a moment to speak.

'I guess I want reliable recipes where I'm not standing over the cooker for forty-five minutes. I want to know how to adapt and improvise with good, fresh, reasonably priced produce ... I want to enjoy food and meals with my young family and teach them how to eat well ...'

Bill nods and smiles at me. Tommy can't seem to hide his discomfort at being ousted from the discussion. I sense in a moment he will need to rant. There are three people here; the seasoned broadcaster, the sharp-tongued MP, or the lowly housewife – easy to see who will be the target here.

'And how is this indicative of what everyone wants? I'll think you find pizza ovens are a great addition to any house.'

'Yeah, if you're running a Pizza Express from your garden.'

Ed sits back in the sofa, seemingly happy to have been ousted from the conversation given that it's much more fun to be a spectator. I watch as Tommy McCoy refuses to face me as he talks, directing his comments elsewhere instead to the person they are truly directed to. I notice his forearms, fake tanned up to his wrists. But there's something so preened about him, it's distracting. I look at Luella for a moment and think about this façade he's built his brand on. Am I really here to bring it down to its knees? To expose him for all his fakery? Or is there something about him which also scratches at my own surface, that resents him for it. I think about one of the first things I ever said to this man. How I knew I was a crap mother and didn't need reminding of the fact. People are talking while I'm thinking and studying his leather-cuffed watch.

'I just don't know how she seems qualified to make such comments.'

I look over at Luella knowing I've missed an important sentence in the middle of all of that.

'God, we know you have four kids, we know you have a busy life but that hardly makes you representative of an entire nation of mothers. The recent tabloids have most certainly told us that.'

I look over at Tommy. The hair. I think it's the hair that is the most annoying. That and the fact he feels the need to think my life deserves some sort of commiseration or indeed judgement.

'The papers have been misinformed.'

Tommy shrugs his shoulders. Keep your cool, Campbell.

'Look, I know I'm no role model for anyone nor am I representative of most mothers. I just don't think mums want your misplaced pity, thinking you have the solutions to our everyday woes.'

Bill smiles at me. I want to hug him.

'I just deal with my life each day as it comes. I cook three meals a day with children hanging off my ankles, asking me to check their spellings, sew on name tags, and get bubble gum out of their hair. I'll think you'll find cooking is a much different thing when under these sorts of circumstances. No mention of how to cook like that in here.'

Ed is laughing at this point. I think about that last answer. I'll admit to a lie in there. I don't sew on name tags any more. I write on labels with special pens or iron them on, sometimes

202

using superglue. Even Bill is gearing up for more of my retorts. I think about what Matt may have put in my coffee this morning, rarely do I feel so energised. Tommy finally turns to face me.

'So show me. You think I can't cook under pressure? I was trained in some of the best kitchens in London. Go on, I challenge you.'

The colour drains from Luella's face as I squint my eyes and look over at him on the sofa. He may as well be wearing chaps and spurs. A challenge?

'You and me on live national television. Both cooking the same meal, on the same budget, same time, being taste tested by a panel of families.'

Bill looks over at me, telling me to back away. You can have as many retorts and well-informed opinions on food as you like. You can be the poorer, down to earth mother who can tell him how it really is when cooking for a family. But don't cook against the man. I have no intention to do so in any case. This is him resorting to bullying tactics. He can't take me down with his tongue and his glossy book, but he always could in the kitchen. I smile and shake my head.

'No, thanks.'

'Well, then what she says means nothing, really. I thought this was a discussion about food. Not for some housewife to come on here and spout anecdotal rubbish about her own experiences.'

Bill puts his hand in the air.

'Now, Tommy, come on. There's no need for that …'

'No, Bill. I won't have some half-arsed mother come on here and tell me how to do my job.'

But at this point, I know what I have to do.

'And I don't need you telling me how to do mine. Name your place. I'm in if you are.'

CHAPTER NINETEEN

'How about cheese on toast? You make good cheese on toast.'

I'm staring at Adam in our kitchen as he sips his tea. Adam, whose biggest culinary dilemmas involve whether to go all out and have the vindaloo, or to christen his bacon sarnie with red or brown sauce. I think he owns a saucepan. I think at present it's handling the overflow from a leaking cistern. He's peering over at the list on the kitchen door. Everything from tuna pasta bake to lamp chops to chicken stir fries to jacket potatoes with baked beans (Ted's contribution). Yes, I can see that now. I prick a baking potato and stand in front of the oven for an hour reading a magazine as it cooks. That would make for great television. Still, at least it would fill in the time as opposed to the ten minutes it'd take me to whip up cheese on toast.

'No need for sarcasm.'

Adam looks up incredulous at the thought.

'Shit, Jools. No, you ask Ben. When we were little you always did the best cheese on toast. It was always crisp and you could hold it. Mine's always …'

'Flaccid?'

I laugh at him as he creases his eyes at me and goes back to reading the list. It's been here for a week, since the gauntlet was thrown down, in front of the nation no less. Twelve suggestions later and we're still no closer to finding something in my basic cooking repertoire that I'll be able to cook in front of millions. Maybe cheese on toast is the way forward, tomato slices to boost the nutritional content, a splosh of Worcestershire sauce, and a dusting of mixed herbs so it looks vaguely well presented. Talk about grasping at straws.

Following my foolish, impulsive need to prove a point and commit social suicide on live television, this week has bordered on the insane. Next to the usual juggling act that is my life, I have the papers debating about this epic battle with one saying it has the potential to be the TV moment of the year. Is that a proper award? Would I be able to attend a ceremony, wear an inappropriately cut Lipsy dress, and rub shoulders with the cast of Corrie? For the most part, the papers have been encouraging. McCoy's bullying tactics are being made more evident to the critics and viewing public, and his approval ratings (whatever those are) have plummeted since. Even Dad has mentioned the McCoy sauces in his local Tesco are part of a two for one promotion. Still, he takes the opportunity to use this bit of public attention well.

In the past week I've counted six interviews with him talking about everything from his public support for meals on wheels being made healthier, to his new business venture – a new line in non-stick baking tins in his own patented colour of McCoy maroon. Kitty is also in on the act, waving her baby foods about and also, deliberately Luella tells me, wearing loose clothing so people will conjecture if she's pregnant again (the answer is no; she's still healing from her last stomach shaping operation). Most days I wonder what I was thinking, others I ask Luella if we could ask Gordon Ramsay to don a wig and fake boobs and take my place. For now though, it consumes my life, my house, my family. If I have a moment of clarity on a busy day, the thought creeps over me and starts to throw me into a panic. Because it's there in my mental things to focus on list today, along with cutting the twins' toenails, squeezing a blackhead on my chin, weaning Millie off her bottle, making three school play costumes, and fixing my relationship with my husband. That's all.

'Ben's going to fucking freeze out there.' Adam gestures over to the end of the garden where Ben nervously puffs away on a cigarette (that better be a cigarette), kicking old sandpit toys. Both brothers have been more regular fixtures at the house since the whole business with our mother has reared its ugly head. Not that I mind at all – though completely different, we've always had each other's backs, yet we seem unable to know how to deal with anything. Adam I worry less about, yet Ben seems to internalise all that worry. You see it today in the way he jogs from side to side and inhales between his teeth. I watch him staring at an old, unpainted fence panel, his baby face masked in thick slivers of cloudy confusion, and ache to hold him like a big sister should. He approaches the back door and I pretend not to have been staring.

'So, where's Dad taken Gia?'

'Tea dance at the church hall.'

Adam pulls a face and roots through my bread bin.

'One day that'll be you ... now hands off my crumpets, they're tomorrow's breakfast.' He doesn't listen and heads for the toaster. I hear the distant thunder of steps as Matt attempts to dress the kids. Ben hovers by the door.

'Where is your effing coat? You'll catch your death.'

Ben doesn't respond. I glance over and he's looking at my wonky kitchen clock.

'Ben?' He's quiet as Adam rustles through the cupboards looking for jam.

'Are you guys free now? Just for a little bit.' His face is slightly ashen, a little despondent. Adam nods. I go over to give Ben a hug and feel his head rest against my shoulder. 'I'm really sorry, Jools,' he whispers into me.

I peel his body away from me and look down at his face. Adam stands there clutching a jar of strawberry conserve, unwilling to get involved in the embrace but knowing something is wrong.

'What's up? Are we having more talks about she-who-can-not-be-named?'

I snigger a little imagining her as Voldermort's older sister. Ben looks over at Adam. 'Are the kids going to be around?'

I nod. 'I can get Matt to take them to the park. What is this about?'

Ben puts his head around the kitchen door. 'No, no, no ... it's probably best they're here. I mean ...'

'Ben, spill.'

And then it's like magic. A doorbell. 'I really am sorry. Seriously. But you said you didn't mind so I rang the newspaper and they put me in touch ... and well, we've been talking ...'

'Ben!' Adam and I literally shriek in unison and pop our heads around the door. 'What the fuck have you done?' Adam crumples his crumpet in his fist. A shadowy figure hangs by the front door and my heart doesn't stop. It goes into some strange somersault mode where I can feel it resonate in my eyeballs. 'You didn't. Seriously? My house? You invited her to my house?'

This isn't supposed to happen here. It's supposed to happen on a pier. In the rain. Not now when my monologue isn't prepared, when my hair isn't brushed, when my toilet isn't cleaned, when my kids ... I can't think. The doorbell goes again.

'Jools! Get the door!' I hear footsteps on the stairs and recognise the light, skippy gait as Hannah. No, no, no, no. I run into the hall.

'Han, I need something upstairs. Please get it for me.'

'What?'

'A pen. Any pen. Just get me a pen.'

She screws her face up and retreats up to her room. I panic. The shadowy figure has seen me. My voice goes into pitchy, sing-song mode, 'I'll be there in a minute.' I dart back into the kitchen. Adam maniacally clutches a box of Cheerios for help and stuffs them into his mouth hoping if he fills his mouth enough, or I guess chokes, then he won't have to deal with this. 'I'm not doing this, end of. You bugger for making me do this. You little bugger. You tell her I hate her.'

'Sure. Any other messages you want to pass on?'

'No, that will do for now. Bugger.' He pushes past me, knowing the only escape is upstairs. Deep down, somewhere, there's little Adam who used to stare at Mum's picture on the mantle and tell her about his day. But today he has been ambushed. We have both been ambushed. I glare at Ben. This was never going to be a good idea. Ever. Why now? I can't.

We shuffle to attention, hearing the muffle of footsteps upstairs and voices through the wall. Ben's heartbeat radiates through the air like sonar.

'Benny?'

Shit. Matt. No. Not yet. 'Nope. Matt. Campbell. Sorry

you've had to wait. I thought … wait, you're …'

I can see Matt's face now: Firstly, you thought I was Ben? Wrong hair colour, wrong age, but you've thought I'm six years younger than I really am so I'll take that. But you look familiar. You kind of look like my wife.

'Dorothy. Juliet and Benny's mother.'

Then nothing. I wonder what's going on in her head. Is she being rude in her silence? Are they hugging, shaking hands? Maybe Matt's staring her out. I hear him hesitate before remembering he's the gentlemanly sort and telling her to come in. 'I didn't know you were expected but I guess it's a pleasure to meet … I think I'll go and get …' Ben looks at me and takes my hand. I follow him.

She's how she looked in the newspaper so there are no big surprises there. But she is shorter than I remembered her, her jewellery is brash and I suspect Elizabeth Duke cheap. She's wearing khaki slacks and black ballet pumps, a floral shirt, and pashmina. And well, not ill like I might have expected from all the sullen photos she'd posed for in the papers. Matt stands behind her holding her handbag and raincoat, looking a little like he might be in shock. I see him and giggle nervously. But I can't look at her. This wasn't my plan, it was Ben's and he doesn't hesitate. He launches himself at her and hugs her in the same way that Ben does most people, with genuine heart, arms wrapped round like an orangutan. I see his body shudder as he's hung over her shoulders and my eyes glaze over.

'Oh, don't cry, love.'

She looks over at me.

'Juliet.'

I nod, still silent, feeling too much to want to launch myself at her lest I knock her to the floor and bang her head against the floor repeatedly. Matt sees me, confused, then glares up to the ceiling understanding why Adam might be hiding with the boys. He looks concerned. I look lost. She's here.

'I'll get some tea on, maybe?' he says.

The next five minutes are a cloud because I block myself out of the conversation and the room. I don't want this to be a part of any memory in my head, I don't want to betray Dad, I don't want to say anything I'm not prepared to say. I focus on aspects of the room: how that stain got on the sofa, the film of dust over the television. There's that missing bit of puzzle I opened the vacuum cleaner to find. Ben just launches into his line of questioning, feeling so happy to be able to tell her about what he's been up to; university and life goals. He's healing over those little life cracks that have made his foundations so unstable for so long.

'Jools, Mum asked you something.'

I come back into the room.

'Where are the kids?'

Matt comes in with tea and biscuits and shouts up the stairs. I have an urge to barricade the door and not let my children see her. Does she deserve to see them? *I'm* not even ready for this. They thunder down the stairs, loitering by the doorframe while Matt encourages them to enter. The twins bounce into the room while Hannah stays by the door. Matt looks over at the twins and nods his head encouraging them to come forward.

'Boys, we have a guest.'

'I'm Jake. Who are you?'

'Jake – I'm your grandmother. You can call me Dot.'

The boys seem a little perplexed. Hannah's head swings around, glaring at me.

'We thought you were dead,' says Ted coolly. A little bit of tea bubbles out of my nose. 'That's what Uncle Adam told us.'

'Well, she's not dead is she,' adds Matt.

'She could be a zombie,' says Jake. Matt has no response. My mum smiles politely. Not a zombie, more a ghost.

Ted retrieves something from his back pocket.

'Well, I made this for Mum but you can have it. It's a flower. It's made out of toilet paper.'

I hold my breath for a bit, wondering if Adam fashioned it upstairs and may have rubbed his backside with said paper before telling the twins to give it to her. But it's the same flowers they were taught to make for Mother's Day last year, with little stalks made out of glittery pipe cleaners. My mother takes them, looking very surprised at the gesture, and pats their heads. Hannah's reaction is more cautious. She stands by the door and carefully studies the faces of everyone in the room. Matt goes upstairs to retrieve Millie.

'I got you kids some presents.'

This makes the boys perk up and they jut their heads out, staring at her as she goes for her handbag in the corridor. Hannah comes over and sits in my lap.

'Honey, what's up? You OK?'

She nods and takes a chunk of my hair to twizzle in her fingers. Ben puts a hand to my kneecap. He looks elated, free of anything that may have sat on his shoulders for that moment too long. She returns with little immaculately wrapped boxes. Cars for the boys, hairclips for the girls. The boys tug at me to open them up, loyalties bought. Hannah is taking her time though.

'Do you like them, Hannah?'

'I suppose. Thank you very much.'

Hannah smiles at her while Millie is brought in for inspection. My mum puts the hairclips in her hand.

'You shouldn't do that.'

The room freezes except for the boys, who zoom their cars over the sofa and across the skirting. Ben looks over at Hannah, I squeeze her body tightly.

'Millie eats hairclips and earrings and stuff. You shouldn't do that.'

I smile and nod, taking the present off my mum. My hand skimming past hers to feel her skin, still Fairy soft like it used to be. I flinch. Mum feels it instantly and looks up at me. Ben pushes the plate of biscuits over to Mum as she goes to pour the tea.

'How do you take it, Benny?'

Hannah interrupts.

'Two sugars with lots of milk. Mum has hers with one sugar.'

Her tone is indignant and she crosses her arms. I hold her close to me.

'Han, why don't you, Daddy, and the boys go upstairs for a bit?'

The boys hear this and scamper away but Hannah doesn't

seem to budge. Matt looks over at me. Where do the boundaries of common courtesy and allowing someone to just be able to have a natural reaction to someone merge? She doesn't have to do anything she doesn't want to but her unwillingness to befriend my mother makes me ask to what extent she can read the papers or at least has picked up on what's been happening in the house. Ben urges Hannah to come and sit with him and she sits in his lap as he cradles her head underneath his chin. Matt holds on to Millie, who's staring curiously at my mother as she nibbles away on a biscuit.

'So where's Adam today?'

I interrupt Hannah before she has a chance to say he's upstairs in the boys' bedroom. Ben reaches over to Mum, nestling his hand in hers. I simultaneously admire and despise how he can be so tactile with her.

'He's not ready, Mum. I think he's going to need more time before ...'

Before what, Ben? There's something in Ben's tone which makes me think he's talking about a time after all this. When we meet again? When we sit down together around a table and forget certain life events didn't have majorly altering consequences? Never mind Adam not being ready, I don't think I am. My little brother has well and truly ambushed me and made me confront my biggest fear, the saddest part of my life story. Here, in my own house. Surrounded by kids I have to explain things to, a husband who doesn't know what's going on, and an overwhelming urge to go medieval on her ass. What is Ben saying? Does he want her to be a part of his life further on from now? I thought he had questions. I have many but they have no form or structure and if I attempt to speak now, I'm fearful they'll just come out in tearful Neanderthal monosyllables. I'm studying Hannah's hair in another bid to distract me. Is that a nit or a bit of fluff?

'Well, it was nice to be invited round, to be able to see you all after all this time and tell you ...'

Eeeks. Cloying moment here. Mainly because you weren't invited by me, at least. But what do you need to tell us? You're sorry? If you could you would turn back time and do everything differently? I am tempted to hold my hands up to my ears like earmuffs. Ben seems to be on tenterhooks, holding on to her every word.

'I thought it was time I came here and was totally upfront with you. About why I left. I mean, I have to apologise for the papers. So much of that article was untrue but ... the part about wanting to be in touch. That bit was correct.'

Ben nods. I want to ask about motives, money, betrayal. Still, I say nothing. Ben pipes up.

'I guess the first thing I wanted to know is if you are all right now. We didn't know if you were still ill or in remission. The papers didn't make it clear.'

She pauses.

'I had breast cancer. But they caught it early, stage one. I'm better now, thanks.'

She makes it sound like a touch of flu. The article made it sound as though she'd been on her deathbed and we'd been at home playing Scrabble not really giving two hoots.

'I guess Jools and I both ... I mean, if we'd known, then we would have liked to have lent some support.'

Ben grabs my kneecap, hoping he can get me to nod along. Would I? I guess. My heart is not completely made out of stone. I think.

'Oh, well. Brian and the boys were there and we got by. But thank you for saying that.'

And that is when the room freezes. Like a big giant tableau. Brian with the David Bellamy beard we knew about, but there was something lobbed on the end of that sentence. And the boys. Ben looks over at me. I look over at Matt.

'Which boys?' says Ben

'Well, I ... thought you knew. Scott and Craig, my other sons.'

She dives into her handbag to retrieve her phone, scrolling through menus, then holds a photo up to Ben.

'So this is us in Turkey last year; that's Brian and Scott and Craig. I think he looks a lot like you, Benny.'

I can't seem to move my face. The colour drains out of Ben's and Hannah's little hand slips into mine and grasps my fingers tightly like barbed wire. Who? What?

'You mean your father never told you?'

Ben and I are on mute. Matt steps inside the room.

'Ummm, I don't think Frank did, no.'

Her tone becomes quite matter of fact, almost like she's telling us what she had for breakfast.

'I mean, it was the hardest choice I've ever had to make. Leaving you all and starting anew. But I loved Brian, he was my soulmate, the person I was supposed to be with. I couldn't stay here knowing my heart wanted to be elsewhere. So I left. I didn't want to make things hard for your dad and I'm sorry about the pain I caused him but I thought the best thing I could do was to leave you with him. I loved you kids but …'

Leave us with him? Like a consolation prize? I say the first thing I've said to her since she got here.

'But you loved him more.'

She looks down at the picture.

'A year later we had Scott and Craig and moved to Suffolk. I never forgot about you lot but I think it worked out for the best. You all seemed happy. I was happy. I left it at that.'

Ben can't suppress his emotion any more and tears rain down his chin, falling as little black dots all over his jeans. I can't quite believe what she's saying. My breath just sits loose in my mouth, neurones fire anger, hate, fury emotions through my skull. Get out of my house. How were we happy without a mother for a majority of our childhood? And she was happy? Fucking good for her. Happy without us. That's just great. Because happiness and us as your kids is surely something that can't co-exist. God, even if new love beckoned elsewhere, she could have made some attempt to still have us as part of her life, to not have it engrained into our skulls that we made someone so sad with their lot in life that we forced them out of it. Yet I can't tell her this. Matt looks over at us and is also at a loss for words.

'Awww, Benny. I didn't want to upset you. The boys are keen to get to know you. I'm willing to build bridges so you and your brothers can be friends. This is our place in Turkey, you're welcome any time.'

I still can't talk. Because this wasn't even about abandoning the three children she already had, this was about replacing them. Ben who was always the baby was now lumbered in the middle somewhere. Hannah sees how upset he is and turns to throw her hands around his neck. Ben has no option but to hold on to her. I sit there still taking it all in. We're all silent for a moment. Until one person dares speak.

'His name is Uncle Ben. No one calls him Benny. If you were his mummy, you'd know that.'

Air rushes up my nostrils as she says it. Ben doesn't respond. Matt looks mortified.

'Hannah! Upstairs now!'

'It's all right, think we're both gonna go,' announces Ben, and he bundles Hannah away as they both exit the room. My mum follows them with her eyes and I watch Hannah give her evils as she exits. Now I'm sitting here with my husband not knowing where to look and what he should be doing. And my mother.

'I'm sorry. I didn't mean to upset anyone.'

I still can't bring myself to talk to or at her. I look down at my hands, fiddling with the creases in my fingers, studying the dirt caked into my fingernails. No, to drop a bombshell like that on us after twenty years, of course that wouldn't have upset us. We sat here like lemons, almost apologising to you about not being there when you were ill, and now you sit here defiant that abandoning your children twenty years ago was all right. You were in love, that excuses everything. There's nothing about how sorry you are, how we are, or any questions pertaining to our schooldays, our graduations, our relationships. She just swans in and tells us life's fine and dandy for her because it's all new and we're not part of it. She turns to Matt.

'Matthew. I just wanted to let them know the truth. After all this time, I thought they'd be able to deal with it.'

The air, dry and raspy, rises from my throat.

'My husband's name is Matteo.'

It's only been in the papers every week, if she'd bothered to read anything about me. She studies my face, frozen with shock.

215

'That's Italian, isn't it? That's nice.'

Matt nods slowly.

'If you were my mother you'd know that.'

She stares over at me and for once I look her straight in the eye. I see so many things. I see Adam's forehead and Ben's lips. I see that little mole about an inch into her chin. The eyes. The eyes are mine. I see a lot of things, but mostly a woman. Just someone I used to know.

'I wasn't happy, Juliet. I was stifled, verging on depressed, but couldn't see a way out. No one needs a mother like that.'

'No. We just needed a mother.'

I stare at her, taking in every word and every millimetre of her face so I can preserve this memory for ever. Because I know now that this is the last time I will ever see her. I'm not sure if I had a memory of her before then that pertained to that. Just a jumble of images, all the good ones that I plastered on to some sort of collective montage that made me think there was a good and valid reason as to why she left. But there wasn't. Only her own fear of an unfulfilled life, a quick get-out clause based on instinct and lust that meant she abandoned three young children. It was selfish, it lacked any true thought for those she was supposed to have loved and had a responsibility for. There's anger simmering away in there but also a fair amount of disappointment. It turns into tears that roll bulbous down my cheeks. Matt looks at them and I see him get her coat from the rack in the hallway.

'Dorothy. I think it's best if you left.'

She shrugs her shoulders; the nonchalance almost overpowering me to pick up a teacup and chuck it at her head. But she picks up her coat and takes one last look at me before she leaves.

'You're doing very well for yourself, Juliet. With all that cooking stuff. You and your brothers are a credit to your father.'

And then she goes. The door clicks softly, I hear her footsteps down the path and then all I feel are Matt's arms clamped around me as I sit in a ball on the living room floor dousing his shoulders with tears.

Later that night, Dad returns to find me in the kitchen clutching on to a glass full of whisky and flat Coke. Matt is upstairs sleeping with the kids while Adam and Ben have adjourned to the nearest bar/pub to get plastered. The news has come as no huge shock to Adam, who expected the worst and might as well have told us so, but Ben has understandably not taken the news well. He had his arms out wide like a great big love-filled albatross only to be taken down over the high seas. He's now quiet, withdrawn, not the Ben I know. Adam's solution is thus to fill him to the brim with alcohol to numb the shock, or at least help him to pull so he can replace these feelings with regret from a dodgy one-night stand.

Dad comes in and puts on the kettle.

'So guess who came around today?'

'You finally got that gas man round?'

'Nope, guess again.'

'Not 'effing McCoy?'

I shake my head.

'Dorothy.'

He doesn't turn to face me. He stands there resting his head slightly against the kitchen cabinets.

'Ben ambushed me. In my own house.' He remains silent. 'Invited her round for tea.'

He gets two mugs out of the cupboard.

'Did you know about the other two?'

He looks over at me and returns to watching the kettle bubble and hiss.

'About the other two boys? I'd heard.'

I want to ask him why he'd never said anything but I know. Why kick us when we were already down? He did it to protect us, to not invoke any more hate and bad blood between us. Still, we were adults. Well, I was. Don't know about the other two.

'How was she?'

'Not sure I was part of the conversation for long enough to find out.'

'Are you seeing her again?'

He says it a little resigned, like one hour with our mother

would mean everything between us was going to have changed and we'd head off with her to go and play happy bigger families. I shake my head resolutely.

'I don't think I will be. Plus, who needs more brothers? Two is enough for me.'

He smiles. There is a huge wall of emotion that I need to knock down, but not here, not now. The woman has taken up far too much of my time this evening. Given she's someone I have no love for, who has drummed up nothing in me tonight except bile and tears, I just want rid of her in my brain. Tonight, I've realised being a mother is more than nature, the fact I lived inside her once. The relationship is symbiotic, it needs nurturing, it needs care and attention that she stopped providing twenty years ago. Dad comes up behind me and puts a hand on my shoulder.

'Where are they? How's Ben?'

'Not good. They're out drinking'

He inhales deeply and closes his eyes.

'I just didn't know how to go about it with you three. I did what I thought was best. I always hoped she'd come back or put in an appearance when it mattered but … And you? How are you?'

I shrug my shoulders. I should still be crying but I think I've been drained of tears tonight. Nothing has been levelled out, questions still line my brain like tissue paper. I change the subject for some sense of release.

'So did Gia enjoy the dancing?'

Dad looks at me for a while. He knows when not to dig, he knows that I'm the sort who in time will come forth with how I feel but first I like to file through my head and come to resolutions of my own accord; twenty years of seeing me through my teens has taught him that much. He smiles at me.

'She's quite graceful. Ned took a liking to her.'

'He would. The pervy old twat. Did you finally ask Alma to dance tonight?'

He goes through my drawers and finds the spoons nestled amongst the children's cutlery. He pours the water over the teabags and steeps them for just long enough.

'You know, there's been talk. Apparently, she drove her last husband to drink and her hair smells of Horlicks.'

I laugh under my breath. He goes to the fridge, glancing at the list on the door before opening it to retrieve the milk.

'Any closer to finding this dish you're gonna prepare then?'

I look at him as he splashes just enough milk into the cup, stirring it in and clinking the spoon on the side of the cup three times like he always does. There are so many questions for Dad too. Was there a reason Mum felt so stifled? Why didn't you remarry? Do you still love her? But as much as I can fire the questions at him, I know deep down none of this was ever his fault. He just did what he was supposed to do. He had his moments like any parent (he left Ben in a Tesco once; he thought tinned peaches was an unacceptable dinner). But he was there. Always there.

'I was thinking, well, hoping, you could teach me how to cook your chilli. Maybe I could do that.'

He looks at me and smiles, before putting his hand in mine as we sip our tea in perfect silence.

CHAPTER TWENTY

It's a Thursday and lo and behold, I'm in the kitchen. Only this time I'm not cooking, I'm being resourceful. A quick trip into Kingston this morning to buy some deli goodies for dinner also found me two light grey Primark handbags that will eventually become rhino costumes for the annual school play. In Primark, I was also asked for my autograph by an old woman scouring for tights. After I had scribbled on the back of her phone bill, she told me I seemed like a lovely young girl and she hoped I was going to kick that bugger into next week with my cooking. The fact she thought me both young and capable of such a feat made my day. So now I'm cutting into the handbags with garden shears and going crazy with the superglue, calling the boys in every so often for fittings. Gia stands by the hob doing interesting culinary things with courgettes while Donna is also by for a coffee, grumbling because Ciara has been cast as a dolphin, one of the starring roles but with an infinitely more difficult costume predicament. Justin, on the other hand, is a tree and she is debating just dying his little afro green so all he'll have to do is wear some brown cords and he's all set to go. In between, she also reads out from a newspaper on the table that is comparing the big cooking showdown.

'Shit, Jools. Didn't know he had them fuckin' Mitchin stars things. Four, apparently.'

I smile watching Gia hunch her shoulders to hear Donna swear. Gia is perfectly polite to Donna's face but is slightly intimidated by all the jewellery and skin-tight denim. I look over the article to see Tommy there in his chef whites, standing in front of his Bristolian eatery, Maison de Gout, recently named one of the best places to eat in the South West. Though as Luella has pointed out, it really does sounds like the House of the Medical Gout, which isn't so inaccurate given his love

221

for sprinkling a little truffle butter over everything. Next to the riverside bistro he has in London, Mangetout, and the gastro pub he owns in Hampshire, The Petits Pois (not least his penchant for bastardising the French language), he also has mentions in *Egon Ronay*, the *AA Food Guide*, and yes, his four Michelin stars. This isn't even David and Goliath any more. This is *Star Wars*. And I'm not even Princess Leia in a gold bikini. I'm Yoda. I have my wits about me but I'm shrivelled and small and green with fear at what the future holds for me. Because my cooking is not Michelin star haute cuisine, I'm comparable to a Little Chef. It's sometimes a bit of a gamble eating there but it's always there, it fills a gap, it makes you smile. I hope.

'Have you heard? He's bought his own cow for mincing and he's having organic avocadoes brought in to make guacamole with a recipe from the best Mexican chef in London.'

I smile, cutting big, garish buckles off the handbag in my hands. My guacamole will be made from a recipe my dad has cultivated over the years that began life on the back of an Old El Paso box. Donna can sense from the way that I'm handling my shears that the subject needs to be changed.

'Well, who fucking cares, eh? I heard organic doesn't mean nothing any more. Just means they pile even more horse crap on the stuff to make them grow bigger. Ain't that right, Gigi?'

Gia smiles, putting on her 'I'm-so-shocked-that-I'm-going-to-pretend-I'm-so-foreign-I-didn't-understand-that' face. Donna has pilfered parts of my handbag in order to make Ciara some sort of headdress. At the moment all she has is a grey swimsuit, leggings, and silver Crocs. I am attempting to make some rhino horns out of old kitchen towel tubes and some Tippex pens. The boys come running in on the hunt for food and I place one of my homemade masks over Ted's head, catching him like a fish.

'So what do you think?'

Gia looks suspiciously at my handiwork while Donna giggles under her breath. These masks are crucial, because all I have next to them are some cheap, light grey tracksuits. The patched pieces of grey leather have been stapled together haphazardly and the horn superglued on in the middle.

'They're a bit S&M, love.'

'What's that, Mummy?' cries a suspicious voice from out of the mask.

I shake my head so as not to have to answer the question. Ted looks like an executioner/professional wrestler as his little eyes peer out of the holes.

'Can we have some Coke, Mum?'

'Erm, no?'

'Louis Prince gets to drink Coke before he goes to bed.'

'Yep, and the little bugger has black teeth like he smokes thirty a day,' adds Donna.

I go to the fridge and pour three glasses of milk, which they down with impressive speed before scampering off again. Donna's still laughing while Gia stares at me from the kitchen sink, still doing that weird thing where she watches me like I might be part of some sort of sociological study. Subject laughs: reason unknown; hair still unwashed. Luckily, Donna just assumes it's typical of our in-law relationship and carries on regardless. I look back at Gia, wondering what is going on in that little Italian mind of hers, thinking how she must be processing everything. And I think back to her and Matt's Italian exchange the other week and what he said the other night, pretty much confirming what I'd known all along: all the justification and persuasion in the world could never erase the fact I took her son from her before his time. She notices me looking and takes a courgette, forcibly hacking one of the ends off. I look away.

The back door suddenly opens and Annie pops her head around the doorway.

'Only me. Thought I'd drop by and see how things were.'

My shoulders lighten to see her. Annie's heard from Matt about meetings with my mother and has been trying to encourage me the best she can since I decided to take my cooking face-off up one notch. Gia is always pleased to see her, given I suspect she likes her influence on me more than Donna. Either that or she secretly wishes Matt had married some highflying, well-styled hotshot like her.

'Annie! You stay for dinner maybe?'

Annie needs little persuasion, as does anyone who's invited to share in Gia's cooking, and comes to give me a hug.

'How are you? How's things?'

'You know. Drama, drama, drama.'

Millie reaches up to give Annie a bit of her biscuit. Annie gives her curls a long, prolonged kiss and sniff. Sometimes, if the room is silent enough and the scent of baby lotion is strong enough in the air, you can hear her uterus skip a beat.

'Well, I just came from the docs. Looks like we're going to go ahead with the IVF.'

'Really? It's only been a year. What happened with the acupuncturist?'

'He was supposed to activate my ovaries but I always left with the shits.'

Donna smiles over at her. She glances at Millie.

'Sorry, TMI. Can I have this one? That would still leave you with three.'

She strokes Millie's head and holds her close to her. I always feel for Annie, wondering how and what I can say that won't sound condescending given my fortune when it's come to popping sprogs. She can't have Millie, of course, but maybe she could take the twins every other Saturday. She then does what Annie does best and that is to change subject in order to snap out of her baby slump.

'Anyway, I read an article recently that says McCoy's babies aren't even his.'

I turn to face her. Any dredge of gossip at the moment about McCoy is more than welcome to cheer me up, especially as I glance down at the article Donna was reading to see a picture of McCoy handpicking his own beans.

'Turns out all that cooking left his balls all shrivelled up and spermless so Kitty had to resort to using bank sperm, which is why if you look at all those kids they all look slightly different.'

Donna snorts with laughter and I swear I see Gia's shoulders shudder a bit at the sink. She comes over and puts a cup of tea in front of Annie. Donna suddenly perks up.

'People were saying that about Paula Jordan at school, you know. Apparently, she ain't got a belly button because they botched her lipo after Harriet so Toby is some kid they adopted from Estonia.'

Annie laughs so much a little bit of tea dribbles through her nose. Donna grabs me by the hand.

'Oi, I meant to talk to you about that. Ciara mentioned that Tyrrell girl has been bringing them newspapers into school – all the ones you've been in and it's caused some fuss.'

Annie, Gia, and I pause to take it in.

'You what?'

'They've been trying to get on Hannah's case about it. Remember Lynne Fry ran off with the bloke who delivered her fridge? Comet Colin, Dave calls him. Well, it's started a thing with their class where to get on kids' cases they start badmouthing their mums and dads and throwing words like "divorce" about.'

I shake my head and close my eyes. My little Hannah Banana. I'm not sure how I thought children her age would deal with information like this, how they'd use it. Not very well, it would seem. And from the very mouth of Jen Tyrrell – Donna's recent nemesis and Queen Bee of the school playground. I have half a mind to storm around to her house now and give her a good, hard slap.

Gia intervenes, 'Hannah is OK?'

'Oh, I wouldn't worry about Han. Ciara says she's taking it all on the chin, like properly stands up for herself, tough cookie. But thought you should know.'

'No, I'm glad.'

It's good to hear something reassuring like that, given the circumstances, but really I need to sit down and speak to that girl. Never mind bullying, I feel there are residual issues there with my mother that need clarifying. We've found out snippets of what she thought after her outburst the other day – she told Ben she wasn't very nice to people who weren't nice back – a logic so clarified and innocent that I wondered if I should just use that as my mantra from now on. But she also seemed defensive, almost a little angry, and angry tweens are not a good thing. I look over at Gia, who's now doing the cold and silent thing given her granddaughter has been caught in the firing line of some primary school slanging match. Shit, that's not a happy face. Annie notices it too and stands to attention.

'Gia? Is there anything I can do?'

'You can grate courgette?'

I think about Annie's one-hundred pound manicure and possibly two-hundred pound suit that I don't have a pinny to cover. She just looks at me and smiles, takes her rings off, and gets tucked in. True friendship if ever I saw it. The doorbell rings and Donna gets up.

'This might be Dave, he's finishing early today so he said he might pop in to say hello.'

She scoots up as I sit there and watch Millie lick biscuit out the nooks and crannies of her fingers, how I think all biscuits deserve to be eaten. Is there anything I need to do with you? Check the progress of teeth growing and research what hairstyles best suit curly and ginger. She nods faintly in agreement.

It's then I suddenly hear it. Or more like I don't hear it. Silence. A few minutes ago I swore I heard boys throwing themselves around the living room and the TV blaring, but it's been replaced by the hiss of a pot on the stove and the mild whisper of a conversation outside. Donna and Dave? I get up to see what's going on. I see the front door half open and Donna gesticulating wildly to someone halfway up our pathway. The other person is unclear in the haze of the glass.

'Seriously, mate. Fuck off out of here.'

I swing the door open when I hear it, not imagining who it could be. My first guess is a reporter, the second is a Jehovah's witness. He was really not very high up on the list at all.

'Richie?'

'Jools?'

When I see his face, the air gets sucked out of my nostrils like a hoover hose and I stand there not knowing what to say to him. The last time I saw him, bar newspapers and Facebook, was in Leeds during finals in our first year. Let's just be friends. I'm not sure about us. We've just got so much of this life to see. I cringe now to think of the cliché of it all. He dumped me in my student flat, kissing me on my forehead before leaving. I rushed to the window to see him disappear down my road. From matchstick, to pin, to dot. I love you, Richie Colman, I love you so, so much. Please don't leave me. I crumpled to the floor thinking it was the worst thing anybody could do to anyone, wallowing in self-pity about being abandoned and unlovable and putting on Radiohead while I sat in my darkened student room.

Yet that was almost ten years ago. Now he just stands here dressed in jeans and a generic bad slogan Topman T-shirt. The shoes are bad: leather and laced and trainers but not. Once I finally get round to looking him in the eye, they're the same – green like mushy peas. I shake my head if only to wake myself into speaking.

'Richie? What the hell are you doing here?'

This wasn't Putney. This isn't nearly in the same vicinity as Putney.

'My mum told me you lived here. She's not been well. She had an operation a few days back.'

'Is she all right?'

He nods. Peg Colman. She had big, wild Kate Bush hair and used to partake regularly in local amateur dramatics. She used to joke and call me the daughter she never had. I was, of course, won over by statements like that, especially when they came with fondant fancies and bottles of Irn Bru. I decide not to dig any deeper. Donna stands behind me, arms crossed, looking like she could take on the world. To my right, I see three faces pressed against the glass, belonging to the twins and Donna's little Justin. Something suddenly became more interesting than *Ben 10*.

'I wanted to pop by and say hello.'

I shrug, rather well truth be told, in how nonchalant I appear to be when really I'm seized by shock.

'Well, hello. Give my regards to your mum.'

Donna cackles behind me.

'Told you, mate. She don't want anything to do with you.'

He glares at her while he approaches me and leans in, his arm brushing against mine. It throws me for a loop and I end up staring at him for longer than I need to.

'I was hoping we could have a chat? Catch up?'

There is something very different about him from our days at university. The hair, the tapered jeans. But there is that feeling in my gut as well. Guilt. That part of my subconscious somewhere rings loud: that small part of my brain that was always registered to him. When I had fights with Matt and my insides brewed with resentment, I always replaced Matt in my mind with Richie. The person who really knew me and was far better suited to me and had been my star-crossed lover in my youth, lying across his bed, snogging until our jaws went numb, telling me we were going to be together for ever. Yet at this moment, all I want to do is kick him really hard. Why the monkeys are you here? You should remain some figment of my imagination, an online acquaintance, someone I once knew. You don't belong here. Another person appears from behind me. Richie looks up to greet her.

'Abbie, right? Hey.'

Annie gives me a look of pure horror.

'It's Annie. What the … why are you here?'

'I was in the neighbourhood. Mum told me you hadn't moved very far.'

He makes me sound like I've lived in Kingston all my life. I mean, it is the truth, but it's not like a flat share in Putney is any more exotic or far removed from here. Annie suddenly sees the kids and runs inside the house to peel them away from the glass.

'Richie, it's really not a good time.'

My hands are clammy, my temples sticky from having to confront him here on my doorstep. This fantasy had always played out a little better in my head. I had a better monologue prepared, I was wearing Louboutins to make my calves look more shapely, and maybe some control knickers. My mother-in-law wouldn't appear behind me at such moments either.

Gia, in a pinny and with a courgette in each hand, her face lightly dusted in semolina.

And neither would my husband. Matt! Hello, dear! And how was work?

'Hello, can I help you?' he says, casual as anything.

And this should be the moment when Doctor Who arrives in

228

his TARDIS and the meeting of these two worlds should result in some sort of time-continuum anomaly whereby we all get sucked into another dimension. Or not. Instead we all stand still in incredibly awkward silence. Until Matt recognises who it is.

'You're kidding me, right?'

At this moment, I should be trying to be diplomatic and separate the two men as they edge dangerously closer. Instead, I am comparing them. Matt has better hair, cool headphones, and is three centimetres taller. I win.

'Matteo? Who this?' Gia still seeks out answers from Donna who is silently watching on, maybe a little entertained.

'Seriously. Please leave.'

'I was actually here to see Jools, not you.'

'Invited, were we?'

I shake my head resolutely. The air is thick with testosterone and the faint smell of Gia's antipasti in the kitchen. Little boys watch the conversation rocket back and forth like a tennis match. Donna reaches over my shoulder.

'Don't worry, Matt. I told him to sling his hook.'

Richie scowls back at Donna. Matt and Richie both look at me like they want me to take sides. I just want to stand here, on my own in my confusion, embarrassment, and hyper-emotionality.

'You have the temerity to one, flirt with my wife online and two, talk crap to the papers and now show up on my doorstep, where I live, where my kids live?'

'Mate, whatever happened was between me and Jools.'

'Whatever happened was totally inappropriate. I warned you last time and I'll do it again. She's mine.'

I jolt when I hear it. When was I last a possession? He sounds like he does when he's claiming the last biscuit on a plate. Still, there is an element of truth. I step a little closer to Matt. I look up at this display of manhood as Richie rolls his eyes.

'Yep, last time when you hit me. What a big man you are.'

And this is when it should all kick off, the taunting, the insults, the primitive claiming of womenfolk as their own. But Matt catches a glimpse of his sons at the window and stops, his stares bouncing between wife and former lover of wife with such intensity I swear he could bore holes in our foreheads. I, for one, would just like Richie to leave. Richie existed before on some existential level, my alternative reality, my greener grass. But now he's here, in the flesh, and to be honest, I don't really fancy it. I just want to bid him adieu and go back to the sanctuary of what is real, of what works. Thanks for dropping by and reminding me of the fact, thanks for being someone I couldn't give a toss about. Please, please just go away. But someone hasn't had their say. Confused, I see her consulting a flustered-looking Annie at the door. An Annie who realises she shouldn't have said anything, because when she does a little old lady storms down my pathway, pushing Donna into our box hedge, and proceeds to pummel Richie Colman with a courgette. The world stops. Matt smiles. I'm surprised how courgettes make for quite robust truncheons.

'YOU!'

It takes all of Matt's strength to hold her back.

'*Mamma! Cosa fai?*'

Donna and Annie stand there silently in awe.

'This the boy from newspaper. Why? Why you sell story?'

Richie shields his face, cowering as he's attacked by vegetables.

'The newspapers were not very accurate, ma'am. They twisted my words and manipulated our friendship.'

'What friendship? If you both friends, when a newspaper ring you, you tell them it is *stronzo* of you to comment like you know this girl. You respect her family!'

'Yes but …'

Matt and I look at each other when she says this, wondering where such clarity on the situation came from, wondering when this man ever became as big of a problem as he did. I stand back to hear Gia so vehemently defend our family. Maybe it was never about her and me. Maybe it was always about bigger pictures: little people, a home, a family. Richie looks at me for help. I just smile as Gia responds with a gesture so crude that I cup my hand over my mouth to keep the laughter in. Richie goes a whiter shade of pale. Donna cheers her on.

'I don't care to hear this. She had *bambini,* she have husband now. You are selling your story for the money? You make my Matteo sound like common thug. I am feeling sorry for you.'

Richie is lost for words while Matt sidles up to her, trying to curl her offending finger back into her palm. Richie turns back to me.

'Babe, honestly I'm so sorry. I came here today to talk and see if there was anything I could do to make it up to you.'

Could he cook? Maybe I could put him in a pinny and go up against McCoy. Money. Money would also be good. I think I also bought him an MP3 player for his eighteenth birthday using my wages from working Saturdays at WHSmith. Could I have that back?

'Gia's right. Just …'

But I'm not sure what to say. Gia's breath down my neck, Matt glaring, ready to pounce, I am silent. I loved you once. Fairytale, nonsensical love that made you listen to Al Green thinking your life could be condensed into a song. Little girl love. But after you, I met someone else. Life became a full-on musical, sometimes the numbers are fast and furious, sometimes they are slow and they drag, in between are the moments of drama that make the air cloud with despair. And it's a work unfinished, still in progress. So thank you for cutting me off when you did. A year sooner may have been better, given me that year to snog randoms and enjoy being a fresher a bit more but then hell, I never would have met Matt. Hannah would never have been made. So thank you for being someone I used to care about. You are just a man in a cheap T-shirt with a paunch.

'Just … *vaffanculo!*'

Matt chuckles to himself as Gia begins to wave courgettes in Richie's face again. I'm assuming she wasn't inviting him in for a cup of tea.

'Seriously, lady, I have no idea who you are, this has nothing to do with you.'

And this. This is where it all kicks off.

'I AM GIA CAMPBELL! This is my family!'

And Richie starts to edge towards the gate, tripping

backwards over the dodgy loose stone as Gia chases him out and starts to follow him down the pavement.

'I see you here again … *ti taglio i testicoli e li faccio in una zuppa*!'

I hear nothing in that sentence bar the word for soup and testicles. Matt follows her out on to the pavement but Richie feels the idiotic need to have one last jab.

'Like mother, like son.'

And this is when Gia's eyes turn a funny shade of black like she's been inhabited by a force unknown to this world. Richie sees it. He runs. Gia chases. Holding her courgettes. With exceptional speed given she's in velour house slippers. Matt chases Gia. I chase Matt. I watch as Richie's body turns the corner past the mini-mart and stand there outside Louisiana Crispy Chicken on the High Street as he weaves through the crowd from matchstick, to pin, to dot, Gia gesticulating wildly behind him as he half gallops, half trips into the Tesco Metro. Goodbye, Richie Colman. Really, goodbye.

CHAPTER TWENTY-ONE

'Really, Vernon? Well, first we're going to fry off this onion until it's translucent and the smell is starting to develop.'

Vernon doesn't look too impressed. Well, that would be the case when Vernon is being played by a microwave and the tasting panel are a jar of spatulas. I stir my empty pan and look up to the kitchen wall. I hear laughing come at me from behind with its very best North West accent.

'So what goes in now, love? Is that garrrlic? Lovely.'

'You sound Cornish.'

Never mind that he is also two foot shorter than Vernon Kay. Ben punches me on the arm.

'So Vernon Kay, why not Dermot? At least there'd be someone interesting to look at then.'

I don't know why Vernon. The fact is McCoy has handpicked everything from presenter to jingly music to set colours and even though I got to choose what we will be cooking, I'll just be the filler in the middle to make Tommy McCoy look like the fantastic, all-singing, *wunderkind* celebrity he is. Luella says not to worry but that doesn't mean every day when I have two minutes to myself, I'm not talking to the microwave. Sometimes the bread bin. I shrug as Ben picks up the pile of DVDs from beside me. Luella sends one every day for inspiration and to help me 'form my own sense of brand' she says. At the moment, she wants to hype me up as a female Nigel Slater with kids but without the poncy foodie vocab, the facial hair, or the orgasmic expressions over freshly roasted cuts of meat.

'*Hot Guys Who Cook* – this sounds like porn. Good porn. Are they naked?'

'No, but you can have it. Have worked out I'm most definitely not a hot guy who cooks.'

He takes that and some early Delia – back when she used to only wear red jumpers in her conservatory – and a show involving Aussie blokes cooking in their swimwear, an eclectic mix, but that has always been Ben. He locks an arm into mine and puts a head on my shoulder. He looks different today. The clothes are always impeccable, the right side of fashion victim with the blazer and vintage jeans, but the face is a little more hopeful. I've only seen him a couple of times since the whole situation with Mum. Adam took it upon himself to be counsel in that matter, medicating him with liquor and, bless him, accompanying him to gay bars to help him feel better, even having the gall to complain when he wasn't hit on.

The fact was, I didn't know what to say to him because my feelings about the matter were still mixed. No way was I ready to accommodate more brothers in my life, but neither did I know what side of the fence I sat on. I didn't quite hate her, all my initial anger had been replaced by more important emotions, yet I wasn't quite ready to stand there with open arms and welcome her back into my life. I felt nothing, literally nothing about the situation, which was worse than probably feeling hate. So I hugged Ben and furnished him with love and doleful looks and left it to Adam and his bilious rage to help him get over his mother-based woes. And maybe, just maybe, it's worked. Today he radiates an energy that is very old Ben. But then you would if you'd also just graduated with a 2.1 from Queen Mary and Westfield. I brim over with pride.

'That's a very chic outfit, sis.'

'You sound surprised.'

'Frankly, I am. Where from?'

'Oasis trousers, M&S top.'

'M&S? How mumsy.'

I push his shoulder slightly as he helps me rearrange my belt, making sure it sits on my waist rather than being something my tits are perched on.

'So, you? You're all right?'

He nods without uttering a word. We don't have to mention her on today of all days but I need to know this isn't a façade; that underneath the thought of our mother doesn't bubble away and itch at his psyche. He grabs my face and plants a kiss on my cheek.

'I thought I needed a mother. I don't.'

His answer seems very definite, for which I'm glad, though I suspect this will not be the end of his need to grasp some sense of belonging to her as a child. Still, for now, he's resigned himself to the fact our family works without her. The kids burst in as we smile and embrace. I hope to good god they didn't hear the part about not needing a mother. Many an argument about picking up toys would love that tagged on the end. The boys have a present wrapped up in newspaper.

'We wrapped it ourselves.'

It shows, given the newspaper has been coloured in and stuck together with dinosaur stickers. Ben opens it up as the boys look on. A box of Uncle Ben's rice. We all laugh, the boys look very proud of themselves as Ben holds it close to his chest.

'I will treasure this for ever.'

Thanks, boys, because now I realise I'm a dinner down tomorrow. And that in the congratulatory present stakes, I have let Ben down quite badly, dragging him along to the kids' school play to sit amongst the video cameras and proud parent types. However, the boys look quite amusing in their matching grey tracksuits and patchwork handbag masks.

'Let's play Quidditch, Uncle Ben!'

I look over curiously at Ben, who shrugs his shoulders. The boys 'fess up.

'Uncle Ben showed us. You can do it with the hoover and a tennis ball.'

I shake my head. 'No time for Quidditch! Shoes on.'

They leave, running past Gia who stands behind her with a handbag and the biggest camera known to man.

'Gia, looking glamorous as always.'

Always a sucker for a compliment, she bows her head and smiles. In her hands, a copy of last week's *The Sun* that she seems to have surgically attached to her. She urges Ben to come and have a look at her newfound fame: a picture of her chasing Richie Colman down the road, with Matt and I in tow looking like we're practising for a 4x4 relay down my local parade of shops. Still, Gia is quite happy to be in print and has shown the article to everyone who has walked through the door.

CAMPBELL MAFIA MOTHER-IN-LAW

Ben's eyes open widely as he whispers out the side of his mouth.

'Jesus, is she chasing him with a dildo?'

I half choke, half nudge him with my elbow.

'It's a courgette.'

'Well, whatever gets you off.'

Gia looks curiously at Ben, who just grabs her by the shoulders and gives her perm a kiss.

'Well, I think it's brilliant you gave him what for. Never liked him.'

'I went out with him for four years!'

'Well, I always thought he was slightly homophobic and he had awful taste in shoes.'

The latter I cannot argue with. I look at the picture – Luella's biggest bugbear about it is that Matt and I seem to be standing outside a fried chicken takeaway looking worryingly out of breath. A bit of cropping and this picture could ruin us, she says. But to be honest, I'm not sure if it didn't do the very opposite. After chasing my ex down the street, we got Gia home and it was only then we realised why she had been staying with us for so long. It was neither to impart cooking wisdom nor rearrange my spice jars, but to fiercely protect and look after a small little family unit she had grown quite fond of. While she may always have her doubts about Matt and myself, she believed in our family and her goal was to hold together what ratty newspaper articles would wish to set asunder – all with the power of a couple of courgettes. So she's been here to prop us up, lend support, cook her little heart out. And I think I like it; I feel it's marked a shift in our relationship. Her validating my family makes me believe for the first time in nine years that maybe she doesn't hate me too much.

'Ta-dah!'

Hannah suddenly makes an entrance in the kitchen, looking far too old in her hula outfit. Matt went protective father figure and vetoed coconut shells on an eight-year-old whereas I vetoed the thermal vest under the coconut shells to save Hannah's street cred, so we have settled for a house plant that has been stapled onto an old swimming costume, that she now wears with black plimsolls, sport socks, and a lei that Matt wore on a stag do and smells a little of cider. Ben grabs Hannah, declaring her the most beautiful hula dancer in the land. I fiddle with earrings and change bags and my rhino sex shop masks while Ben watches on.

'So the boys are elephants? Cute.'

With Matt meeting us at school, I arrive in good time (very unlike me) so that we don't draw too much attention to ourselves and can nab the best seats. Dad isn't coming to avoid a repeat of last year when he fell asleep and left a wet patch on Matt's shoulder. Adam would rather pull teeth. I've positioned us centre left so I can see the children through a column of curtain-less space before they go on stage and have a good escape route should Millie decide to wail her way through the performance. As soon as Donna sees us, she scoots over.

'I've got some Piriton in my bag? Doped Alesha up so she won't get too moody.'

I decline the offer of soft baby drugs as Ben reaches over for air kissing. The parents arrange themselves as I would have guessed. The Tyrrells and Jordans together second row from the front so they can look over the teachers' shoulders and be party to gossip and flaunt their dedicated parent act. Hugh 'Huge' Tyrrell might as well have brought the BBC wildlife division with him for the size of the camera he has propped on his equally large shoulder. Paula has Greg Jordan in tow, the sort you can tell plays tennis in Cliff Richard polyester shorts and pulls his ankle socks up so they're just under his kneecaps. Out of all of them, Greg is the only one to gesture hello by saluting me like a Girl Guide. I salute back. Parents like me, the Liquorice Allsorts who come with babies, cameras that don't work, and don't feel important enough to go too near the front, fill the middle. Pooja's mum always waves with both hands, still in dusky pink fleece; Billy Tate's mother, who I know doesn't use tampons, comes over and we have a chat about

McCoy; and I also get to chat to Eve Lingham, mother of Alfie who called Jake a pube. She's got large corkscrew curls and a fondness for maxi dresses in a bid to make her look like a trendy earth mama. To prove this, she embraces me and tells me a lot of the mums at school are really behind me. I shake my head and tell her it's a storm in a teacup. She returns with looks that either suggests I'm crazy, this thing is huge and you're going to get steamrolled, or that I'm trying to be politely modest.

The rest of the parents are best described as a motley crew. I always like the dads in the work overalls, the ones who bring aunts, uncles, and second cousins, the couples obviously mid-separation who sit seats apart.

And then you get to the back of the school hall, the mothers with even younger babies who are trying to breastfeed using the school polyester curtains as cover and the au pairs who reserve two seats for parents who will no doubt be late and slip in when they can. And the nameless few, not paps I think, as Mrs Whittaker stands there by the door with a big stick (really, I'm told it's a prop for the play) making sure. One woman keeps looking over at me and smiling. She's pretty in a fresh, sprightly way which makes me think she's not a mother or has had plastic surgery. When Matt comes in, he's obviously run a fair bit as his hair is frizzy, his tie skewed over his right shoulder. He pats Millie on the head and goes in for a well done hug with Ben.

'So how's it been? The vultures out yet?'

He stares over at the Tyrrell/Jordan collective as he says it. Vultures being not far off given the cardigan Jen Tyrrell wears, with its bizarre feathered cuffs and collar. We had anticipated a bit of a free for all after her and Donna's altercation but so far everything has remained decidedly civil. There have been looks, and we've had to trap Donna into a seat by the wall so she can't go anywhere, but there are no asides, no nasty remarks. Even the other parents do not seem to be too concerned about me; they smile and whisper but not in a necessarily malicious way. Just in a way to make me think I need to check my teeth.

There are actually more comments directed towards single

238

mothers, play away fathers, and one mother rumoured to be profiteering from running special masseuse services out of her front room (not in my kids' class; she used the local rags to advertise her wares and got found out by another dad – small world etc.). So, me cooking on national television and looking like I've spent a few bob on some better fitting clothes actually isn't that big of a deal. And for some reason, this is actually quite comforting to me.

In actual fact, the biggest thing to explode that evening is the homemade volcano at the back of the stage. Clifton Primary has gone all out this year with the lights, the papier-mâché backdrops, and baking powder volcanoes.

It's a sweet if completely nonsensical play. Two of the eldest children narrate in the style of a Julia Donaldson book about a giraffe who's tall and feels left out and is befriended by a dolphin who shows him the world and they become good friends etc. I'm not sure how Attenborough would deal with the biological inaccuracies, but hell, these animals talk, sing, and wear masks made out of Primark handbags. Ciara does a good job of being the dolphin, wearing a silver swimming cap with fins made out of said handbag. Hannah does a commendable hula number and Matt takes a million and one photos while I simply sit and stare at the poor girl whose mother made her hula skirt out of a green plastic bag through which you can see her pastel pink knickers. When my boys come on, I hold my breath waiting for them to start charging at the stage. A narrator starts:

'The giraffe was unhappy, misunderstood,
But those old baboons were just up to no good.
They wanted giraffe!
They wanted her out!
They didn't understand what she was about.
So dolphin told the rhinos,
All wrinkly and grey,
You must go and help her,
You must save the day!'

As much as I'm not sure that I like the fact my sons are being cast as non-verbal lackeys, they do a hilarious job of charging up and down the stage and making ghastly grunting noises. Matt and Ben find it hilarious as do most of the audience. Gia's clicking finger can't move fast enough. This only goads them on to show off more until I see a teacher flap her hands about in the wings telling them to calm down. It's then I notice the baboons in the production. One of them has a mini fur coat on, neither have made an attempt to make their buttocks shine pink: Maisy Tyrrell and Harriet Jordan. I point it out to Matt and we both look at each other then over at the vultures who don't seem wholly impressed at the way my five-year-old twins have confined them to a big hole in the savannah. And there things draw to a close, with Ciara banging out a lovely doleful duet with her giraffe friend (namely the tallest boy in school dressed in what looks like the remnants of an old sofa). Then everyone comes on stage to sing along to what sounds like a do-gooder's rehash of a Michael Jackson anthem. They all wave their hands, from hula dancers, to scuba divers, to rhinos, to sea anemone, and the poor lad who got cast as the sun and was made to wear canary yellow tights. Nobody seems to care though, parents take photos and children look bemused, my twin boys jump up and down at the side of the stage and punch each other in the arm. I think I'm proud. I think about what this means. If Donna is the wily and graceful dolphin and Jen and Paula are the gossiping baboons, surely that makes me the big clunky rhino with my weathered skin and surly eyes. I pout a little. Even a hippo would have been better than that.

Play over, we all assemble in the school hall where I get excited over the prospect of custard creams and tea served out of a big silver urn. I always think there's a lovely retro quality to having tea at school. I dig around for egg mayo sandwiches but the budget doesn't seem to have stretched to that this year. I pocket more biscuits to make up for that and hang around with Ben, Matt, Gia, and Millie. The Tyrrells and Jordans stand to the side of the room turning their noses up at the UHT milk. Ben skims through the photos on his camera phone, giggling.

'Jools, those twins are fricking hilarious.'

I smile back. After the group finale had finished, Ted

thought it a good idea to launch himself off the stage in the style of Kung Fu Panda, shouting out how no one was to mess with him. In the process he toppled a teacher off her chair and tore a large hole in his tracksuit so everyone could see his underwear. No doubt, this will be what everyone talks about for years to come. I suspect clips will make their way on to some Saturday night outtakes show. The children come running in at this point, past us and to the table filled with flimsy cups of neon squash. When they see us they wave and we give them all hugs for their efforts before they fly off again to play with friends. A tap on my shoulder and I turn around to see the sprightly young lady from before. Matt looks her up and down.

'I'm sorry. I just wanted to introduce myself … given you've been sleeping with my husband and all …'

Matt, Ben, and I freeze as she laughs. Gia looks like she might throw her cup of tea at her.

'I'm Lindsay. Sam Pringle's wife.'

Matt still can't seem to move his face whereas I finally get the joke and laugh nervously so that I cloud the air with biscuit crumb. I go to shake her hand. Ben goes to explain everything to Gia in a hurried mix of what sounds like Spanish and GCSE French.

'Jools. Campbell. I am so sorry about all of that. I was mortified that events got so twisted.'

She puts an arm on my shoulder.

'Oh, we had a good laugh about it. The school made a statement on our behalf as well. I just wanted to wish you luck for Friday. Sam and I are rooting for you. We even have that poster from *The Sun* on our kitchen fridge.'

Yes, *The Sun* poster. An A3 monstrosity that came with yesterday's issue which you could stick on your front window, fridge, or as I saw it yesterday, in a car window to pledge your allegiance. 'Campbell's SouperMum!' or 'Masterchef McCoy!' For one, I'm worried my new moniker looks a bit like a really bad typo. The picture is of me waving my finger at McCoy on the BBC sofa, mid-gurn and looking like I have multiple chins.

'That's very kind. To be honest, I need all the help I can get.'

She smiles as Mr Pringle approaches us, buoyant at the success of the play and that Ted falling off the stage was the only minor mishap. There are kisses and congratulations all round.

'I mean Ben studied drama so he knows his stuff.'

Ben nods even though I know this is far removed from the experimental, nouveau-street theatre he is normally accustomed to being involved in. Mr Pringle is all smiles; this isn't the first time I've seen him since our whole newspaper debacle but he's been very good at glossing over any awkwardness for Hannah's sake and making light of the situation. His wife's hand goes into his while Matt and I let the initial panic of her introductions wash over us. They're a sweet couple, in those early throes of new marriage where I suspect frequent sex and date nights still figure quite highly. I notice her look over my shoulder and suddenly grimace.

'So are they the ones, Sam?'

I turn to see Paula, Jen, and their family entourages standing behind me, collectively mocking the biscuit selection with old lady carryalls. I smile at Matt. Mr Pringle nods but whispers something under his breath. Ben realises this is his cue to leave and stand next to Gia and Millie while Matt and I lean in to try and make out what he said.

'I have half a mind to ...'

'Linds, seriously not here.'

I sense the urgency in his voice and back down, fake smiling like I might not be interested in what she says next. She turns to me and whispers into my hair, 'You know it was them, right? The ones who took the photos of you and Sam and sold them to the papers.'

My head swings round to face them. Matt's nostrils flare quite unattractively.

'Another mother dobbed them in. Completely pathetic if you ask me. And as for their other behaviour ...'

Their what? It was them, really? Was this payback for having given Paula's kids fish fingers? My mind spins as I try to decide how I should deal with this news. Lindsay gets in there first, and before I know it she's waving at Paula, who sashays over. Of course, she ignores me and has done ever since McCoy labelled me a food cretin, but now I know why. Guilt. Do I miss her? Christ, no. But I miss the satisfaction that comes from looking after her kids. Their guts must be aching for a bit of gluten right about now.

'Hello. I'm Paula Jordan. And you are?'

'Lindsay Pringle. We spoke once. I think you called my house once at three in the morning?'

What? Did she just say that? Or have I eaten too many custard creams? Paula goes a shade of pomegranate while Matt and I take two sidesteps to the left. I hand Matt a chocolate bourbon. There is some fantastically awkward silence. Greg looks at his wife curiously. Mr Pringle tries to pull his wife away, as Ben acts as Gia's dodgy interpreter. Plus, he's holding a sandwich. There are sandwiches?

'We've been calling about school matters, actually,' says Paula, not very convincingly. 'I find your insinuations quite curious.'

Lindsay looks like she's gearing up for a retort while her husband stands there, eyes to the school parquet flooring. Ben has a selection of sandwiches – tuna, cheese and pickle, and, ka-ching, egg mayo. I scan the room with one eye on sandwich alert while the other scans the conversation in front of me.

'Important school matters, actually.'

It's a voice so loud and haughty I look to the ceiling to see if it is God himself. No, just Jen Tyrrell. I've never spoken to Jen Tyrrell in my life. Mainly because she's the sort of person who doesn't let you get a word in edgeways but also because there's an air about her as though she think she's better than you and everyone else in the room. She strides over with her husband, Hugh Tyrrell, the heavy treader in all this, the muscle, though I can't make out if he ever has an opinion on anything or is simply henpecked into submission. Ben shifts me a look, less confused, more excited that his graduation present is going to contain an actual live fight. He takes Gia and Millie off to stand behind the curtains.

'Well, if by that you mean ringing at eleven thirty in the evening after you've downed a bottle of red to tell my husband how you haven't had sex in a year then that sounds particularly pertinent to school matters, yes.'

Lindsay Pringle in your lemon yellow tea dress and Monsoon cardigan – you are officially my most favourite person who exists. I see Sam Pringle turn a lovely shade of beetroot. Ben chokes on his tea, Matt's eyes open up like they could fall out of their sockets. I want more! Who hasn't had sex in a year? But from the way Paula's face drains of colour (which isn't actually that hard given how pale she is) I think I know the answer. You drink wine? I thought you only drank mung bean tea. Our post-play date conversations could have been far more interesting if you'd told me you drank alcohol. Jen Tyrrell makes a valiant attempt to spare her BFF'S blushes.

'Your husband has been a confidante to all the mothers in the class.'

'But how is that his job? His responsibilities are to look after your kids, not you.'

'Linds …' Sam grabs her arm but she hasn't had her say.

'And to top it all off and make your coffee mornings all the more interesting, you make up stories about him and Mrs Campbell to entertain you and earn you a quick buck. Frankly disgusting behaviour.'

Hey, that's me! Jen Tyrrell glances over at me a little evilly. Not knowing what to do, I put a hand up in the air like I'm acknowledging my name has just been said. Lindsay just shakes her head. Paula sidles up to her at this point, trying to draw attention away from her sexless marriage. Parents next to us have started to crowd around like they're here to watch a hanging. Sam Pringle finally gets a word in.

'Mrs Tyrrell, Mrs Jordan. I am appreciative that you want to involve me in your kids' lives but I am a teacher, there are boundaries, and to make up stories is just plain wrong and completely inappropriate. It sends a really bad message out to the kids.'

It's a statement so official that I wonder if he's been trained by Luella. But it's a final word on the matter, we don't have to draw it out any further. Maybe I can go and find a sandwich. Or not.

'I'm inappropriate? Really?'

Mr Pringle's shoulders seem to slump back into their sockets as he realises what he's done has not so much drawn a line in the sand but created a sandstorm of angry mother.

'What I meant was …'

'If I'm inappropriate then what about Mrs Campbell here?'

Woah, that's me again! But I'm inappropriate? Is it this top? I pull a shocked and confused face. Angry and Scottish to the left of me barges in.

'Excuse me?' he half bellows.

Matt is ready to charge at her like a, well, rhino, but I hold his arm back.

'Ever since her little rant in the supermarket, I can't think of anyone more inappropriate than her. Flaunting herself in the public eye, all those stories about her mother and her ex-boyfriends and family.'

Paula nods, still trying to detract from the fact that good ol' Greg Jordan can't bear to sleep with her. Lindsay Pringle looks at me and smiles in support. Matt might be foaming a little out the corners of his mouth.

'What sort of message is she giving my kids? That it's all right to get pregnant when you're twenty, marry someone you hardly know, and reject your own mother?'

Silence descends over the crowd like fog. Jen Tyrrell has been publicly put down and man, is she coming back with a vengeance. Damn Donna leaving early. I am quiet, my jaw is locked. I look over at Gia, who obviously doesn't understand half of what has gone on but wishes she could get involved. I look over at Matt, who's speechless with rage, and I look over at my kids standing by the doors to the hall. Jake and Ted at the front, Hannah towards the back, squash in hands trying to make out words from behind reinforced glass panels. Matt and I look at them and realise retaliation is futile when they're party to these events. They've already endured so much at school, they don't need this. We have to take the high road.

'We all know what you're about, Jools Campbell. You're trying to make out you're some celebrity mother or chef but I can't think of anyone less qualified to talk about such things.'

And there it is, the final poisonous dart fired, leaving me reeling from the fact it's been let out into the air like that. I feel my eyes glaze over, like skin over custard.

'And who are you again?'

I don't recognise the voice at first; maybe because he's made an effort to sound authoritative like a knighted Oscar-nominated actor – a bit Gandalf trying to scare off a dragon. I turn and he slips a hand into mine.

'Jennifer Tyrrell. And you are?'

'Ben Hartley. Jools's brother. Can I ask your qualifications as a mother then?'

'Well, I … that's not what I meant.'

'Well, from where I was standing, it sounded like you may have a masters on the subject, a doctorate perhaps?'

He turns to face the crowds in the same way one might in the Globe during a meaningful soliloquy. I can tell he more than half likes the attention and the wonderful acoustics.

'Trust me, half of what you read in the papers is rubbish, much like a lot of what just came out of your mouth.'

Jen Tyrrell glares at Ben, framed by her husband and her furry cardigan. What possesses a woman to buy a garment like that? What possesses a mother to have such a sour personality? The people around us stand to attention.

'And are you a parent? You know then what it's like to have kids and have experience on the subject?'

'No. I am not a parent.'

'Then how does this concern you?'

'Because I'm the person in this room who probably knows Jools the best. Yes, as you've kindly pointed out to everyone today, she was twenty years old when she became a mother …'

I look over at Ben, who refuses to look me in the eye else I collapse into floods of tears.

'But trust me, she was also a mother long before Hannah ever came on the scene.'

He pauses, half pouting, half trying to hold back what I hope are not drama student tears.

'So to berate her in front of everyone here only shows your insecurities, your jealousy, and is a great insult to someone I hold very dear.'

I grab his arm and pull down on his sleeve, trying hard not to cry. The crowd is moved. Unfortunately, this only eggs Ben on.

'And I am very proud of her. Better to go out into the world and have a dignified opinion on parenthood as opposed to having a career as a tanorexic middle-aged woman in badly fitting Matalan, spreading gossip to entertain herself.'

Lindsay Pringle snorts a little. Matt stands there immensely proud of his brother-in-law, his chest out. I close my eyes in preparation for the inevitable Tyrrell comeback.

'And how old are you?'

'I'm not sure how that's relevant but I am twenty-one.'

'Because I take great insult from someone half my age spouting diatribes about my life. Your youth reeks of ignorance.'

You can tell half the crowd are doing some simple maths in their head.

'Your age reeks of regret, bitterness, shades of vindictiveness.'

I look over at Jen, who is running out of words, out of plausible ways to defend herself in the face of such eloquence and calm. She panics.

'Well, at least I knew my husband before I married him.'

If Matt was a cartoon character he'd go ten rounds with this woman like Popeye. But he is restrained for the kids and his mother and simply shakes his head and holds my hand in response. I'm surprised if his tongue is still attached given how much he'll have to bite into it. I want to be angry, so angry. But for some reason I refuse to be. I can't think of anything bad to say when my kids are glaring at me like that from that door. If they weren't, though, it would be too damn easy to just lay into her. You want to talk about husbands? From what I hear Greg Jordan shags the nanny at the park! In the bushes by the tennis courts! Donna also reckons Hugh Tyrrell has a fondness for trying on his wife's shoes. Other parents around us think differently and are aghast at the low blow, others are just glad for the entertainment.

'You're telling me you knew you were going to marry some

overweight, hirsute man? Wow. I applaud your good taste, lady,' adds Ben.

The room shudders a little with laughter. Surprisingly, a sweat patch-addled Hugh Tyrrell doesn't flinch. Paula and Greg seem less interested in being involved in this fight now. Greg's eyes seem to dart around the room with worry that everyone might think he's impotent, Paula knowing she'll never be able to take on the verbal prowess of my little brother. Jen just stands there, boiling in her furry cardigan, part furious, part indignant that her family life is being picked apart bit by bit. Welcome to my world, Jen Tyrrell, welcome.

'Just … just … go to hell, you jumped up little fag!'

I'm not sure what happens next. Speaking for myself, all I know is that the little part of my brain that is dedicated to loving my family and being a mother, that goes all lioness when people try and infringe on my little unit, starts to fizz in my head. This deserves a breaking of silence. I'm gearing up for a McCoy style rant. I look over at the Pringles, all open-mouthed in shock. I look over at Matt whose eyes are so wide they almost glow white. Ben stands there, eyebrows raised from not having heard that word since the late nineties. Words line my throat as I go to speak. But I'm too late.

'That's IT! Get the hell out of my school. NOW!'

People suck in air like vacuums. I turn to see Mrs Whittaker, face red like rhubarb, quite literally. Even her ears pulsate bright pink. Mr Pringle steps in and holds her hand back.

'Alice, please, you'll …'

This isn't even a tumbleweed moment. Parents, children, and other teachers stand about like this is huge game of Stuck in the Mud. Jen opens her mouth so wide you can see she still has some old metal fillings at the back.

'In all my years of teaching, I have never met a more malicious and small-minded woman. I will just about tolerate your tattle-mongering but you have just sat through a play about diversity and come out with language like that. You owe Mr Hartley an apology.'

'Never.'

I'm not sure exactly what to do. Even Millie has paused to

absorb all the drama. You can see it in Jen Tyrrell's eyes. Get out of my way. Ben looks to the floor in shame. Gia's eyes pop out from behind the curtains.

'How dare you! I will be talking to the school governors about this on Monday.'

Her eyes are all demonic at this point, so much so I can't bear to look at her.

'Please do. Alice Whittaker. Do you want me to spell that for you?'

'This is a disgrace.'

'What? Your behaviour? I couldn't agree more. Now leave.'

Jen stares her down before finally caving and dragging her sorry entourage out of the room. Everyone breathes again as they leave. Children run into parental arms. My mouth is still open, crumbs of custard cream all over my bottom lip and in my hair. Matt looks at me and over at Mrs Whittaker, whose glasses have fogged up, her face still pink, massaging her liver-spotted hands as Mr Pringle drapes his arms over her, embracing her tight.

'Alice, you shouldn't have said …'

'I know. But that wench has had it coming. I'm sorry, Mr Hartley, that you had to hear that in our school. And I'm sorry, Mrs Campbell, that I couldn't do more to step in earlier.'

I shake my head. She did enough. Enough to have given the conversation some finality. Ben, on the other hand, tips his head to one side. I know he'd never be offended by an offhand insult from someone he didn't even know. But I know what he's thinking. That was bloody awesome! Best graduation present ever! When do I usually have the chance to accost and publicly harass middle-aged harpies? When do I have the chance to have such an attentive audience? Can I come again next year? Then he looks over at me and gives me one of those big, colourful Ben smiles, the sort I like, the sort that makes it impossible for me to hate him, or at least think there was something in the middle of all of that that was meant just for me.

CHAPTER TWENTY-TWO

'Daddy! We need more of a smile. Lu, can we get Daddy to relax?'

I'm looking over at Matt perched on the end of the sofa, mouth curled up like he might be passing wind or trying not to swear in front of the children. Darius, the photographer, head to toe in black with strange, studded trainers stands there with his hip out and a glazed look in his eyes. This isn't high fashion with Kate Moss nor über cool David Bailey portraiture, this is a family photo with two boys who can't keep their tongues in their mouths. Foundation runs slick down my face as I try to garner some Campbell family spirit.

'C'mon, guys. Just one photo. Let's do this and then we can all get ice cream.'

The children freeze. Matt doesn't look convinced. I'm trying to think if I have any ice cream. Luella keeps gesturing over at Matt, who looks a bit Wallace and Gromit. Then for a split second, we all turn to the camera, we are all still. C'mon you wanky Shoreditch twat, take the sodding photo. Snap. Breathe. The children launch themselves off to the kitchen. Darius bobs his head around as he previews the image.

'Yeah, we might have something, Lu. Guess it's better than nothing.'

Matt looks like he wants to stamp on his camera in a Jude Law style frenzy. I put an arm around him.

'Think of the money.'

It's not six figures. It's not four figures, but even I can see in Matt's face that nothing is worth this embarrassment. He rolls his eyes about and I try to catch his gaze as people scurry about us. Look at me, please. Things with Matt still remain at this big juncture where we don't talk about the important, key points of our relationship but just keep calm and carry on. Richie Colman was a hiccup in the greater scheme of things, chased out of our lives by Gia, but deep down, I think we both know we still have to take the time to sit down and lay ourselves bare, to validate our relationship to ourselves. But now is not the time or the place. I just watch as he gets up to leave, following the children into the kitchen as I hear the scraping of the freezer drawers in search of ice cream that isn't there.

Today is the day I finally allowed photographers into my house instead of having them jump out of bushes at me. The cooking showdown looms in one and a half weeks and now, Luella says, is the time to up the ante. Even more now since the appearance of Tommy's nine page spread in *Hello!* of him and the McCoy collective curled up looking smiley and glowing in their second home in Cornwall. But it's OK! Quite literally. Because Luella has bargained us a deal with the other side. It will make me come across better to the public, she reckons, instead of having my photos nestled against photos of polo matches and Pippa Middleton. However, given my house is not some bio-degradable, greenhouse gas friendly Skandium furnished lighthouse in the middle of Cornwall, Luella's had to give the house a slight cosmetic makeover, hence the fluffy purple pillows and luxury throws. Never mind the kids, who are Monsoon-tastic. I watch as Millie sits on the throw and rolls her fingers over it. What is this material? This is not polyester? She drools in admiration, leaving a mark that makes me think we won't be able to return it to Heals tomorrow.

'So Jools, this is Polly from *OK!* and she'll be doing the interview segment. Will Matt be joining us?'

I can hear him next door, also frustrated by the lack of creamy frozen goodness. He's trying to placate the children with fruit. This will never work. I also hear Gia's voice in the background telling the children she has gum in her handbag. The kids have started a mutiny.

'Maybe later?'

Luella senses discord and quickly covers up any blemishes.

'Sure. I mean, you guys don't have nannies to help you out so they might need to juggle. Hope that's OK, Polly.'

She shrugs and sits down. I nearly sit on Millie. Luella

scoops her up in time and expertly places her on my lap. I laugh. I'm not sure why. Luella looks from behind Polly's shoulder like I need to take this more seriously or not laugh like I'm a giggly drunk.

'So thanks for inviting us to your home and giving us the chance to meet your family. You've kept them out of everything so far, is there a reason for this?'

What I should say: Well, yeah, they're kids. I'm their mother, not their pimp. To whore them out for my own purposes would be bordering on exploitation. It's what McCoy does all the time and to be honest, I find it disgusting.

'Ummm, this little media circus that's erupted around us is a little intimidating and a lot of stuff that's been written has been quite harsh. I want to protect them from that. As for my husband, he's a little shy and private and I respect that he's not asked for any of this.'

Luella does a mini thumbs up.

'So why involve them today?'

Because Luella told me to?

'I guess people are interested in my family, so to have a candid peek at what my house is like can't hurt. Rather they're photographed in the comfort of their own home as opposed to in the street or outside school.'

Polly seems fine with this answer. I look at her curiously. She's all tulip skirt and Victoriana blouse with men's brogues. She's making me, in my comfy leggings and big jumper, look a little unfashionable and shapeless.

'I respect that. So tell me about your house. How long have you lived here for?'

I pause for a moment. This was not in the list of anticipated questions that Luella had prepared for me. I am wondering what she wants to know, my interior designer preferences? The year of building? Why, yes, I believe this corner feature is inspired by the famous Swedish designer, Johannes Ikea – your classic Billy bookcase.

'We've been here for seven years now, since we moved back to London after university and it's, well, a little cosy for six but it's home.'

Millie smiles at this point, which warms me to think she approves of this little hobbit hole we've decided to raise her in. Not sure she'll be as accommodating in five years when we realise we don't have a bedroom for her and she'll have to sleep in the hallway.

'Any reason you decided to live south? You went to uni in Leeds, right? And your hubby is Scottish.'

I feel ambushed again in a Kitty McCoy kind of way. I wanted to live near my dad? At the time, I was scared of Matt's mother? A voice interrupts.

'It was a work thing. Kept us down here, plus having grown up in Edinburgh, I'm not sure I wanted to expose my children to the cold just yet.'

Polly smiles. Was that rude to Edinburgh? Matt has in his hands a multipack of Cornettos that was either hiding in the icy depths of my freezer or bought by Gia down the petrol station on the corner. He offers them around and Luella looks slightly worried, like we should be offering the fancy reporter type espresso as opposed to a strawberry ice cream cone. Polly doesn't seem too fazed.

'Oooh, haven't had a Cornetto in ages. Yes, please. How retro.'

Cornettos are retro? I always thought that was the job of the Feast. Matt smiles and comes to sit down next to me, offering Millie a little bit of cone and chocolate sauce. Millie, being Millie and a Campbell, doesn't refuse. I wonder if this will make its way into the article.

'So, Matt? What are your thoughts on your wife's sudden rise in the celebrity world?'

Matt looks over at me thoughtfully.

'Well, it's been a bit of a shock but I think she's handled herself very well in the press.'

I look over at him and grab his ice cream free hand. Polly notes this down. Suddenly, three extra children descend on the room, ice creams in hand and around mouths. Luckily, this might keep them quiet but I see Luella's eyes go to the soft furnishings, especially with Ted who brandishes his ice cream like a sword.

'You don't mind, do you? I can get them back in the kitchen.'

I am all too aware I've made my children sound like a pack of dogs but Polly laughs and shakes her head.

'Oh no! Actually, I have some questions for them if that's OK?'

Hannah sits to attention. The twins twist their noses up like they've been asked to recite their spellings.

'So, tell me. What do you think of Mummy's cooking?'

The room freezes for a moment. The twins look thoughtful like this might be a trick question. Matt grabs my thigh. Millie drools into her father's lap. Hannah is the only one to speak.

'I like her spaghetti carbonara.'

Matt swizzles his head around. I look into space, thinking about all the dishes in the world. Hannah has never professed a liking for that one.

'I like spaghetti with creamy sauces and she does that one well and it's not from a jar.'

Polly laughs. The twins still seem to be registering what they like to eat. Please don't say baked beans, please don't say toast.

'Mummy makes good mashed potatoes,' says Ted.

'... and the best scrambled eggs,' adds Jake.

That could have been better, that could have been worse.

'Well, tell me what you had for dinner tonight.'

The boys realise this is more straightforward and Ted sticks his chest out, knowing he has the answer.

'We had fruity chicken with couscous.'

Polly nods her head, almost impressed, and looks my way.

'So do the children eat a lot of international cuisine?'

Again, I am ambushed. It's couscous, it's hardly a tagine cooked over a wood fire. I cook couscous because it's my friend – damn that I didn't think to cook that against McCoy: pour hot stock over it, it's done, and the kids like it. Though it'd be good if they could keep it on their forks, I can see a big clump of it on the bottom of Matt's sock and some in Millie's hair. I wonder if Polly will write how my kids had big, fat, couscous-shaped nits.

'I try.'

Though again, the chicken part is only half Moroccan because I put a pinch of cumin in it and some chopped-up apricots. In my house, international extends to Greek (feta and black olives), French (brie and a whole head of garlic), and Hawaiian (a tin of pineapple rings).

'Well, we certainly have a lot of Italian with my background but Jools does a good stir fry, fajitas, and we've tried the kids with mild curries and things like satay and sushi.'

Yes, indeed we have. Matt is being so diplomatic given the sushi was fresh from the supermarket and the curries were ignored with the children opting for the poppadums and mango chutney. I'm wondering why I can't remember anything. Luella looks mightily pleased with herself and the way the interview is going.

'But the sushi tasted like the sea. It wasn't so great,' pipes Jake.

Hannah elbows him in the ribs. Polly leans in close to him.

'Don't worry, I'm not a fan either.'

Jake laughs and pulls a face at Hannah.

'And what do you guys think about Mummy cooking on the television against Mr McCoy?'

The room goes silent again. We haven't told the children that much about what's been happening, trying to keep things as normal and stress-free for them as possible. Hannah looks over at me.

'That man from the supermarket? You're cooking against him? Like a competition?'

The children raise their eyebrows at me. Even they know what a completely deranged idea it is.

'Who?' asks Ted.

Hannah whispers into his ear and Ted realises who she's speaking about.

'Him? I hope you beat him, Mummy. He wasn't very nice to you. And he has silly hair.'

Polly smiles. Jake starts to laugh deep from inside his nostrils.

'Yeah, I hope you get to cook like a ninja and take him down.'

Now it's Matt's turn to giggle. Yes, why didn't I think of that? We could cook in ninja pyjamas. There could be knife throwing involved. Jake has his hands out ready to karate chop. Polly shows Ted an article about McCoy in her folder, talking about how all the pork in his restaurants have regular massages in cherry brandy and walk in lush green pastures with dandelions and views of the sea. He turns his nose up to see McCoy's face. I love you, Ted.

'So Mummy, what do you win at the end?'

It's a very good question. My self-respect, perhaps, a moment to go back to at the end of my days and say hey, Warhol was right. I had my fifteen minutes but they weren't wasted in *Big Brother* or singing karaoke week after week; I beat McCoy to a pulp and won a small battle for hard done by mothers across the land.

'Well, nothing. But …'

'Then why do it?'

Polly looks at me curiously. I freeze. Because in all of this, I have been starting to question my double standards. Matt looks down at his knee knowing that from the start he's always had his reservations about my dalliance with this intrusive, media-based career. So why? I only agreed to this stupid cook-off because McCoy provoked me. I should have done what I tell the kids to do, back down and smile sweetly, take it all on my blotchy chin. I should try and reclaim some sense of normality for the kids to avoid them being bullied at school, to not let them question whether their family is falling apart. Am I doing this for the money? The promise of a book deal? Meagre sums for guest appearances on UKTV food channels that no one will really watch? I don't even know any more.

There was a lie I told myself that maybe I was doing this for me, to prove that beyond being this half-baked mother to four children, there was a university-educated girl with goals and aspirations higher than building things out of Meccano and learning how to reverse park into really small spaces outside a school gate. Was this my breakout chance for a career? To do something for myself? Yet the ritual humiliation that this is entailing is hardly boosting my morale in any way. My pause is long. Hannah sits up.

'Because mummies would rather listen to her than some silly man with silly hair.'

Matt and I give each other looks, wishing there was a way we could push the words back in. Polly laughs. Luella falls off the end of the sofa. They boys are satisfied with such explanations. Matt continues.

'Hannah's right in a way. The best thing about my wife is that she's not perfect and she acknowledges it and lets other mothers know it's fine. I'm not sure how it's come to be that someone like McCoy with all his sanctimony can be so popular.'

Hannah smiles, knowing she's been vindicated but unsure what half those words meant. Polly's hand starts to move quicker across the page. Luella cranes her neck around to see what she's scribbling.

'So is that how you feel about McCoy, Jools?'

Again, diplomacy addles my brain so much that I can't think of what I need to say about him. All that filters through my mind is wanker, wanker, wanker.

'I think we lead very different lives.'

Polly nods, expecting more, but I'm not going to give it. I just smile. I think it riles her a little, especially when she comes up with her next question.

'So Matt, you mentioned before your wife isn't perfect? What did you mean by that?'

Matt hesitates, especially as we see the kids sitting next to us, paused, eating Cornetto crumbs off the fronts of their jumpers.

'I mean, she's human. We're all flawed.'

His tone is abrupt, edging towards Angry Scot. He might need another Cornetto. I give Polly a forced smile through grinding teeth.

'I mean, our relationship is not some glossy magazine editorial. We've never been about keeping up appearances and purporting to always get it right. We don't. We just keep it real and work damn hard.'

I pause as he says that. How do we do that exactly? It's

funny how nine years down the line, you wonder what's changed. How has our relationship ever evolved? I'm not sure how it was supposed to – does love envelop and change you from the person you once were? Is it maintained by big monumental events that I can't remember? I'm quiet because I'm not sure how damn hard I've been working on us. Polly looks at me curiously.

'So is that how you're different from McCoy?'

Matt nods repeatedly.

'Seriously, to tell people you sit in your Cornish lighthouse and everything is organic and fine and dandy all the time is just a crock of sh …'

'It's just very far removed from their experiences,' pipes in Luella.

'I mean, what was that in their article in *Hello!*' Polly shudders to hear her rival's name uttered. 'We're so in tune … we never fight … we bring out the inner calm in each other. Seriously?'

Luella laughs under her breath. I give Matt a look wondering where and when he's been reading *Hello!* Polly turns to the kids at this point.

'So do your Mummy and Daddy fight then?'

Daddy glares at Polly, nostrils flared. Three words dart through my head: death by brogue. Hannah looks thoughtful. Ted looks a little proud of himself.

'They fight when Daddy leaves wet towels on the bed. Mummy says he's disgusting.'

Matt blushes a light rose. Jake pipes in.

'And once Daddy caught Mummy eating crisps in bed and called her a heifer.'

My turn to blush. Hannah joins in.

'But they don't fight like other mummies and daddies. Billy Tate said his mum chased his dad down the road with the iron once. My mummy's never done that.'

Polly nods. I wonder what Fiona Tate intended to do with the iron. I, for one, am slightly unnerved by what could be said, but Matt's priorities are obviously the children and how Polly's journalistic tactics are trying to dig for information via our kids, no less.

'Kids, why don't you go and see Nonna in the kitchen?'

They all get up to leave, Ted hugging Polly as he goes.

'Do you eat crisps in bed?' he asks, trying to gage the normality of the situation. Polly blushes, which I take to mean a yes – I'm guessing prawn cocktail. And with that he runs off. Matt closes the door behind them. Luella looks worried. He comes and sits down next to me.

'We do fight. Nothing to be ashamed of. I don't mind my kids seeing the cracks in our relationship as long as they see how we resolve arguments. To send the message out that everything is perfect 100% of the time is the wrong message.'

Luella is satisfied with this answer and nods at Matt's logic. Polly looks like she wants to dig further. Please Polly, don't.

'So with everything that has been in the press regarding past relationships, the details of your own and such, you mean you don't mind your kids reading about that?'

Oh no, she didn't. A big fat lump gets forged in my throat as I see Luella trying to catch her breath. The next response is critical. I should get in there first. But I don't.

'I mind the fact a lot of it is a load of made-up crap.'

Was that bad? I can't tell any more. Matt, strangely, is not fuming like he's been known to recently. He's on a light, animated simmer.

'So if I was to say the name Richie Colman to you …'

He would throw a cup of coffee at the wall and get his mother to chase them down the road. I hear the sound of Matt's teeth molars possibly shattering inside his mouth. Must speak.

'I would say he was someone from my past.'

Matt's eyes drop to the floor.

'Someone from a completely different time in my life. I thought it was incredibly tactless of him to have gone to the media with his story.'

Polly is not as much listening to me but watching Matt squirm in his seat. I put a hand on his knee to reassure him.

'I can see Matt is quite uncomfortable talking about him … Does he have a hold over your relationship?'

I look at Matt, straight in the eye.

260

'No.'

He looks at me, reading my face from the constellation of acne on my forehead to the curve of my chin. The squirming stops.

'Well, if we can get back to how you guys first met? People have been focused on how you were very young when you got together, how it was all a bit shotgun. Would you agree?'

I nod, even though I'm not sure what I'm nodding at given I know this issue has always hung around us like a pesky fly, doubt that just refuses to shift. I feel Matt's fingers interlock with mine and squeeze a little. I look over and he takes a deep breath.

'I'd agree. We were young, it was all a bit manic. But I did the right thing at the end of the day.'

I pause to hear what he has to say next. He did the right and honourable thing and that was to marry the girl he knocked up. He could have had a very different life had he not. He could have persuaded me to go the Marie Stopes round the corner and deal with things, he could have just up and left, but he was a good man. He did the right thing.

'I married, and have always stood by, someone I was completely in love with.'

And the room stops. Not that it was moving much. But my face goes a little numb. Luella's eyes shift from badass publicist to glazed over and affected. Polly has no choice but to smile.

'Love at first sight then?'

I turn to face him.

'Maybe. I think you can spend little more than a week with someone and know – everything's different. No pretence or games, it just works. And that's how it's always been with Jools. It just fits.'

Don't cry, don't cry. Too late. I tear up a little and pick at my eyelashes, pretending it's my mascara.

'And next to all the love stuff, we seem to work well together when it comes to parenting and running a house. Like good sidekicks, really.'

Luella laughs. Maybe at the idea of Matt in Batman tights.

'You OK, Jools? Do you feel similarly?'

I nod. There is so much to say. I never knew you saw our relationship so clearly, so logically. I love Matt. Of course I do. But I know I entered into our relationship tentatively – to say otherwise would be lying. I went with a gut feeling that everything would pan out all right, that he was a decent enough bloke to stick around. Matt looks over at me, eyes almost yearning for me to say something of equal emotional impact. This is the one and only time I will say something remotely loved up and mushy to you, woman. Time to 'fess up your true emotions. But I am mute. Was I really too blind to see how much he's loved me from the start? Has he always thought my love for him has been different – borne from obligation? Borne from a need to surround myself with a family of my own – repairing my own mother's mistakes?

'Yeah. I guess, it's just … I am very lucky.'

Polly nods, not quite believing me. 'That you are.'

Matt just looks down, the sound of a large gulp sounds like someone throwing a boulder off a cliff. I was the love of his life. And he is mine, he must be. But with Richie, there was the real sense of loss at the time, real emotions being stirred into motion. With Matt, it's always been plain sailing. And for someone as emotionally manic as myself, I do wonder about this lack of passion. Is it because it's lacking? Is it because I feel any less for him than I would another?

'To be honest, I envy relationships like yours.'

Everyone pauses. Polly scribbles away, not realising she's said something of greater significance than she's realised.

'What do you mean?' I ask.

'You got a man to commit to something at the age of twenty, my boyfriend is twenty-nine and we can't even get a cat together.'

Luella smiles at me and nods.

'Here you have someone uncomplicated, who obviously adores you, who gets you despite everything. That is very rare.'

I smile and look over at Matt, eyes still pointed at the carpet. I get it. You're here because you didn't want to be your mother. You stay here because it's convenient, because I gave you no other choice. But no. Nine years down the line, it can't be.

'He's right. It always fit. We got off to some strange, intense start but we fit. We've got on with life. Ninety-nine per cent of my life is just pure insanity and drama and then there's Matt who has just always been ...'

The epicentre of all that is normal, sane, and logical. And I cry. Because I'm not sure where I would have been for the past nine years without him. Sitting in a messy kitchen without the four maddest kids in the world, sidekick-less, without the love of my life. And it's as if something clicks and rains over my brain with guilt, with love, with a newly clarified logic about us.

'... he's always been the one thing that makes perfect sense ...'

There's no drama because when it comes to us, there's never been the need. Luella smiles and nods. Polly scribbles away, not realising she's done what we may have paid a therapist thousands to do. And for the first time, Matt looks up at me and smiles and even though he'd never admit to it, that might be a little tear in the corner of his eye.

CHAPTER TWENTY-THREE

Exactly thirty-six hours until T-Day, until I go on the television and try my damnedest to survive the cook-off from hell. Jake was right, why am I doing this? In the run-up, the newspapers and columnists are having a field day. There will be live blogs and William Hill have me at odds of 25-1 that I will cook McCoy under the table. Of course, McCoy is 3-1 to win the whole thing and by this time next year no one will ever remember who I am. The paps are back in my life. Mrs Whittaker (currently under review for bollocking Jen Tyrrell but assured to have her reputation bolstered by ninety-nine per cent of the parents at the school) regularly chases them out of the giant wheelie bins round the back of the school but a faithful few sit in cars by the hedges opposite the house. Mrs Pattak next door now has her curtains closed all day and when she sees me she says something in Hindi which sounds like either a curse or a prayer. I probably deserve both. This morning, the papers are all about McCoy. Apparently, because the recent floods in South East Asia are not nearly as important, McCoy has dyed his hair for the occasion. He's gone platinum blond. There are pictures of him exiting a salon with Kitty, who has had matching highlights done, others as he goes and makes an appearance at his gastropub, a final one of him kissing a baby. Below is a picture of me picking up the kids from school, make-up-free, book bags in one hand, Millie in the stroller covered in raisins, Hannah in a mood because I wouldn't let her go to a friend's house, and the twins pulling faces. The picture is circled by Luella, who sent it around this morning. A message is written underneath. MASCARA! IF YOU DON'T HAVE THE TIME, AT LEAST USE MASCARA! BRUSH YOUR HAIR! MAKE THE BOYS WALK BEHIND YOU! Adam comes in and sees me studying the picture, reading the message. He perches his chin on my shoulder.

'You don't look that bad. C'mon, McCock, the nineties called, they want their hair back.'

I laugh and put the paper down. Adam grabs a freshly baked muffin in one hand and a cup of coffee in the other, all Gia's doing, of course. Adam is here, he says, to lend support, but truth is he's here for the baked goods. He flicks through another McCoy article in *The Sun* while simultaneously feeding Millie bits of panettone.

'Apparently, he's been invited over to the United States to speak at fat camps and cook at the Oscars,' I inform him.

'Maybe he can stay there,' adds Adam.

I have no response because he's not going anywhere in the next couple of days. I just grab a muffin and stuff it whole and warm into my mouth. Carbs may be my only consolation in all of this. Maybe I can eat myself into a sugar coma and not have to do it. As I put my plan into action, Gia enters, eyeballing me because the baked goods are for the guests. My brother does what he always does when he sees Gia, which is to semi curtsey.

'Adam … you see *OK!* magazine?'

I roll my eyes as she gets her copy out from under the fruit bowl where I'd been hiding it and flicks through to the interview and the glossy pictures. Of course, it could have been a lot worse. They didn't mention the fact that Matt and I were snivelling wrecks declaring our admiration for each other, nor the fact that the kids thought McCoy had stupid hair. No, but they did say my family were colourful and spirited – I'm guessing code for hyper and uncontrollable. Adam scans through the photos, before a bit of baked goods flies out of his mouth.

'Did they? No, they didn't …'

Yes, they did. For some reason, which I attribute totally to McCoy's camp of media interventionists, they decided to Photoshop Millie's hair. She was now positively Ronald McDonald. Matt was fuming that they had the gall to digitally alter his daughter but didn't think his squinty eyes needed fixing in any way. Gia takes the magazine back.

'I think the family all very *bellisimo*. I like. I showing all the family in Italy.'

I nod, still a little on edge and stressed out. Gia hooks her arm into mine.

'I wash the stuffed toys and I throw away that plant in the bathroom, it smelling funny. Is there anything you are wanting me to do?'

I smile. Lots. You could run over McCoy, set fire to one of his restaurants, cook a chilli and pop it through a specially installed trap door on set halfway through, or bestow on me some special cooking power like a genie. I shake my head and pop in another muffin. White chocolate chips and raspberries dull the horror for now.

'You know I had a dream last night that halfway through your cooking, Tommy got Mum to appear through a curtain.'

I don't laugh. I don't even say a word. The fact is I wouldn't put it past him. Gia gives Adam a look.

'It was a joke, sis.'

I get a finger and jab it into his armpit, which makes Millie laugh to no end. I do it again. I haven't really spoken much to Adam since the whole mother reappearing from nowhere debacle but it doesn't looks like anything has fazed him too much in the ordeal. His psyche had already filtered her out and dealt with her not being part of his life. I half hate him for his psychological efficiency. It still nags at me a little, still pops into consciousness every so often and makes me stare at wall space for moments too long.

'So you heard anything more from ol' Dottie?' he asks.

I shake my head.

'Me neither, in case you were wondering.'

'I wasn't.'

Gia sits down quietly, pretending that wiping Millie's mouth needs far more concentration than it does. Adam then does what Adam does which is to squish my shoulders from the side in a half-hearted attempt at a hug. He's never quite enveloped me like Ben does but it's his way of letting me know he's on my side. I squish back. Adam looks out the back window of the kitchen, as far as his reflection.

267

'What did they look like?'

'The others?'

The brothers. I'm not sure if I gave the picture a second look but one of them was attempting to grow one of those bum fluff beards, the other had a tie-dye T-shirt on. I shrug my shoulders.

'I'm picturing two lads out there who are just carbon copies of me and Ben.'

'Another two of you? I shudder at the thought.'

He pushes my arm a little and gives me a look. Adam's looks are not as playful and bright as Ben's – they just seem to be loaded with something I can never quite make out, some level of emotion he's too scared to ever want to express. There's always a lot of nodding.

'I swear though, I never want to see Ben that fucked up again ... sorry, Gia.'

He turns to apologise but Gia has her hand in the air, almost as if she's allowing it for now. She catches my eye and gives me a smile. Gia has been particularly tactful regarding the situation with my mother, staying permanently on the side-lines through the furore, looking on as my brothers and I broke down in front of her and argued our way through it. Yet she was quiet, saddened, by the events. I only saw her comment to Matt, so he could translate for her how significant it was.

'She is a silly woman,' she suddenly adds.

Silly might be an understatement but Adam nods in appreciation of the fact that it's not just him who thinks so.

'I am sorry she is not the woman you want her to be. She is silly to not see how lucky she is to be having children like you.'

And then silence as Adam and I digest that final sentence. I smile. Gia, Gia, Gia – only three weeks ago you were bordering on being the mother-in-law cliché. But then something happened. You championed my family, you chased the ghosts of ex-boyfriends away, you kicked ass with copious amounts of homemade pasta. And while your visits used to be filled with awkwardness, a shade of forced sentiment, now there is something warming about having you around, the comforts you have provided from my kitchen, the way you organise my saucepans so they fit together like Russian dolls. Adam is still a little silent.

'Come, you must go for your rehearsal, no?'

I nod. She has her hand faced upwards and goes to touch my face like she's blessing me. I respect you now, mother of my grandchildren – go back into the world with the recipes I have bestowed upon you and continue your good work. But no. Instead, she places something in my palm.

'This for you, for tomorrow. Have faith, *mia.*'

I look down at my palm and open it to find a small, gold cross there on a chain. Adam, holding Millie, can barely contain himself from bursting into hysterics to see it. Yep, that's what I need. A fucking miracle.

12.36 p.m.

I'm not entirely sure where I pictured this Armageddon-style cooking showdown taking place. I thought I'd at least get a set of someone's house that wasn't actually mine but no, this place is bloody huge. The studio is cavernous, the walls all intertwined and not unlike the inside of the spaceship in *Alien*. If anything is going to intimidate me, it's all these wires and the metal hanging down like some sort of industrial accident waiting to happen.

'Seven minutes left!'

I'm here for a mini run-through with Luella. I am dolled up in a fifties-style dress with heels and accessories and my only audience member is Annie, who's here on her lunch break because her office is ten minutes away. To be honest, I'm not sure how today is helping me in any way, apart from making me very on edge. What seems to be most telling is that I cannot seem to cook under this sort of pressure. Leisurely *Saturday Kitchen* cooking where half of it is done for me, I can do. Four kids pulling my arms and hanging off my hips, I can do, but with Luella telling me constantly that I have minutes left, under the heat of the lights, and with people scrutinising my every move with questions, I fail miserably. I don't know why I cut my avocadoes like that. I just do. Jake would never give me

269

such a hard time. A voice booms on to set.

'Wow, Tommy! That smells amazing!'

I look over to the empty worktop next to me where Tommy McCoy is being played by a broom and Vernon is a microphone stand.

'You have to not appear distracted, Jools! Vernon will throw lines around like this and you can't let it get to you.'

I'm more distracted by the fact my salsa looks like it's been pissed on. Why is it so watery? I can't tell from this lighting either whether my guacamole is going grey or just looks rubbish. I squeeze more lemon on it. I then stand there for a moment staring at everything. Luella looks highly concerned.

'You have to appear proactive! Maybe wash something up?'

I look confused. Do I have to? This is the time at home when I'd be letting the food simmer away and sitting down to have a glug of tea and a read of a magazine. I nod and chuck things in the sink. Then I drain the rice and plate up.

'Three minutes!'

If Ted did this at home, I'd be tempted to throw him out the kitchen window. I spoon everything onto the plate as required and even have time to fold a napkin on the side. What's that thing that chefs do with their tea towels? Don't they wipe the sides of the plate down? I try to do that but it ends up an even bigger smudge on the side of the plate. I wipe it with my finger and see Annie laughing.

'Thirty seconds … twenty-eight …'

I'm done. I stand there and put my hands behind my back. I'm not going to wash up because I don't want to. I just grab some coriander and chuck it on the side.

'Ten, nine …' I let the other numbers wash over me so Luella can have her dramatic finish.

'STOP COOKING!'

Annie makes a faux angry face, which makes me giggle, and they both come down from their chairs to my workspace. I swizzle my hands around, presenting my food like I'm inviting them to play their cards right. They both look at it curiously.

'Well, you want to try it?'

Annie shrugs her shoulders and tucks in. Luella puts a

notebook down on the side where I can see that in the past hour, she's dedicated two A4 pages to my failings. She picks up a fork and fluffs at my rice.

'It's all right, Jools. Perfectly good chilli. Maybe a bit more spice, a bit more chilli powder?' says Annie. She comes and gives me a hug. Luella's lips twist around each other.

'Rice needs more seasoning, maybe, and I'd be tempted to ditch the coriander – devil's herb. The guacamole is a touch too sour as well.'

I nod. It's all entirely constructive so I'm sure I can use it to my advantage.

'But I have other things.'

I hold my breath.

'One. You can't wave at the audience with a big cat grin, the people at home won't know what you're doing and it'll just make you look demented.'

I was trying to be funny given my only audience member was Annie, but never mind.

'Second, I'm tempted to rethink the dress. You kept doing this plié-style bending at the knees like you were either breaking wind or had some issues down there.'

Annie laughs and salsa flies out her mouth.

'It's just, I'm not used to this set up. I'm usually on all fours getting saucepans out of cupboards so I find myself reaching down to get them.'

Luella pulls a confused face and nods.

'Well, maybe we'll have you in something a bit comfier. We look like we're trying too hard to turn you into Bree Van de Kamp. And we'll rethink the tribal bangles, you just kept getting shit caught in them.'

I nod. Annie grips on to my hand tightly.

'And I think we need to work on presentation and plating up. Nothing too artsy fartsy but this looks a little crude. A little like …'

A dollop of technicolour cat sick? I think about how I usually plate up, and that's to arrange the fruit into smiley faces.

'A little amateurish?'

'But she is an amateur,' Annie informs her.

'True. But this is school dinner plonked on a white plate, it's a little dull.'

Annie cocks her head from side to side. 'We could get some pretty earthen crockery to jazz it up a bit,' she adds.

Luella nods and takes notes.

'They do those great tapas-style plates with all the different sections; that could work?' she adds.

'Or maybe we could also bring in a mariachi band and ply the tasting panel with margaritas?' I tell them.

They both laugh yet Luella's eyes seem to question whether this could indeed be possible.

7.16pm

After my run through, I dashed across London to pick the kids up and found that Hannah's class had made me a good luck card. It made me cry for reasons I wasn't sure of – today, people were telling me I was headed for disaster and that the only things that would get me through were miracles, luck, and alcohol. So I went with the latter; got home, opened up a bottle of white wine, and started drinking.

So now, I am completely relaxed and watching *The One Show* for I suspect the same reason everyone else does, because it's before the good telly and there's nothing else on the other channels except news. Luella has been here with her last-minute pep talks and is now gone. The children potter about the house, Dad cooks dinner with Millie, and I am getting drunk. This feels almost surreal. Like any other day. Not that I'd be midweek drinking – there are still a hundred and one things to do before day's end. It feels like nothing and everything could happen tomorrow. Yet I still feel nothing. I down another glug of wine. Maybe it's the wine. I slump into the sofa and feel a lovely, oozy, warm feeling about my shoulders. This midweek drinking has happened a lot recently. Not sure if I've done this much since I was a student. I sit there and think about what's changed since then. For one, I don't dye my hair stupid colours any more. I don't use batik wraps as curtains nor drink two

272

pound bottles of wine from Spar. But some things remain the same. Matt, my poor attempts at an exercise regime, the fact I still don't have a mother, and that I have big, fat debts hanging over my head. I down half a glass of Chile's finest. A little person comes in and sits down next to me, snuggling their head into my armpit. Hannah.

'Is that Kitty McCoy?'

I am so half-drunk, I hadn't noticed. Yes, it is. She's talking about tomorrow and wears a strange tabard-style shift under which you can see her bra. Are people allowed to do that at her age? I think about the greying quality of my bras in the drawers upstairs: the comfortable cotton, the downy bits of lace, the dying nursing bras stained with old milk. Then I have a thought that maybe I can wear one tomorrow and the shock of seeing something so horrific would mean no one would look at my cooking. I look back at Kitty. Even her elbows shine like she's been polished. Her hair is so golden and glistening, the studio lights make her look like Christmas. I nod.

'I'm glad she isn't my mummy.'

I stop for a moment and look at Hannah and smile.

'Why's that then?'

'She just doesn't look like that much fun.'

I infer this to mean I might be fun. I'm not skinny or blonde or boobsy but I am fun. I'll take that.

'Harriet's mum's like that. When we head out the house, she's got to make sure her shoes match her outfit and Harriet says she won't leave the house without lipstick, not even to go and buy milk.'

She stares at the screen with an inquisitive brow as I sigh thinking how glad I am she perceives such vanity over one's looks to be a failing. Then I sigh again thinking how I've sometimes gone into that petrol station on the corner with a pyjama top tucked into my jeans and a beanie over my bed hair.

'So are we coming to the TV place tomorrow?'

I nod.

'Yep, Uncles Adam and Ben are coming too … and Aunty Annie. You'll all be there to watch.'

She snuggles in close. Watch as your mother suffers a

breakdown in front of the nation. Who wouldn't want their eight-year-old there to witness that?

'Then why are you sad, Mummy? Don't be sad. Has Tommy McCoy been saying nasty things again?'

Well, kind of, but I don't tell her that. I shake my head.

'Is this about your mummy?'

I shake my head again, wondering where all this empathic insight came from.

'You think my mummy makes me sad?'

Hannah shrugs her shoulders and nods.

'You like to cry. Like when people die on *EastEnders*. Or when we watch *X Factor* and people talk about their kids and stuff. You get sad a lot.'

She makes me sound like a big blubbering fool. Is it healthy for your child to see that much crying?

'Well, people can be sad sometimes about stuff. You sad about anything at the moment?'

She shakes her head. This fills me with a big sense of relief.

'I get sad when you're sad. That's all.'

Big swirls of white wine push something inside my brain and the tears start to fall and roll down my cheeks. Hannah's face turns to ash to think she might have said something untoward in all of that. She jumps on my lap and holds me tight. I call them thunderstorm hugs – they crush your ribs and make your tongue stick out of your mouth like a frog. I look down at her body laid over mine. When did she get so tall? She literally takes up three quarters of me. When did her brain get so big and full of information? I remember the days when we used to sit in our bedsit in Leeds and spend the time looking through library books, and she'd test me on theories of pro-social behaviour and short term memory. Now she is so many things. She has more hair. She doesn't spend all day in her pyjamas. She has a small overbite that will probably need braces in three or four years' time. Little Hannah Banana. Maybe you are the reason why things are as they are now. If you hadn't been conceived, would I still be with Matt? Would I have four kids? Would I be married and about to appear on national television? Probably not. She doesn't seem to notice me staring at her, questioning the effects of her existence. She just hangs on tight and I squeeze her back. Dad enters the room and looks over at us. He sees my tears, he sees the half empty wine bottle on the floor. He nods his head and leaves the room, mouthing something as he goes.

'Dinner's up.'

'What we having, Grandpa?'

He smiles, oven gloves in hand.

'Fish finger pie. Ready when you are.'

I laugh so hard snot flies out my nose and into Hannah's hair.

2.34am

It's today, it's today, it's today. I look over at the clock. Technically, it is today but I don't sleep. I can't, I won't, I shan't. Occasionally I do drift off but the dreams I have are such horrific versions of possible events involving me spontaneously combusting, shitting myself, and severing digits that aren't my own that I wake up in cold sweats and find the room awash in that weird navy-blue colour that drowns out every sound and scent and makes me think I'm losing my grip on my sanity. Now I'm worried; that sort of pre-birth worry that everything on the other side of this event may be changed and irreparable for ever. Is this going to be one of those TV moments that live for eternity so in years to come, people will point and mock? So I don't sleep. I just lie there in my bed and think about all the things that fill me with dread and panic. My mum. My dad. My kids. Losing my kids. Kids being snatched off streets. Matt. Losing Matt. Matt having imaginary affairs with skinny women in his office who don't exist. Women who have nice shoes and don't wear knickers. Adam never finding love. Ben becoming some poor, slovenly actor who never gets a break. The fact my kids might grow up to hate me, or start carrying knives, or buy drugs from the ice cream van near the cemetery. Never being able to pay off our mortgage.

'Are you up? Go to sleep, Jools. You need to sleep.'

'I can't. I'm really cacking it.'

'The amount you drank tonight I thought you'd be dead to the world by now.'

After the wine came another bottle at dinner and then a glass of warm brandy before bed. Enough alcohol to have me miss a couple of stairs, not enough to make me comatose. I think about those fish fingers warming my guts, orange waves of artificial breadcrumbs partying with the white wine. My stomach churns.

'Talk to me, please.'

Matt rolls over and spoons me. I feel the warmth of his breath nest into the back of my neck, hands grab on to post-baby love handles. He does this so he knows he can sleep and I will talk into blank air like he's listening.

'Kitty McCoy was on television tonight. She's selling Baby Ganoush in tubs now. And a whole new range of fruit dips.'

'That's nice.'

'I've never made a fruit dip in my life.'

'Because there is no need to dip fruit. You can just eat it as it is.'

Silence.

Matt's quiet, his breath slowing down as he tries to fall back to sleep.

'What if I throw up on the food?'

'Parsley. Covers up everything.'

I nudge him in the ribs, thinking about that chilli I made today. Maybe vomit might help? I can feel Matt rubbing his feet together under the duvet. It helps him sleep. Little Hobbit hairs rub against my ankles as he does it.

'Do you think I can beat McCoy?'

He's quiet, asleep? He mumbles something I can't quite make out. I turn to face him.

'What was that?'

I see his eyes clamped shut. I put my finger up his nose.

'I think you're the bravest person I know for doing this but …'

But what, you half-finishing sentence fool? He looks me straight in the eye and then goes to hug me. I'm not sure what to feel. On the one hand, Matt has always been brutally honest with me. Yet on the other, I want him to tell me I will take McCoy down. I will cook him under the fake countertops and come out so victorious people will hold parades in my honour. Maybe I'll even get to wear a little crown. I want him to believe I'm at least capable. Why am I doing this then? To be a pawn in McCoy's media game, proving he's better than everyone? To put myself through this for the sake of bravery? I'm still thinking this as we're mid-embrace, wondering how this came to be, a semi-decent cook taking on the biggest chef in the land with his numerous accolades and bestselling tomes, when I feel something against my leg. My imminent failure has made my husband hard? I push him away.

'I'm glad the fact that I'm going to make a tit of myself on national television is so arousing.'

He laughs. Again, not very morale boosting. He brushes my hair from my face and looks at me again, the way Matt does, like he's studying my face for something I'm not sure is there. He then goes to kiss me so I won't press him for the answer he's not yet given me. Idiot. Idiot because it's almost working. This is not kissing like he normally does. It's soft, drawn-out, and attentive like we're in the back of a cinema. His hands are in a new place. Not on my boobs like they normally are, squeezing them like oranges. On my face, cupping my chin, tracing the outline of my cheeks. You bastard. Trying to distract me with nice kissing. He rolls on to me, our legs straddling each other, feet touching. His weight on me, he whispers into my ear.

'It will be fine.'

The sex or the cooking? I'm too tired to ask him which. I just let him cup my buttocks in his hands, trying to remove my knickers and kick them off the edge of the bed. It's always the same with Matt, safe, warm sex, like a hot water bottle except without the knobbly bit that gets stuck in your back. Even better than that. Maybe this will help me get to sleep.

7.10 a.m.

The sex did help me get to sleep. It was like being on a ship rocking its way to shore on a light current. Matt fell asleep inside me without coming, until I pushed him off and literally tucked him in. Then I rolled over and passed out myself. This time my dreams involved cooking on a boat like Keith Floyd, surrounded by wine and drinking myself into oblivion under the Greek sun until I didn't really care about what I was cooking. To be honest, it was very comforting.

The only thing is next morning, while Matt and I are in our semi-states of undress, we're woken up by Luella. Quite literally. She bursts into our bedroom, no knocking, no tea.

'Up, guys. Your dad let me in.'

She rubs her hands together as Matt tries to position himself under the duvet as so to not let on that's he's stark bollock naked under there. My dad?

'Action stations. Gia and your dad are downstairs making the breakfast and the twins are already watching *Rastamouse*. Chop chop. Hahahaha, how appropriate.'

She exits the room as I realise she was standing on my half-worn underwear at the foot of the bed. Outside, the sky is grey and the clouds hang low as if they know what today will bring. I feel my forehead to see if I am warm enough to carry a fever. No such luck.

Today is to be run with military precision, we know this as Luella printed out itineraries for us that she laminated and attached to every wall in the house. The children will go to school as normal. A people carrier will arrive at 12 p.m. to take myself and Luella to the TV studio. Dad and Gia, who are too nervous to be present, are going to stay at home with Millie and watch on our TV. Three o'clock and the kids will be picked up by Uncle Ben in another people carrier and dropped at the studio. Uncle Adam, Annie, and Matt will meet us at the studio at 6-ish. The live telecast will begin at 8 p.m.

So, for a day that starts at midday, I am curious as to why Luella is here at the crack of dawn. I pull on knickers and a dressing gown and find Millie sitting in her cot, hearing all the commotion. She puts her arms up to me, her hair all matted onto her face like a little red helmet. It's sad she won't be there to see this thing through with me. She was there at the beginning, when it all started. She faced off against Kitty McCoy like a faithful mini henchman. She endured a Photoshop disaster. Now she'll have to see the end via a television next to my dad. She puts her head against my chest and gives me what I'm going to call a hug. I'm here for you Mum, you can do this. That, and I need a new nappy.

Downstairs, the kitchen boils over with excitement and baked goods. Gia and Dad felt it necessary to start the day with stacks of doughnuts, pastries, and bacon sandwiches so the kitchen table is stacked high. Dad, who tells me he didn't sleep a wink last night either, came round early to help get the party started, as he puts it. He's jittery, too much coffee, too many nerves; so much so he's decided to unload my drawers and start rearranging the middle one, home to my potato masher and whisks. Next to the kitchen table are flowers. From Aunt Sylvia to Hugh Fearnley-Whittingstall to Mrs Pattak next door, there seems to be a torrent of good luck cards and floral arrangements. It's slightly funereal and a little overwhelming.

Next to that lies a big pile of newspapers Luella has presented for our deliberation. Matt is already at the table with *The Sun* that has my face opposite McCoy's like we're about to go five rounds. It's the headline and large picture usually reserved for World Cup Semi-finals or reality show finales. IT'S WAR! There might be some people in the Middle East who dare to question that.

I peer over Matt's shoulder and we have a two page spread with people's comments and columnists giving their predictions. One is very pro-McCoy, telling us that it's hardly worth the television minutes, while the other urges me on, trying to hype up the underdog. I pick up *The Guardian* and I've got Charlie Brooker giving his column's worth of opinion on the matter. It is as it usually is. A sprinkling of clever profanity mixed with his acerbic nonchalance about people and the world in general, but he is also profoundly anti-McCoy ('*he makes me wants to cut my eyes out, sauté them lightly with balsamic, and then squeeze lemon juice into my empty sockets*') so he wants me to win and while I'm at it '*put his testicles through a garlic press.*' Will do, time permitting. Outside we have four paps waiting in their cars and by the time the laptop is out, Twitter and Facebook (or Twitface as it's come to be collectively known in our house) is ablaze with comments and good wishes from the unknown. It's all a bit much. So I stuff my face with croissant and watch as everyone mills about. Croissants. Last time I ate one of these was in Sainsbury's, leaving big flaky pastry warts on my chin. I stop eating out of paranoia and grab a doughnut instead. Maybe I can resort back to the plan where if I eat enough sugar-based gluten products then I still have time to slip into some sort of coma, which means I won't have to be a participant in today's events. Maybe. I'm not sure what I feel. I am sure there is deep-rooted primal fear that will come to paralyse me as soon as cameras come on and I'm baked in foundation and fake tan (Luella's suggestion given I was starting to come across a bit *Twilight* undead). But for now I feel nothing. I feel numb with nothing. I think I might need to pee. That's about it. I don't think I want to cry, nor laugh, nor collapse into a big huddle of tears. I definitely want to run. But I'm not sure where to. Luella chatters like she's being run off a generator.

'You've got to love Brooker. Remind me we should send him something. Maybe some steaks.'

I nod. I should feel differently, I think. I should be jogging up and down the hallway and firing myself up, boxing the walls and gathering the family around for prayer as we hold hands and chant together. But nothing. It doesn't feel like Christmas, nor like the morning of a big exam. God, do I feel calm? The urgency to need to pee tells me otherwise. I hear the children next door fly off the sofa. Hannah enters and picks up a pain au chocolat, her hair like a fuzzy banshee.

'They're talking about you on the television, Mummy.'

Luella runs into the next room. Hannah comes over and drapes her arms around my neck. I stare out of the window and over the hedges to where there is a small sliver of sky in the distance, framed by telephone poles and untrimmed trees. Matt puts his hand into mine and looks in to my eyes, the same way he did last night before our clumsy attempts at passion. And he says nothing. I don't think he needs to. I just grab his fingers really hard until little crescents are left in his palm. The boys suddenly rush through the door and their eyes light up at all the baked goods. Everything is very quiet bar Ted sneezing from all the flowers. He jerks a sneeze right into Luella's coffee. No bogies, maybe she won't notice. Jake goes over and pesters my dad for a spatula that he can hit his brother with. Hannah turns to me, chocolate all over her fingers and smeared across her face like war paint.

'Tommy McCoy is such a gobshite.'

Huh? Matt chokes on his pastry.

'Han, where did you learn that word?'

'Bloke on the television just called him that.'

Matt shrugs his shoulders and smiles.

'Just don't use it again, all right?'

Hannah smiles. I am, however, in that state of confusion where I need to rub my temples. What the fuck is happening today? Where the hell am I? I move Hannah from my lap and go upstairs, into the family bathroom, and back against the door. I hear Luella's voice on the landing.

'Jools? Jools?'

I hear footsteps creak up. Shit, I need five minutes out of this. I need to breathe. There's a soft knocking.

'Please, Luella. I just need five minutes. This is all a little messed up.'

'Jools, it's me. It's your dad.'

I reach up and unlatch the door, going to sit on the edge of the bath. He comes and joins me, our toes embedded in the shag pile that Matt and I have never had the money nor time to replace even though we suspect it's been harbouring mould.

'Talk about your circus come to town.'

'Not my imagination then?'

Dad shakes his head and puts a hand on my knee.

'Do you still want to do this?'

'It's not a case of want, Dad. I have to. I signed a contract with the production company.'

He nods his head slowly. Maybe we can fake some appendicitis, get your hand stuck in a blender. He's also scanning through his well-rehearsed list of phrases meant to boost my spirits and make me feel better. He has many. Failed German GCSE mocks (not the end of the world, only Germans speak German); being dumped by Richie Colman (other fish in the sea); finding out I was pregnant with twins (could be worse, could be triplets). He's none too inventive but I've always felt, since Mum left, I've been his only key for tapping into the female psyche. It's meant he's always been cautious, never too judgemental else he'd scare me off too. I await my Dad Phrase of the Week.

'Then do it, love. Do it properly. Get your arse out there and hold your head up high. I'm not having some poxy bell-end of a TV chef make a fool out of my daughter. You go out there and show that wazzock what you're made of.'

I say nothing. I just fall backwards into the bath as we both collapse into fits of giggles.

CHAPTER TWENTY-FOUR

By the end of the morning, the nervous energy still bubbles over but in a nice Jacuzzi style rather than as before, when the bubbles were spitting violently and boiling over the edge of the pan. Hearing my dad's fighting talk and falling into the bath quite ungracefully, legs akimbo, shifted something. There's a little fighting spirit in me, mostly from the realisation that this hoopla surrounding the situation had mostly been orchestrated by McCoy to get at me and trigger the sort of response that would have me backed on to bathroom doors declaring I never wanted to see the outside world again. The bastard may have got to me just that little bit but I was surrounded by people who would pick me up again, the only people whose opinions I cared about. The kids were a huge pick-me-up as they left with their hugs and declarations of support, Matt even more so. So as people arrived to pluck, wash, and polish me down to within an inch of my life, I suddenly felt like I could take on the day and come out the other end. Maybe.

In the car over to the studio, I can't tell if Luella feels the same. She's quiet and seems to have my life down to two purple A4 lever arch files which she scans every so often, not while shouting to the driver to avoid flyovers and high streets because of the shitty traffic. I forget that this day probably means quite a lot to her in terms of getting one over on an ex-love.

Since she mentioned her history with McCoy I've let things lie, not wanting to drag the matter out nor bring to mind the fact she might be living vicariously through me. The driver goes over a bump and things fall out of her Mulberry bag, including a wallet and some photos. I help her scoop things up, glancing at her French husband and designer children in their matching Vertbaudet raincoats.

'In a parallel universe, they'd be named Cinnamon and

Fennel.'

I laugh, a little too much, and snort. Sleep deprivation and nerves make me a tad delirious. I look at her as she studies the picture and smiles.

'Have you met McCoy's kids before?'

She shakes her head at me, her mouth pointed to a pout.

'Only Ginger and Kitty when we did *This Morning* but as the collective happy family? No. Actually, that morning at BBC was the first time I'd seen him since ...'

My mouth is open, realising what she's saying. Since he dumped her, broke off their engagement, and left her for dust to marry a skinnier, blonder vixen. Is this wise? There will be knives in the vicinity. I'm starting to question what scenes of chaos may ensue in between me chopping onions and frying up beef. She senses my unease and laughs.

'Don't worry. That ship has sailed. You know there was a time I'd gladly have pickled his balls and given that wife of his a good slap but it's over ... different chapter of my life.'

I nod, the driver wincing a little to hear talk of pickled testicles.

'I mean, you know how it is with a past love. He'll always have been a part of my life but the emotion has changed. The story's moved on.'

I pause to hear her say that. I forget Luella has been witness to every part of my life so far. Up to this point she's remained impartial, very professional about everything, but sometimes she says a comment like that to let me know she's had her ear in.

'Not that you taking him on and kicking his chef arse into next week won't give me some pleasure, but this is about you today. You're my lucky horse.'

I hope that's not a reference to the size of my backside, and smile as she grabs my hand. Luella Bendicks and her pornstar name and her sleek bob. Would I be here if it wasn't for you? Maybe. But I'd know far less about organic farming and be wearing cheap tights that would stick to my dress and ride up to show the whole world my gusset. I grasp back to thank her. The driver peers over the seat.

'Oi, oi. Big kerfuffle up front.'

Luella stares out the front window as a sea of people part for the car to pass. At first I don't register why they're there. Maybe an accident, a rally. Then the flashes start flashing, people call my name. For me? Luella goes into panic mode tidying all her things away, reminding me to cross my legs and shade my eyes so the flashes don't make my eyes pop like I've got a thyroid condition. Don't celebs put things over their heads at this point? Or is that only for weddings and unnamed prisoners headed for court?

'Just get through the gates! We'll go round the back.'

'I can't get through! They're lying across the sodding bonnet.'

Luella turns to me.

'Remember, legs together. Follow me. Say hello to everyone, tell them you're very excited and raring to go. Nothing else. And whatever you do, don't listen to them.'

I nod as she opens the car door and follow her instructions to the letter. The cacophony of noise is deafening. Where are your kids? Is your hubby/mother/lover coming? What do you think of McCoy? Really? I just smile and wave and bid everyone a good afternoon. Luella pulls my arm along as we get to the doors and I turn to wave goodbye and for some reason curtsey. Luckily, the photographers find that amusing. And then we go inside. If I were a horse, I think that would be my viewing time in the enclosure. All bets are off.

2.39 p.m.

I have a dressing room with my name on. Not since I was twelve have I had a door with my name on so I am a little excited. It's a strange old room. It's not lined in orchids, white damask, and bowls of sweets where all the green ones have been removed. But I have a mini fridge with little bottles of water and Diet Coke which Luella tells me to avoid as it might discolour my teeth and she doesn't think I need the caffeine. Before, Vernon popped by to say hello. He was properly tall.

Like basketball player, looking-up-to-the-sun tall. He was nice enough and gave me a hug, which made me feel like a three-foot midget. But for now, I sit here. I've had a nice chicken salad sandwich for lunch with posh crisps. I've flicked through some magazines and talked to the wall, pretending to chop an onion that isn't there. I've also used my en-suite loo. The toilet paper was even quilted.

A knock at the door sees me jolt out of my seat and I go to answer it, partly glad for the distraction. Another celebrity maybe? Please be Ant and Dec. Or maybe a tea lady with nice biscuits? I'm almost excited until the door opens and I stand there for a good five seconds and stare.

Ambushed. Again. Really?

'Hi, Jools. How's it going? Just thought I'd pop by and wish you well.'

At this point, my first instinct is to shout for Luella like when you're a kid and there's someone at the door you don't know. The second is to shut the door really hard and see if I can't take off a couple of his toes.

'Tommy. Hi.'

It's like a stand-off with a chugger. No, get out of my way, I don't care that every five seconds a donkey dies. Behind him stands a man in a suit carrying a briefcase who gestures a hello with a nod of his balding head.

'We were wondering if we could come in and have a chat?'

I look down the long and winding halls to find Luella is nowhere to be seen.

'I mean, are you busy? We can come back later.'

He pops his head through the door to see my empty dressing room, just my handbag and some bread crusts keeping me company. Bastard. This is why people have entourages. I could do with Donna here right now.

'Well, I'm not but I guess ...'

He takes this as his cue to enter and rolls his eyes around my dressing room as he does, judging my lack of view of the Thames and Xbox, no doubt. I invite them to sit down and grab a chair, feeling a little on edge, a little like I want to lay into this man and grab fistfuls of his newly bleached hair. But I don't.

'So, this is Roger Kipling, he's my lawyer and we just wanted to come and chat to you today and see how everything's going. Feeling ready?'

A lawyer. I have a lawyer. Her name's Annie. She's not here yet and she doesn't have a comb over. One point to me.

'I guess.'

I eyeball the lawyer and his fancy suit. Annie would wear cashmere. That is obviously from Burton. Another point to me.

'Well, that's great. You're a fighter, I like that.'

I nod.

'So, I'm good. Is that it? Can I help you with anything else today?'

Maybe he wants to apologise, maybe he wants to have a continued discussion about the benefits of frying salmon. My heart beats out of my chest for some reason. I half expect the lawyer to have a gun in there. Maybe he wants to sue me.

'Well, I just wanted to apologise for the media. It has gotten way out of hand – all the stories being dragged through the press, it really has been quite upsetting.'

Upsetting for him? I'm sure.

'In what way?'

'No one likes to see their family undergo all that scrutiny.'

'Well, from what my publicist has told me, you had quite a hand in getting some of those stories to press.'

He smirks a little. I spy the fire extinguisher in the corner of my eye and wonder if I can bash his head in with it. I'm sure I've seen that on *CSI*.

'Your publicist?'

'Luella Bendicks. She was with me at the BBC thing. I believe you might know her.'

He rolls his tongue over his top teeth and says nothing.

'She's been really good in telling me how this media game works. I've learnt a lot from her.'

'I'm sure.'

The room is deathly silent for all of ten seconds. The lawyer coughs to break the silence. I get up and retrieve a bottle of water from the fridge. The only thing I can think to do to display my level of anger is not to offer them anything – no

Diet Coke for you, tossers. The lawyer whispers something to Tommy and he then looks at me.

'Jools, we're here today because everything has been blown out of proportion. I came here because I am genuinely sorry at how big this has become and how I forced you into a corner to cook and participate in this competition.'

I stand there and quietly sip from my bottle before returning to my chair. This is getting better. Apologies. They might be better in a newspaper or on live television but at least here I can gauge their sincerity. The lawyer reaches into his briefcase and retrieves a printed document.

'So I want to offer you money as recompense for all the embarrassment I've put you through.'

They slide the document over to me with a fancy looking cartridge pen. It sits there on my low-lying coffee table and I notice the rectangular piece of paper attached to the front. I choke. Fifty thousand pounds. For me. With my name on.

'Please, take it.'

They both nod. There's a catch. There has to be. I pick up the papers and start reading. No, no, no. You must be joking. I read it again.

'This sort of money could really be good for you and your family. Please consider it.'

I scan through the one sentence to have captured my attention. I read it over and over and over till the words blur.

'You're bribing me? It says here I have to lose the cook-off tonight and then the money will be mine.'

They both nod. The lawyer pushes the cartridge pen towards me. Fifty fricking thousand pounds. Bye bye, some of the mortgage, hello, new car! Hello, computer and a shopping spree. Hello, proper fitting shoes and music lessons for the kids. Bye bye, dignity.

'This is a hell of a lot of money. Do you desperately need me to lose tonight?'

Roger Kipling adds his authoritative five pence share.

'Mrs Campbell, Mr McCoy is offering this money in goodwill. From reading about your history and familial situation, we sense this money may be of huge benefit to you.'

I sit there open-mouthed, pained by the fact they look down on my family so. Pained that they think a bit of money and my life would be perfect. They look so incredibly smug, so convinced that they have some sort of power over me. All I'm thinking of now is trapping parts of their manhood in that suitcase. The door flies open and Luella stands there.

'Hello?!'

Tommy and Luella look at each other for a while as I rise from my chair.

'Jools? Is everything all right in here?'

I nod.

'Yep, Mr McCoy and his lawyer were just leaving.'

They don't take their documents. They leave them on the table. I watch as Tommy smiles at me on the way out, a weird smile that a fox might give a farmyard goose before killing it. I don't smile back.

5.35 p.m.

'Give me the bloody phone, I'm going to call *The Sun* now. They can get this on their website before day's end.'

Matt is not happy. He stands there wrinkling bits of paper in his hands and stomping about as Luella hisses in unison and Annie grabs bits of the document and casts her lawyerly eye over them. Ben and the children play some card game in the corner of the room, feasting on snacks and looking stylish and trendy in GAP and Converse. Adam found a make-up girl he took a fancy to a while back so we've lost him to the studio corridors. I go over and sit with the children and Ben puts an arm around me.

'Well, think about it. McCoy thought you could actually beat him and he was so intimidated he was willing to pay you to lose.'

That's one idea. Could I seriously win this thing? He thought so enough to pay a visit to a lawyer and have him run up important-looking documents. I think about the money. That money could be so useful to my family right now, my kids most of all would be the chief benefactors and maybe that's what's important. Matt, however, thinks it's shameful – the fact that his ability to provide for his family has been brought into question. He's stomping in the corner of the room. Luella pours him another plastic cup of champagne (brought by Annie to loosen the place up). Ben has even brought Valium that he got from a flatmate, except I refuse to take them given that he tells me they could possibly be something else, their bathroom cabinet not familiar with a labelling system. I sip my champagne slowly and deliberatively. The twins come over and sniff at cups for drinks. I grab on to Jake sitting in front of me. They gelled his hair before so it's now all crispy and shiny. I miss his chocolate mound of fluffy hair. Jake always had the best hair even when he was a baby. He knew it as well. He looked over at Ted and his wispy strands of hair and looked very pleased with himself. Ted came back and half smiled, showing off two deep dimples like they'd been carved into his cheeks. I remember thinking nothing. I had a baby in each arm, still high off pethidine. I thought Ted had six toes on his left foot. I just inhaled. It was like a drug. I grab Ted with my other arm and put them both in a headlock and kiss them on their foreheads, which they immediately wipe off.

'Jools! Don't mess the hair!' Luella shouts from across the room. I glance over and she is trying to calm Matt down and pointing at a pair of shiny trousers laid out for him. I don't have to hear what Matt is saying about them. All I hear is the word 'guttering.' Still, I think I like him the way he is, Ramones T-shirt and battered trainers, the right side of trendy dad.

'Where's his dressing room? I have a good mind to take this round to him and tell him to stick it where the sun don't shine.'

I look over and smile. I stuff a whole hand of crisps in my mouth to soak up the champagne as Annie saunters over.

'He's done his groundwork.'

'But what if she loses anyway?' asks Ben.

Annie gives him a look.

'Well, she'd get the money anyway but at what cost, Benjamin?'

Ben nods his head from side to side.

'But the document is saying here that Jools could drop out, forfeit, or simply not show up and still get the money so ... the decision is yours. But there is more ...'

My ears prickle.

'He wants you to just go away. Not follow up on this celebrity thing, just fade away and never have existed.'

'What do you think?' I ask my sagacious lawyer friend.

'I think he's a tit. This is obviously to protect himself and his interests. I think it's got little to do with recompensing you and is all about him being threatened by someone who is much more likeable and could steal his foodie thunder.'

Ben nods in agreement. Matt still stomps in the corner of the room. I'm not sure if it's about the money or the guttering trousers any more but I can see that fury, that blind rage in his eyes that surfaces at very few moments: moments when emotions have properly been stirred up by something significant, something of worth to him. I guess that would be me. I stand up, look at the clock, and think long and hard about why I am here. Was it money? Was it pride? Or was it for some other reason – thought up by some raging, braless woman in a supermarket one Monday morning. Because McCoy is not me, he will never be me, and I will never be him. When did I lose sight of that? I get up.

'Luella, there's that press call in the studio in five minutes. We'd better get down there.'

Everyone looks at me in surprise. Even I'm surprised. I am calm. Did Ben sprinkle the Valium on the crisps? But I know why. I stroll up to Matt waving the cheque in the air and tear it into four. The room freezes. So do I.

6 p.m.

Fifteen minutes later and my hands are shaking a little from having had a winning lottery ticket and ripping it to shreds. Everyone in that room stared at those four bits of paper on the floor for the longest time as all our dreams of holidays, well-fitting jeans, and extensions faded into nothing. I have my pride, I have my pride. She says. So now, a little shell shocked, we're all in the studio having our photographs taken. This has been my only demand in all of this. While McCoy was keen to get our clans out in the open, I wanted my kids out of this so bartered with the production company that they could have a couple of photos and that's it. As we're led out the twins are obviously the most excited, given their recent school play success, so bounce on to the set. Hannah stays close, Matt holds my hand. The twins notice the other children first: one girl preened like a peacock in a tulle party dress and ballet slippers, the boys in matching Fair Isle jumpers. The boys, who like company, bound over but the children are ushered away by a bosomy woman. I know that woman: the McCoy's nanny from *This Morning*. So they must be Basil, Mace, and Clementine. Hannah goes over to 'Baz' who's got a Nintendo DS and looks over his shoulder. He immediately turns his back to her. Matt hurries over and puts an arm around her.

'Gobshites, the lot of them.'

Hannah laughs in shock while Baz runs off behind a curtain, revealing a melee of people behind it, one of whom strides in, clad in denim, and rushes over to shake my hand. I hear cameras click all the quicker. I see Matt's foot ready to trip him up.

'Jools! How are we doing? Are we set?'

I shake his hand and say nothing, turning my head to smile, watching Luella from the side-lines telling me to show some teeth.

'I'm good. These must be your kids.'

The children flutter on, followed by skinny Kitty who gives Matt an evil look. Not in camera shot of course. The children are weirding me out. Before, they had the look of death drones ready to kill. Now they've all gone a bit *Stepford* as they position themselves against their dad. Even little Ginger seems to know how to rest her little head by her dad's knee.

'You have one missing. The redhead.'

'She's at home with her grandparents. She's retired from the media. It was all too much for her.'

The photographers laugh a little while Tommy goes stony-faced for a second to think that maybe I was directing that at him and his constant pimping out of his clan. He keeps standing in front of me, knowing I'm much too short to look at him directly in the face, even with heels. It's like a boxer's weigh in, without the scales, thank God. Matt just stands behind me and puts his hand on my shoulder. This is the first time he's meeting the McCoys and unlike them and their media charade, he's not as good at hiding his true emotions, especially with everything that's happened in the past hour. I know, as Luella keeps trying to gesture over at him to stop flaring his nostrils. As for my kids, they are less familiar with standing correctly for this picture jigsaw so the twins simply flank me while Hannah bends down by my knees. Kitty keeps smiling, maybe at how unpractised we are. A production crew member strides on to set.

'Right, let's finish up now. We still have some things to discuss with our guests.'

Everyone with a camera is ushered away as Luella runs on and the producers dressed like mime artists with clipboards make an appearance as if from nowhere. As soon as the last photographer disappears, so does the *Stepford* act. The McCoy kids' shoulders slump and Kitty's face curls into a snarl. Tommy's entourage stalk the stage like Stormtroopers, adjusting lights and laying out his organic produce. McCoy just stands there listing demands.

'So we have some knives we want to use. A German brand who are looking for promotional consideration and I want to wear my chef whites.'

Matt and I look at Luella, who's shrugging her shoulders. I don't think I have a problem with fancy knives nor McCoy trying to remind everyone again that HE IS A CHEF. To make a point, he starts stripping in front of us and slips his whites on over his oily torso. It's the Chippendales, restaurant style. I notice Luella looking a moment too long at his shiny chest, no hair – that means he must wax. Eeks.

'And we want the kids to be on set when I cook. Kitty too.'

Again, Luella shrugs and rolls her eyes. I look at Matt whose fingers grip mine so tightly I can feel the pulse in my thumb.

The producer looks to me for my similar needs for the day.

'Well, I want to wear a sombrero and have a bottle of tequila on hand.'

Everyone laughs except the McCoy clan, of course.

'And what about your family? Will they be joining you on set?'

I look over at Luella who always has advice to give me on such matters but knows when it's down to my family then the ball's always in my court. I see Kitty give her the once over, no doubt knowing who she is. I turn to the producer.

'No. I don't really see the point, to be honest.'

A producer can't hide his glee at my statement and Matt sniggers under his breath. Luella smiles the biggest smile I've ever seen on her as the McCoys are ushered away, out of earshot of my defamatory remarks. Ben, who stands nervously behind Luella, ushers the kids away.

'I love you. Really fucking love you. Did you see the greasy chest? He's pulled out all the stops. I want you to go back and jiggle your tits about. Idiots.'

She storms off. Matt's hand is still in mine as people mill about and we're left standing in my side of the fake kitchen. I stand at the counter and look into the lens of the still camera, rubbing my hands up and down the pale wood like it might give me luck. Matt stands opposite and looks down at my boobs.

'They'll do.'

I grab them and push them up manually. They could do with an inch of hoisting but that is really way down on the priority list. I look up and Matt just smiles at me.

'Do you remember when you gave birth to Millie? Weren't we watching McCock on the telly?'

'Yup.'

'Didn't you scream at him that he was a Mockney shite and you didn't want him to be the first person our child saw?'

I laugh but I don't answer. That was when it all started. When we became the family we are now, when life got crazy and busy and mental. He gets it. I think I do too. And I just smile as he kisses me on the forehead and we walk off set together.

CHAPTER TWENTY-FIVE

'So we all know the gauntlet has been laid down today. McCoy vs Campbell … any final words before we get down to it?'

Vernon is still tall. Heels are useless against someone so tall. I should have brought along that footstool in my bathroom that the boys teeter on to pee. The thought makes me smile.

'May the best man win.'

I'm still thinking about that footstool and the time that we told Ted he had to stand on it to pee and he did just that without the toilet bowl to aim in. I found him standing in his own puddle of piss scratching his head, wondering how he'd failed. I laugh. No one else does. What was that? Best man. But I'm a woman.

'May the best person win.'

The selected few in the studio laugh as Vernon whoops and presses the comedy red button, big numbers count down in the background like as soon as we've finished cooking the ground will swallow us up and nuclear warheads will be released. That would be go-go-go then.

It's strange. I am seriously calm. All the nerves and panic has subsided. I am focussed. I think about the kids, who are watching all of this from the comfort of my dressing room with a DVD of *Toy Story* playing alongside. Uncle Adam, who can't bear to watch, sits with them and keeps them topped up with apple juice. As requested, McCoy's kids are on set, watching from the side-lines with Kitty looking a little Von Trapp in that they might break into song at any moment. I only have Matt, Luella, and Ben watching from out of shot, each of them with their hands over their mouths. Ben puts his thumbs up every so often. I watch as Mace McCoy mimics him from across the set and Kitty laughs. I wonder if these knives are made for throwing.

So where was I? Chilli Con Carne. I need to chop an onion. Vernon is over with Tommy at the moment, picking his brains over chopping without crying and red vs white. I just get down to it and a cameraman comes close up to my hands as I start to peel. I flash him a hint of manicure and he smiles. Onion peeled, I go to chop and my technique is slightly laboured but better than before all of this. Great knife! Like a blade going through hot butter. I gain a little bit of speed and look over at McCoy who's smashing his garlic and being a smarmy g … shitty shit shit. I look down and see that next to chopping onions, I've also been chopping fingers. Crap bags. I flinch as the cameraman realises what I've done and jumps back, waving his hands in the air to a producer. I panic, waving my hand about and watching as blood drips onto the chopping boards. I still have a finger but I have a deep cut on the joint, blood gushing from it without ebb. A producer runs on, grabs my finger, and puts it under the sink, whispering into my ear.

'Are you all right? Do you want us to go to break?'

Vernon looks over, as does McCoy. I see Kitty smile in the background.

'Just get me a plaster.'

The producer, one of those bouncy, glossy-haired types, does as she's told with the help of someone running about with a big green box. We wrap it up as best we can so that my finger is completely straight and unmanageable but I will soldier on. Like those people who save whole platoons with great big pieces of shrapnel in their legs. Ben has disappeared. Luella looks down to the floor. But Matt is still there. A little paler but still there. I hear McCoy next to me.

'So most would use your bog standard mince beef for this sort of thing but the best meat you can use is chuck steak in largish chunks so this becomes a real man's chilli.'

I look down at my pink straggles of mince in their black container. Focus girl, focus.

'And I think it's important to keep the ingredients authentic, so I'm using Mexican chipotle as opposed to plain chilli powder, fresh chillies, and some streaky bacon for depth of flavour.'

I keep chopping my celery and carrots, wondering how the hell he kept within the ten pound budget we were given. My finger looks ridiculous. Luella is squatting on the floor looking like she might be hyperventilating. I am focussed, I can do this. A hand on my shoulder makes me jump a little and my carrot falls out of my hand and rolls on to the floor. Nice cameraman picks it up and hands it back to me and I go and wash it. Bloody Vernon. I hear a small child snigger in the background.

'Sorry, love. How's it going? How are you feeling? Calm down. You're doing great. Been through the wars already?'

I laugh and hold my finger up.

'Must be the knives. Not sure if I'm too keen on this brand. Bloody death traps.'

I see McCoy slam a saucepan down. That would be your promotional consideration gone. I hear Matt softly laughing and Luella go to stand like that might have saved me.

'But you're soldiering on, tell me about your chilli.'

I look down at my simmering hob and up to the big black hole that is the camera. Hi, Dad! Hi, Gia! Hi, Millie!

'Well, it's my dad's recipe. He's been cooking it ever since we were kids. I'm just going to sweat some veg then add the mince and all the herbs and stuff.'

Look at me! I'm 'sweating veg!' How technical of me. Vernon plays with my spice jars and ingredients bag.

'Chocolate! In a chilli! Are you mad?'

I thought Dad was too. But apparently that's what he's been using for years.

'Yeah. We've got cinnamon, chilli powder, garlic, and cumin, and at the end I melt a few squares of really dark chocolate to really draw out the flavour.'

And I'm drawing out flavour too! Just give me that Michelin star now. I see McCoy grinding things in a pestle and mortar, staring at me. Does he have chocolate too? Kitty's neck is craned over so far over her kids' heads that I see how haggard her neck is. She's all designer, with big shoulder pads and leather trousers. Luella let me have trousers too: black and skinny with a tunic dress. I think they're comfortable. I'm not sure if I've breathed much since this all started so I assume so.

But I've made a concerted effort not to bend at the knees so much this time, also because I fear the trousers may split. Vernon is nodding and staring at my beef. It's very bloody. Unreasonably so. Is it off? I then stare at a tiny blood trail on my countertop and realise the blood from my cut dripped onto the meat a little. Shit. I'm cooking human blood chilli. Vernon doesn't seem to have noticed.

'And what's that you're adding there?'

A dash of AB positive, fresh I'll have you know.

'Some Worcestershire sauce. Sometimes I'll put some soy sauce in too.'

Vernon smiles. I see blood. Did anyone else see the blood? I just stir until everything in my pan goes a uniform dark brown. I'm cooking with blood, sweat, and tears, quite literally.

'And what are you serving with it?'

'Well, usually Mexican night for us is this with rice, tortillas, and some dips so I'm doing some easy guacamole and a bit of salsa. I mean, it's the reason I chose this dish … it's a great midweek meal.'

'Well, it's looking great and I sincerely wish you both the best of luck. There's half an hour left on the clock so we'll leave you to get cooking and go to a break. See you in five.'

Lights switch off. Vernon's hands go to my shoulders.

'Calm down, love. It'll be fine.'

I look up at him, just seeing a shadow of big man, and nod enthusiastically. Luella runs on set and grabs my finger. I wince in pain.

'How are you? Do we need to change the dressing?'

I shake my head with no time for words, getting to grips with my avocados. Yet because I have an aversion to the stupidly sharp knives, I'm just grabbing at the seeds with my fingers, clawing at them so the avocado flesh turns to mush. I look over at McCoy chopping at herbs and deseeding chillies. Then I turn around. Matt. He grabs a tin opener to help me out with my tomatoes. He says nothing. Of course, the McCoys would never stand for this. Kitty storms over.

'Excuse me, the deal here was that we'd be cooking solo. No help. This is a clear infringement of the rules.'

Matt doesn't seem to register she's standing there and carries on regardless. Luella butts in as I would have guessed she would. I hope none of them bring up the issue of the bribe, surely that would be the biggest infringement of any rulebook.

'Give her a break, she's just sliced her finger open on a knife that your husband pushed on her. He's just opening a tin.'

He's also giving my rice a stir but there is no room for compassion here. Kitty clicks her fingers and from the side-lines a small Hispanic-looking man with a strange, evil beard runs on in Crocs and checked trousers, brandishing a paring knife, going straight for the limes.

'What the fuck?'

Kitty shrugs her shoulders with a sardonic smile, which Luella mimics before swearing at her turned back.

'We'll see about that bitchbag.'

Luella's hands are a blur over my countertop as she starts emptying little measured-out pots over my mince. Everything gets tossed in maniacally. Including the chocolate.

'Noooooo!'

But I'm too late and as soon as I see it melting, it sticks to the bottom of the pan, becoming a hot, dark brown mess. Shit. Quite literally. I see Kitty's head bob with laughter as the three of us stand over the pan, Matt having the good sense to chuck the tomatoes in to try and save it. But this only makes the burnt chocolate rise to the top in flakes. Matt turns to me saying nothing while two producers look on at me, my foundation starting to melt from the heat.

'And we're back in one minute.'

I look over at McCoy; aromas drifting over from his side of the set, his little sous-chef making light work of a head of lettuce. I look at my lettuce in the colander in the sink, already drooping as if it knows it's going to be on the losing side. This can't be it, can it? No. I grab the tin of kidney beans and empty them into the pan to hide the chocolate. It's a non-simmering pot of boggy mess, Matt has the good sense to try and find me a cover while I whisper to Luella.

'The blood. Did my blood go in the mince?'

Her face goes ashen and she doesn't even have time to

answer before a producer runs on to usher Matt, Luella, and beardy sous-chef away.

'So we're back. McCoy vs Campbell in our live cook-off, seeing if we can pit culinary genius against stay-at-home street smarts, and I'm here with Jools Campbell. So chilli's on, can I take a look?'

I grab at Vernon's sleeve as he goes to reach for the pot. He flinches back.

'It's hot. Here, why don't you try some guacamole?'

I hold a spoon up to his mouth, flicking a bit of green onto his shirt. I see Luella in the corner of my eye putting her hands to her face. He nods and gives me a thumbs up to tell me he approves. Or maybe he just doesn't want to be rude. He then starts with the questions.

'So tell me, love. What is your best money-saving tip for mums out there when cooking a dish like this?'

I pause for a moment as I wrestle with my limes, squirting juice all over myself.

'Ummm, wow. Well, to be honest I would never make something like this from scratch.'

The set freezes. I'm going against the Channel 4 Organic Ethos. They all assume it's a reference to takeaways or buying a ready meal or worse, serving it from a tin; time to dig myself out with my wooden spoon in hand.

'I mean, chilli in our house is usually a leftovers kind of meal. Like, I'll have a savoury mince left over from a bolognaise or something and then I'll just fry up some kidney beans and spices to bulk it out and then I've got another meal.'

I look over and Matt smiles at how efficient I sound. Truth is, sometimes I just tip a tin of baked beans over some mince and pass it off as chilli. They're kids. If you put things on sticks and tell them it's kebabs, they listen. I don't tell Vernon that.

'That's genius. Great tip. So a savoury mince is like onions and …'

'Celery, carrots, any bits of old veg at the bottom of the fridge. Fry with mince, add your seasoning and herbs, and pour some stock over. Great base for loads of dishes.'

Vernon smiles. Your Tess does this too, doesn't she?

'I mean, our man McCoy is talking about chuck steak, chipotle, and fresh chilli but seriously, if you're cooking a chilli for a family, you've got to think about spice level for little people and your budget.'

Vernon gets me. We nod and talk about mince accompaniments, everything from polenta to potato and I sound almost like I know what I'm doing, apart from the fact I'm scared of polenta and my chilli is hissing. Instead, I lean against my counter chatting away, trying to block everything out when really I should be slicing and dicing. Better still is seeing McCoy behind Vernon, looking over and wondering why he isn't getting any attention. Up yours, McCoy! Vernon likes me more!

'And so we've heard from Jools and after the break we're going back to Tommy. Guys, we have approximately eighteen minutes left. We'll see you after this.'

Another break already? The fact is I was so busy chatting to Vernon I didn't realise I was also here to cook. Luella runs on again and opens the pot to examine the chilli. It's actually not so bad. The kidney beans mask the burnt chocolate bits and the tomatoey bit is simmering down to a thicker pulp. Matt comes along and stirs my rice again, which Kitty observes from her thirty paces away and orders bearded sous-chef back on to set to help arrange plates and open pots of sour cream.

'That was fab. You're doing great. Keep up with the answers. I'll forget you just pelted Vern with avocado.'

I smile knowing the chilli is going to have to do wondrous things in that pot for it to taste decent. I put my guacamole in the fridge and see my face in the oven door looking a little like I might have a sweat moustache. Hopefully, the foundation will just soak that up. Back at my countertop, Kitty has stridden over again, purposeful and decidedly nosey. Little Clementine is with her, a child with wavy, honey-glossed hair like she's borrowed it off Jennifer Aniston. She puts her fingers up on the counter and peeks over at what I'm doing.

'Really, this is out of bounds, Kitty. I believe this is an infringement of the rules.'

I walk up to the counter to find Luella glaring at her nemesis

301

with a sweet smile but eyes like a death hawk. She must get some sense of supreme satisfaction from laying into her like this, yet I think a smidgeon of jealousy overwhelms. Would Luella use today to bring the subject up? They stand there for a few seconds while Kitty dares to look through my spice rack. Matt looks like he wants to slap her hand.

'Oh, you've bought your tortillas? That's nice.'

I smile at her. A daughter named after an orange? That's nice. I can't understand her little interruption. For a moment I thought it might be she's here to make amends and apologise too. Let's just all cook and be happy! But no. She scans my dishes as producers come on yet again to usher everyone to their rightful places and Vernon comes running on like he's just been away to have a pee.

'And we're back! Twelve minutes left, people. And I'm with Tommy McCoy! How's it going? Tell us what's happening with your rice.'

I block this bit out. I don't need to hear him teach Vernon how to feel up an avocado or why your beef should be a bit fatty. I just need to concentrate on my food.

'So I think you'll find a real Mexican chilli would never have kidney beans in it.'

I spy my empty tin on the corner of the counter and throw it in the bin. I get out my tomatoes to make my salsa. At least there will be salsa. And I stir the rice again. It looks all right. But the pan is a little static. I stir it again and see Matt on the side-lines flicking his fingers up and down like the way he used to dance in the mid-noughties. I crease my eyes to look at him and watch his mouth. Find? Fight? Fire? Fire? What about the fire?

It's bloody off, that's what it is. What? How? I bend down to start flicking at switches and knobs. But it wasn't off when Matt stirred it before. It's been on since ... since Kitty came over with her daughter who was poking around my workstation. I stare over at the little doughy-cheeked girl and her glossy, horsetail hair and she waves to me. Gobshites! Kitty pats her on the head as I get my water to go back on the boil again. Matt is whispering something to Luella given he must have realised

302

what happened and she storms off to the producers in her harem pants and shoes combination like an angry genie. The rice is still hard. Ten and a half minutes left.

This can still be done. Soldier on, Campbell. But I can't. He's won. I am defeated. For the love of God, don't cry on live TV. Don't you dare.

I look over at McCoy. And then I look at Matt. Down by his side, the children sprout from behind his back. Little faces watching the lights, the cameras, the action, and waving like I've just come back from war. And he sees me and smiles, that smile I've come to know and love and appreciate. Look at this mess we've got ourselves into. But I'm here, you're here. I've got your back. I will always root for you. And tears that may have been there dry over, the breath stuck in my throat escapes. And I do what Luella tells me not to; I grin back like a demented cat, waving.

I love you, he mouths. I nod. And then he bends down to talk to Hannah. She then whispers something to Jake, who like a wave passes it on to his twin. Why are they coming over? Why? Luella stands there watching them slowly and I know what she's thinking. Why is Jake's hair sticking up at the back? Where is that Fat Face cardigan I gave Hannah? The kids look nervous and I go over to meet them at the end of my worktop.

'We're reinforcements,' Hannah says smiling.

'Daddy said you shouldn't be doing this alone.' I run a hand over the top of her head, feeling both terrible they're in front of this camera but slightly relieved that they're here: familiar, warm, and smiley. The twins grab on to my legs and I embrace them either side of me. Ted tugs me down to his level. 'Can we help?'

I look over at hot pans and sharp German knives and twist my lips. 'Lettuce? You can tear the lettuce?' Jake doesn't seem overly excited about the task in hand but they head to the counter and do as they're told. I see Kitty to one side of me, her collection of children dumbfounded. Hannah slips a hand into mine.

'Stir the dinner before it burns.' And I laugh. I'm not sure why. Maybe it's because this happens a lot. Maybe I've got this far because half the time, when I'm preoccupied with things it's usually Hannah acting as egg-timer. She hangs off my arm like she does and we do that strange rocking dance we do when she's bored or cruising for a hug. I hold her close to me. My kids. My crazy monkey-faced kids. Over on the other side of the kitchen, I see Kitty whisper orders to Baz, who walks over to his father and hugs him around the midriff. McCoy says something to him I can't make out but there's a look and he goes to sit down again, shrugging his shoulders. I smile. And that's when I realise, when I have my lightning bolt moment about me, about the way I cook, about the way I should have been winging this all along. I turn to Hannah.

'You think you could lay my table for me? Fold some napkins?' Hannah smiles and nods, doing as she's told.

'So tell me about school today?'

'I learnt about Florence Nightingale. But I didn't get all my tables right. It was the nines.' And for one small moment, I forget where I am.

'Didn't I show you that trick? With your hands?' I go behind her and hold out her hands. 'One times nine is, see the fingers.'

I hear her laugh. And that's all I hear as McCoy's corner is suspiciously quiet, competing for noise and attention. I see the cameraman smile. I claw at my hands with her hair and kiss her on the forehead. The boys run up to me.

'We've done the lettuce ... and Ted ate some.' Ted hits Jake. I separate them and tear off a bit of kitchen towel, wiping something off Jake's nose.

'We don't hit in this house.'

'We're not in a house.'

'Smart alec ... you want to help me with the coriander?'

'More green stuff?' Jake turns his nose up and I mimic him. They go over to the chopping board and Jake sticks coriander up his nose and sneezes it out.

'Jake!' I give the rice a stir then open the pot of chilli. But geez, what is that smell? I see it thick, swampy, and a strange orangey colour. That is not going to win anything. The bottom is starting to form that familiar rubbery crust, the blackened flecks of chocolate seem to cling to the kidney beans, making them like they've got some strange bean pox. This would be the moment I'd turn off the gas, let it congeal so it'll be easier to chuck in the bin, and head to the freezer. For some fish fingers. I smile.

And then a hand falls on my shoulder. I turn.

'That looks like the contents of one of Millie's nappies.' I laugh and put the pot lid back on. The cameraman looks away. Luella stares over at all of us and puts a thumb up at me.

'You're going to be on TV. You're going to be one of those TV saps you hate.'

Matt smiles. 'Well, at least we'll be on together, like Sonny and Cher.'

'Like Richard and Judy.' He laughs. He takes a lock of hair that's been dangling over my left eye and brushes it away from my face. And it's over. I know that. I haven't won. I'm nowhere close. But I'm all right. I always have been. I laugh under my breath, wipe off my brow, and find Jake, one eye on me, one on my tortilla chips.

'Muuuuum, Ted and me are really hungry ...'

'Well, guess we better sort that out, eh?'

SIX MONTHS LATER

I'm curious to know what Christmas is like in other houses. I always imagine it's a very civilised affair. There are big, towering trees, Bing Crosby, and large glazed turkeys that are carved by the man of the house while everyone sits around drinking mulled wine and exchanging presents, the children revelling in the joy of Jesus and Santa. My Christmas starts with Ted at the end of the bed crying.

'Santa didn't come, Mum! I said I was sorry for all those horrible things I did.'

I wake up and usher him in under the duvet given the house is like an icebox. The clock reads 4.56 a.m.

'Ted, he hasn't got to our house yet. Go back to sleep.'

Santa has actually left the stockings in our wardrobe to avoid a repeat of last year, where the boys went downstairs first and opened all the presents before anyone else got up. Matt and I had to re-wrap all of Hannah's presents in newspaper and tin foil. Ted seems happy with what I've said and nestles into my armpit but I can't sleep. Turkey anxiety. Is it all right there in the fridge? What are those timings again? I do bad turkey maths in my head and think about other Christmas style woes (exploding puddings; uncrispy potatoes) until I realise I'm never going to fall back to sleep again. Neither is Millie, who heard her brother come into our room and stands in her cot, eyes piercing the darkness like a little jungle tiger. I pick her up and go to the wardrobe, collecting the pressies, and head downstairs to do some ho-ho-hoing.

It is frigging cold in my house so I put on my slippers and dressing gown, Millie on one arm all sleepy and warm, a big IKEA sack in the other. I head over to the fireplace and arrange the presents at jaunty angles along with a note that Matt has written in charcoal. I then eat the mince pie the kids left out for him, neck the Baileys, and return the carrot to the fridge. Millie gives me a look like I may be scarring her for life.

'Mummy! What are you doing?'

Shit, shit, shit. It's Jake: one pyjama leg up, the other down, the hair bouffant about his ears. I wipe crumbs from my mouth.

'Jake? What are you doing up?'

'I'm waiting for Santa.'

'You've just missed him.'

'Really? Oh man! What did he say?'

'We had a chat about stuff. He liked our tree.'

Jake looks over at it. We left our tree buying a little late this year so it's a little scarce on the fir, a little lopsided given we've had to squash it in a corner. Jake suspects that last sentence was a lie.

'Go back to sleep, honey. You know the rules, we all open pressies together.'

He doesn't protest too much. I watch him go up to our room and throw himself onto our bed. I then go into the kitchen and prod at the turkey in the fridge and decide to take it out. Pale and pimply, like me circa the late nineties. He goes in the sink and I put on the kettle. The door opens and Matt enters.

'Jesus Christ!'

I shrug. 'No, but it is his birthday.' He laughs sleepily then takes Millie from me while I make us some tea.

'Merry Christmas then …'

He gives me a kiss next to my ear and I repay the gesture with milk and one sugar. We sit down and he looks at the homemade name place cards that Hannah made, enough glitter on them to keep the tooth fairy in business for a year. Next to them, some cards from the faithful few: lewd naked Santas from Donna, Annie's sonogram framed in holly, full-out nativity from Gia. Next to them, our Christmas present from Luella: a trendy wooden frame with an excerpt from some newspaper review of the year.

Villain Of The Year - Tommy McCoy

The worst of times for chef McCoy, who tried to boost a flagging career with a series of attacks on a lowly mother-of-four. The nadir came on a live televised cook-off where the chef was cringeworthy in his victory, only made worse when it was clear he had sabotaged her efforts and bribed her to lose. With book sales plummeting, restaurant reviews floundering, and a wife who's now taking a misguided foray into baby fashion (neon jumpsuits for babies?) things Chez McCoy have become seemingly desperate, the ploys for attention delving to all-time lows, the empire which once shined so Michelin bright becoming a victim of its own success.

Hero Of The Year - Jools Campbell

The mother-of-four who took on the McCoys and may have lost (we all saw the blood drip into the mince; we're glad she told the tasting panel they shouldn't eat it) but won a place in all of our McCoy-hating hearts. Even though her personal life was dragged through the tabloid mincer (her only response being – 'no affairs here', she Tweeted), she came through the other end of such mauling with respect, appearing dignified for not jumping on the celeb bandwagon. Instead she put her energies into a family cookbook with a twist: it's actually been written by her family – a heart-warming compendium of recipes from her dad's chilli recipe to her mother-in-law's ultimate lasagne al forno, recently voted best family recipe in Good Food magazine. A new housewives' fave; endearing, honest, and not a child with a food-based name in sight.

Next to some vintage vinyl and perhaps the kids, this has become Matt's favourite thing in the whole house. I'm still staring at the turkey, thinking if they let those cameras in here today, then reviews would be a whole lot different; what did Nigella do? Doesn't she put her turkey in a bath or something? I'm sure Heston starts roasting his the previous night. Matt logs on to Facebook to wish his anonymous friends seasonal greetings and then logs on to Amazon. He likes to sit there and read reviews and badmouths the ones who call my book a big pile of pap.

'Look at this! People who bought your book also bought The Best of Girls Aloud.'

What the hell? Is it terrible to think that in all of these months, this might be the most venomous thing anyone has said to me? Matt is laughing at me while I glare at the screen. They also bought *Delia's Christmas*, box sets of *Family Guy*, and Kerplunk! As you do. Matt grabs my hand and smiles. I'd like him to say something corny at this point to make this a proper Jimmy Stewart Christmas moment, where imaginary bells will ring and clouds of snow will fill the kitchen window. This is going to be the best Christmas ever! You're all I need this Christmas day! But he says nothing, like Matt does. That is until he sees the turkey.

'Why is the turkey all frozen?'

The turkey was frozen. I had wedged it too far into the fridge so half of it had been frozen and crushed against the back wall. This meant we had to find a bucket where we could dunk half of it in tepid water to defrost and have its unfrozen legs akimbo, sticking out the top like a small, chubby, hairless mole. So in all the turkey chaos, the whole day becomes a terrible mess of mistiming and temperamental oven. The parsnips are black and sticky because I've forgotten honey burns so they get taken out to the garden by Dad who returns to tell me he's buried them at the site of our annual bonfire. The Brussel sprouts are that weird dark green that tells me they're going to taste like fart, and the potatoes are a little underdone. Crispy because of that goose fat I spent a fiver on but a little al dente. Can potatoes be al dente? Hell, I'm a celebrity chef now. Yes, they can. Thank God for Matt and his bacon and chestnut stuffing. Thank God for sausages that you just plop on a foiled baking tray and are lovely and bite-sized and you can just pop in your mouth when it's all become a little too stressful.

When we do sit down to eat, we have an old family tradition where we save a present to open at the table. It draws the present excitement out for the day, otherwise the kids go into withdrawal and start clawing at newspaper, catalogues etc. just so they can hear the sound of paper tearing. As is tradition, Dad and the boys all get socks and there's laughter because they're all matching. Ben's date, Leo, a scruffy Bohemian with hair like steel wool and a cravat, laughs like a pair of bellows. Millie's not keen and starts crying. I pick her up and the kids dig in.

Hannah throws her hands around me when she sees I will be taking her to some ice musical thing involving Disney tweens. She's happy. I am less so but it's nothing some gin and earplugs won't get me through.

The boys, who have yet to get as excited over pieces of paper, have got a Scalextric thing which I suspect Matt may have bought more for his own desires. Adam's eyes light up to see it. The boys are slightly manic now. The question is, will they eat? Which will probably be yes, given I haven't fed them a thing since breakfast unless they've nabbed the last of the chocolate Christmas tree decorations. Millie is last and Hannah rips the paper open for her. She gets one of those talking computer things which at the time of purchase I thought would charge her brain up to Einstein capacity but really will just annoy me with stupid animal noises and American accents.

Still, the children are happy and their faces glow with commercial festive joy. There's a small attack of the fuzzies given the fact we've sometimes skimped with Christmas when funds have been low. But the book has meant we can go all out this year. I even have luxury crackers. Some of the mortgage has been paid off, we got ourselves a new car. And a new sofa which got wrecked the next day by Ribena, but that's nothing turning the cushions over didn't solve. Matt and I always exchange our presents now. I'm very proud of mine. Matt quit his job last month. He'd worked so hard for so long in a job he hated, he resigned and let me bear some of the financial responsibility of the family until my star runs out. And so, while he has this career break to decide what he wants to do next, I've enrolled him in some night courses. He's always wanted to learn Japanese so he's on a course for ten weeks at our local college. I've even bought him a new pencil case. When he opens it, he takes one look at it and smiles. He smiles more these days. We have a kiss, which Jake declares disgusting and Ben agrees so they all clamour together and rip open crackers, we trade unfunny jokes (luxury does not extend to humour it would seem), and hats get worn and mostly end up on the floor. I keep looking at Matt who does his best to look at Millie and cut up bits of potato for her. Nothing for me then? I twist my lips around each other. It's not like this hasn't happened before. We've had present droughts: crappy boxes of chocolates for birthdays, even shittier anniversaries where he declares he's giving me himself. Inside, I pout and cross my arms, but outside I try and pretend that having my family around me is all the present I need. Yeah, whatever.

'Mum! Jake's got more stuffing than me!'

Of course my kids would also be fighting over the stuffing, not the rest of the dinner I've made. I try and appease Ted with another sausage. We do what we always do in our family; Adam takes more potatoes than is polite, Dad floods his plate with gravy, Hannah thinks I don't know that she hides her sprouts in her napkin. I look down and my plate is full, overloaded, and foaming over with food. It's no glossy picture in a food editorial but it's enough for me to smile and get my fork ready. I see a bit of cracker foil on a sausage and go to pick it out. Wait. A ring? Ooooh, maybe these luxury crackers were worth their money. Shit, it's actually quite nice. A vintage feel to it with a lovely little stone set in the centre. Perfect. I like cheapo jewellery that looks better than it is. Why the hell is Matt grinning at me? He keeps looking at the ring. Not my fault you got a pocket calculator. But then the penny drops, as does the ring, back into my stuffing.

'A ring? For me?'

He nods back at me. 'That engagement ring you never had. The one we were never too bothered about having. Until now.'

Talk about warm and fuzzy, I'm a hair's breadth away from crying, from throwing myself at him. But I don't. I'm not sure Dad's folding table, already teetering under the weight of dinner, could take it. I just smile.

'Eat up, love. What's wrong?'

Dad looks over as Matt puts a hand into mine. Dad is chewing slowly, waiting for me to announce that the turkey must be spat out because I've done something to it.

'Nothing. Just …'

I look down at my plate to find, extract, and wear the ring. I hear coughing next to me.

'Ted?'

I automatically take a hand to his back. He stops coughing and looks up at me, his face all blueberry.

'Something hard in your stuffing, Mum. Nearly couldn't swallow it.'

THE END

Jo Bartlett

Somebody Else's Boy

Will Nancy and Jack be allowed to embrace the future, or will their histories forever bind them to the past?

Drama teacher Nancy O'Brien puts her ambitions on hold to support her family, and returns to her idyllic seaside home town, St Nicholas Bay. Jack has his own reasons for heading to the Bay; a young widower desperate to come to terms with his loss, he hopes setting up home there with baby son, Toby, might just enable him to survive the future.

As Nancy and Jack become closer, not everyone is thrilled, in particular Toby's grandmother, who can't bear to see her late daughter 'replaced'. When Spencer – the only man Nancy's ever really loved – reappears, her living arrangements with Jack seem set for disaster.

Kate Field

The Magic of Ramblings

Local journalist Cassie is getting married to hot-shot, reliable Timothy and his mother Sylvia nicknamed 'Monster-in-Law' wants to plan the entire wedding. When Sylvia books the exclusive ID Images to take photographs of the extravagant do, Cassie has no idea what she's walking into.

The elusive JM, ID Images' newest photographer, just so happens to be Jared, Cassie's first love and ex-fiancé, who broke off their engagement to travel and take photos of far-reaching wonders. He's back to pay for his next wild adventure.

Cassie decides it's best to pretend not to know him, but when she's asked to write an article for her newspaper, she's tasked with a column surrounding all things wedding related. When Cassie jokingly writes a column meant for herself depicting her situation, a co-worker submits it in place of the real article and it's soon making headlines, with readers asking the age old question - Who Will She Choose?

Rosie Orr

Something Blue

Anna has a grown-up son, an ex-husband somewhere in Australia, and a feckless married lover. Sporting new scarlet underwear, and not much else, she is horrified to open her door one afternoon not to lover Jack but to son Sam and his girlfriend. They have come to announce their engagement – and to tell her that their wedding is only weeks away!

Anna is soon in the throes of preparations for a traditional Irish wedding: keeping at bay the Versace-wearing mother of the bride, dealing with the return of her ex-husband, and wondering whether Jack will ever have the gumption to leave his wife. And then the big day arrives, bringing hotel cats, destroyed crème brûlée and a surprisingly attractive photographer…

Jenny Kane

Another Glass of Champagne

Fortysomething Amy is shocked and delighted to discover she's expecting a baby – not to mention terrified! Amy wants best friend Jack to be godfather, but he hasn't been heard from in months.

When Jack finally reappears, he's full of good intentions – but his new business plan could spell disaster for the beloved Pickwicks Coffee Shop, and ruin a number of old friendships... Meanwhile his love life is as complicated as ever – and yet when he swears off men for good, Jack meets someone who makes him rethink his priorities...but is it too late for a fresh start?

Author Kit has problems of her own: just when her career has started to take off, she finds herself unable to write – and there's a deadline looming, plus two headstrong kids to see through their difficult teenage years...will she be able to cope?

A follow-up to the runaway success Another Cup of Coffee.

Debby Holt

The Soulmate

A novel about love, loss and starting again.

Widower Henry Drummond is marking time, drifting towards retirement, until he accidentally saves a life.

His daughter Maddie is at a wedding with the love of her life. But he is the groom and she is not the bride.

They both decide they need to change their lives, preferably with a soulmate by their sides. But as Henry's mother tells him, 'Love is a complicated business and it is not for the easily discouraged.' Strange encounters, humiliations and excitements come along and romance keeps eluding them. Soon family crises get in the way. But their quest has taken on a life of its own, with surprising consequences for all concerned.

For more information about **Jenny Kane**

and other **Accent Press** titles

please visit

www.accentpress.co.uk